PRAISE FOR JAMES DASHNER AND THE MAZE RUNNER SERIES

More Than 10 Million Copies in Print!

A #1 *New York Times* Bestseller
A *USA Today* Bestseller
A *Kirkus Reviews* Best Teen Book of the Year
An ALA-YALSA Best Fiction for Young Adults Book
An ALA-YALSA Quick Pick

"[A] mysterious survival saga that passionate fans describe as a fusion of *Lord of the Flies, The Hunger Games,* and *Lost.*" —EW.com

"[A] nail-biting must-read." —Seventeen.com

"Wonderful action writing—fast-paced . . . but smart and well observed." —*Newsday*

"Breathless, cinematic action." —*Publishers Weekly*

"Heart-pounding to the very last moment." —*Kirkus Reviews*

"Exclamation-worthy." —*Romantic Times*

★ "James Dashner's illuminating prequel [*The Kill Order*] will thrill fans of this Maze Runner [series] and prove just as exciting for readers new to the series." —*Shelf Awareness*, Starred

"Take a deep breath before you start any James Dashner book." —*Deseret News*

BOOKS BY JAMES DASHNER

The Mortality Doctrine Series
The Eye of Minds
The Rule of Thoughts
The Game of Lives

The Maze Runner Series
The Maze Runner
The Scorch Trials
The Death Cure
The Kill Order
The Fever Code

The 13th Reality Series
The Journal of Curious Letters
The Hunt for Dark Infinity
The Blade of Shattered Hope
The Void of Mist and Thunder

THE SCORCH TRIALS

JAMES DASHNER

DELACORTE PRESS

This is a work of fiction. Names, characters, places, and incidents either are the product of the author's imagination or are used fictitiously. Any resemblance to actual persons, living or dead, events, or locales is entirely coincidental.

Text copyright © 2010 by James Dashner
Cover art copyright © 2010 by Philip Straub
Cover typography by Joel Tippie

All rights reserved. Published in the United States by Delacorte Press, an imprint of Random House Children's Books, a division of Random House LLC, a Penguin Random House Company, New York.
Originally published in hardcover by Delacorte Press, New York, in 2010.

Delacorte Press is a registered trademark and the colophon is a trademark of Random House LLC.

Visit us on the Web! randomhouse.com/teens

Educators and librarians, for a variety of teaching tools, visit us at RHTeachersLibrarians.com

The Library of Congress has cataloged the hardcover edition of this work as follows:
Dashner, James.
The Scorch Trials / James Dashner. — 1st ed.
p. cm.
Sequel to: The maze runner.
Summary: After surviving horrific conditions in the Maze, Thomas is entrapped, along with nineteen other boys, in a scientific experiment designed to observe their responses and gather data believed to be essential for the survival of the human race.
ISBN 978-0-385-73875-0 (hc) — ISBN 978-0-385-90745-3 (glb) —
ISBN 978-0-375-89611-8 (ebook)
[1. Survival—Fiction. 2. Science fiction.] I. Title.
PZ7.D2587Sc 2010
[Fic]—dc22
2010021189

ISBN 978-0-385-73876-7 (tr. pbk.)

Printed in the United States of America

Random House Children's Books supports the First Amendment and celebrates the right to read.

For Wesley, Bryson, Kayla and Dallin. Best kids ever.

CHAPTER 1

She spoke to him before the world fell apart.

Hey, are you still asleep?

Thomas shifted in his bed, felt a darkness around him like air turned solid, pressing in. At first he panicked; his eyes snapped open as he imagined himself back in the Box—that horrible cube of cold metal that had delivered him to the Glade and the Maze. But there was a faint light, and lumps of dim shadow gradually emerged throughout the huge room. Bunk beds. Dressers. The soft breaths and gurgly snores of boys deep in slumber.

Relief filled him. He was safe now, rescued and delivered to this dormitory. No more worries. No more Grievers. No more death.

Tom?

A voice in his head. A girl's. Not audible, not visible. But he heard it all the same, though never could he have explained to anyone how it worked.

Exhaling a deep breath, he relaxed into his pillow, his razor-edged nerves settling down from that fleeting moment of terror. He spoke back, forming the words with his thoughts.

Teresa? What time is it?

No idea, she replied. *But I can't sleep. I probably dozed for an hour or so. Maybe more. I was hoping you were awake to keep me company.*

Thomas tried not to smile. Even though she wouldn't be able to see it, it would be embarrassing all the same. *Didn't give me much choice in the matter, did you? Kind of hard to sleep when someone's talking directly into your skull.*

Waa, waa. Go back to bed, then.

No. I'm good. He stared at the bottom of the bunk above him—featureless and darkly fuzzy in the shadow—where Minho was currently breathing like a guy with ungodly amounts of phlegm lodged in his throat. *What've you been thinking about?*

What do you think? Somehow she projected a jab of cynicism into the words. *I keep seeing Grievers. Their disgusting skin and blubber bodies, all those metal arms and spikes. It was way too close for comfort, Tom. How're we gonna get something like that out of our heads?*

Thomas knew what he thought. Those images would never leave—the Gladers would be haunted by the horrible things that had happened in the Maze for the rest of their lives. He figured that most if not all of them would have major psychological problems. Maybe even go completely nutso.

And above it all, he had one image burned into his memories as strongly as a branded mark from a searing hot iron. His friend Chuck, stabbed in the chest, bleeding, dying as Thomas held him.

Thomas knew he would *never* forget that. But what he said to Teresa was: *It'll go away. Just takes a little time, that's all.*

You're so full of it, she said.

I know. How ridiculous was it that he loved hearing her say something like that to him? That her sarcasm meant things were going to be okay? *You're an idiot,* he told himself, then hoped she didn't hear that thought.

I hate that they separated me from you guys, she said.

Thomas understood why they had, though. She was the only girl and the rest of the Gladers were teenage boys—a bunch of shanks they didn't trust yet. *Guess they were protecting you.*

Yeah. I guess. Melancholy seeped into his brain with her words, stuck to them like syrup. *But it sucks being alone after everything we went through.*

Where'd they take you, anyway? She sounded so sad that he almost wanted to get up and look for her, but he knew better.

Just on the other side of that big common room where we ate last night. It's a small room with a few bunks. I'm pretty sure they locked the door when they left.

See, told ya they wanted to protect you. Then he quickly added, *Not that you need protecting. I'd put my money on you against at least half these shanks.*

Only half?

Okay, three-quarters. Including me.

A long stretch of silence followed, though somehow Thomas could still sense her presence. He *felt* her. It was almost like how, even though he couldn't see Minho, he knew his friend lay only a few feet above him. And it wasn't just the snoring. When someone is close by, you just know it.

Despite all the memories of the last few weeks, Thomas was surprisingly calm, and soon sleep overpowered him once more. Darkness settled on his world, but she was there, next to him in so many ways. Almost . . . touching.

He had no concept of time passing while in that state. Half asleep, half enjoying her presence and the thought that they'd been rescued from that horrible place. That they were safe, that he and Teresa could get to know each other all over again. That life could be good.

Blissful sleep. Hazy darkness. Warmth. A physical glow. Almost floating.

The world seemed to fade away. All became numb and sweet. And the darkness, somehow comforting. He slipped into a dream.

He's very young. Four, maybe? Five? Lying in a bed with blankets pulled to his chin.

A woman sits next to him, her hands folded in her lap. She has long brown hair, a face just beginning to show signs of age. Her eyes are sad. He knows this even though she's trying very hard to hide it with a smile.

He wants to say something, ask her a question. But he can't. He's not really here. Just witnessing it all from a place he doesn't quite understand. She begins to talk, a sound so simultaneously sweet and angry it disturbs him.

"I don't know why they chose you, but I do know this. You're special somehow. Never forget that. And never forget how much"—her voice cracks and tears run down her face—"never forget how much I love you."

The boy replies, but it's not really Thomas speaking. Even though it *is* him. None of it makes sense. "Are you gonna be crazy like all those people on TV, Mommy? Like . . . Daddy?"

The woman reaches out and runs her fingers through his hair. Woman? No, he can't call her that. This is his mother. His . . . mommy.

"Don't you worry about that, honey," she says. "You won't be here to see it."

Her smile has gone away.

Too fast the dream faded into blackness, leaving Thomas in a void with nothing but his thoughts. Had he seen another memory crawl up from the depths of his amnesia? Had he really seen his mom? There'd been something about his dad being crazy. The ache inside Thomas was deep and gnawing, and he tried to sink further into oblivion.

Later—how much later he had no idea—Teresa spoke to him again.

Tom, something's wrong.

CHAPTER 2

That was how it started. He heard Teresa say those three words, but it seemed from far away, as if spoken down a long and cluttered tunnel. His slumber had become a viscous liquid, thick and sticky, trapping him. He became aware of himself, but realized he was removed from the world, entombed by exhaustion. He couldn't wake up.

Thomas!

She screamed it. A piercing rattle in his head. He felt the first trickle of fear, but it was more like a dream. He could only sleep. And they were safe now, nothing to worry about anymore. Yeah, it had to be a dream. Teresa was fine, they were all fine. He relaxed again, let himself drown in slumber.

Other sounds snuck their way into his consciousness. Thumps. The clang of metal against metal. Something shattering. Boys shouting. More like the echo of shouts, very distant, muted. Suddenly they became more like screams. Unearthly cries of anguish. But still distant. As if he'd been wrapped in a thick cocoon of dark velvet.

Finally something pricked the comfort of sleep. This wasn't right. Teresa had called for him, told him something was wrong! He fought the deep sleep that had consumed him, clawed at the heavy weight pinning him down.

Wake up! he yelled at himself. *Wake up!*

Then something disappeared from inside him. There one instant, gone the next. He felt as if a major organ had just been ripped from his body.

It had been her. She was gone.

Teresa! he screamed out with his mind. *Teresa! Are you there?*

But there was nothing, and he no longer felt that comforting sense of her closeness. He called her name again, then again, as he continued to struggle against the dark pull of sleep.

Finally, reality swept in, washed away the darkness. Engulfed in terror, Thomas opened his eyes and shot to a sitting position on his bed, scooted out until he got his feet under him and jumped up. Looked around.

Everything had gone crazy.

The other Gladers in the room were running around, shouting. And terrible, horrible, awful sounds filled the air, like the wretched squeals of animals being tortured. There was Frypan, pointing out a window, his face pale. Newt and Minho were running to the door. Winston, hands held up to his frightened, acne-plagued face like he'd just seen a flesh-eating zombie. Others stumbling over each other to look out the different windows, but keeping their distance from the glass. Achingly, Thomas realized he didn't even know most of the names of the twenty boys who'd survived the Maze, an odd thought to have in the middle of all that chaos.

Something at the corner of his eye made him turn to look toward the wall. What he saw immediately wiped away any peace and safety he'd felt talking to Teresa in the night. Made him doubt such emotions could even exist in the same world in which he now stood.

Three feet from his bed, draped by colorful curtains, a window looked out into a bright, blinding light. The glass was broken, jagged shards leaning against crisscrossed steel bars. A man stood on the other side, gripping the bars with bloody hands. His eyes were wide and bloodshot, filled with madness. Sores and scars covered his thin, sunburnt face. He had no hair, only diseased splotches of what looked like greenish moss. A vicious slit stretched across his right cheek; Thomas could see teeth through the raw, festering wound. Pink saliva dribbled in swaying lines from the man's chin.

"I'm a Crank!" the horror of a man yelled. "I'm a bloody Crank!"

And then he started screaming two words over and over and over, spit flying with every shriek.

"Kill me! Kill me! Kill me! . . ."

CHAPTER 3

A hand slammed down on Thomas's shoulder from behind; he cried out and spun around to see Minho staring past him at the maniac screaming through the window.

"They're everywhere," Minho said. His voice had a gloom to it that perfectly matched how Thomas felt. It seemed as if everything they'd dared hope for the previous night had dissolved to nothing. "And there's no sign of those shanks who rescued us," he added.

Thomas had lived in fear and terror the past few weeks, but this was almost too much. To feel safe only to have that snatched away again. Shocking even himself, though, he quickly set aside that small part of him that wanted to jump back into his bed and bawl his eyes out. He pushed away the lingering ache of remembering his mom and the stuff about his dad and people going crazy. Thomas knew that someone had to take charge—they needed a plan if they were going to survive this, too.

"Have any of them gotten in yet?" he asked, a strange calm washing over him. "Do all the windows have these bars?"

Minho nodded toward one of the many lining the walls of the long rectangular room. "Yeah. It was too dark to notice them last night, especially with those stupid frilly curtains. But I'm sure glad for 'em."

Thomas looked at the Gladers around them, some running from window to window to get a look outside, others huddling in small groups. Everyone had a look of half disbelief, half terror. "Where's Newt?"

"Right here."

Thomas turned to see the older boy, not knowing how he'd missed him. "What's goin' on?"

"You think I have a bloody clue? Bunch of crazies want to eat us for breakfast, by the looks of it. We need to find another room, have a Gathering. All this noise is driving nails through my buggin' skull."

Thomas nodded absently; he agreed with the plan but hoped Newt and Minho would take care of it. He was eager to make contact with Teresa—he hoped her warning had just been part of a dream, a hallucination from the drug of deep and exhausted slumber. And that vision of his mom . . .

His two friends moved away, calling out and waving their arms to collect Gladers. Thomas took a tremulous glance back at the shredded madman at the window, then looked away immediately, wishing he hadn't reminded his brain of the blood and torn flesh, the insane eyes, the hysterical screaming.

Kill me! Kill me! Kill me!

Thomas stumbled to the farthest wall, leaned heavily against it.

Teresa, he called out again with his mind. *Teresa. Can you hear me?*

He waited, closing his eyes to concentrate. Reaching out with invisible hands, trying to grasp some trace of her. Nothing. Not even a passing shadow or brush of feeling, much less a response.

Teresa, he said more urgently, clenching his teeth with the effort. *Where are you? What happened?*

Nothing. His heart seemed to slow until it almost stopped, and he felt like he'd swallowed a big hairy lump of cotton. Something had happened to her.

He opened his eyes to see the Gladers gathered around the green-painted door that led to the common area where they'd eaten pizza the night before. Minho was jerking on the round brass handle to no avail. Locked.

The only other door was to a shower and locker room, from which no other exits existed. There was that, and the windows. All with those metal bars. Thank goodness. Each one had raging lunatics screaming and yelling on the other side.

Even though worry ate at him like spilled acid in his veins, Thomas gave up momentarily on trying to contact Teresa and joined the other Gladers. Newt was having a go at the door, with the same useless result.

"It's locked," he muttered when he finally gave up, his arms falling weakly to his sides.

"Really, genius?" Minho said, his powerful arms folded and tensed, veins bulging all over the place. Thomas thought for a split second he could actually see the blood pumping through them. "No wonder you were named after Isaac Newton—such an amazing ability to think."

Newt wasn't in the mood. Or maybe he'd just learned long ago to ignore Minho's smart-aleck remarks. "Let's break this bloody handle off." He looked around as if he expected someone to give him a sledgehammer.

"I wish those shuck . . . Cranks would shut up!" Minho yelled, turning to glower at the closest one, a woman who looked even more hideous than the first man Thomas had seen. A bleeding wound crossed her face, ending on the side of her head.

"Cranks?" Frypan repeated. The hairy cook had been silent until then, barely noticeable. Thomas thought he looked even more frightened than when they'd been about to battle the Grievers to escape the Maze. Maybe this was worse. When they'd settled into bed last night, everything had seemed good and safe. Yeah, maybe this *was* worse, to have that suddenly taken away.

Minho pointed at the screaming, bloody woman. "That's what they keep calling themselves. Haven't you heard it?"

"I don't care if you call 'em pussy willows," Newt snapped. "Find me something to break through this stupid door!"

"Here," a shorter boy said, carrying a slender but solid fire extinguisher he'd taken off the wall—Thomas remembered seeing it earlier. Again, he felt guilty for not even knowing this kid's name.

Newt grabbed the red cylinder, ready to pile-drive the door handle. Thomas stood as close as he could, eager to see what was on the other side of the door, though he had a very bad feeling that whatever it was, they weren't going to like it.

Newt lifted the extinguisher, then slammed it down on the round brass handle. The loud crack was accompanied by a deeper crunch, and it took only three more whacks before the entire unit of the handle crashed to the floor with a jangle of broken metal pieces. The door inched outward, cracked open just enough to show darkness on the other side.

Newt stood quietly, staring at that long, narrow gap of blackness as if he expected demons from the underworld to come flying through. Absently, he handed the extinguisher back to the boy who'd found it. "Let's go," he said. Thomas thought he heard the slightest quaver in his voice.

"Wait," Frypan called out. "We sure we wanna go out there? Maybe that door was locked for a reason."

Thomas couldn't help but agree; something felt wrong about this.

Minho stepped up to stand right next to Newt; he looked back at Frypan, then made eye contact with Thomas. "What else're we gonna do? Sit here and wait for those loonies to get in? Come on."

"Those freaks aren't breaking through the window bars anytime soon," Frypan retorted. "Let's just *think* for a second."

"Time for thinking's done," Minho said. He kicked out with his foot and the door swung completely open; if anything, it seemed to grow even darker on the other side. "Plus, you should've spoken up *before* we blasted the lock to bits, slinthead. Too late now."

"I hate when you're right," Frypan grumbled under his breath.

Thomas couldn't quit staring past the open door, into the pool of inky darkness. He felt a now-all-too-familiar clench of apprehension, knowing that something had to be wrong or the people who'd rescued them would've come for them a long time ago. But Minho and Newt were right—they had to go out there and find some answers.

"Shuck it," Minho said. "I'll go first."

Without waiting for a response he walked through the open door, his body vanishing in the gloom almost instantly. Newt gave Thomas a hesitant look, then followed. For some reason Thomas thought it should be up to him to go next, so he did.

Step by step, he left the dorm room and entered the darkness of the common area, hands reaching out in front of him.

The glow of light coming from behind didn't do much to illuminate things; he might as well have been walking with his eyes squeezed shut. And the place smelled. Horrible.

Minho yelped up ahead, then called back. "Whoa, be careful. Something . . . weird's hanging from the ceiling."

Thomas heard a slight squeak or groan, something creaking. As if Minho had bumped into a low-hanging chandelier, sending it swaying back and forth. A grunt from Newt somewhere to the right was followed by the squeal of metal dragging across the floor.

"Table," Newt announced. "Watch out for tables."

Frypan spoke up behind Thomas. "Does anyone remember where the light switches were?"

"That's where I'm heading," Newt responded. "I swear I remember seeing a set of them somewhere over here."

Thomas continued walking blindly forward. His eyes had adjusted a little; where before, everything had been a wall of blackness, now he could see traces of shadows against shadows. Yet something was off. He was still a little disoriented, but things seemed to be in places they shouldn't be. It was almost as if—

"Bluh-huh-huh," Minho groaned, a shudder of repulsion, like he'd just stepped in a pile of klunk. Another creaking sound cut through the room.

Before Thomas could ask what had happened, he bumped into something himself. Hard. Awkwardly shaped. The feel of cloth.

"Found it!" Newt shouted.

A few clicks were heard; then the room suddenly blazed with fluorescent lights, temporarily blinding Thomas. He stumbled away from the thing he'd bumped into, rubbing his eyes, ran into another stiff figure, sent it swaying away from him.

"Whoa!" Minho yelled.

Thomas squinted; his vision cleared. He forced himself to look at the scene of horror around him.

Throughout the large room, people hung from the ceiling—at least a dozen. They'd all been strung up by the neck, the ropes twisted and trenched into purple, bloated skin. The stiff bodies swung to and fro ever so slightly, pale pink tongues lolling out of their white-lipped mouths. All of them had eyes open, though glazed over with certain death. By the looks of it, they'd been that way for hours. Their clothes and some of their faces looked familiar.

Thomas dropped to his knees.

He knew these dead people.

They were the ones who'd rescued the Gladers. Just the day before.

CHAPTER 4

Thomas tried not to look at any of the dead bodies as he stood up. He half walked, half stumbled over to Newt, who was still by the bank of light switches, his terrified gaze darting between the corpses hanging throughout the room.

Minho joined them, swearing under his breath. Other Gladers were emerging from the dorm room, shouting as they realized what they were seeing; Thomas heard a couple of them throw up, gagging and spitting. He felt the sudden urge himself, but fought it. What had happened? How could everything be taken away from them so fast? His stomach tightened up as despair threatened to bowl him over.

Then he remembered Teresa.

Teresa! he called out with his mind. *Teresa!* Again and again, mentally screaming it with his eyes closed and jaw clenched. *Where are you!*

"Tommy," Newt said, reaching out to squeeze his shoulder. "What's bloody wrong with you?"

Thomas opened his eyes, realized he was doubled over, arms wrapped around his stomach. He slowly straightened, tried to push away the panic eating him inside. "What . . . what do you think? Look around us."

"Yeah, but you looked like you were in pain or something."

"I'm fine—just trying to reach her in my mind. But I can't." He wasn't fine. He hated reminding the others that he and Teresa could speak telepathically. And if all these people were dead . . . "We've gotta find where they put her," he blurted out, grasping urgently for a task to clear his mind. He scanned the room, trying his best not to focus on the corpses, looking for a door that might lead to her room. She'd said it was across the common area from where they'd all slept.

There. A yellow door with a brass handle.

"He's right," Minho said to the group. "Spread out, find her!"

"Might've already." Thomas was on the move, surprised at how quickly he'd recovered his senses. He ran toward the door, dodging tables and bodies. She had to be in there, safe like they'd been. The door was closed; that was a good sign. Probably locked. Maybe she'd fallen into a deep sleep like him. That was why she'd been quiet, unresponsive.

He had almost reached the door when he remembered that they might need something to break into the room. "Someone grab that fire extinguisher!" he yelled over his shoulder. The smell in the common area was horrendous; he gagged as he sucked in a deep breath.

"Winston, go get it," Minho ordered behind him.

Thomas reached the door first and tried the handle. It didn't budge, locked tight. Then he noticed a small, clear-plastic display hanging on the wall to the right, about five inches square. A sheet of paper had been slipped into the thin slot, several words typed on its surface.

Teresa Agnes. Group A, Subject A1.
The Betrayer.

Oddly, the thing that stood out the most to Thomas was Teresa's last name. Or at least, what appeared to be her last name. Agnes. He didn't know why, but it surprised him. Teresa Agnes. He couldn't think of anyone within the splotchy knowledge of history floating in his still-scarce memories who matched that name. He himself had been renamed after Thomas Edison, the great inventor. But Teresa Agnes? He'd never heard of her.

Of course, all their names were more of a joke than anything, probably a callous way for the Creators—WICKED or whoever had done this to them—to distance themselves from the *real* people they'd stolen from *real* mothers and fathers. Thomas couldn't wait until the day he learned what he'd been called at birth, what name lay stamped in the minds of his parents, whoever they were. Wherever they were.

The sketchy memories he'd initially regained from going through the Changing had made him think that he didn't have parents who loved him. That whoever they were, they didn't want him. That he'd been taken from horrible circumstances. But now he refused to believe it, especially after having dreamed about his mom during the night.

Minho snapped his fingers in front of Thomas's eyes. "Hello? Calling Thomas? Not a good time to daydream. Lots of dead bodies, smells like Frypan's pits. Wake up."

Thomas turned to him. "Sorry. Just thought it was weird that Teresa's last name was Agnes."

Minho clucked his tongue. "Who cares about *that*? What's this freakin' stuff about her being the Betrayer?"

"And what's 'Group A, Subject A1' mean?" This was Newt, who handed over the fire extinguisher to Thomas. "Anyway, your turn to break a buggin' door handle."

Thomas grabbed it, suddenly angry at himself for wasting even a few seconds thinking about the stupid label. Teresa was in there, and she needed their help. Trying not to be bothered by the word *betrayer*, he gripped the cylinder and slammed it against the brass knob. A jolt ran up his arms as the clang of metal against metal rang through the air. He'd felt it give a little, and two smashes later the handle fell off and the door popped open an inch or two.

Thomas threw the extinguisher to the side and grabbed the door, swung it all the way out. Itchy anticipation mixed with dread at what he might find. He was the first to step into the lighted room.

It was a smaller version of the boys' dorm, just four bunk beds, two dressers and a closed door, presumably leading to another bathroom. All the beds were made up nicely except one, its blankets tossed to the side and a pillow hanging off the edge, the sheet rumpled. But there was no sign of Teresa.

"Teresa!" Thomas called out, his throat straining with panic as he yelled.

The swirly, swooshing sound of a toilet flushing came through the closed door and a sudden relief burst through Thomas. It was so strong he almost had to sit down. She was here, she was safe. He steadied himself and started walking toward the bathroom, but Newt reached out and grabbed his arm.

"You're used to living with a bunch of boys," Newt said. "I don't think it's polite to go stomping into the bloody ladies' room. Just wait till she comes out."

"Then we need to get everybody in here and have a Gathering," Minho added. "It doesn't stink in here, and there aren't any windows for Cranks to scream at us."

Thomas hadn't noticed the lack of windows until that moment, though it should've been the most obvious thing, considering the chaos of their own dorm room. Cranks. He'd almost forgotten.

"I wish she'd hurry up," he murmured.

"I'll get everyone over here," Minho said; he turned and walked back into the common area.

Thomas stared at the bathroom door. Newt and Frypan and a few other Gladers pushed their way into the room and took seats on the beds, all of them leaning forward, elbows on knees, rubbing their hands together absently, the anxiety and worry evident in their body language.

Teresa? Thomas said in his mind. *Can you hear me? We're waiting for you out here.*

No response. And he still felt that bubble of emptiness, as if her presence itself had been permanently taken away.

There was a click. The handle on the door to the bathroom turned; then the door opened, swinging toward Thomas. He stepped forward, ready to pull Teresa into a hug—he didn't care who was there to see it. But the person who walked into the dorm room wasn't Teresa. Thomas stopped midstride and almost tripped. Everything inside him seemed to fall.

It was a boy.

He wore the same kind of clothes they'd all been given the night before—clean pajamas with a button-up shirt and flannel pants, light blue. He had olive skin, and his dark hair was cut surprisingly short. The look of innocent surprise on his face was the only thing that prevented Thomas from grabbing the shank by the collar and shaking him until some answers came out.

"Who are you?" Thomas asked, not caring that the words sounded harsh.

"Who am I?" the boy responded, somewhat sarcastically. "Who are *you?*"

Newt had gotten back to his feet, actually standing even closer to the new guy than Thomas was. "Don't bloody mess around. There are a lot more of us than there are of you. Tell us who you are."

The boy folded his arms, a defiance coming over his whole body. "Fine. My name's Aris. What else you wanna know?"

Thomas wanted to punch the guy. Him acting all high and mighty while Teresa was *missing*. "How'd you get here? Where's the girl who slept here last night?"

"Girl? What girl? I'm the only one here, and it's been that way since they put me here last night."

Thomas turned to point back in the direction of the door to the common area. "There's a sign right out there that *says* this is her room. Teresa . . . Agnes. No mention of a shank named *Aris*."

Something in his tone must've made the boy realize this wasn't a joke. He held out his hands in a conciliatory gesture. "Look, man, I don't know what you're talking about. They put me in here last night, I slept in *that* bed"—he pointed to the one with the rumpled sheet and blanket—"and I woke up about five minutes ago and took a pee. Never heard the name Teresa Agnes in my life. Sorry."

The brief moment of relief Thomas had felt when he'd heard the toilet flush officially shattered. He shared a look with Newt, not knowing what to ask next.

Newt shrugged slightly, then turned back to Aris. "*Who* put you in here last night?"

Aris threw his arms up in the air, then let them come back down and slap against his sides. "I don't even know, man. A bunch of people with guns who rescued us, told us everything would be okay now."

"Rescued you from what?" Thomas asked. This was getting weird. Really, really weird.

Aris looked down at the floor and his shoulders fell. It looked as if a wave of some terrible memory had washed over him. He sighed, then finally looked back up at Thomas and answered.

"From the Maze, man. From the Maze."

CHAPTER 5

Something softened in Thomas. This kid wasn't lying—he could just tell. The look of horror that had taken hold of Aris was one he knew well. Thomas had felt it himself and had seen it on too many other faces. He knew exactly what kind of terrible memories made someone look like that. He also knew that Aris had no clue what had happened to Teresa.

"Maybe you should sit down," Thomas said. "I think we have a lot to talk about."

"What do you mean?" Aris asked. "Who are you guys? Where'd *you* come from?"

Thomas let out a slight laugh. "The Maze. The Grievers. WICKED. You name it." So much had happened, where could he start? Not to mention that worry over Teresa was making his head spin, making him want to run out of the room and search for her immediately, but he stayed.

"You're lying," Aris said, his voice having dropped to a whisper, his face now a full shade paler.

"No, we're not," Newt responded. "Tommy's right. We need to talk. Sounds like we've come from similar places."

"Who's that guy?"

Thomas turned around to see that Minho had returned, a pack of Gladers standing behind him on the other side of the doorway. Their faces were scrunched up in disgust at the smell out there, their eyes still full of the terror of seeing what filled the room just behind them.

"Minho, meet Aris," Thomas said, taking a step to the side and gesturing toward the other boy. "Aris, meet Minho."

Minho stuttered out a few unintelligible words, as if he couldn't quite decide where to start.

"Look," Newt said. "Let's take down these top beds and move them around the room. Then we can all sit and figure out what's bloody going on."

Thomas shook his head. "No. First, we need to go find Teresa. She must be in some other room."

"Isn't one," Minho said.

"What do you mean?"

"I just checked this whole place out. There's the big common area, this room, our dorm room, and some seriously shucked doors that lead outside—where we came in from the bus yesterday. Locked and chained from the *inside*. Doesn't make any sense, but I don't see any other doors or exits."

Thomas shook his head in confusion. It felt like a million spiders had just spun cobwebs through his brain. "But . . . what about last night? Where'd the food come from? Didn't anyone notice other rooms, a kitchen, anything?" He looked around, hoping for an answer, but no one said a word.

"Maybe there's a hidden door," Newt finally said. "Look, we can only do one thing at a time. We need to—"

"No!" Thomas shouted. "We've got all day to talk to this Aris guy. The label by the door said Teresa should be here somewhere—we need to find her!"

Without waiting for a response, he headed for the door back to the common area, pushing his way past boys until he was through. The smell hit him as if a bucket of raw sewage had been spilled over his head. The bloated and purple bodies hung like carcasses of game set out by hunters to dry. Their lifeless eyes stared back at him.

A familiar, sickening tickle of revulsion filled his stomach and triggered his gag reflex. Closing his eyes for a second, he willed his insides to settle. When they finally did, he began his search for some sign of Teresa, concentrating with all his might on *not* looking at the dead people.

But then a horrible thought struck him. What if she . . .

He ran through the room, searching the faces of the bodies. None of them was her. Relief dissolved the fleeting moment of panic, and he focused on the room itself.

The walls surrounding the common area were as plain as could be; smooth plaster painted white, no decoration of any kind. And for some reason, no windows. He walked quickly around its entire circumference, running his left hand along the wall as he did so. He came to the door to the boys' dorm room, went past it, then made it to the big entrance through which they'd come the day before. There had been a torrential downpour at the time, which seemed impossible now, considering the bright sun he'd seen shining behind the crazy man earlier.

The entrance—or exit—consisted of two large steel doors, their surfaces a shiny silver. And just like Minho said, a massive chain—with links a full inch thick—had been threaded through the handles on the doors and pulled tight, two big key locks snapped shut to keep it that way. Thomas reached out and pulled on the chains to check their strength. The metal felt cool under his hands, and it didn't give at all.

He expected thumps from the other side—Cranks trying to get in just as they were at the windows in the dorm room. But the room remained silent. The only sounds were muted and coming from the two dorms—distant shouts and screams from the Cranks and murmurs of conversation from the Gladers.

Frustrated, Thomas continued his trek along the walls until he made it back to the room that was *supposed* to be Teresa's. Nothing, not even a crack or seam to indicate another exit. The large room wasn't even a square—it was a big oval, round and cornerless.

He was completely perplexed. He thought back to the night before, when they'd all sat there and eaten pizza like the starved people they'd been. Surely they'd seen other doors, a kitchen, something. But the more he thought about it, the more he tried to picture what things had looked like, the fuzzier it became. An alarm went off in his head—their brains had been tinkered with before. Had it happened again? Had their memories been altered or wiped?

And what had happened to Teresa?

Desperate, he thought about crawling across the floor to look for a trapdoor or something—some clue to what had happened. But he couldn't spend another minute with all those rotting bodies. The only thing left was the new kid. He sighed and turned back to the small room where they'd found him. Aris had to know something that would help.

Just as Newt had ordered, the top beds had been unhooked from the lower ones and placed around the room against the walls, creating enough space for the nineteen other Gladers and Aris to sit in a circle, everyone facing each other.

When Minho saw Thomas, he patted an empty spot next to him. "Told ya, dude. Have a seat and let's talk. We waited on you. But close that shuck door as much as you can first—smells worse than Gally's rotting feet out there."

Without responding, Thomas pulled the door shut, then walked over and sat down. He wanted to sink his head into his hands, but he didn't. Nothing indicated for sure that any kind of danger threatened

Teresa. Something weird was going on, but there could be a million explanations, and plenty of them included her being okay.

Newt was one bed to the right, sitting so far forward that just the edge of his butt rested on the mattress. "All right, let's get started on the bloody storytellin' so we can get to the real problem—finding something to eat."

Right on cue, Thomas felt a hunger pang, heard his stomach growl. That problem hadn't even occurred to him yet. Water would be fine—they had the bathrooms—but there was no sign of food anywhere.

"Good that," Minho said. "Talk, Aris. Tell us everything."

The new boy was directly across the room from Thomas—the Gladers sitting to each side of the stranger had scooted to the far ends of the bed. Aris shook his head. "No way. You guys go first."

"Yeah?" Minho responded. "How about we all just take turns beating the living klunk out of your shuck face? Then we'll ask you to talk again."

"Minho," Newt said sternly. "There's no reason—"

Minho pointed sharply at Aris. "Please, dude. For all we know this shank could be one of the Creators. Somebody from WICKED, here to spy on us. He could've killed those people out there—he's the only one we don't know and the doors and windows are locked! I'm sick of him acting all snooty when we've got twenty guys to his one. He should talk first."

Thomas groaned on the inside. One thing he knew was that the kid would never open up if Minho terrified him.

Newt sighed and looked over at Aris. "He's got a point. Just tell us what you meant about coming from the buggin' Maze. That's where *we* escaped from, and we obviously haven't met you."

Aris rubbed his eyes, then met Newt's gaze. "Fine, listen. I was thrown into this gigantic maze made out of huge stone walls—but before that my memory was erased. I couldn't remember anything about my life from before. I just knew my name. I lived there with a bunch of girls. There must've been fifty of them, and I was the only boy. We escaped a few days ago—the people who helped kept us in a big gym for a few days, then moved me here last night—but no one explained anything. What's this stuff about you being in a maze, too?"

Thomas barely heard the last few words of what Aris had said over the sounds of surprise coming from the other Gladers. Confusion swirled in his brain. Aris had announced what he'd been through as simply and quickly as describing a trip to the beach. But it seemed crazy. Monumental, if true. Luckily someone voiced exactly what Thomas was trying to sort out in his mind.

"Wait a minute," Newt said. "You lived in a big maze, on a farm, where walls closed every night? Just you and a few dozen girls? Were there creatures called Grievers? Were you the last one to arrive? And did everything go buggin' nuts when you did? Did you come in a coma? With a note that said you were the last one ever?"

"Whoa, whoa, whoa," Aris was saying even before Newt had finished. "How do you know all this? How . . ."

"It's the same shuck experiment," Minho said, the earlier belligerence gone from his voice. "Or same . . . whatever. But they had all girls and one boy, we had all boys and one girl. WICKED must've built two of those mazes, run two different tests!"

Thomas's line of thinking had already accepted that. He finally settled himself enough to speak. He looked at Aris. "Did they call you the Trigger?"

Aris nodded, obviously as perplexed as anyone else in the room.

"And could you . . . ," Thomas began, but hesitated. He felt like every time he brought this up, he was admitting to the world that he was crazy. "Could you speak to one of those girls inside your mind? Ya know, like telepathically?"

Aris's eyes widened, staring deeply at Thomas as if he'd understood a dark secret that only someone else who shared it could understand.

Can you hear me?

The phrase appeared so clearly inside Thomas's mind that at first he thought Aris had spoken aloud. But no—his lips hadn't moved.

Can you hear me? the boy repeated.

Thomas hesitated, swallowed. *Yes.*

They killed her, Aris said back to him. *They killed my best friend.*

CHAPTER 6

"What's going on?" Newt asked, looking back and forth between Thomas and Aris. "Why're you guys looking at each other like you just fell in love?"

"He can do it, too," Thomas answered, not taking his eyes off the new kid, seeing the others only in his peripheral vision. That final statement by Aris had terrified him; if they'd killed *his* telepathy partner . . .

"Do what?" Frypan asked.

"What do you think?" Minho said. "He's a freak like Thomas. They can talk in each other's heads."

Newt was glaring at Thomas now. "Serious?"

Thomas nodded and almost spoke to Aris in his mind again, but said it out loud at the last second. "*Who* killed her? What happened?"

"Who killed who?" Minho said. "No more of your voodoo klunk while we're around."

Thomas, eyes watering now, finally broke his gaze with Aris and looked over at Minho. "He had someone he could do this with, just like I did. I mean . . . *do*. But he said they killed her. I want to know who *they* are."

Aris's head had dropped; his eyes looked closed from where Thomas sat. "I don't really know who *they* are. It's too confusing. I couldn't tell the bad guys from the good guys. But I think somehow they made this girl Beth . . . stab . . . my friend. Her name was Rachel. She's dead, man. She's dead." He covered his face with both hands.

Thomas felt an almost painful prick of confusion. Everything pointed to Aris's having come from another version of the Maze, set up in the same format except with the ratio of girls to boys being switched. But that would make Aris their version of Teresa. And this Beth sounded like their version of Gally, who'd killed Chuck. With a knife. Did that mean that Gally was supposed to have killed Thomas instead?

But why was Aris here now? And where was Teresa? Things that had almost started to click in his mind fell apart again.

"Well, how'd you end up with us?" Newt asked. "Where are all these girls you keep talking about? How many of them escaped with you? Did they bring all of you here or just you?"

Thomas couldn't help but feel sorry for Aris. To get grilled with all these questions after something like that had happened. If the roles were switched, if Thomas had seen Teresa get killed . . . Watching it happen to Chuck had been bad enough.

Bad enough? he thought. *Or was seeing Chuck die worse?* Thomas wanted to scream. At that moment, everything in the world just *sucked*.

Aris looked up finally, wiped a couple of tears from his cheeks. He did it without the slightest hint of shame, and Thomas suddenly knew that he liked this kid.

"Look," the boy said. "I'm just as confused as everyone else. About thirty of us survived, they took us to that gym, fed us, cleaned us up. Then they brought me to this place last night, saying I should be separate since I'm a guy. That's it. Then you sticks show up."

"*Sticks?*" Minho repeated.

Aris shook his head. "Never mind. I don't even know what it means. Just a word they used when I got there."

Minho exchanged a glance with Thomas, half smiling. Looked like both groups had come up with their own vocabulary.

"Hey," one of the Gladers Thomas didn't really know called out. He was leaning against the wall behind Aris, pointing at him. "What's that on the side of your neck? Something black, right below your collar."

Aris tried to look down, but couldn't bend his neck to see that part of his body. "What?"

Thomas saw a dark splotch just above the back neckline of the boy's pajama shirt as he shifted around. It appeared to be a thick line, stretching from the hollow of his collarbone around to his back. And it was broken up, like it might be lettering.

"Here, let me look," Newt offered. He stood from the bed and walked over, his limp—from something in the past he'd never shared with Thomas—showing more than usual. He reached out and pulled Aris's shirt down more so he could see the odd marking better.

"It's a tattoo," Newt said, squinting as if he didn't believe his eyes.

"What's it say?" Minho asked, though he'd already gotten up from the bed and approached to get his own look.

When Newt didn't answer right away, curiosity forced Thomas to his feet, and soon he was right beside Minho, leaning over to see the tattoo himself. What he saw printed there in blocky letters made his heart skip a beat.

Property of WICKED. Group B, Subject B1. The Partner.

"What's that supposed to mean?" Minho asked.

"What does it *say*?" Aris asked, reaching around to feel the skin of his neck and shoulders, pulling his shirt collar down. "I swear it wasn't there last night!"

Newt repeated the words to him, then said, "Property of WICKED?

I thought we'd escaped them. Or you'd escaped them, too. Whatever." He turned around, visibly frustrated, and went back to sit down on his bed.

"And why would it call you the *Partner?*" Minho said, still staring at the tattoo.

Aris shook his head. "I don't have a clue. I swear. And there's no way that was there before last night. I showered, looked in the mirror. I would've seen it. And someone would've noticed it back in the Maze for sure."

"You're telling me they tattooed you in the middle of the night?" Minho said. "Without you noticing? Come on, dude."

"I swear!" Aris insisted. Then he got up and went to the bathroom, probably to try to see the words for himself.

"I don't believe a shuck word he says," Minho whispered to Thomas on his way back to his seat. Then, just as he leaned forward to plop back down on the mattress, his shirt shifted enough to reveal a thick line of black on *his* neck.

"Whoa!" Thomas said. For a second, he was too stunned to move.

"What?" Minho asked, looking at Thomas as if he'd just sprouted a third ear on his forehead.

"Your—your neck," Thomas finally got out. "You have it on your neck, too!"

"What the shuck you talkin' about?" Minho said, pulling at his shirt, face scrunched up as he struggled to see something he couldn't.

Thomas ran over to Minho, slapped his hands away, then pulled the neckline of the shirt back. "Holy . . . It's right there! Same thing, except . . ."

Thomas read the words to himself.

Property of WICKED. Group A, Subject A7. The Leader.

"*What*, dude!" Minho yelled at him.

Most of the other Gladers had gathered in a tight group behind Thomas, squeezing in to get a look. Thomas quickly read the tattooed words out loud, surprised he did it without stumbling on them.

"You're kiddin' me, man," Minho said, standing up. He pushed his way through the crowd of boys to follow Aris to the bathroom.

And then the frenzy began. Thomas felt his own shirt tugged down as he pulled at others. Everyone started talking over everyone else.

"They all say Group A."

"Property of WICKED, just like his."

"You're Subject A-thirteen."

"Subject A-nineteen."

"A-three."

"A-ten."

Thomas was slowly turning in a circle, dazed as he watched the Gladers discover the tattoos on each other. Most of them didn't have the additional designations like Aris and Minho, just the property line. Newt was going from boy to boy, looking for himself, his face set in stone as if he were concentrating on memorizing the names and numbers. Then, quite by accident, the two of them stood facing each other.

"What does mine say?" Newt asked.

Thomas pulled the neckline of Newt's shirt to the side, then leaned over to read the words etched into his skin. "You're Subject A-five and they called you the *Glue*."

Newt gave him a startled look. "The *Glue*?"

Thomas let go of his shirt and stepped back. "Yeah. Probably because you're kind of the glue that holds us all together. I don't know. Read mine."

"I already did—"

Thomas noticed that an odd expression had come over Newt's face.

One of hesitation. Or dread. Like he didn't want to tell Thomas what his tattoo said. "Well?"

"You're Subject A-two," Newt answered. Then he lowered his eyes.

"And?" Thomas pushed.

Newt hesitated, then answered without looking at him. "It doesn't call you anything. It just says . . . 'To be killed by Group B.'"

CHAPTER 7

Thomas didn't really have time to process what Newt had said. He was actually trying to decide whether he was more confused or scared when a clanging bell began ringing throughout the room. He instinctively put his hands to his ears and looked around at the others.

He noticed the perplexed recognition on their faces, and then it hit him. It was the same sound he'd heard back in the Maze right before Teresa had shown up in the Box. That was the only time he'd heard it, and trapped within the confines of a small room it was different—stronger, laced with overlapping echoes. Still, he was pretty sure it was the same. It was the alarm used in the Glade to announce that a Newbie had arrived.

And it wasn't stopping; Thomas already felt a headache forming behind his eyes.

The Gladers milled about the room, gawking at the walls and the roof as if they were trying to figure out the source of the noise. Some of them sat down on the beds, hands pressed to the sides of their heads. Thomas tried to find the source of the alarm as well, but couldn't see anything. No speakers, no heating or air-conditioning vents in the walls, nothing. Just a sound coming from everywhere at once.

Newt grabbed his arm, shouted in his ear. "It's the bloody Newbie alarm!"

"I know!"

"Why's it ringing?"

Thomas shrugged, hoping his face didn't betray how annoyed he was. How was he supposed to know what was going on?

Minho and Aris had reappeared from the bathroom, both of them absently rubbing the backs of their necks as they searched the room for answers. It didn't take long for them to realize that the others had similar tattoos. Frypan had walked over to the door leading back out to the common room and was just about to touch the palm of his hand to the spot where the broken handle used to be.

"Wait!" Thomas shouted on impulse. He ran over to join Frypan at the door, sensing Newt right behind him.

"Why?" Frypan asked, his hand still hovering just inches from the door.

"I don't know," Thomas replied, not sure if he could even be heard over the clanging sounds. "It's an *alarm*. Maybe something really bad is happening."

"Yeah!" Frypan yelled back. "And maybe we need to get out of here!"

Without waiting to see what Thomas said, he pushed the door. When it didn't move, he pushed harder. When it still didn't budge, he leaned up against it with his full weight, shoulder first.

Nothing. It was closed as tight as if it were bricked shut.

"You broke the shuck handle!" Frypan screamed, then slapped the door with the palm of his hand.

Thomas didn't want to shout anymore; he was tired and his throat hurt. He turned and leaned back against the wall, folded his arms. Most of the Gladers seemed as run-down as Thomas—sick of looking for answers or a way out. All of them were either sitting on the beds or standing around with blank expressions on their faces.

Out of desperation more than anything, Thomas called to Teresa again. Then several times more. But she didn't respond, and with all the blaring noise, he didn't know if he could have focused enough to hear her anyway. He still felt her absence; it was like waking up one day with no teeth in your mouth. You wouldn't need to run to the mirror to know they were gone.

Then the alarm stopped.

Never before had silence seemed to have its own sound. Like a buzzing hive of bees, it settled on the room with ferocity, making Thomas reach up and wiggle a finger in each ear. Every breath, every sigh in the room was like an explosion compared to the bizarre haze of quiet.

Newt was the first one to speak. "Don't tell me we're still gonna get bloody Newbies thrown in our laps."

"Where's the Box in this shuck place?" Minho muttered sarcastically.

A slight creak made Thomas look sharply over at the door to the common area. It had swung open several inches, a slice of darkness marking where it now stood ajar. Someone had turned off the lights on the other side. Frypan backed up a step.

"Guessin' they want us to go out there now," Minho said.

"Then why don't you go first," Frypan offered.

Minho had already started moving. "No problem. Maybe we'll have a new little shank to pick on and kick in the butt when we got nothin' else to do." He made it to the door, then paused and looked sideways at Thomas. His voice turned surprisingly soft. "We could use another Chuck."

Thomas knew he shouldn't have been upset. If anything, Minho was trying—in his own strange way—to show that he missed Chuck just as much as everyone else. But being reminded of his friend, and at such an odd moment, made Thomas angry. Instinct told him to ignore it—he was having a hard enough time dealing with the things going on around him. He needed to separate himself from his feelings for a while and just move forward. Step by step. Figure it all out.

"Yeah," he finally said. "You going through or you need me to go first?"

"What did your tattoo say?" Minho responded quietly, ignoring Thomas's question.

"Doesn't matter. Let's go out there."

Minho nodded, still not looking directly at him. Then he smiled, and whatever had been troubling him so deeply appeared to vanish, replaced by his usual laid-back attitude. "Good that. If some zombie starts eating my leg, save me."

"Deal." Thomas wanted him to hurry and get on with it. He knew they were on the edge of yet another great change in their ridiculous journey, and he didn't want to draw it out any longer.

Minho pushed open the door. The single bar of blackness became a wide swath of it, the common area now as dark as it had been when they'd first left the boys' dorm. Minho stepped through the doorway, and Thomas followed right on his heels.

"Wait here," Minho whispered. "No need playing bumper cars with the dead folks again. Let me find the light switches first."

"Why would they have turned them off?" Thomas asked. "I mean, *who* turned them off?"

Minho looked back at him; the light from Aris's room spilled across his face, illuminating the smirk set firmly there. "Why do you even bother asking questions, dude? Nothing has ever made sense and it probably never will. Now slim it and sit still."

Minho was quickly swallowed by the darkness. Thomas heard his soft footsteps on the carpet and the *swish* sound of his hand running along the wall as he walked.

"Here they are!" he shouted from the spot that seemed about right to Thomas.

A few clicks sounded and then lights blazed throughout the room. For the tiniest fraction of a second, Thomas didn't realize what was so starkly different about the place. But then it hit him, and as if that awakened his other senses as well, he realized that the horrible smell of rotting corpses had vanished.

And now he knew why.

The bodies were gone, with no sign that they'd ever been there in the first place.

CHAPTER 8

Several seconds passed before Thomas realized he'd stopped breathing. Sucking in a deep pull of air, he gaped at the now-empty room. No bloated, purple-skinned bodies. No stink.

Newt nudged past him, walking forward with his slight limp until he stood in the very center of the room's carpeted floor. "This is impossible," he said, turning in a slow circle, gazing up at the ceiling where the corpses had hung from ropes only minutes earlier. "Not enough time passed for someone to get them out. And no one else even came into this buggin' room. We would've heard them!"

Thomas stepped to the side and leaned against the wall as the other Gladers and Aris came out of the small dorm room. A hushed sense of awe spread across the group as one by one, each person noticed the missing dead. As for Thomas, he once again felt a numbness, like he just might be done feeling surprised at anything.

"You're right," Minho said to Newt. "We were in there with the door closed for, what, twenty minutes? No way anyone could've moved all those bodies that quickly. Plus, this place is locked from the *inside*."

"Not to mention getting rid of the smell," Thomas added.

Minho nodded.

"Well, you shanks are right smart," Frypan said through a huff. "But take a look around. They're gone. So whatever you think, somehow they got rid of them."

Thomas didn't feel like arguing about it—or even talking about it. So the dead bodies were gone. They'd seen stranger stuff.

"Hey," Winston said. "Those crazy people quit screaming and yelling."

Thomas put his weight back on his feet, listened. Silence. "I thought we just couldn't hear them from Aris's room. But you're right—they stopped."

Soon everyone was running for the larger dorm room on the far side of the common area. Thomas followed, intensely curious to look out the windows and see the world outside. Before, with the Cranks screaming and pressing their faces against the iron bars, he'd been too horrified to get a good view.

"No way!" Minho yelled from up ahead, then, without further explanation, disappeared inside the room.

As Thomas moved in that direction, he noticed that every boy hesitated a second, wide-eyed at the threshold of the door, then went ahead and entered the dorm. He waited as each Glader and then Aris funneled their way inside, then followed.

He felt the same shock he'd sensed from the other boys. As a whole, the room looked much like it had when they'd walked out of it earlier. But there was one monumental difference: at each window, without exception, a red brick wall had been erected just outside the iron bars, completely blocking every inch of open space. The only light in the room came from the panels on the ceiling.

"Even if they were quick with those bodies," Newt said, "I'm pretty sure they didn't have time to bloody throw up some brick walls. What's going on here?"

Thomas watched as Minho walked over to one of the windows and reached through the bars, pressing his hand against the red bricks. "Solid," he said, then slapped at it.

"It doesn't even look fresh," Thomas murmured, stepping up to one himself to get a feel. Hard and cool. "The mortar's dry. Somehow they've tricked us, that's all."

"Tricked us?" Frypan asked. "How?"

Thomas shrugged, that numbness returning. Still wishing desperately that he could talk to Teresa. "I don't know. Remember the Cliff? We jumped into thin air and went through an invisible hole. Who knows what these people can do."

The next half hour passed in a haze. Thomas wandered about, as did everyone else, inspecting the brick walls, looking for signs of anything else that had changed. Several things had, each one just as strange as the next. All the beds in the Gladers' dorm room were made, and there was no sign of the grungy clothes they'd all worn before changing into the pajamas provided the night before. The dressers had been rearranged, though the difference was subtle and some people disagreed that they'd been moved at all. Either way, each one had been stocked with fresh clothes and shoes, and new digital watches for each boy.

But the biggest change of all—discovered by Minho—was the sign outside the room where they'd found Aris. Instead of saying *Teresa Agnes, Group A, Subject A1, The Betrayer*, it now said:

Aris Jones, Group B, Subject B1
The Partner

Everyone observed the new plaque, then wandered away, but Thomas found himself standing in front of it, unable to remove his eyes. To Thomas it felt like the new label made it official—Teresa had been taken from him, replaced by Aris. None of it made sense, and none of it mattered anymore. He went back to the boys' dorm, found the cot he'd slept on during the night—or at least, the one he *thought* he'd slept on—

and lay down, putting the pillow over his head, as if that would make everyone else go away.

What had happened to her? What had happened to *them*? Where were they? What were they supposed to do? And the tattoos...

Turning his head to the side, then his whole body, he squeezed his eyes shut and folded his arms tightly, pulling his legs up until he lay in the fetal position. Then, determined to keep trying until he heard back from her, he called out with his thoughts.

Teresa? A pause. *Teresa?* A longer pause. *Teresa!* He shouted it mentally, his whole body tensing with the effort. *Teresa! Where are you? Please answer me! Why aren't you trying to contact me? Ter—*

Get out of my head!

The words exploded inside his mind, so vivid and so strangely audible within his skull that he felt lances of pain behind his eyes and in his ears. He sat up in bed, then stood. It was her. It was definitely her.

Teresa? He pressed the first two fingers of both hands against his temples. *Teresa?*

Whoever you are, get out of my shuck head!

Thomas stumbled backward until he sat down once again on the bed. His eyes were closed as he concentrated. *Teresa, what are you talking about? It's me. Thomas. Where are you?*

Shut up! It was her, he had no doubt, but her mental voice was full of fear and anger. *Just shut up! I don't know who you are! Leave me alone!*

But, Thomas began, completely at a loss. *Teresa, what's wrong?*

She paused before answering, as if collecting her thoughts, and when she finally spoke again, Thomas sensed an almost disturbing calm in her.

Leave me alone, or I'll hunt you down and cut your throat. I swear it.

And then she was gone. Despite her warning, he tried calling for her again, but the same emptiness he'd felt since that morning returned, her presence having vanished.

Thomas fell back on the bed, something horrible burning through his body. He quickly buried his head in the pillow again and cried for the first time since Chuck had been killed. But the words from the label outside her door—*The Betrayer*—kept popping up in his mind. Each time, he pushed them away.

Amazingly, no one bothered him or asked him what was wrong. His stifled sobs finally faded into an occasional hitched breath, and eventually he fell asleep. Once again, he dreamed.

He's a little older this time, probably seven or eight. A very bright light hovers above his head like magic.

People in strange green suits and funny glasses keep peeking at him, their heads momentarily blocking the brilliance that shines down. He can see their eyes but nothing else. Their mouths and noses are covered by masks. Thomas is somehow both himself at that age and yet, as before, observing as an outsider. But he feels the boy's fear.

People are talking, voices muted and dull. Some are men, some are women, but he can't tell which is which or who is who.

He can't understand much of it at all.

Only glimpses. Fragments of conversation. All of it terrifying.

"We'll have to cut deeper with him and the girl."

"Can their brains handle this?"

"This is so amazing, you know? The Flare is rooted inside him."

"He might die."

"Or worse. He might live."

He hears one last thing, finally something that doesn't make him shiver in disgust or fright.

"Or he and the others might save us. Save us all."

CHAPTER 9

When he woke up, his head felt like several chunks of ice had been hammered through his ears and into his brain. Wincing, he reached up to rub his eyes and was hit by a wave of nausea that sent the room tilting around him. Then he remembered the terrible things Teresa had said, then the short dream, and misery engulfed him. Who had those people been? Was it real? What had they meant when they'd said those awful things about his brain?

"Glad to see you still know how to take a nap."

Thomas peeked through a squint and saw Newt standing next to his bed, staring down at him.

"How long's it been?" Thomas asked, forcing thoughts of Teresa and the dream—memory?—into a dark corner of his mind to agonize over later.

Newt looked at his watch. "Couple hours. When people noticed you lie down, it actually kind of relaxed everyone. Not much we can do but sit and wait for something new to happen. There's no way out of this place."

Thomas tried not to groan as he scooted himself into a sitting position, his back against the wall at the head of his bed. "Do we even have any food?"

"No. But I'm pretty sure these people wouldn't go through all this trouble to bring us here, trick us or whatever they've done, just to let us buggin' starve to death. Something will happen. Reminds me of when they sent the first group of us to the Glade. The initial group of me and Alby and Minho and some others. The original Gladers." He said that last part with a not-so-subtle burst of sarcasm.

Thomas was intrigued, surprised he'd never before dug into what that had been like. "How does this remind you of that?"

Newt's gaze was focused on the brick wall outside the closest window. "We all woke up in the middle of the day, lying on the ground around the doors to the Box. It was closed. Our memories had been wiped, just like yours when you came. You'd be surprised at how quickly we pulled ourselves together and quit panicking. There were about thirty of us. Obviously, we had no bloody clue what had happened, how we'd gotten there, what we were supposed to do. And we were terrified, disoriented. But since we were all in the same crappy situation, we organized ourselves and figured out the place. Had the full farm running within days, everybody with their own job."

Thomas was relieved that the pain in his skull had diminished. And he was intrigued to hear about the start of the Glade—the scattered pieces of the puzzle brought back by the Changing weren't nearly enough to form solid memories. "Did the Creators have everything in place already? Crops, animals, all that?"

Newt nodded, still staring at the bricked-up window. "Yeah, but it took a ton of work to get it going nice and smooth. A lot of trial and error before we accomplished anything."

"So . . . how does this remind you of that?" Thomas asked again.

Finally, Newt looked at him. "I guess back then we all just had a sense that there was obviously a *purpose* to us having been sent there. If someone had wanted to kill us, why wouldn't they have just killed us? Why would they send us to a huge place with a house and a barn and animals? And because we had no other choice, we accepted it and started working and exploring."

"But we're already done exploring here," Thomas countered. "No animals, no food, no Maze."

"Yeah, but come on. It's the same concept. We're obviously here for a buggin' purpose. We'll figure it out eventually."

"If we don't starve first."

Newt pointed at the bathroom. "We've got plenty of water, so it'll be at least a few days before we drop dead. Something will happen."

Deep down Thomas believed it, too, and was only arguing to solidify it in his own mind. "But what about all those dead people we saw? Maybe they rescued us for real, got killed, and now we're screwed. Maybe we were *supposed* to do something, but now it's all been messed up and we've been left here to die."

Newt burst out laughing. "You're one depressing piece of klunk, slinthead. Nah, with all those corpses magically disappearing and the brick walls, I'd say this is something more like the Maze. Weird and impossible to explain. The latest and greatest mystery. Maybe our next test, who knows. Whatever's going on, we'll have a chance, just like we did in the bloody Maze. I guarantee it."

"Yeah," Thomas murmured, wondering if he should share what he'd dreamed about. Deciding to save it for later, he said, "Hope you're right. As long as no Grievers suddenly show up, we'll be good."

Newt was already shaking his head by the time Thomas finished. "Please, man. Careful what you buggin' wish for. Maybe they'll send something worse."

The image of Teresa popped into Thomas's mind just then, and he lost all desire to talk. "Who's the cheerful one now?" he forced himself to say.

"You got me," Newt replied, then stood up. "Guess I'll go bug somebody else till the excitement begins, which better be bloody soon. I'm hungry."

"Careful what *you* wish for."

"Good that."

Newt walked away, and Thomas scooted down to lie on his back, staring at the bottom of the bunk above him. He closed his eyes after a while, but when he saw Teresa's face in the darkness of his thoughts, he opened them right up again. If he was going to get through this, he'd have to try to forget about her for now.

Hunger.

It's like an animal trapped inside you, Thomas thought. After three full days of not eating, it felt like a vicious, gnawing, dull-clawed animal was trying to burrow its way out of his stomach. He felt it every second of every minute of every hour. He drank water as often as possible from the sinks in the bathroom, but it did nothing to drive the beast away. If anything, it felt like he was making the thing stronger so it could inflict more misery within.

The others felt it, too, even if most of them kept their complaints to themselves. Thomas watched as they walked around, heads hung low, jaws slack, as if every step burned a thousand calories. People licked their lips a lot. They grabbed at their stomachs, pushed on them, as if trying to calm that gnawing beast. Unless they were going to the bathroom to use it or to get a drink, the Gladers didn't move at all. Like Thomas, they just lay there on the bunk beds, limp. Skin pale, eyes sunken.

Thomas felt all this like a festering disease, and seeing the others only made it worse, a stark reminder that this wasn't something he could just ignore. That it was real, and death waited just around the corner.

Listless sleep. Bathroom. Water. Trudge back to bed. Listless sleep—without any more of the memory-dreams he'd experienced. It became a horrendous cycle, broken up only by thoughts of Teresa, her harsh words to him the only thing that lightened the prospect of death, even if only a little. She'd been the only thing he could grasp for hope after the Maze and Chuck's death. And now she was gone, there was no food, and three long days had passed.

Hunger. Misery.

He'd quit bothering to look at his watch—it only made time drag and reminded his body how long it'd been since he'd eaten—but he thought it was roughly midafternoon of the third day when a humming sound abruptly began from the common area.

He stared at the door leading out there, knew he should get up and go check it out. But his mind had already been slipping into another one of those hazy half-naps, the world around him foggy.

Maybe he'd imagined it. But then he heard it again.

He told himself to get up.

He fell asleep instead.

"Thomas."

It was Minho's voice. Weak, but stronger than it had been the last time he'd heard it.

"Thomas. Dude, wake up."

Thomas opened his eyes, amazed he'd survived another nap without dying. Things were blurry for a second, and at first he didn't believe that what he thought was just a few inches from his face was real. But then its image sharpened, and the red roundness of it, with flecks of green scattered across its shiny surface, made him feel like he was looking on heaven itself.

An apple.

"Where'd you . . ." He didn't bother to finish, those two words alone sapping his strength.

"Just eat it," Minho said, followed by a wet crunch.

Thomas glanced up to see his friend munching on his own apple.

Then, drawing the last remnants of energy from somewhere deep inside himself, he pushed himself up onto an elbow and grabbed the fruit lying on the bed. He lifted it to his mouth and took a small bite. The burst of flavor and juice was a glorious thing.

Moaning, he attacked the rest of it and had eaten down to its stumpy core before Minho had even finished his—despite the head start.

"Slim yourself nice and calm," Minho said. "Eat like that and you'll just throw it right back up. Here's another one—try slowing down this time."

He handed a second apple to Thomas, who took it without saying thank you and chomped a big bite. As he chewed, resolving to swallow before stuffing another chunk in his mouth, he realized he could actually feel the first traces of energy trickling through his body.

"This is so good," he mumbled. "This is so shuckin' good."

"You still sound like an idiot when you use Glader words," Minho responded before taking another bite of his apple.

Thomas ignored him. "Where'd these come from?"

Minho hesitated in the middle of chewing, then resumed. "Found them out in the common room. Along with . . . something else. Shanks who found it all claim they'd just looked a few minutes earlier and nothing had been there, but whatever, I don't care."

Thomas swung his legs off the bed and sat up. "What else did they find?"

Minho took a bite, then nodded toward the door. "Go look for yourself."

Thomas rolled his eyes and slowly stood up. The miserable weakness was still there, like most of his insides had been sucked right out and all he had left were a few bones and tendons to hold himself erect. But he steadied, feeling even after a few seconds that he was already better than the last time he'd made the long, lifeless trek to the bathroom.

Once he thought he had his balance, he walked over to the door and entered the common area. Only three days before, the room had been filled with dead bodies—now it was crowded with Gladers picking things off a big pile of food that had seemingly been dumped there without any order. Fruit, vegetables, small packages.

But he'd barely registered this when an even more bizarre sight on the far side of the room caught his attention. He reached out to steady himself on the wall behind him.

A large wooden desk had been placed opposite the door to the other dorm room.

Behind the desk, a thin man in a white suit sat in a chair, his feet propped up and crossed at the ankles.

The man was reading a book.

CHAPTER 10

Thomas stood there for a full minute, staring at the man casually sitting at the desk, reading. It was as if he'd been reading that way and in that very spot every day for his whole life. Thin black hair combed across a pale, bald head; a long nose, twisted slightly to the right; and shifty brown eyes darting back and forth as he read—the man somehow looked relaxed and nervous at the same time.

And the white suit. Pants, shirt, tie, coat. Socks. Shoes. All white.

What in the *world*?

Thomas looked over at the Gladers munching on fruit and a snack from a bag that looked like a mixture of nuts and seeds. They seemed oblivious to the man at the desk.

"Who *is* that guy?" Thomas called out to no one in particular.

One of the boys looked up, stopped chewing for a second. Then he quickly finished off his mouthful and swallowed. "He won't tell us anything. Told us we had to wait till he's ready." The boy shrugged as if that wasn't a big deal and took another bite of a peeled orange.

Thomas returned his attention to the stranger. Still sitting there, still reading. He turned a page with a whispery scrape and continued scanning the words.

Baffled, and with a stomach rumbling for more food, Thomas still couldn't help but walk toward the man to investigate. Of all the strange things to wake up to . . .

"Careful," one of the Gladers called out, but it was too late.

Just ten feet in front of the desk, Thomas slammed into an invisible wall. His nose hit first, smashing against what felt like a cold sheet of glass. The rest of his body followed suit, bumping against the unseen wall and making him stumble backward. He instinctively reached up to rub his nose as he squinted to see how he could've possibly missed a glass barrier.

But no matter how hard he looked, he couldn't see anything. Not the slightest glare or reflection, not a smudge anywhere. All he saw was air. All the while, the man hadn't bothered to move or give even the least hint he'd noticed anything.

More slowly this time, Thomas approached the spot, holding his hands out. Soon he made contact with the wall of completely invisible . . . what? It felt like glass—smooth, hard and cool to the touch. But he saw absolutely nothing to indicate that something solid stood there.

Frustrated, Thomas moved to the left, then the right, feeling along the unseen yet solid wall. It spanned the entire room; there was no way to approach the stranger at the desk. Thomas finally pounded on it, making a series of dull thumps, but nothing else happened. Some of the Gladers behind him, Aris included, remarked how they'd already tried that.

The strangely dressed man, just a dozen or so feet in front of him, let out an exaggerated sigh as he pulled his crossed feet from the desk and let them drop to the floor. He placed a finger in his book to mark his place and looked up at Thomas, making no effort to hide his annoyance.

"How many times do I have to repeat this?" the man said, his nasally voice a perfect match for his pale skin, thin hair and skinny body. And that suit. That stupid white suit. Oddly, his words weren't muffled at all by the barrier. "We still have forty-seven minutes before I've been authorized to implement Phase Two of the Trials. Please show your patience and leave me alone. You've been given this time to eat and replenish yourselves, and I strongly suggest you take advantage of it, young man. Now, if you don't mind . . ."

Without waiting for a response, he leaned back in his chair and returned his feet to the desktop. Then, opening his book to the spot he'd marked, he resumed reading.

Thomas was truly speechless. He turned away from the man and the desk and leaned against the invisible wall, its hard surface pressing against his back. What had just happened? Surely he was still asleep, dreaming. For some reason, that thought alone seemed to amplify his hunger, and he longingly glanced over at the mound of food. Then he noticed Minho at the door to the dorm room, leaning against its frame with his arms folded.

Thomas jabbed a thumb over his shoulder and raised his eyebrows.

"You met our new friend?" Minho responded, a smirk flashing across his face. "Real piece of work, this guy. I gotta get me one of those shuck suits. Fancy stuff."

"Am I awake?" Thomas asked.

"You're awake. Now eat—you look horrible. Almost as bad as Rat Man over there, reading his book."

Thomas was surprised at how quickly he could set aside the oddness of the guy in the white suit appearing out of nowhere, and the invisible wall. Again that numbness that had become so familiar. After the initial shock, nothing was strange anymore. Anything could become normal. Pushing it all away, he dragged himself over to the food and started eating. Another apple. An orange. A bag of mixed nuts, then a chewy bar of granola and raisins. His body begged for water, but he couldn't get himself to move quite yet.

"You need to slim it," Minho said from behind him. "We've got shanks puking all over the place 'cause they ate too much. That's probably enough, dude."

Thomas stood, relishing the feel of a full stomach. Not missing at all that gnawing beast that had lived inside him for so long. He knew Minho was right—he had to slim it. He nodded at his friend before stepping around him to go get a drink, the whole time wondering what could possibly be in store for them when the man in the white suit was ready to implement "Phase Two of the Trials."

Whatever *that* meant.

A half hour later, Thomas sat on the floor with the rest of the Gladers, Minho to his right and Newt to his left, all of them facing the invisible wall and the weasel of a man sitting at the desk behind it. His feet were still propped up, his eyes still flickering down the pages of his book. Thomas felt the wonderful return of energy and strength slowly building inside him.

The new kid, Aris, had given him a strange look in the bathroom, as if he wanted to speak telepathically with him but was afraid to do it. Thomas had ignored him, and quickly walked to the sink and guzzled down as much water as he could with his now-full stomach. By the time he finished and wiped his mouth on his sleeve, Aris had left. Now the boy sat over by the wall, staring at the floor. Thomas felt sorry for him—as bad as things were for the Gladers, Aris had it worse. Especially if he'd been as close to the murdered girl he'd mentioned as Thomas was to Teresa.

Minho was the first to break the silence. "I think we've all gone psycho like those . . . what'd they call themselves again? Cranks. The Cranks at the windows. We're all sitting here waiting for a lecture from Rat Man like this is totally normal. Like we're at some kind of school. I can tell you this much—if he had anything good to say, he wouldn't need a freaking magic wall to protect him from us, now, would he?"

"Just slim it and listen," Newt said. "Maybe it's all gonna be over."

"Yeah, right," Minho said. "And Frypan's gonna start having little babies, Winston'll get rid of his monster acne, and Thomas here'll actually smile for once."

Thomas turned to Minho and exaggerated a fake smile. "There, you happy?"

"Dude," he responded. "You are one ugly shank."

"If you say so."

"Shut your bloody holes," Newt whispered. "I think it's time."

Thomas looked over to see that the stranger—Rat Man, as Minho so kindly called him—had put his feet on the floor and placed the book on the desk. He scooted his chair back to get a better view of one of the drawers, then pulled it out and rummaged through things Thomas couldn't see. Finally, he pulled out a densely packed manila folder full of messy papers, many of them bent and sticking out at odd angles.

"Ah, here it is," Rat Man said in his nasally voice; then he placed the folder on the desk, opened it up and looked at the boys in front of him. "Thank you for gathering in an orderly manner so I can tell you what I've been . . . instructed to tell you. Please listen carefully."

"Why do you need that wall!" Minho shouted.

Newt reached around Thomas and punched Minho in the arm. "Shut it!"

Rat Man continued as if he hadn't heard the outburst. "You're all still here because of an uncanny will to survive despite the odds, among . . . other reasons. About sixty people were sent to live in the Glade. Well, *your* Glade, anyway. Another sixty in Group B, but for now we'll forget them."

The man's eyes flickered to Aris, then went back to slowly scanning the crowd. Thomas didn't know if anyone else had noticed, but he had no doubt that there'd been a hint of familiarity in that quick look. What did it mean . . . ?

"Out of all those people, only a fraction survived to be here today. I'm assuming you've figured this out by now, but many of the things that happen to you are solely for the purpose of judging and analyzing your *responses*. And yet it's not really an experiment as much as it is . . . constructing a blueprint. Stimulating the killzone and collecting the resultant patterns. Putting them all together to achieve the greatest breakthrough in the history of science and medicine.

"These situations inflicted upon you are called the Variables, and each one has been meticulously thought out. I'll explain more soon. And though I can't tell you everything at this time, it's vital that you know this much: these trials you're going through are for a very important cause. Continue to respond well to the Variables, continue to survive, and you'll be rewarded with the knowledge that you've played a part in saving the human race. And yourselves, of course."

Rat Man paused, apparently for effect. Thomas looked over at Minho and raised his eyebrows.

"This dude's shucked in the head," Minho whispered. "How would escaping a freaking maze save the human race?"

"I represent a group called WICKED," Rat Man continued. "I know it sounds menacing, but it stands for World In Catastrophe, Killzone Experiment Department. Nothing menacing about it, despite what you may think. We exist for one purpose and one purpose only: to save the world from catastrophe. You here in this room are a vital part of what we plan to do. We have resources never known to any group of any kind in the history of civilization. Nearly unlimited money, unlimited human capital and technology advanced beyond even the most clever man's wants and wishes.

"As you make your way through the Trials, you have seen and will continue to see evidence of this technology and the resources behind it. If I can tell you anything today, it is that you should never, ever believe your eyes. Or your mind, for that matter. This is why we did the demonstration with the hanging bodies and the bricked-up windows. All I will say is that sometimes what you see is not real, and sometimes what you do *not* see *is* real. We can manipulate your brains and nerve receptacles when necessary. I know this all sounds confusing and a little scary, perhaps."

Thomas thought the man couldn't have possibly made a greater understatement. And the word *killzone* kept bouncing around his head. His scarcely revived memories couldn't quite grasp what it meant, but he'd first seen it on the metal plaque back in the Maze, the one that had spelled out the words that made up WICKED's acronym.

The man slowly passed his eyes over every Glader in the room. His upper lip shone with sweat. "The Maze was a part of the Trials. Not one Variable was thrown at you that didn't serve a purpose for our collection of killzone patterns. Your escape was part of the Trials. Your battle against the Grievers. The murder of the boy Chuck. The supposed rescue and subsequent trip in the bus. All of it. Part of the Trials."

Anger swelled in Thomas's chest at the mention of Chuck. He'd half risen to his feet before he knew what had come over him; Newt pulled him back down to the floor.

As if spurred by this, Rat Man quickly stood up from his chair, sending it back against the wall behind him. Then he placed his hands on the desk and leaned toward the Gladers.

"*All* of it has been part of the Trials, you understand? Phase One, to be exact. And we are still dangerously short of what we need. So we've had to up the ante, and now it's time for Phase Two. It's time for things to get difficult."

CHAPTER 11

The room lapsed into silence. Thomas knew he should be upset by the absurd notion that up to this point things had been easy for them. The idea should've terrified him. Not to mention the stuff about manipulating their brains. But instead, he was so intensely curious to find out what the man was going to tell them, the words had merely washed across his mind.

Rat Man waited for an eternity, then slowly lowered himself back into the chair and scooted forward to sit behind the desk once more. "You may think, or it may seem, that we're merely testing your ability to survive. On the surface, the Maze Trial could be mistakenly classified that way. But I assure you—this is not merely about survival and the will to live. That's only part of this experiment. The bigger picture is something you won't understand until the very end.

"Sun flares have ravaged many parts of the earth. Also, a disease unlike any before known to man has been ravaging the earth's people—a disease called the Flare. For the first time, the governments of all nations—the surviving ones—are working together. They've combined forces to create WICKED—a group meant to fight the new problems of this world. You are a big part of that fight. And you'll have every incentive to work with us, because, sad to say, each one of you has already caught the virus."

He quickly held up his hands to cut off the rumblings that started. "Now, now! No need to worry—the Flare takes a while to set in and show symptoms. But at the end of these Trials, the *cure* will be your reward, and you'll never see the . . . debilitating effects. Not many can afford the cure, you know."

Thomas's hand instinctively went up to his throat, as if a soreness there were the first indicator that he'd caught the Flare. He remembered all too well what the woman on the rescue bus had told him after the Maze. About how the Flare destroyed your brain, slowly driving you insane and stripping you of the capacity to feel basic human emotions like compassion or empathy. About how it turned you into less than an animal.

He thought of the Cranks he'd seen through the dorm windows, and he suddenly wanted to run to the bathroom and scrub his hands and mouth clean. The guy was right—they had all the incentive they needed to make it through this next phase.

"But enough of this history lesson and time-wasting," Rat Man continued. "We know you now. All of you. It doesn't matter what I say or what's behind the mission of WICKED. You'll all do whatever it takes. Of this we have no doubt. And by doing what we ask, you'll save yourselves by getting the very cure so many people desperately want."

Thomas heard Minho groan next to him and worried about him throwing out another one of his smart-aleck remarks. Thomas shushed him before he could do it.

Rat Man looked down at the messy stack of papers lying in the open folder, picked up a loose piece of it, then turned it over, barely glancing at its contents. He cleared his throat. "Phase Two. The Scorch Trials. It officially begins tomorrow morning at six o'clock. You'll enter this room, and in the wall behind me you will find a Flat Trans. To your eyes the Flat Trans will appear as a shimmering wall of gray. Each of you must step through it by five minutes after the hour. So again, it opens at six o'clock and closes five minutes after that. Do you understand?"

Thomas stared at Rat Man, transfixed. It almost felt as if he were watching a recording—as if the stranger weren't really there. The other Gladers must've felt the same, because no one answered the simple question. What was a Flat Trans, anyway?

"I'm quite certain you can all *hear*," Rat Man said. "Do . . . you . . . under . . . stand?"

Thomas nodded; a few boys around him murmured quiet yeahs and yeses.

"Good." Rat Man absently picked up another piece of paper and turned it over. "At that point, the Scorch Trials will have begun. The rules are very simple. Find your way to open air, then head due north for one hundred miles. Make it to the safe haven within two weeks' time and you'll have completed Phase Two. At that point, and only at that point, you'll be cured of the Flare. That's exactly two weeks—starting the second you step through the Trans. If you don't make it, eventually you'll end up dead."

The room should've erupted into arguments, questions, panic. But no one said a word. Thomas felt as if his tongue had dried up into an old, crusty root.

Rat Man quickly slammed the folder shut, bending its contents even more than before, then put it away in the drawer from which he'd retrieved it. He stood, stepped to the side and pushed the chair underneath the desk. Finally, he folded his hands in front of him and returned his attention to the Gladers.

"It's simple, really," he said, his tone so matter-of-fact one would think he'd just given them instructions on how to turn on the showers in the bathroom. "There are no rules. There are no guidelines. You have few supplies, and there's nothing to help you along the way. Go through the Flat Trans at the time indicated. Find open air. Go one hundred miles, directly north, to the safe haven. Make it or die."

The last word seemed to finally snap everyone out of their stupor, all of them speaking up at once.

"What's a Flat Trans?"

"How'd we catch the Flare?"

"How long till we see symptoms?"

"What's at the end of the hundred miles?"

"What happened to the dead bodies?"

Question after question, a chorus of them, all melding into one roar of confusion. As for Thomas, he didn't bother. The stranger wasn't going to tell them anything. Couldn't they all see that?

Rat Man waited patiently, ignoring them, those dark eyes darting back and forth between the Gladers as they spoke. His gaze settled on Thomas, who sat there, silent, staring back at him, hating him. Hating WICKED. Hating the world.

"You shanks shut *up!*" Minho finally shouted. The questions stopped instantly. "This shuck-face ain't answering, so quit wastin' your time."

Rat Man nodded once toward Minho as if thanking him. Perhaps acknowledging his wisdom. "One hundred miles. North. Hope you make it. Remember—you all have the Flare now. We gave it to you to provide any incentive you may be lacking. And reaching the safe haven means receiving a cure." He turned away and moved toward the wall behind him, as if he planned to walk right through it. But then he stopped and faced them again.

"Ah, one last thing," he said. "Don't think you'll avoid the Scorch Trials if you decide *not* to enter the Flat Trans between six and six-oh-five tomorrow morning. Those who stay behind will be executed immediately in a most . . . unpleasant manner. Better off taking your chances in the outside world. Good luck to all of you."

With that he turned away and once again started inexplicably walking toward the wall.

But before Thomas could see what happened, the invisible wall separating them started to fog up, whitening to an opaque blur in a matter of seconds. And then the whole thing disappeared, once again revealing the other side of the common area.

Except there was no sign of the desk and its chair. And no sign of Rat Man.

"Well, shuck me," Minho whispered next to Thomas.

CHAPTER 12

Once again, the Gladers' questions and arguments filled the air, but Thomas left. He needed some space and knew the bathroom was his only escape. So instead of heading to the boys' dorm, he went to the one Teresa, then Aris, had used. He leaned back against the sink, arms folded, staring at the floor. Luckily, no one had followed him.

He didn't know how to begin processing all the information. Bodies hanging from the ceiling, reeking of death and rot, then gone completely in a matter of minutes. A stranger—and his desk!—appear out of nowhere, with an impossible shield protecting them. Then they disappear.

And these were by far the least of their worries. It was clear now that the rescue from the Maze had been a sham. But who were the pawns WICKED had used to pull the Gladers from the Creators' chamber, put them on that bus and bring them here? Had those people known they were going to be killed? Had they even really *been* killed? Rat Man had said not to trust their eyes or their minds. How could they believe anything ever again?

And worst of all, this stuff about them having the Flare disease, about the Trials earning them a cure . . .

Thomas squeezed his eyes closed and rubbed his forehead. Teresa had been taken from him. None of them had families. The next morning they were supposed to start some ridiculous thing called Phase Two, which by the sound of it was going to be worse than the Maze. All those crazy people out there—the Cranks. How would they deal with them? He suddenly thought of Chuck and what he might say if he were there.

Something simple, probably. Something like, *This sucks.*

You'd be right, Chuck, Thomas thought. *The whole world sucks.*

It had only been a few days since he'd seen his friend get stabbed in the heart; poor Chuck had died as Thomas held him. And now Thomas couldn't help but think that as horrible as it was, maybe that had been the best thing for Chuck. Maybe death was better than what lay ahead. His mind veered toward the tattoo on his neck—

"Dude, how long's it take to drop a load?" It was Minho.

Thomas looked up to see him standing in the doorway to the bathroom. "I can't stand it out there. Everyone talking over everybody else like a bunch of babies. Say what they want, we all know what we're gonna do."

Minho walked over to him and leaned his shoulder against the wall. "Ain't you Mr. Happy? Look, man, those shanks out there are just as brave as you are. Every last one of us will go through that . . . whatever he called it . . . tomorrow morning. Who cares if they wanna crack their throats yappin' about it?"

Thomas rolled his eyes. "I never said jack about me being braver than anybody. I'm just sick of hearing people's voices. Yours included."

Minho snickered. "Slinthead, when you try to be mean, it's just freaking hilarious."

"Thanks." Thomas paused. "Flat Trans."

"Huh?"

"That's what the white-suit shank called the thing we need to go through. A Flat Trans."

"Oh yeah. Must be some kind of doorway."

Thomas looked up at him. "That's what I'm thinking. Something like the Cliff. It's flat, and it *trans*ports you somewhere. Flat Trans."

"You're a shuck genius."

Newt came in then. "What're you two hiding for?"

Minho reached over and slapped Thomas on the shoulder. "We're not hiding. Thomas is just whining about his life and wishin' he could go back to his mommy."

"Tommy," Newt said, not seeming amused, "you went through the Changing, got some of your memories back. How much of this stuff do you remember?"

Thomas had been thinking a lot about that. Much of what had come back after being stung by the Griever had turned cloudy. "I don't know. I can't really picture the actual world outside or what it was like being involved with the people I helped design the Maze. Most of it's either faded again or just gone. I've had a couple of weird dreams, but nothing that helps."

They then went off on a discussion about some of the things they'd heard from their odd visitor. About the sun flares and the disease and how different things might be now that they *knew* they were being tested or experimented on. About a lot of things, with no answers—all of it laced with an unspoken fear of the virus they'd supposedly been given. They finally lulled into silence.

"Well, we've got stuff to figure out," Newt said. "And I need help to make sure the bloody food's not gone before we leave tomorrow. Something tells me we're gonna need it."

Thomas hadn't even thought of that. "You're right. Are people still chowing down out there?"

Newt shook his head. "No, Frypan took charge. That shank's religious about food—I think he was glad to have something to be the boss about again. But I'm scared people might get panicky and try to eat it anyway."

"Oh, come on," Minho said. "Those of us who made it this far got here for a reason. All the idiots are dead by now." He looked sideways at Thomas, as if worried Thomas might think he'd included Chuck in that assessment. Maybe even Teresa.

"Maybe," Newt responded. "Hope so. Anyway, I was thinking we need to get organized, get things back together. Act like we did in the bloody Glade. Last few days have been miserable, everybody moaning and groaning, no structure, no plan. It's driving me psycho."

"What'd you expect us to do?" Minho asked. "Form up in lines and do push-ups? We're stuck in a stupid three-room prison."

Newt swatted at the air as if Minho's words were gnats. "Whatever. I'm just saying, things are obviously going to change tomorrow and we gotta be ready to face it."

Despite all the talk, Thomas felt like Newt was failing to make his point.

"What are you getting at?"

Newt paused while he looked at Thomas, then Minho. "We need to make sure we have a solid leader when tomorrow comes. There can't be any doubt who's in charge."

"That's the lamest shuck-faced thing you've ever barked," Minho said. "You're the leader, and you know it. We all know it."

Newt shook his head adamantly. "Bein' hungry make you forget the bloody tattoos? You think they're just decorations?"

"Oh, come on," Minho retorted. "You really think it means anything? They're just playin' with our heads!"

Instead of answering, Newt stepped closer to Minho and pulled back his shirt to reveal the tattoo there. Thomas didn't have to look—he remembered. It had branded Minho as the Leader.

Minho shrugged off Newt's hand and started his usual rant of sarcastic remarks, but Thomas had already tuned out, his heart's pace having kicked in to a rapid series of almost painful thumps. All he could think about was what had been tattooed on his *own* neck.

That he was to be killed.

CHAPTER 13

Thomas felt it getting late and knew they had to get sleep that night and be ready for the morning. So he and the Gladers spent the rest of the evening making crude packs out of bedsheets for carrying the food and the extra clothes that had appeared in the dressers. Some of the food had come in plastic bags, and the now-empty bags were filled with water and tied off with material ripped from the curtains. No one expected these poor excuses for canteens to last very long without leaking, but it was the best idea anyone could come up with.

Newt had finally convinced Minho to be the leader. Thomas knew as well as anybody that they needed someone to be in charge, so he was relieved when Minho grudgingly agreed.

Around nine o'clock, Thomas found himself lying in bed, staring at the bunk above him once again. The room was strangely silent even though he knew no one had fallen asleep yet. Fear surely gripped them as much as it did him. They'd been through the Maze and its horrors. They'd seen close up what WICKED was capable of doing. If Rat Man was correct, and all that had happened was part of some master plan, then these people had forced Gally to kill Chuck, had shot a woman at close range, had hired people to rescue them only to kill them when the mission was complete . . . the list went on and on.

Then, to top it all off, they gave them a hideous disease, with the cure as bait to lure them to continue. Who even knew what was true and what was a lie. And the evidence continued to suggest that they'd singled Thomas out somehow. It was a sad thought—Chuck was the one who had lost his life. Teresa was the one missing. But taking those two away from him . . .

His life felt like a black hole. He had no idea how he would muster the will to go on in the morning. To face whatever WICKED had in store for them. But he'd do it—and not just to get a cure. He would never stop, especially now. Not after what they'd done to him and his friends. If the only way to get back at them was to pass all their tests and trials, to *survive*, then so be it.

So be it.

With thoughts of revenge actually comforting him in a sick and twisted way, he finally fell asleep.

Every Glader had set the alarm on his digital watch for five o'clock in the morning. Thomas woke up well before that and couldn't go back to sleep. When beeps finally started filling the room, he swung his legs off the bed and rubbed his eyes. Someone turned on the light and a yellow blast lit up his vision. Squinting, he got up and headed for the showers. Who knew how long it'd be before he could clean himself again.

At ten minutes till the time appointed by Rat Man, every Glader sat in anticipation, most holding a plastic bag full of water, the bedsheet packs at their sides. Thomas, like the others, had decided he'd carry the water in his hand to make sure it didn't spill or leak. The invisible shield had reappeared overnight in the middle of the common area, impossible to pass through, and the Gladers settled just on the boys' dorm side of it, facing where the stranger in the white suit had said a Flat Trans would appear.

Aris was sitting right next to Thomas, and spoke for the first time since . . . well, Thomas couldn't remember the last time he'd heard the boy's voice.

"Did you think you were crazy?" the new kid asked. "When you first heard her in your head?"

Thomas glanced at him, paused. For some reason, up until that moment he hadn't wanted to talk to this guy. But suddenly the feeling vanished completely. It wasn't Aris's fault that Teresa had disappeared. "Yeah. Then when it kept happening, I got over it—only I started worrying about *other* people thinking I was crazy. So we didn't tell anyone about it for a long time."

"It was weird for me," Aris responded. He looked deep in thought as he stared at the floor. "I was in a coma for a few days, and when I woke up, speaking out to Rachel seemed the most natural thing in the world. If she hadn't accepted it and spoken back, I'm pretty sure I would've lost it. The other girls in the group hated me—some of them wanted to kill me. Rachel was the only one who . . ."

He trailed off, and Minho stood up to address everyone before Aris could finish what he was saying. Thomas was glad for it, because hearing about the trippy alternate version of what he himself had been through only made him think of Teresa, and that hurt too much. He didn't want to think about her anymore. He had to concentrate on surviving for now.

"We've got three minutes," Minho said, for once looking completely serious. "Everybody sure they still wanna go?"

Thomas nodded, noticed others doing the same.

"Anybody change their mind overnight?" Minho asked. "Speak now or never. Once we go wherever we're going, if some shank decides he's a sissy pants and tries to turn back, I'll make sure he does it with a broken nose and smashed privates."

Thomas looked over at Newt, who had his head in his hands and was groaning loudly.

"Newt, you got a problem?" Minho asked, his voice surprisingly stern. Thomas, shocked, waited for Newt's reaction.

The older boy seemed just as surprised. "Uh . . . no. Just admiring your bloody leadership skills."

Minho pulled his shirt away from his neck, leaned over to show everyone the tattoo there. "What does that say, slinthead?"

Newt glanced left and right, his face blushing. "We know you're the boss, Minho. Slim it."

"No, you slim it," Minho retorted, pointing at Newt. "We don't have time for that kind of klunk. So shut your hole."

Thomas could only hope that Minho was putting on an act to solidify the decision they'd made for him to be the leader, and that Newt understood. Though if Minho *was* acting, he was sure doing a good job of it.

"It's six o'clock!" one of the Gladers shouted.

As if this proclamation had triggered it, the invisible shield turned opaque again, fogging to a splotchy white. A split second later it vanished altogether. Thomas noticed the change in the wall opposite them instantly—a large section of it had transformed into a flat, shimmering surface of murky, shadowy gray.

"Come on!" Minho yelled as he pulled the strap of his pack onto his shoulder. He was gripping a water bag in his other hand. "Don't mess around—we only have five minutes to get through. I'll go first." He pointed at Thomas. "You go last—make sure everyone follows me before you come."

Thomas nodded, trying to fight the fire burning through his nerves; he reached up and wiped the sweat off his forehead.

Minho walked up to the wall of gray, then paused right in front of it. The Flat Trans seemed completely unstable, impossible for Thomas to focus on. Shadows and swirls of varying shades of darkness danced across its surface. The whole thing pulsed and blurred, as if it might disappear at any second.

Minho turned to look back at them. "See you shanks on the other side."

Then he stepped through, and the wall of gray murk swallowed him whole.

CHAPTER 14

No one complained as Thomas herded the rest of them behind Minho. No one even said anything, just exchanged flickering, frightened looks as they approached the Flat Trans and went through it. Without fail, every Glader hesitated a second before taking the final step into the murkiness of the gray square. Thomas watched each of them, swatting them on the back right before they disappeared.

After two minutes, only Aris and Newt were left with Thomas.

You sure about this? Aris said to him inside his mind.

Thomas choked on a cough, surprised by the flow of words across his consciousness—that not-quite-audible yet somehow audible speech. He'd thought—and hoped—that Aris had gotten the hint that he didn't want to communicate that way. That was something for Teresa, not anybody else.

"Hurry," Thomas muttered out loud, refusing to answer telepathically. "We've gotta hurry."

Aris stepped through, a hurt look on his face. Newt followed right on his heels; just like that, Thomas was alone in the big common room.

He glanced around one last time, remembered the dead, swelling bodies that had hung there just a few days earlier. Thought about the Maze and all the klunk they'd been through. Sighing as loudly as he could, hoping someone, somewhere could hear it, he gripped his water bag and his bedsheet pack full of food and stepped into the Flat Trans.

A distinct line of coldness traveled across his skin from front to back, as if the wall of gray were a standing plane of icy water. He'd closed his eyes at the last second and opened them now to see nothing but absolute darkness. But he heard voices.

"Hey!" he called out, ignoring the sudden burst of panic in his own voice. "You guys—"

Before he could finish, he stumbled on something and fell over, crashing on top of a squirming body.

"Ow!" the person yelled, pushing Thomas off. It was all he could do to hold tight to the water bag.

"Everyone be still and shut up!" This was Minho, and the relief that washed through Thomas almost made him shout for joy. "Thomas, was that you? Are you in here?"

"Yes!" Thomas regained his feet, blindly feeling around him to make sure he didn't bump into someone else. He felt nothing but air, saw nothing but black. "I was the last one to come through. Did everyone make it?"

"We were lining up and counting off nice and easy till you came stumbling through like a doped-up bull," Minho responded. "Let's do it again. One!"

When no one said anything, Thomas yelled, "Two!"

From there, the Gladers counted off until Aris went last and called out, "Twenty."

"Good that," Minho said. "We're all here, wherever here is. Can't see a shuck thing."

Thomas stood still, sensing the other boys, hearing their breaths, but scared to move. "Too bad we don't have a flashlight."

"Thanks for stating the obvious, Mr. Thomas," Minho replied. "All right, listen up. We're in some kind of hallway—I can feel the walls on both sides, and as far as I can tell, most of you are to my right. Thomas, where you're standing is where we came in. We better not take any chances of accidentally going back through the Flat Trans thingamajiggy, so everyone follow my voice and come toward me. Not much choice but to head down this way and see what we find."

He'd started moving away from Thomas as he said those last few words. The whispers of shuffling feet and rustling packs against clothes told him that the others were following. When he sensed that he was the last one remaining, and that he wouldn't step on anybody again, he moved slowly to his left, reaching his hand out until he felt a hard, cool wall. Then he walked after the rest of the group, letting his hand slide along the wall to keep his bearings.

No one spoke as they moved forward. Thomas hated that his eyes never adjusted to the darkness—there wasn't even the slightest hint of light. The air was cool, but smelled like old leather and dust. A couple of times he bumped into the person directly in front of him; he didn't even know who it was because the boy didn't say anything when they collided.

On and on they went, the tunnel stretching ahead without ever turning to the left or right. Thomas's hand against the wall and the ground below his feet were the only things that kept him tied to reality or gave him a sense of movement. Otherwise, he would've felt as if he were floating through empty space, making no progress whatsoever.

The only sounds were the scrapes of shoes on the hard concrete floor and occasional snatches of whispers between Gladers. Thomas felt every thump of his heart as they marched down the endless tunnel of darkness. He couldn't help but remember the Box, that lightless cube of stale air that had delivered him to the Glade; it had felt much like this. At least now he had a portion of solid memory, had friends and knew who they were. At least now he understood the stakes—that they needed a cure and would probably go through awful things to get it.

A sudden burst of intense whispering filled the tunnel, seemed to come from above. Thomas stopped dead in his tracks. It hadn't been from any of the Gladers, he was sure of it.

From up ahead, Minho shouted for the others to halt. Then, "Did you guys hear that?"

As several Gladers murmured yeses and started asking questions, Thomas tilted his ear toward the ceiling, straining to hear something beyond those voices. The flash of whispering had been quick, just a few short words that had sounded as if they came from a very old and very sick man. But the message had been completely indecipherable.

Minho shushed everyone again, telling them to listen.

Even though it was perfectly dark and therefore pointless, Thomas closed his eyes, concentrating on his sense of hearing. If the voice came again, he wanted to catch what it said.

Less than a minute passed before the same ancient voice whispered harshly once more, echoing through the air as if huge speakers were installed on the ceiling. Thomas heard several people gasp, like they'd gotten it this time and were shocked by what they'd heard. But he still hadn't been able to isolate even one or two of the words. He opened his eyes again, though nothing changed in front of him. Utter darkness. Black.

"Did anybody get what it said?" Newt called out.

"Couple of words," Winston replied. "Sounded like 'go back' right in the middle."

"Yeah, it did," someone agreed.

Thomas thought about what he'd heard, and in retrospect, it did seem like those two words had been in there somewhere. *Go back.*

"Everybody slim it and listen real hard this time," Minho announced. The dark hallway lapsed into silence.

The next time the voice came, Thomas understood every single syllable.

"One-chance deal. Go back now, you won't be sliced."

Judging by the reactions in front of him, everyone else got it this time, too.

"Won't be sliced?"

"What's that supposed to mean?"

"He said we can go back!"

"We can't trust some random shank whispering in the dark."

Thomas tried not to think about how ominous the last four words had been. *You won't be sliced.* That didn't sound good at all. And not being able to see anything made it worse. Driving him crazy.

"Just keep going!" he shouted up to Minho. "I can't take this much longer. Just go!"

"Wait a minute." Frypan's voice. "The voice said this was a one-chance deal. We have to at least think about it."

"Yeah," someone added. "Maybe we should go back."

Thomas shook his head even though he knew no one could see it. "No way. Remember what that guy at the desk told us. That we'd all die horrible deaths if we go back."

Frypan pushed. "Well, what makes him any more in charge than this whispering dude? How're we supposed to know who to listen to and who to ignore?"

Thomas knew it was a good question, but going back just didn't feel right. "The voice is just a test, I bet. We need to keep going."

"He's right." This was Minho from up in front. "Come on, let's go."

He'd barely said the last word when the whispering voice whooshed through the air again, this time laced with an almost childish hatred. *"You're all dead. You're all going to be sliced. Dead and sliced."*

Every hair on Thomas's neck stood up straight and a chill tickled his back. He expected to hear even more calls to go back, but once again the Gladers surprised him. No one said a thing, and soon they were all walking forward again. Minho had been right when he'd said all the sissies had been weeded out.

They made their way deeper into the darkness. The air warmed a bit, seemed to thicken with dust. Thomas coughed several times and was dying to take a drink, but he didn't want to risk untying his water bag without being able to see it. That was all he needed, to spill it all over the floor.

Forward.

Warmer.

Thirsty.

Darkness.

Walking. Time passed ever so slowly.

Thomas had no idea how this hallway could even be possible. They had to have journeyed at least two or three miles since last hearing the creepy whisper of warning. Where *were* they? Underground? Inside some massive building? The Rat Man had said they needed to find open air. How—

A boy screamed a few dozen feet in front of him.

It started out as an abrupt shriek, like simple surprise, but then escalated into pure terror. He didn't know who it was, but the kid was now screaming his throat raw, screeching and squealing like an animal at the old Blood House in the Glade. Thomas heard the sounds of a body thrashing on the ground.

He ran forward on instinct, pushing past several Gladers who seemed frozen by fear, moving toward the inhuman sounds. He didn't know why he thought he'd be able to help more than anyone else, but he didn't hesitate, not even taking care with his steps as he sprinted through the darkness. After the long insanity of walking blindly for so long, it was as if his body craved the action.

He made it, could hear that the boy now lay right in front of him, his arms and legs thrashing on the concrete floor as he struggled against who knew what. Thomas carefully set his water bag and shoulder pack far to the side, then timidly reached forward with his hands to find a grip on an arm or leg. He sensed the other Gladers crowding behind him, a loud and chaotic presence of shouts and questions that he forced himself to ignore.

"Hey!" Thomas yelled at the squirming boy. "What's wrong with you?" His fingers brushed the kid's jeans, then his shirt, but the boy's body convulsed all over the place, impossible to catch, and his shrieks continued to pierce the air.

Finally, Thomas went for broke. He dove forward, launching himself fully onto the body of the thrashing kid. With a jolt that knocked the breath out of him, he landed, felt the squirming torso; an elbow dug into his ribs, then a hand slapped his face. A knee came up and almost got him square in the groin.

"Stop it!" Thomas shouted. "What's wrong!"

The screams gurgled to a stop, almost like the kid had just been pulled underwater. But the convulsing didn't ease in the slightest.

Thomas put an elbow and forearm on the chest of the Glader for leverage, then reached out to grab his hair or his face. But when his hands slid over what was there, confusion consumed him.

There was no head. No hair or face. Not even a neck. None of those things that *should've* been there.

Instead, Thomas felt a large and perfectly smooth ball of cold metal.

CHAPTER 15

The next few seconds were beyond strange. As soon as Thomas's hand made contact with the odd metal ball, the boy stopped moving. His arms and legs stilled and the stiffness in his twitching torso went away in an instant. Thomas felt a thick wetness on the hard sphere, oozing up from where the kid's neck should've been. He knew it was blood, could smell the coppery scent of it.

Then the ball slipped from under Thomas's fingers and rolled away, making a hollow grating sound until it thumped into the closest wall and came to a stop. The boy lying below him didn't move or make a sound. The other Gladers continued to shout questions into the dark, but Thomas ignored them.

Horror filled his chest as he pictured the boy, what he must look like. Nothing about it made sense, but the kid was obviously dead, his head cut off somehow. Or . . . turned into metal? What in the world had happened? Thomas's mind spun, and it took a moment before he realized that warm fluid was flowing over the hand he'd pressed to the floor when the ball slipped away. He freaked.

Scooting backward away from the body, wiping his hand on his pants, he shouted but wasn't able to form words. A couple of Gladers grabbed him from behind and helped him to his feet. He pushed them away, stumbled against a wall. Someone gripped his shirt at the shoulder, pulled him closer.

"Thomas!" Minho's voice. "Thomas! What happened?"

Thomas tried to calm himself, take hold of things. His stomach lurched; his chest tightened. "I . . . I don't know. Who was that? Who was down there screaming?"

Winston answered, his voice shaky. "Frankie, I think. He was right next to me, just making a joke, and then it was like something yanked him away. Yeah, it was him. Definitely him."

"What happened!" Minho repeated.

Thomas realized he was still wiping his hands on his pants. "Look," he said before taking a long breath. Doing all this in the dark was maddening. "I heard him screaming, and ran up here to help. I jumped on him, tried to pin his arms down, find out what was wrong. Then I reached for his head to grab him by the cheeks—I don't even know why—and all I felt was . . ."

He couldn't say it. Nothing could possibly sound more absurd than the truth.

"What?" Minho shouted.

Thomas groaned, then said it. "His head wasn't a head. It was like a . . . a big . . . metal *ball*. I don't know, man, but that's what I felt. Like his shuck head had been swallowed by . . . by a big metal ball!"

"What're you talking about?" Minho asked.

Thomas didn't know how he could convince him or anyone else. "Didn't you hear it rolling away right after he stopped screaming? I know it—"

"It's right here!" someone shouted. Newt. Thomas heard a heavy scrape again, then Newt grunting with effort. "I heard it roll over here. And it's all wet and sticky—feels like blood."

"What the *klunk*," Minho half whispered. "How big is it?" The other Gladers joined in with a chorus of questions.

"Everybody slim it!" Newt yelled. When they quieted, he said flatly, "I don't know." Thomas heard him carefully handling the ball to get a feel for it. "Bigger than a buggin' head for sure. It's perfectly round—a perfect sphere."

Thomas was baffled, disgusted, but all he could think about was getting out of that place. Out of the darkness. "We need to run," he said. "We need to go. Now."

"Maybe we *should* go back." Thomas didn't recognize the voice. "Whatever that ball thing is, it sliced off Frankie's head, just like the old shank warned us."

"No way," Minho responded angrily. "No way. Thomas is right. No more dinkin' around. Spread out a couple of feet from each other, then run. Hunch down, and if something comes near your head, hit the living crap out of it."

No one argued. Thomas quickly found his food and water; then some unspoken communication permeated the group and they set off running, far enough apart not to trip over each other. Thomas wasn't in the very back anymore, not wanting to waste time to get back in order. He ran, ran as hard as he remembered ever running in the Maze.

He smelled sweat. He breathed dust and warm air. His hands grew clammy and gooey from the blood. The darkness, complete.

He ran and didn't stop.

A death ball got one more person. It happened closer to Thomas this time—got a kid he'd never spoken one word to. Thomas heard a distinct sound of metal sliding against metal, a couple of hard clicks. Then the screams drowned out the rest.

No one stopped. A terrible thing, maybe. Probably. But no one stopped.

When the screams finally cut off with a gurgling halt, Thomas heard a loud clonk as the ball of metal crashed onto the hard ground. He heard it rolling, heard it clank against a wall and roll some more.

He kept running. He never slowed.

His heart pounded; his chest hurt from deep, ragged breaths as he desperately gulped the dusty air. He lost track of time, had no sense of how far they'd gone. But when Minho called for everyone to stop, the relief was almost overwhelming. His exhaustion had finally won out over the terror of the thing that had killed two people.

Sounds of people panting filled the small space, and it reeked of bad breath. Frypan was the first one to recover enough to speak. "Why'd we stop?"

"'Cause I almost broke my shins on something up here!" Minho shouted back. "I think it's a stairway."

Thomas felt his spirits lift, but immediately squashed them back down. Getting his hopes up was something he'd sworn never to do again. Not until all this was over.

"Well, let's go up 'em!" Frypan said far too cheerfully.

"Ya think?" Minho responded. "What would we do without you, Frypan? Seriously."

Thomas heard the heavy stomps of Minho's footsteps as he ran up the stairs—it made a high-pitched ringing like they were made of thin metal. Only a few seconds passed before other footsteps joined in, and soon everyone was following Minho.

When Thomas reached the first step, he tripped and fell, banging his knee against the second one. He put his hands down to regain his balance—almost bursting his bag of water—then popped back up, skipping a step every once in a while. Who knew when another metal thing might attack, and hope or no hope, he was more than ready to move on to a place that wasn't pitch-black.

A bang sounded from above, a deeper thump than the footsteps, but it still sounded like metal.

"Ow!" Minho yelled. Then there were a few grunts and groans

as Gladers bumped into each other before they could stop themselves.

"You okay?" Newt asked.

"What'd . . . you hit?" Thomas called up through heavy breaths.

Minho sounded irritated. "The shuck top, that's what. We hit the roof, and there's nowhere else . . ." He trailed off, and Thomas could hear him sliding his hands along the walls and ceiling, searching. "Wait! I think I found—"

A distinct click cut him off, and then the world around Thomas seemed to ignite into pure flame. He cried out as he covered his eyes with his hands—a blinding, searing light shone down from above. He'd dropped his water bag, but he couldn't help it. After so long in pitch-darkness, the sudden appearance of light overpowered him—even through the protection of his hands. Brilliant orange burst through his fingers and eyelids, and a wave of heat—like a hot wind—swept down.

Thomas heard a heavy scrape, then a *clonk,* and the darkness returned. Warily, he dropped his hands and squinted; spots danced across his vision.

"Shuck me," Minho said. "Looks like we found a way out, but I think it's on the freaking sun! Man, that was bright. And hot."

"Let's just open it a crack and let our eyes get used to it," Newt said. Then Thomas heard him walk up the stairs to join Minho. "Here's a shirt—wedge it in there. Everybody shut your eyes!"

Thomas did as he was told and covered them with his hands again. The glow of orange returned and the process began. After a minute or so, he lowered his hands and slowly opened his eyes. He had to squint, and it still seemed like a million flashlights were pointed at him, but it had become bearable. A couple of minutes more and everything was bright but fine.

He could now see that he stood about twenty steps down from

where Minho and Newt crouched just beneath the door in the ceiling. Three shining lines marked the edges of the door, broken only by the shirt they'd stuffed in the right corner to keep it open. Everything around them—the walls, the stairs, the door itself—was made of a dull gray metal. Thomas turned around to look back in the direction from which they'd come, saw that the stairs disappeared into darkness far below them. They'd climbed up a lot more than he'd imagined.

"Anybody blind now?" Minho asked. "I feel like my eyeballs are roasted marshmallows."

Thomas felt that, too. His eyes burned and itched, kept tearing up. The Gladers around him were all rubbing their eyes.

"So what's out there?" someone asked.

Minho shrugged as he peeked through the slit of the open door with a hand half-shielding his vision. "Can't really tell. All I can see is a lot of bright light—maybe we *are* on the shuck sun. But I don't think there're any people out there." He paused. "Or Cranks."

"Let's get out of here, then," Winston said; he was two steps below Thomas. "I'd rather get a sunburn than get my head attacked by some ball of steel. Let's go!"

"All right, Winston," Minho replied. "Keep your undies on—I just wanted to let our eyes adjust first. I'll throw the door all the way open to make sure we're okay. Get ready." He moved up a step so he could press his right shoulder against the slab of metal. "One. Two. Three!"

He straightened his legs with a grunt and heaved upward. Light and heat burst down the stairwell as the door opened with a terrible squeal of grinding metal. Thomas quickly looked toward the ground and squinted. The brightness seemed impossible—even if they *had* been wandering along in perfect darkness for hours.

He heard some shuffling and pushing above him and looked up to see Newt and Minho moving to get out of the square of blinding sunlight coming through the now-open door. The whole stairwell heated up like an oven.

"Aw, man!" Minho said, a wince on his face. "Something's wrong, dude. It feels like it's already burning my skin!"

"He's right," Newt said, rubbing the back of his neck. "I don't know if we can go out there. We might have to wait until the sun goes down."

Groans of complaint sounded from the Gladers, but then they were overcome by a sudden outburst from Winston. "Whoa! Watch out! Watch out!"

Thomas turned to look at Winston down the stairs. He was pointing at something right above him as he backed up a couple of steps. On the ceiling, just a few feet above their heads, a big glob of liquid silver was coalescing, seeping out of the metal as if melting into a large teardrop. It grew bigger and bigger as Thomas stared at it, forming in a matter of seconds into a wavering, slowly rippling ball of molten goop. Then, before anyone could react, it detached from the ceiling and fell away.

But instead of splatting on the steps at their feet, the sphere of silver defied gravity and flew horizontally, directly into Winston's face. His horrific screams filled the air as he fell and started tumbling down the stairs.

CHAPTER 16

Thomas had a sickening thought as he pushed his way down the stairs after Winston. He didn't know if he was going because he wanted to help him or because he couldn't control his curiosity about this silvery monster-ball.

Winston eventually thumped to a stop, his back coming to rest by chance on one of the steps; they were still nowhere close to the bottom. The brilliant light from the open door up top illuminated everything with perfect clarity. Both of Winston's hands were at his face, pulling at the silver liquid—the ball of molten metal had already melded with the top of his head, consuming the part above the ears. Now its edges were creeping downward like thick syrup, lipping over the ears and covering his eyebrows.

Thomas jumped over the boy's body and spun around to kneel on the step directly below him; Winston pulled and pushed at the silver goop to keep it off his eyes. Surprisingly, it seemed to be working. But the boy was screaming at the top of his lungs, thrashing, his feet kicking the wall.

"Get it off me!" he yelled, his voice so strangled that Thomas almost gave up and ran away. If the stuff hurt that bad . . .

It looked like a very dense silver gel. Persistent and stubborn—like it was alive. As soon as Winston pushed a portion of it up and off his eyes, some of it would slip around his fingers from the side and try again. Thomas could see glimpses of the skin on his face when he did this, and it wasn't pretty. Red and blistering.

Winston cried out something unintelligible—his tortured screams could have been in another language altogether. Thomas knew he had to do something. Time had run out.

He threw the pack off his shoulders and dumped the contents; fruits and packages scattered and thumped down the stairs. He took the bedsheet and wrapped it around his hands for protection, then went for it. As Winston swiped at the molten silver right above his eyes again, Thomas grabbed for the sides that had just gone over the boy's ears. He felt heat through the cloth, thought it might burst into flame. He braced his feet, squeezed the stuff as hard as he could, then yanked.

With a disturbing sucking sound, the sides of the attacking metal lifted several inches before slipping out of his hands and slapping back down onto Winston's ears. Impossibly, the boy screamed even louder. A couple of other Gladers tried to move in to help, but Thomas shouted for them to back off, thinking they'd only get in the way.

"We have to do it together!" Thomas yelled at Winston, determined to get a stronger hold this time. "Listen to me, Winston! We have to do it together! Try to get a grip on it and lift it off your head!"

The other boy didn't show any sign of understanding, his whole body convulsing as he struggled. If Thomas hadn't been on the step below him, he would've tumbled down the rest of the way for sure by now.

"On the count of three!" Thomas yelled. "Winston! On the count of three!"

Still no sign he'd heard. Screaming. Thrashing. Kicking. Slapping at the silver.

Tears welled up in Thomas's eyes, or maybe it was sweat trickling down from his forehead. But it stung. And he felt like the air had heated up to a million degrees. His muscles tensed; lances of pain shot through his legs. They were cramping.

"Just do it!" he yelled, ignoring it all and leaning in to try again. "One! Two! Now!"

He gripped the sides of the stretching silver, felt its odd combination of soft toughness, then yanked once again up and away from Winston's head. Winston must've heard, or maybe it was luck, but at the same time, he pushed at the goop with the heels of his hands, like he was trying to rip off his own forehead. The entire mess of silver came off, a wobbly, thick and heavy sheet of the stuff. Thomas didn't hesitate; he flung his arms up and threw the junk over his head and down the stairwell, then spun around on his heels to see what happened.

As it flew through the air, the silver quickly formed back into a sphere, its surface rippling for a moment, then solidifying. It stopped just a few steps down from them, hovered for a second, like it was taking a long and lasting look at its victim, perhaps thinking over what had gone wrong. Then it shot away, flying down the stairway until it disappeared in the darkness far below.

It was gone. For some reason, it hadn't attacked again.

Thomas sucked in huge gasps of air; every inch of his body felt drenched with sweat. He leaned his shoulder against the wall, scared to look back at Winston, who was whimpering behind him. At least the screams had stopped.

Thomas finally turned around and faced him.

The kid was a mess. Curled up into a ball, shaking. The hair on his head had vanished, replaced with raw skin and spots of seeping blood. His ears were cut and ragged, but whole. He sobbed, surely from the pain, probably also from the trauma of what he'd just been through. The acne on his face looked clean and fresh compared to the raw wounds on the rest of his head.

"You okay, man?" Thomas asked, knowing it had to be the dumbest question he'd ever spoken aloud.

Winston shook his head with a quick jerk; his body continued to tremble.

Thomas looked up to see Minho and Newt and Aris and all the other Gladers just a couple of steps above them, all staring down in complete shock. The brilliant glare from above shadowed their faces, but Thomas could still see their eyes—wide like those of cats stunned by a spotlight.

"What was that shuck thing?" Minho murmured.

Thomas couldn't bring himself to speak, just shook his head wearily.

Newt was the one to answer. "Magic goop that eats people's heads, that's what it bloody was."

"Has to be some kind of new technology." This came from Aris, the first time Thomas had seen him participate in a discussion. The boy looked around, obviously noticing the surprised faces, then shrugged as if embarrassed and continued. "I've had a few splotchy memories come back. I know the world has some pretty advanced techno stuff—but I don't remember anything like flying molten metal that tries to cut off body parts."

Thomas thought about his own sketchy memories. Certainly nothing like that came to mind for him, either.

Minho pointed absently down the stairwell past Thomas. "That crap must keep gelling around your face, then eat into the flesh of your neck until it cuts clean through it. Nice. That's real nice."

"Did you see? Thing came right out of the ceiling!" Frypan said. "We better get out of here. Now."

"Couldn't agree more," Newt added.

Minho glanced down at Winston with a look of disgust, and Thomas followed his gaze. The kid had quit shaking, and his sobs had calmed to a stifled whimper. But he looked awful, and was surely scarred for life.

Thomas couldn't imagine hair ever growing back on the red, raw mess of his head.

"Frypan, Jack!" Minho called out. "Get Winston on his feet, help him along. Aris, you gather the klunk he dropped, have a couple of guys help you carry it. We're leaving. I don't care how bright or brutal that light is up there—I don't feel like having my head turned into a bowling ball today."

He turned around without waiting to see if people followed his orders. It was a move that, for some reason, made Thomas think the guy would end up making a good leader after all. "Come on, Thomas and Newt," he called over his shoulder. "The three of us are going through first."

Thomas exchanged glances with Newt, who returned a look that had a little fear in it but was mostly full of curiosity. An eagerness to move on. Thomas felt it himself, and hated to admit that anything seemed better than dealing with the aftermath of what had happened to Winston.

"Let's go," Newt said, his voice rising on the second word, as if they had no choice but to do what they were told. Though his face revealed the truth: he wanted to get away from poor Winston just as much as Thomas did.

Thomas nodded and carefully stepped over Winston, trying not to look at the skin on his injured head again. It was making him sick. He moved to the side to let Frypan, Jack and Aris past him to do their jobs, then started up the stairs, two at a time. Following Newt and Minho to the top, where it seemed like the sun itself waited just outside the open door.

CHAPTER 17

The other Gladers moved out of their way, seemingly more than happy to let the three of them be the ones to see what was outside. Thomas squinted and then shielded his eyes as they got closer. It was getting hard to believe they could actually step through the door into that horrible brightness and survive.

Minho stopped on the last step, just short of the direct line of the light. Then he slowly held his hand out until it entered the square of brilliance. Despite the boy's olive complexion, it looked to Thomas as if Minho's skin shone like white fire.

After only a few seconds Minho pulled his hand back and shook it at his side like he'd hit his thumb with a hammer. "That's definitely hot. Definitely hot." He turned to face Thomas and Newt. "If we're gonna do this, we better have something wrapped around us or we'll have second-degree sunburns in five minutes."

"Let's empty out our packs," Newt said, already taking his off his shoulder. "Wear these sheets like buggin' robes as we check things out. If it works well enough, we can stuff the food and water into half our sheets and use the other half for protection."

Thomas had already freed his sheet to help Winston. "We'll look like ghosts—scare away any bad guys out there."

Minho didn't take the same care as Newt; he just upended his pack and let everything drop. The Gladers closest to them scrambled on instinct to stop the stuff from tumbling down the stairs. "Funny boy, that

Thomas. Let's just hope we don't have some nice Cranks to greet us," he said as he started untying the knots he'd made in the bedsheet. "I don't see how anyone could just be hanging out in that heat. Hopefully there'll be trees or some kind of shelter."

"I don't know," Newt said. "Then they might be hiding, bloody waitin' to get us or something."

Thomas was just itching to check things out. Quit making guesses and see for himself what they were up against. "We won't know till we investigate. Let's go." He whipped out his sheet, then pulled it over himself and wrapped it tightly around his face like an old woman in a shawl. "How do I look?"

"Like the ugliest shanky girl I've ever seen," Minho responded. "You better thank the gods above you were born a dude."

"Thanks."

Minho and Newt did as Thomas had done, though both of them took more care to grip the sheet with their hands under it so they were completely covered. They also held it out to make sure their faces were shaded. Thomas followed suit.

"You shanks ready?" Minho asked, looking at Newt, then Thomas.

"Kind of excited, actually," Newt responded.

Thomas didn't know if that was quite the right word, but he felt the same urge to act. "Me too. Let's go."

The remaining steps above them went all the way to the top, like an exit from an old cellar, the last few glowing with the brilliance of the sun. Minho hesitated, but then ran up them, not stopping until he'd disappeared, seemingly absorbed into the light.

"Go!" Newt yelled, smacking Thomas on the back.

Thomas felt a rush of adrenaline. Blowing out a deep breath, he took off after Minho; he heard Newt right on his heels.

As soon as Thomas emerged into the light, he realized that they might as well have been draped in see-through plastic. The sheet did nothing to block the blinding light and searing heat beating down from above. He opened his mouth to speak and a raw plume of dry warmth shot down his throat, seeming to obliterate any air or moisture in its path. He tried desperately to pull in oxygen, but instead it felt like someone had lit a fire in his chest.

Although his memories were few and scattered, Thomas didn't think the world was supposed to be like this.

With his eyes screwed shut against the white brilliance, he bumped into Minho and almost fell down. Regaining his balance, he bent his knees and squatted, tenting the sheet entirely over his body as he continued to fight for breath. He finally caught it, sucking air in and puffing it out rapidly as he tried to compose himself. That first instant after exiting the stairway had really panicked him. The other two Gladers were also breathing heavily.

"You guys all right?" Minho finally asked.

Thomas grunted a yes, and Newt said, "Pretty sure we just arrived in bloody hell. Always thought you'd end up here, Minho, but not me."

"Good that," Minho replied. "My eyeballs hurt, but I think I'm finally starting to get kind of used to the light."

Thomas opened his own eyes into a squint and looked down at the ground just a couple of feet below his face. Dirt and dust. A few gray-brown rocks. The sheet lay draped completely around him, but it glowed so white it was like some odd piece of futuristic light technology.

"Who you hidin' from?" Minho asked. "Get up, ya shank—I don't see anybody."

Thomas was embarrassed that they thought he was cowering there— he must look like a small child whimpering under his blankets, trying not to be seen. He stood up and very slowly lifted the sheet until he could peek out at their surroundings.

It was a wasteland.

In front of him, a flat pan of dry and lifeless earth stretched as far as he could see. Not a single tree. Not a bush. No hills or valleys. Just an orange-yellow sea of dust and rocks; wavering currents of heated air boiled on the horizon like steam, floating upward, as if any life out there were melting toward the cloudless and pale blue sky.

Thomas turned in a circle, didn't see much change until he faced the opposite direction. A line of jagged and barren mountains rose far in the distance. In front of those mountains, maybe halfway between there and where they now stood, a cluster of buildings sat squatting together like a pile of abandoned boxes. It had to be a town, but it was impossible to tell how big it was from this distance. Hot air shimmered in front of it, blurring everything close to the ground.

The white-hot sun above already lay far to Thomas's left, and seemed to be sinking toward that horizon, which meant that way was west, which meant that the town ahead and the range of black and red rock behind it had to be due north. Where they were supposed to head. His sense of direction surprised him, as if a piece of his past had risen from the ashes.

"How far away do you think those buildings are?" Newt asked. After the echoing, hollow sounds their speaking had made in the long dark tunnel and stairway, his voice was like a dull whisper.

"Could that be a hundred miles?" Thomas asked no one in particular. "That's definitely north. Is that where we have to go?"

Minho shook his head under his sheet-hood. "No way, dude. I mean, we're supposed to go that way, but it's not even close to a hundred miles. Thirty at most. And the mountains might be sixty or seventy."

"Didn't know you could measure distance so well with nothing but your bloody eyeballs," Newt said.

"I'm a Runner, shuck-face. You get a feel for stuff like that in the Maze, even if its scale was a lot smaller."

"The Rat Man wasn't kidding about those sun flares," Thomas said, trying not to let his heart sink too much. "Looks like a nuclear holocaust out here. I wonder if the whole world is like this."

"Let's hope not," Minho responded. "I'd be happy to see one tree right about now. Maybe a creek."

"I'd settle for a patch of grass," Newt said through a sigh.

The more Thomas looked, the closer that town appeared. Thirty miles might even have been too much. He broke his gaze and turned toward the others. "Could this be any more different from what they put us through in the Maze? There, we were trapped inside walls, with everything we need to survive. Now we have nothing holding us in, but no way to survive unless we go where they told us to. Isn't that called irony or something like that?"

"Something like that," Minho agreed. "You're a philosophizing wonder." He nodded back toward the exit from the stairway. "Come on. Let's get those shanks out here and start walking. No time to waste letting the sun suck all the water out of us."

"Maybe we should wait until it goes down," Newt suggested.

"And hang out with those shuck balls of metal? No way."

Thomas agreed that they should get moving. "I think we're okay. Looks like sunset's only a few hours away. We can be tough for a while, take a break, then go as far as possible during the night. I can't stand another minute down there."

Minho nodded firmly.

"Sounds like a plan," Newt said. "For now, let's just make it to that dusty old town and hope it's not full of our Crank buddies."

Thomas's chest hitched at that comment.

Minho walked back to the hole and leaned over it. "Hey, you bunch of sissy, no-good shanks! Grab all the food and get up here!"

Not one Glader complained about the plan.

Thomas watched as each one of them did the same things he'd done when he first exited the stairway. Struggling gasps for breaths, squinty eyes, looks of hopelessness. He bet that each one of them had hoped the Rat Man was lying. That the worst times had been back in the Maze. But he was pretty sure that after the crazy head-eating silver things and then seeing this wasteland, no one would ever have such hopeful thoughts again.

They had to make some adjustments as they readied for the journey—the food and water bags were stuffed more tightly into half of the original packs; then the free bedsheets were used to cover two people as they walked. All in all, it worked surprisingly well—even for Jack and poor Winston—and soon they were marching across the hard, rock-strewn ground. Thomas shared his sheet with Aris, though he didn't know how it had ended up that way. Maybe he was just refusing to admit that he'd wanted to be with the boy, that he might be the only possible connection to figuring out what had happened to Teresa.

Thomas held one end of the sheet up with his left hand and had a pack draped around his right shoulder. Aris was to his right; they'd agreed to trade off the now-much-heavier pack every thirty minutes. Step by dusty step, they made their way toward the town, the heat seeming to suck a full day of their life away every hundred yards.

They didn't talk for a long while, but Thomas finally broke the silence. "So you've never heard the name Teresa before?"

Aris looked sharply at him, and Thomas realized he'd probably had a less-than-subtle hint of accusation in his voice. But he didn't back down. "Well? Have you?"

Aris returned his gaze forward, but there was something suspicious there. "No. Never. I don't know who she is or where she went. But at least you didn't see her die right in front of you."

That was a punch to the gut, but for some reason it made Thomas like Aris more. "I know, sorry." He thought for a second before he asked the next questions. "How close were you guys? What was her name, again?"

"Rachel." Aris paused, and for a second Thomas thought the conversation might be over already, but then he continued. "We were way more than close. Things happened. We remembered stuff. Made new memories."

Thomas knew Minho would've laughed his face off at that last comment, but to him it sounded like the saddest three words he'd ever heard. He felt he had to say something—offer something. "Yeah. I did see a really good friend die, though. Every time I think about Chuck I get ticked off all over again. If they've done the same thing to Teresa, they won't be able to stop me. Nothing will. They'll all die."

Thomas stopped—forcing Aris to as well—shocked that those words had just come out of his own mouth. It was like something else had taken over him and said those things. But he did feel it. Very strongly. "What do you think—"

But before he could finish the thought, Frypan started shouting. He was pointing at something.

It only took a second for Thomas to realize what had gotten the cook all excited.

Far ahead, from the direction of the town, two people were running toward them, their bodies like ghostly forms of darkness in the heat mirage, small plumes of dust rising from their feet.

CHAPTER 18

Thomas stared at the runners. He sensed that the other Gladers around him had stopped as well, as if there'd been an unspoken command to do so. Thomas shivered, something that seemed completely impossible in the sweltering heat. He didn't know why he felt the tickle of cold fear along his back—the Gladers outnumbered the approaching strangers almost ten times over—but the feeling was undeniable.

"Everyone pack in tighter," Minho said. "And get ready to fight these shanks the first sign of trouble."

The blurry mirage of upward-melting heat obscured the two figures until they were only a hundred yards or so away. Thomas's muscles tensed when they came into focus. He remembered all too well what he'd seen through the barred window just a few mornings ago. The Cranks. But these people scared him in a different way.

They stopped just a couple of dozen feet in front of the Gladers. One was a man, the other a woman, though Thomas could only tell this from the lady's slightly curvy figure. Other than that, they had the same build—tall and scrawny. Their heads and faces were almost completely covered in wrappings of tattered beige cloth, small ragged slits cut for them to see and breathe through. Their shirts and pants were a hodgepodge of filthy clothing sewn together, tied with ratty strips of denim in some places. Nothing was exposed to the beating sun but their hands, and those were red and cracked and scabby.

The two of them stood there, panting as they caught their breath, a sound like sick dogs.

"Who are you?" Minho called out.

The strangers didn't respond, didn't move. Their chests heaved in and out. Thomas observed them from under his makeshift hood—he couldn't imagine how anyone could run so far and not die of heat exhaustion.

"Who *are* you?" Minho repeated.

Instead of answering, the two strangers split apart and started walking in a broad circle around the bunched-up Gladers. Their eyes, hidden behind the slits in those odd mummy wrappings, stayed fixed on the boys as they made their way in a wide arc, as if sizing them up for a kill. Thomas felt the tension inside him rise, hated when he could no longer see both of them at once. He turned around and watched as they met back up behind the group and once again faced them, standing still.

"There are a whole lot more of us than there are of you," Minho said, his voice betraying his frustration. To threaten them so soon seemed desperate. "Start talking. Tell us who you are."

"We're Cranks."

The two words came from the woman, a short burst of guttural annoyance. For no discernible reason she pointed across the Gladers back toward the town from which they'd run.

"Cranks?" Minho said; he had pushed his way through the crowd to be closest to the strangers again. "Just like the ones that tried to break into our building a couple days ago?"

Thomas cringed—these people would have no idea what Minho was talking about. Somehow the Gladers had traveled a long way from wherever that place had been—through the Flat Trans.

"We're Cranks." This time from the man, his voice surprisingly lighter and less gruff than the woman's. But there was no kindness in it.

He pointed over the Gladers just like his companion had done. "Came to see if you're Cranks. Came to see if you've got the Flare."

Minho turned to look at Thomas and then a few others, his eyebrows raised. No one said anything. He turned back. "Some dude told us we had the Flare, yeah. What can you tell us about it?"

"Don't matter," the man responded; the strips of cloth wrapped around his face jiggled with every word. "You got it, you'll know soon enough."

"Well, what do you bloody want?" Newt asked, stepping up to stand next to Minho. "What's it matter to you if we're Cranks or not?"

The woman responded this time, acting as if she hadn't heard the questions. "How'd you get in the Scorch? Where'd you come from? How'd you get here?"

Thomas was surprised at the . . . intelligence evident in her words. The Cranks they'd seen back at the dorm had seemed absolutely insane, like animals. These people were aware enough to realize that their group had appeared out of nowhere. Nothing lay in the opposite direction from the town.

Minho leaned over to consult with Newt, then turned and stepped closer to Thomas. "What do we tell these people?"

Thomas had no clue. "I don't know. The truth? It can't hurt."

"The truth?" Minho said sarcastically. "What an idea, Thomas. You're freaking brilliant, as usual." He faced the Cranks again. "We were sent here by WICKED. Came out of a hole just a little while that way, from a tunnel. We're supposed to go one hundred miles to the north, cross the Scorch. Any of that mean a thing to you?"

Once again, it was as if they hadn't heard a word he'd said.

"Not all Cranks are gone," the man said. "Not all of them are past the Gone." He said that last word in a way that made it sound like the name of a place. "Different ones at different levels. Best you learn who to make friends with and who to avoid. Or kill. Better learn right quick if you're coming our way."

"What's your way?" Minho asked. "You came from that town, right? Is that where all these Cranks live? Is there food and water there?"

Thomas felt the same urge as Minho—to ask a million questions. He was half tempted to suggest they capture these two Cranks and *make* them answer. But for the moment the pair didn't seem intent on helping at all, and they split again to circle back around to the side of the Gladers closest to the town.

Once they met up in the spot where they'd first spoken, the distant town almost seeming to float between them, the woman said one last thing. "If you don't have it yet, you'll have it soon. Same with the other group. The ones that're supposed to kill you."

The two strangers then turned around and ran back toward the cluster of buildings on the horizon, leaving Thomas and the other Gladers in stunned silence. Soon, any evidence of the running Cranks was lost in a blur of heat and dust.

"Other group?" someone said. Maybe Frypan. Thomas was in too much of a trance staring at the disappearing Cranks and worrying about the Flare to notice.

"Wonder if they're talking about my group." This was definitely Aris. Thomas finally forced himself to snap out of his gaze.

"Group B?" he asked him. "You think they've already made it to the town?"

"Hello!" Minho snapped. "Who cares? You'd think the little part about them supposedly killing us would be the attention getter. Maybe this stuff about the Flare?"

Thomas thought of the tattoo on the back of his neck. Those simple words that scared him. "Maybe when she said 'you' she didn't mean all of us." He jabbed a thumb over his shoulder, pointing down at his menacing mark. "Maybe she meant me specifically. Couldn't tell where her eyes were looking."

"How's she gonna know who you are?" Minho retorted. "Plus, doesn't matter. If someone tries to kill you, or me, or anyone else, they might as well try to get all of us. Right?"

"You're so sweet," Frypan said with a snort. "Go ahead and die with Thomas. I think I'll sneak away and enjoy living with the guilt." He cast his special look that meant he was only kidding, but Thomas wondered if a little truth might be hiding in there somewhere.

"Well, what do we do now?" Jack asked. He had Winston's arm around one of his shoulders, but the former Keeper of the Blood House seemed to have recovered some of his strength. Luckily the sheet covered the hideous parts of his head.

"What do you think?" Newt asked, but then he nodded at Minho.

Minho rolled his eyes. "We keep going, that's what. Look, we don't have a choice. If we don't go to that town, we're gonna die out here of sunstroke or starvation. If we *do* go, we'll have some shelter for a while, maybe even food. Cranks or no Cranks, that's where we're going."

"And Group B?" Thomas asked; he glanced over at Aris. "Or whoever they were talking about. What if they really do wanna kill us? All we have to fight with are our hands."

Minho flexed his right arm. "If these people are really the girls Aris was hanging out with, I'll show 'em these guns of mine and they'll go runnin'."

Thomas kept pushing. "And if these girls have weapons? Or can fight? Or if it's not them at all but a bunch of seven-foot-tall grunts who like to eat humans? Or a thousand Cranks?"

"Thomas . . . no. Everybody." Minho let out an exasperated sigh.

"Would everyone just shut their holes and slim it? No more questions. Unless you have an idea that doesn't involve absolute certain death, then quit your pipin' and let's take the only chance we got. Get it?"

Thomas smiled, though he didn't know where the impulse came from. Somehow in a few sentences Minho had cheered him up, or at least given him a little hope. They just had to go, to move, to do. That was it.

"That's better," Minho said with a satisfied nod. "Anybody else wanna pee their pants and cry for Mommy?"

A few snickers broke out, but no one said anything.

"Good. Newt, you lead up front this time, limp and all. Thomas, you in the back. Jack, get someone else to help with Winston to give you a break. Let's go."

And so they did. Aris held the pack this time, and Thomas felt as if he were almost floating along the ground, it felt so good. The only hard part was holding that sheet up, his arm growing weak and rubbery. But on and on they went, sometimes walking, sometimes jogging.

Luckily, the sun seemed to gain weight and drop more quickly the closer it got to the horizon. By Thomas's wristwatch, the Cranks had only been gone an hour when the sky turned a purplish orange and the intense glare of the sun started to melt away into a more pleasant glow. Not long after that, it disappeared below the horizon altogether, pulling nighttime and stars across the sky like a curtain.

The Gladers kept moving, heading toward the faint twinkle of lights coming from the town. Thomas could almost enjoy it now that he wasn't holding the pack and they'd put the sheet away.

Finally, when every last trace of dusk had gone, full darkness settled on the land like a black fog.

CHAPTER 19

Soon after dark, Thomas heard a girl screaming.

At first he didn't know what he was hearing, or if maybe it was just his imagination. With the thumps of dry footsteps, the rustling of the packs, the whispers of conversation between heavy breaths, it was hard to tell. But what had started as almost a buzz inside his head soon became unmistakable. Somewhere ahead of them, maybe all the way in the town but more likely closer, a girl's screams tore through the night.

The others had obviously noticed it, too, and soon the Gladers quit running. Once everyone caught their breath, it became easier to hear the disturbing sound.

It was almost like a cat. An injured, wailing cat. The kind of noise that made your skin crawl and made you press your hands to your ears and pray it went away. There was something unnatural about it, something that chilled Thomas inside and out. The darkness only added to the creepiness. Whoever the source, she still wasn't very close, but her shrill screeches bounced along like living echoes, trying to smash their unspeakable sounds against the dirt until they ceased to exist in this world.

"You know what that reminds me of?" Minho asked, his voice a whisper with an edge of fear.

Thomas knew. "Ben. Alby. Me, I guess? Screaming after the Griever sting?"

"You got it."

"No, no, no," Frypan moaned. "Don't tell me we're gonna have those suckers out here, too. I can't take it!"

Newt responded, just a couple of feet to the left of Thomas and Aris. "Doubt it. Remember how moist and gooey their skin was? They'd turn into a big dust ball if they rolled around in this stuff."

"Well," Thomas said, "if WICKED can create Grievers, they can create plenty of other freaks of nature that might be worse. Hate to say it, but that rat-lookin' guy said things were finally going to get tough."

"Once again, Thomas gives us a cheerful pep talk," Frypan announced; he tried to sound jovial, but it came out more like a spiteful rub.

"Just saying it how it is."

Frypan huffed. "I know. And *how it is* sucks big-time."

"What now?" Thomas asked.

"I think we should take a break," Minho said. "Fill our little tummies and drink up. Then we should book it for as long as we can stand it while the sun is still down. Maybe get a couple hours' sleep before dawn."

"And the psycho screaming lady out there?" Frypan asked.

"Sounds like she's plenty busy with her own troubles."

For some reason that statement terrified Thomas. Maybe the others, too, because no one said a word as they slipped the packs off their shoulders, sat down and began eating.

"Man, I wish she'd shut up." It was about the fifth time Aris had said that as they ran along in the darker-than-dark night. The poor girl, somewhere out there, getting closer all the while, was still crying her fretful, high-pitched wails.

Their meal had been quiet and somber, the talk drifting toward what the Rat Man had said about the Variables and how their responses to them were all that mattered. About creating a "blueprint," about finding the "killzone" patterns. No one had any answers, of course, only meaningless speculations. It was odd, Thomas thought. They now *knew* they were being tested somehow, put through WICKED's trials. In some ways it felt like they should behave differently because of this, and yet they just kept going, fighting, surviving until they could get the promised cure. And that was what they'd keep doing; Thomas was sure of it.

It had taken a while for his legs and joints to loosen up once Minho got everyone moving again. Above them, the moon was a sliver, barely providing any more light than the stars. But you didn't need to see much to run along flat and barren land. Plus, unless it was his imagination, they were actually starting to reach the lights from the town. He could see that they flickered now, which meant they were probably fires. Which made sense—the odds of having electricity in this wasteland hovered around zero.

He wasn't sure when it happened exactly, but suddenly the cluster of buildings they were running toward seemed a lot closer. And there were a lot more of them than he or anyone else had thought. Taller, too. Wider. Spread out and organized in rows and in an orderly fashion. For all they knew, the place might've once been a major city, devastated by whatever had happened to the area. Could sun flares really inflict that much damage? Or had other things caused it during the aftermath?

Thomas was starting to think they'd actually reach the first buildings sometime the next day.

Even though they didn't need the cover of their sheet at the moment, Aris still jogged right next to him, and Thomas felt like talking. "Tell me more about your whole Maze thing."

Aris's breaths were even; he seemed to be in just as good shape as Thomas. "My whole Maze thing? What's that supposed to mean?"

"You've never really told us the details. What was it like for you? How long were you there? How'd you get out?"

Aris answered over the soft *crunch, crunch, crunch* of their footsteps on the desert ground. "I've talked with some of your friends, and it sounds like a lot of it was exactly the same. Just . . . girls instead of guys. Some of them had been there for two years, the rest had shown up one at a time, once a month. Then came Rachel, then me the next day, in a coma. I barely remember anything, just those last few crazy days after I finally woke up."

He went on to explain what had happened, and so much of it matched what Thomas and the Gladers had been through, it was just plain bizarre. Almost impossible to believe. Aris came out of his coma, said something about the Ending, the walls quit shutting at night, their Box stopped coming, they figured out the Maze had a code, on and on and on until the escape. Which went down almost the same as the Gladers' terrifying experience, except less of the girl group died—if they were tough like Teresa, this didn't surprise Thomas in the least.

In the end, once Aris and his group were in the final chamber, a girl named Beth—who'd disappeared days earlier, just like Gally had—killed Rachel, right before rescuers came in and whisked them away to the gym Aris had mentioned before. Then the rescuers took him to the place where the Gladers had finally discovered him—what had been Teresa's room.

If that was what had happened. Who knew how things worked anymore, after seeing what could happen at the Cliff and the Flat Trans that had taken them to the tunnel. Not to mention the bricked-up walls and the name change on Aris's door.

It all gave Thomas a big fat headache.

When he tried to think of Group B and imagine their roles—how he and Aris were basically switched, and how Aris was actually Teresa's counterpart—it twisted his mind. The fact that Chuck had been killed in the end instead of him . . . that was the only major difference that stood out in the parallels. Were the setups meant to instigate certain conflicts or provoke reactions for WICKED's studies?

"It's all kind of freaky, huh?" Aris asked after letting Thomas digest his story for a while.

"I don't know what the word for it is. But it blows me away how the two groups went through these trippy parallel experiments. Or tests, trials, whatever they were. I mean, if they're testing our responses, I guess it makes sense that we were put through the same thing. Weird, though."

Right when Thomas stopped speaking the girl in the distance let out a shriek even louder than her now-regular cries of pain and he felt a fresh rush of horror.

"I think I know," Aris said, so quietly Thomas wasn't sure he'd heard him correctly.

"Huh?"

"I think I know. Why there were two groups. *Are* two groups."

Thomas looked over at him, could barely see the surprising look of calm on his face. "You do? What then?"

Aris still didn't seem very winded. "Well, actually I have two ideas. One is I think these people—WICKED, whoever they are—are trying to weed out the best of both groups to use us somehow. Maybe even breed us or something like that."

"What?" Thomas was so surprised he almost forgot about the screaming. He couldn't believe anyone would be so sick. "*Breed* us? Come on."

"After going through the Maze and what we just saw happen in that tunnel, you think *breeding* is far-fetched? Give me a break."

"Good that." Thomas had to admit that the kid had a point. "Okay, so what was your other theory?" As he asked it Thomas could feel the weariness brought on by the run settling in; his throat felt like someone had poured a glassful of sand down his gullet.

"Kind of the opposite," Aris responded. "That instead of wanting survivors from both groups, they only want one group to live through to the end. So they're either weeding out people from the guys *and* the girls, or an entire group altogether. Either way, it's the only explanation I can think of."

Thomas thought about what he'd said for quite some time before responding. "But what about the stuff the Rat Man said? That they're testing our responses, building some kind of blueprint? Maybe it's an experiment. Maybe they don't plan for any of us to survive. Maybe they're studying our brains and our reactions and our genes and everything else. When it's all done, we'll be dead and they'll have lots of reports to read."

"Hmm," Aris grunted, considering. "Possibly. I keep trying to figure out why they had one member of the opposite sex in each group."

"Maybe to see what kind of fights or problems it would cause. Study people's reactions—it's kind of a unique situation." Thomas almost wanted to laugh. "I love how we're talking about this—like we're deciding when we need to stop for a klunk."

Aris actually did laugh, a dry chuckle that made Thomas feel better—actually made him like the new kid even more. "Man, don't say that. I've had to go for at least an hour."

It was Thomas's turn to snicker, and right on cue, like he'd heard Aris calling for it, Minho yelled out for everyone to stop.

"Potty break," he said with his hands on his hips as he caught his breath. "Bury your klunk and don't do it too close. We'll rest for fifteen, then we'll just walk awhile. I know you shanks can't keep up with Runners like me and Thomas."

Thomas tuned out—he didn't need directions on how to use the bathroom—and turned to get a look at where they'd stopped. He took a deep, full breath, and when he relaxed his eyes caught on something. A dark shadow of a shape a few hundred yards in front of them, but not directly in the path of their journey. A square of darkness against the faint glow of the town up ahead. It stood out so distinctly he couldn't believe he hadn't noticed it until now.

"Hey!" he yelled, pointing toward it. "Looks like a little building up there, just a few minutes away, to the right some. You guys see it?"

"Yeah, I see it," Minho responded, walking up to stand next to him. "Wonder what it is."

Before Thomas could respond, two things happened almost simultaneously.

First, the haunted screams of the mystery girl stopped, instantly, cut short as if a door had closed on her. Then, stepping out from behind the dark building up ahead, the figure of a girl appeared, long hair flowing from her shadowed head like black silk.

CHAPTER 20

Thomas couldn't help it. His first instinct was to hope it was her, call out to her. To hope that against all odds she was there, just a few hundred yards away, waiting for him.

Teresa?

Nothing.

Teresa? Teresa!

Nothing. The abscess left when she disappeared was still in his head—like an empty pool. But . . . it *could* be her. Might be her. Maybe something had happened to their ability to communicate.

Once the girl had stepped out from behind the building, or more likely from *inside* the building, she just stood there. Despite being obscured completely by shadow, something about her stance made it obvious she was facing them, staring at them with arms folded.

"You think that's Teresa?" Newt asked, as if he'd read Thomas's mind.

Thomas nodded before he knew what he was doing. He quickly looked around to see if anyone had noticed. Didn't seem so. "No clue," he finally said.

"You think *she* was the one screaming?" Frypan asked. "It stopped right when she walked out."

Minho grunted. "Better bet is she was the one torturing somebody. Probably killed her and put her out of her misery when she saw us coming." Then for some reason he clapped his hands once. "Okay, then, who wants to go meet this nice young lady?"

How Minho could be so lighthearted at times like this just baffled Thomas. "I'll do it," he said, way too loudly. He didn't want to make it obvious that he hoped it was Teresa.

"I was just kidding, shuck-face," Minho said. "Let's all go over there. She could have an army of psycho girl ninjas hiding in that shack of hers."

"Psycho girl ninjas?" Newt repeated, his voice showing he was surprised, if not annoyed, by Minho's attitude.

"Yeah. Let's go." Minho started walking forward.

Thomas acted on a sudden and unexpected instinct. "No!" He lowered his voice. "No. You guys stay here—I'll go talk to her. Maybe it's a trap or something. We'd be idiots to all go over there and fall right into it."

"And you're *not* an idiot for going by yourself?" Minho asked.

"Well, we can't just walk on by without checking it out. I'll go. If something happens or gets suspicious, I'll call for help."

Minho paused for a long moment. "All right. Go. Our brave little shank." He whacked Thomas on the back with his open palm and it stung.

"This is bloody stupid," Newt interrupted, stepping forward. "I'll go with him."

"No!" Thomas snapped. "Just . . . let me do this. Something tells me we need to be careful. If I cry like a baby, come save me." And before anyone could argue, he took off at a fast walk toward the girl and her building.

He closed the distance quickly. His shoes crunched against the gritty dirt and rocks, breaking the silence. He sniffed the raw smells of the desert mixed with a distant scent of something burning, and as he stared at the silhouette of the girl next to the building, he suddenly knew for sure. Maybe it was the shape of her head or body. Maybe it was her stance, the way she held her folded arms crooked to one side, her hip jutting the other direction. But he knew.

It was her.

It was Teresa.

When he reached a point just a few feet from her, right before the faint light would finally reveal her face, she turned around and went through an open door, disappearing inside the small building. It was a rectangle, a slightly tilted roof tenting in the middle, longways. As far as he could tell, it had no windows. Large black cubes were hanging from the corners—speakers, perhaps. Maybe the sound had been broadcast, been a fake. That would explain why they could hear it from so far away.

The door, a big slab of wood, stood all the way open and rested against the wall. It was even darker inside than out.

Thomas moved. He walked through the door, realizing even as he did so how reckless and stupid it might be. But it was her. No matter what had happened, no matter the explanation for her disappearance and refusal to speak with him through their thoughts, he knew she wouldn't hurt him. No way.

The air was noticeably cooler inside, almost moist. It felt wonderful. Three steps in, he stopped and listened in the complete darkness. He could hear her breathing.

"Teresa?" he asked aloud, pushing away the temptation to ask for her in his mind again. "Teresa, what's going on?"

She didn't respond, but he heard a short intake of breath, followed by a halting sniff, as if she were crying but trying to hide it from him.

"Teresa, *please*. I don't know what's happened or what they did to you, but I'm here now. This is crazy. Just talk to—"

He cut off when a light blazed to life with a quick flare that then dulled to a small flame. His eyes naturally went straight to it, to the hand holding a match. He watched as it dropped, slowly, carefully, to light a candle resting on a small table. When it caught, and the hand flicked the match until it went out, Thomas finally looked up and saw her. Saw that he'd been right after all. But the short and almost overpowering thrill of seeing Teresa alive was soon cut short, replaced by confusion and pain.

She was clean, every part of her. He'd expected her to be filthy like he must be after all this time in the dusty desert. He'd expected her clothes to be ratty and torn. He'd expected greasy hair and a smudged and sunburned face. But instead she wore fresh clothes; her clean hair cascaded to her shoulders. Nothing marred the pale skin of her face or arms. She was more beautiful than he'd ever seen her in the Maze, than any memories he could pull from the murky goop of what he'd recovered after the Changing.

But her eyes sparkled with tears; her lower lip trembled with fear; her hands shook at her sides. He saw recognition in her eyes, saw that she hadn't forgotten him again, but behind that there was pure and absolute terror.

"Teresa," he whispered, knotting up inside. "What's wrong?"

She didn't respond, but her eyes flickered to the side, then back to him. A couple of tears trickled out, slipping down her cheeks, then falling to the floor. Her lips trembled even more, and her chest lurched with what could only be a stifled sob.

Thomas stepped forward, put his hands out to her.

"No!" she screamed. "Get away from me!"

Thomas stopped—it was like something massive had just slammed him in the gut. He held his hands up. "Okay, okay. Teresa, what . . ." He didn't know what to say or ask. Didn't know what to do. But that terrible feeling of something breaking inside him intensified, threatened to choke him as it swelled in his throat.

He stilled, scared to set her off again. All he could do was lock eyes with her, try to communicate how he felt, beg her to tell him something. Anything.

A very long moment passed in silence. The way her body shook, the way she almost seemed to struggle against something unseen . . . it reminded him of . . .

It reminded him of how Gally had been acting, right after they'd escaped from the Glade and he'd entered the room with the woman in the white shirt. Right before everything had gone crazy. Right before he'd killed Chuck.

Thomas had to speak or he'd burst. "Teresa, I've thought about you every second since they took you away. You—"

She didn't let him finish. Rushing forward, she was in front of him in two long strides and reaching out, grabbing his shoulders and pulling herself close to him. Shocked, Thomas wrapped his arms around her and squeezed, embracing her so tightly he suddenly worried she couldn't breathe. Her hands found the back of his head, then the sides of his face, making him look at her.

And then they were kissing. Something exploded within his chest, burning away the tension and confusion and fear. Burning away the hurt of seconds earlier. For a moment it felt like nothing mattered anymore. Like nothing would matter ever again.

But then she pulled away. She stumbled backward until she hit the wall. The terror returned to her face, possessed it like a demon. And then she spoke, her voice a whisper but laced with urgency.

"Get away from me, Tom," she said. "All of you need to get . . . away . . . from me. Don't argue. Just leave. Run." Her neck tensed with the effort to get those last few words out.

Thomas had never hurt so badly. But he shocked himself by what he did next.

He knew her now, *remembered* her. And he knew that she was telling the truth—something wasn't right here. Something was terribly wrong—far worse than he'd first imagined. Staying, arguing with her, trying to force her to come with him would be a slap in the face to the incredible amount of willpower it must've taken her to break away and warn him. He had to do what she said.

"Teresa," he said. "I'll find you." Tears now welling in his own eyes, he turned from her and ran from the building.

CHAPTER 21

Thomas stumbled away from the now-dark building, squinting through tear-blurred eyes. He went back to the Gladers and refused to answer their questions. Told them they had to go, run, get away as fast as possible. That he'd explain later. That their lives were in danger.

He didn't wait for them. He didn't offer to take the pack from Aris. He just started toward the town, sprinting till he finally had to slow down to a manageable pace, blocking the others out, blocking the whole world out. Running away from her was the hardest thing he'd ever done, he had no doubt of it. Showing up at the Glade with his memories wiped, adapting to life there, being trapped in the Maze, fighting Grievers, watching Chuck die—none of it matched what he felt now.

She was there. She'd been in his arms. They'd been together again.

They'd kissed and he'd felt something he would've thought impossible.

And now he was running away. Leaving her behind.

Choked sobs burst from him. He groaned, heard the miserable sound of his voice crack. His heart felt a pain that almost made him stop, collapse to the ground and give up. Sorrow consumed him, and more than once he was tempted to go back. But somehow he held true to what she'd ordered him to do, and he held on to the promise he'd made to find her again.

At least she was alive. At least she was alive.

That was what he kept telling himself. That was what kept him running.

She was alive.

His body could only take so much. At some point, maybe two hours after he'd left her, maybe three, he stopped, sure his heart would explode out of his chest if he went one more step. Turning, he looked behind him and he saw shadows moving far in the distance—the other Gladers, way back. Breathing huge gulps of dry air, Thomas knelt, planted his forearms on one knee, then closed his eyes to rest until they caught up.

Minho reached him first, and their leader wasn't happy. Even in the faint light—dawn was just starting to brighten the eastern sky—he visibly fumed as he walked around Thomas three full times before he said anything.

"What . . . Why . . . What kind of a shuck idiot are you, Thomas?"

Thomas didn't feel like talking about it. About anything.

When he didn't answer, Minho knelt down next to him. "How could you do that? How could you just come out of there and take off like that? Without explaining anything? Since when is that how we do things? You slinthead." He let out a big sigh and fell back to sit on his butt, shaking his head.

"Sorry," Thomas finally muttered. "It was kinda traumatizing."

The other Gladers had reached them by now, half of them doubling over to catch their breaths, the other half pressing in to hear what Thomas and Minho were talking about. Newt was right there, but he seemed content to let Minho do all the digging to find out what had happened.

"Traumatizing?" Minho asked. "Who did you see in there? What did they say?"

Thomas knew he had no choice—this wasn't something he could or should keep from the others. "It was . . . it was Teresa."

He expected gasps, exclamations of surprise, accusations of being a freaking liar. But in the silence that followed, you could hear the morning winds scuttle across the dusty lands surrounding them.

"What?" Minho finally said. "You're serious?"

Thomas simply nodded, staring at a triangular-shaped rock on the ground. The air had brightened considerably in just the last few minutes.

Minho was understandably shocked. "And you *left* her there? Dude, you need to start talking and tell us what happened."

As much as it pained him, as much as the memory of it tore at his heart, Thomas told the story. Seeing her, how she trembled and cried, how she acted like Gally—almost possessed—before he killed Chuck, the warning she'd given. He told it all; the only thing he left out was the kiss.

"Wow," Minho said in a weary voice, somehow wrapping it all up with that one simple word.

Several minutes passed. The dry wind scratched across the ground, filling the air with dust as the bright orange dome of the sun crested the horizon and officially started the day. No one spoke. Thomas heard sniffs and breaths and a few coughs. The sounds of people drinking from their water bags. The town seemed to have grown during the night, its buildings stretching toward the cloudless, purple-blue sky. It would only take another day or two to reach it.

"It was some kind of trap," he finally said. "I don't know what would've happened, or how many of us would've died. Maybe all of us. But I could see that there wasn't any doubt in her eyes when she broke away from whatever restrained her. She saved us, and I bet they make her . . ." He swallowed. "I bet they make her pay for it."

Minho reached out and squeezed Thomas's shoulder. "Dude, if those shuck WICKED people wanted her dead, she'd be rottin' under a big pile of rocks. She's just as tough as anybody else, maybe tougher. She'll survive."

Thomas took in a deep pull of air and let it out. He felt better. Impossibly, he felt better. Minho was right. "I know. Somehow I know."

Minho stood up. "We should've stopped a couple hours ago to get some sleep. But thanks to Mr. Desert Runner down here"—he lightly whacked Thomas in the head—"we ran ourselves ragged till the freaking sun came back up. I still think we need to rest for a while. Do it under the sheets, whatever, but let's try."

It ended up being no problem at all for Thomas. The brightening sun making the backs of his eyelids a murky black-splotched crimson, he fell asleep instantly, a sheet pulled all the way over his head to protect him from sunburn—and from his troubles.

CHAPTER 22

Minho let them sleep for almost four hours. Not that he had to wake many people up. The rising and intensifying sun raged its heat down on the land, and it became unbearable—impossible to ignore. By the time Thomas was up and had the food repacked after breakfast, sweat already drenched his clothes. The smell of body odor hung over them like a stinky mist, and he just hoped he wasn't the worst culprit. The showers back at the dorm seemed like pure luxury now.

The Gladers remained sullen and quiet as they readied for the journey. The more Thomas thought about it, the more he realized that there wasn't much to be happy about. Still, two things kept him going, and he hoped they did the same for the others. First, an overwhelming curiosity to find out what was in that stupid town—it looked more and more like a city as they got closer. And second, the hope that Teresa was alive and well. Maybe she'd gone through one of those Flat Trans things. Maybe she was ahead of them now. In the city, even. Thomas felt a swell of encouragement.

"Let's go," Minho said when everybody was ready. Then they were off.

Across the dry and dusty land they walked. No one needed to say it, but Thomas knew everyone was thinking the same thing—they no longer had the energy to run while the sun was up. And even if they did, they didn't have enough water to keep them alive at a faster pace.

So they walked, sheets held over their heads. As food and water dwindled, more of the packs became available to use for protection from the sun, and fewer Gladers had to walk in pairs. Thomas was one of the first to be alone, probably because no one wanted to talk to him after hearing the story about Teresa. He certainly wasn't going to complain—solitude was bliss for now.

Walking. Breaks for food and water. Walking. Heat, like a dry ocean through which they had to swim. That wind, blowing stronger now, bringing more dust and grit than relief from the heat. It whipped at the sheets, made it harder to keep them in place. Thomas kept coughing and rubbing chunks of accumulated grime from the corners of his eyes. He felt as if every swallow of water only made him want more, but their supplies had reached dangerously low levels. If there wasn't fresh water in the city when they reached it . . .

There was no good way for him to finish that line of thought.

They kept going, each step becoming just a little more agonizing, and quiet set in. No one talked. Thomas felt like even saying a couple of words would expend too much energy. It was all he could do to put one foot in front of the other, over and over and over, staring lifelessly at their goal—the ever-nearing city.

It was as if the buildings were alive, growing right before their eyes as they got closer. Soon Thomas could see what had to be stone, windows glimmering in the sunlight. Some seemed to be broken, but far less than half. From Thomas's vantage point, the streets seemed empty. No fires burned during the day. As far as he could tell, not one tree or any other kind of plant existed in the place. How would it, in this climate? How could people possibly live there? How would they grow food? What would they find?

Tomorrow. It had taken longer than he'd thought, but Thomas had no doubt they'd reach the city tomorrow. And though they'd probably be better off going *around* it, they had no choice. They needed to replenish their supplies.

Walking. Breaks. Heat.

When nightfall finally came, the sun disappearing below the far western horizon at a maddeningly slow pace, the wind picked up even more, and this time brought the slightest chill. Thomas enjoyed it, grateful for any relief from the heat.

By midnight, however, when Minho finally called on them to stop and get more sleep, the city and its now-burning fires ever closer, the wind had become even stronger. It blew in gales, whipping and curling with increasing power.

Soon after they stopped, as Thomas lay on his back, sheet tucked around him and pulled up tightly to his chin, he looked up at the sky. The winds were almost soothing, lulling him to sleep. Just as his mind got hazy from exhaustion, the stars seemed to fade away, and sleep brought him another dream.

He's sitting in a chair. Ten or eleven years old. Teresa—she looks so different, so much younger, yet it's still clearly her—sits across from him, a table between them. She's about his age. No one else is in the room, a dark place with only one light—a dull square of yellow in the ceiling directly overhead.

"Tom, you need to try harder," she says. Her arms are folded, and even at this younger age, it's a look he doesn't find surprising. It's very familiar. As if he has already known her a long time.

"I *am* trying." Again it's him speaking, but not really him. It doesn't make sense.

"They'll probably kill us if we can't do this."

"I know."

"Then try!"

"I am!"

"Fine," she says. "You know what? I'm not speaking out loud to you anymore. Never ever again until you can do it."

"But—"

Not inside your mind, either. She's talking in his head. That trick that still freaks him out and he still can't reciprocate. *Starting now.*

"Teresa, just give me a few more days. I'll get it."

She doesn't respond.

"Okay, just one more day."

She only stares at him. Then, not even that. She looks down at the table, reaches out and starts scratching a spot in the wood with her fingernail.

"There's no way you're not gonna talk to me."

No response. And he knows her, despite what he just said. Oh, he knows her.

"Fine," he says. He closes his eyes, does what the instructor told him to do. Imagines a sea of black nothingness, interrupted only by the image of Teresa's face. Then, with every last bit of willpower, he forms the words and *throws* them at her.

You smell like a bag of crap.

Teresa smiles, then replies in his mind.

So do you.

CHAPTER 23

Thomas woke up to wind beating at his face and hair and clothes. It felt like invisible hands were trying to rip them off. It was still dark. And cold, too, his whole body shivering from it. Getting up on his elbows, he looked around, hardly able to see the huddled shapes sleeping near him, their sheets pulled tightly against their bodies.

Their sheets.

He let out a frustrated yelp, then jumped to his feet—at some point in the night his own sheet had slipped loose and flown off. With the tearing wind, it could be ten miles away by now.

"Shuck it," he whispered; the howl of the wind stole the words before he could even hear them. The dream came back to him—or was it a memory? It had to be. That brief glimpse into a time when he and Teresa had been younger, learning how to do their telepathy trick. He felt his heart sink a little, missing her, feeling guilt over yet more proof that he'd been part of WICKED before going to the Maze. He shook it off, not wanting to think about it. He could block it out if he tried hard enough.

He looked up at black sky, then sucked in a hurried breath as the memory of the sun vanishing from the Glade came rushing back. That had been the beginning of the end. The beginning of the terror.

But common sense soon calmed his heart. The winds. The cool air. A storm. It had to be a storm.

Clouds.

Embarrassed, he sat back down, then lay on his side and curled into a ball, his arms wrapped around himself. The cold wasn't unbearable, just a vast change from the horrible heat of the last couple of days. He probed his mind and wondered about the memories he'd had lately. Could they be lingering results of the Changing? Was his memory coming back?

The thought gave him mixed feelings. He wanted his memory block finally cracked for good—wanted to know who he was, where he came from. But that desire was tempered by fear of what he might find out about himself. About his role in the very things that had brought him to this point, that had done this to his friends.

He needed sleep desperately. The wind a constant roar in his ears, he finally slipped away, this time to nothing.

The light woke him to a dull, gray dawn that finally revealed the thick layer of clouds covering the sky. It also made the endless expanse of desert around them look even more dreary. The city was so close now, only a few hours away. The buildings really *were* tall; one of them even stretched up and disappeared in a low-hanging fog. And the glass in all those broken windows was like jagged teeth in mouths open to catch food that might be flying about in the stormy wind.

The gusty air still tore at him, and a thick layer of dirt seemed forever baked onto his face. He rubbed his head and his hair felt stiff with wind-dried grime.

Most of the other Gladers were up and about, taking in the unexpected shift in the weather, deep in conversations he couldn't hear. There was only the roar in his ears.

Minho noticed him awake and came over; he leaned into the wind as he walked, his clothes flapping around him. "'Bout time you woke up!" He was fully shouting.

Thomas rubbed the crust out of his eyes and got to his feet. "Where'd this all come from!" he yelled back. "I thought we were in the middle of a desert!"

Minho looked up at the roiling gray mass of clouds, then back at Thomas. He leaned closer to speak directly in his ear. "Well, guess it has to rain in the desert *sometime*. Hurry and eat—we gotta get going. Maybe we can get there and find a place to hide before we're soaked by the storm."

"What if we get there and a bunch of Cranks try to kill us?"

"Then we'll fight 'em!" Minho frowned as if disappointed that Thomas had asked such a stupid question. "What else you wanna do? We're almost out of food and water."

Thomas knew Minho was right. Plus, if they could fight dozens of Grievers, a bunch of half-mad, starved sicklings shouldn't be too much of a problem. "All right, then. Let's go. I'll eat one of those granola things while we walk."

A few minutes later, they were once again heading for the city, the gray sky above them ready to burst and bleed water at any moment.

They were only a couple of miles away from the closest buildings when they came across an old man lying in the sand on his back, wrapped in several blankets. Jack had been the one to spot him first, and soon Thomas and the others were packed in a circle around the guy, staring down at him.

Thomas's stomach turned as he studied the man more closely, but he couldn't look away. The stranger had to be a hundred years old, though it was hard to tell—the wear and tear of the sun might've made him just look that way. Wrinkled, leathery face. Scabs and sores where his hair should've been. Dark, dark skin.

He was alive, breathing deeply, but he gazed at the sky with an emptiness in his eyes. As if he was waiting for some god to come down and take him away, end his miserable life. He showed no sign he'd even noticed the Gladers approach.

"Hey! Old man!" Minho shouted, always the tactful one. "What're you doing out here?"

Thomas had a hard enough time hearing the words over the ripping wind; he couldn't imagine that the ancient guy could make anything out. But was he blind as well? Maybe.

Thomas nudged Minho out of the way and knelt down right beside the man's face. The melancholy there was heartbreaking. He held his hand out and waved it right above the old guy's eyes.

Nothing. No blink, no movement. It was only after Thomas pulled his hand back that the man's eyelids slowly drooped closed, then open again. Just once.

"Sir?" Thomas asked. "Mister?" The words sounded strange to him, conjured up from the murky memories of his past. He certainly hadn't used them since being sent to the Glade and the Maze. "Can you hear me? Can you talk?"

The man did that slow blink again, but didn't say anything.

Newt knelt next to Thomas and spoke loudly over the wind. "This guy's a bloody gold mine if we can get him to tell us stuff about the city. Looks harmless, probably knows what to expect when we go in there."

Thomas sighed. "Yeah, but he doesn't even seem to be able to hear us, much less have a long talk."

"Keep trying," Minho said from behind them. "You're officially our foreign ambassador, Thomas. Get the dude to open up and tell us about the good ol' days."

For some odd reason Thomas wanted to say something funny back, but he couldn't think of anything. If he'd been funny in his old life, every scrap of humor had certainly vanished in the memory swipe. "Okay," he said.

He scooted as close to the man's head as he could, then positioned himself so their eyes were square, just a couple of feet apart. "Sir? We really need your help!" He felt bad for shouting, worried the old man might take it the wrong way, but he had no choice. The wind was gusting stronger and stronger. "We need you to tell us if it's safe to go inside the city! We can carry you there if you need help yourself. Sir? Sir!"

The man's dark eyes had been looking past him, up at the sky, but now they shifted, slowly, until they focused on his. Awareness filled them like dark liquid poured slowly into a glass. His lips parted, but nothing came out except a small cough.

Thomas's hopes lifted. "My name is Thomas. These are my friends. We've been walking through the desert for a couple of days, and we need more water and food. What do you . . ."

He trailed off when the man's eyes flicked back and forth, a sudden hint of panic there.

"It's okay, we won't hurt you," Thomas quickly said. "We're . . . we're the good guys. But we'd really appreciate it if—"

The man's left hand shot out from beneath the blankets wrapped around him and clasped Thomas's wrist, gripping it with a strength far greater than seemed possible. Thomas cried out in surprise and instinctively tried to pull his arm free, but couldn't. He was shocked by the man's strength. He could barely budge against the man's iron manacle of a fist.

"Hey!" he shouted. "Let go of me!"

The man shook his head, those dark eyes full more of fear than any kind of belligerence. His lips parted again, and a rough, indecipherable whisper rose from his mouth. He didn't loosen his grip.

Thomas gave up the struggle to free his arm; instead, he relaxed and leaned forward to put his ear close to the stranger's mouth. "What'd you say!" he shouted.

The man spoke again, a dry rasp that was unsettling, spooky. Thomas caught the words *storm* and *terror* and *bad people*. None of them sounded very inspiring.

"One more time!" Thomas yelled, his head still cocked so his ear rested only inches above the man's face.

This time Thomas understood most of it, missing only a few words. "Storm coming . . . full of terror . . . brings out . . . stay away . . . bad people."

The man shot up into a sitting position, his eyes full and white around his irises. "Storm! Storm! Storm!" He didn't stop, repeating the word over and over; a mucus-thick strand of saliva finally crested over his bottom lip and swung back and forth like a hypnotist's pendulum.

He released Thomas's arm, and Thomas scooted back on his butt to get away. Even as he did so, the wind intensified, seemed to go from strong gusts to outright hurricane-strength gales of terror, just like the man had said. The world was lost in the sound of roaring, screaming air. Thomas felt as if his hair and clothes might rip off at any second. Almost all of the Gladers' sheets went flying, flapping over the ground and into the air like an army of ghosts. Food skittered in all directions.

Thomas got to his feet, an almost impossible task with the wind trying to knock him over. He stumbled forward several feet until he leaned back into it; invisible hands held him up.

Minho stood nearby, frantically waving his arms as he tried to get everyone's attention. Most saw and gathered around him, including Thomas, who fought off the panic creeping along his insides. It was only a storm. Far better than Grievers or Cranks with knives. Or ropes.

The old man had lost his blankets to the wind, and he huddled now in the fetal position, his skinny legs squeezed against his chest, eyes closed. Thomas had the fleeting thought that they should carry him someplace safe, save him for at least attempting to warn them about the storm. But something told him the man would fight tooth and nail if they tried to touch him or pick him up.

The Gladers were now packed together. Minho pointed at the city. The closest building was within a half hour if they ran at a good pace. The way the wind tore at them, the way the clouds above thickened and churned and bruised to a deep purple, almost black, the way dust and debris flew through the air, reaching that building seemed the only sane choice.

Minho started running. The others fell in, and Thomas waited to bring up the rear, knowing that was what Minho wanted him to do. He finally broke into a brisk jog, glad they weren't going directly into the wind. Only then did a few of the words the old man had said pop into his mind. They made him break into a sweat that quickly evaporated, leaving his skin dry and salty.

Stay away. Bad people.

CHAPTER 24

As they approached the city, it became harder for Thomas to actually see it. The dust in the air had thickened into a brown fog, and he felt it in every breath. It was crusting in his eyes, making them water and turning into goop that he had to keep wiping away. The large building they were shooting for had become a looming shadow behind the cloud of dust, towering taller and taller, like a growing giant.

The wind had gained a rough edge, pelting him with sand and grit until it hurt. Every once in a while a larger object would fly by, scaring him half out of his wits. A branch. Something that looked like a small mouse. A piece of roofing tile. And countless scraps of paper. All swirling through the air like snowflakes.

Then came the lightning.

They'd halved the distance to the building—maybe more than that—when the bolts came from nowhere, and the world around him erupted in light and thunder.

They fell from the sky in jagged streaks, like bars of white light, slamming into the ground and throwing up massive amounts of scorched earth. The crushing sound was too much to bear, and Thomas's ears began to go numb, the horrific noise fading to a distant hum as he went deaf.

He kept running, almost blind now, unable to hear, barely able to see the building. People fell and got back up. Thomas stumbled but caught his balance. He helped Newt regain his feet, then Frypan. Pushed them forward as he kept on. It was only a matter of time before one of the thick daggers of lightning struck someone and fried them to a blackened char. His hair stood on end despite the ripping wind, the static in the air raging and prickly as flying needles.

Thomas wanted to scream, wanted to hear his own voice, even if it was only the dull vibrations inside his skull. But he knew the dust-riddled air would choke him; it was hard enough to take short, quick breaths through his nose. Especially with the storm of lightning crashing to the ground all around them, singeing the air, making everything smell like copper and ash.

The sky darkened further, the dust cloud thickened; Thomas realized he couldn't see everyone anymore. Just those few directly in front of him. Light from the strikes flashed against them, a short burst of brilliant white illuminating them for the briefest instant. It all added together to blind Thomas even more. They had to reach that building. They had to get there or they wouldn't last much longer.

And where was the rain? he wondered. Where was the rain? What kind of a storm was this?

A bolt of pure white zigzagged from the sky and exploded on the ground right in front of him. He screamed but couldn't hear himself, squeezing his eyes shut as something—some burst of energy or wave of air—threw him to the side. He landed flat on his back, the breath knocked from his chest, as a spray of dirt and rocks rained down on him. Spitting, wiping at his face, he gulped for air as he scrambled onto his hands and knees, then his feet. The air finally flowed, and he pulled it deep into his lungs.

He heard a ringing now, a steady, high-pitched buzz that felt like nails in his eardrums. The wind tried to eat his clothes, dirt stung his skin, darkness swirled around him like living night, broken only by the flashes of lightning. Then he saw it, a horrific image made even spookier by the on-again-off-again source of light.

It was Jack. He lay on the ground, inside a small crater, writhing as he clutched his knee. There was nothing below that—shin, ankle, and foot obliterated by the burst of pure electricity from the sky. Blood that looked like black tar gushed from the hideous wound, making a paste of horror with the dirt. His clothes had been burned off, leaving him naked, injuries spreading across his whole body. He had no hair. And it looked like his eyeballs had . . .

Thomas spun around and collapsed to the ground, coughing as he spit up everything in his stomach. There was nothing they could do for Jack. No way. Nothing. But he was still *alive*. Though the thought shamed him, Thomas was glad he couldn't hear the screams. He didn't know if he could bear to even look at him again.

Then someone was grabbing him, pulling him to his feet. Minho. He said something, and Thomas focused enough to read his lips. *We have to go. Nothing we can do.*

Jack, he thought. *Oh, man, Jack.*

Stumbling, his stomach muscles sore from throwing up, his ears ringing painfully, in shock from the terrible sight of Jack ripped to shreds by lightning, he ran after Minho. He saw lumps of shadow to the left and right, other Gladers, but only a few. It was too dark to see very far, and the lightning came and went too fast to reveal much. Only dust and debris and that looming shape of the building, almost on top of them now. They'd lost any hope of organization or staying together. It was each Glader for himself now—they just had to hope everyone could make it.

Wind. Explosions of light. Wind. Choking dust. Wind. Ringing in his ears, pain. Wind. He kept going, his eyes glued to Minho just a few steps ahead of him. He didn't feel anything for Jack. He didn't care if he was permanently deaf. He didn't care about the others anymore. The chaos around him seemed to siphon away his humanity, turn him into an animal. All he wanted was to survive, make it to that building, get inside. *Live.* Gain another day.

Searing white light detonated in front of him, throwing him through the air again. Even as he flew backward, he screamed, tried to regain his footing—the explosion had happened right where Minho was running. Minho! Thomas landed with a jarring thump that felt like every joint in his body came loose, then popped back into place. He ignored the pain, got up, ran forward, his vision full of darkness mixed with blurry afterimages, amoebas of purplish light. Then he saw flames.

It took a second for his brain to compute what he was seeing. Rods of fire dancing about like magic, hot tendrils whipping to the right from the wind. Then it all collapsed to the ground, a heap of thrashing flame. Thomas reached it and understood.

It was Minho. His clothes were on fire.

With a shriek that sent sharp pains through his head, he fell to the ground next to his friend. He dug into the earth—thankfully loose from the explosion of electricity that hit it—and shoveled it on top of Minho with both hands, scooping frantically. Aiming for the brightest points of flame, he made progress as Minho helped by rolling around and beating at his upper body with both hands.

In a matter of seconds, the fire went out, leaving behind charred clothing and countless angry wounds. Thomas was glad he couldn't hear the wails of agony that appeared to be coming from Minho. He knew they didn't have time to stop, so Thomas grabbed their leader by the shoulders and dragged him to his feet.

"Come on!" Thomas shouted, though the words felt like a couple of noiseless throbs in his brain.

Minho coughed, winced again, but then nodded and wrapped one of his arms around Thomas's neck. Together they moved as fast as they could toward the building, Thomas doing most of the work.

All around them, the lightning continued to fall like arrows of white fire. Thomas could feel the silent impact of the explosions, each one rattling his skull, shaking his bones. Flashes of light all around. Past the building toward which they stumbled and struggled, even more fires had sprung up; two or three times he saw lightning make direct contact with the upper reaches of a structure, sending a rain of bricks and glass falling to the streets below.

The darkness began to take on a different tone, more gray than brown, and Thomas realized that the storm clouds must've really thickened and sunk toward the ground, pushing the dust and fog out of their way. The wind had lessened slightly, but the lightning seemed stronger than ever.

Gladers were to the left and right, all heading in the same direction. They seemed fewer in number, but Thomas still couldn't see well enough to know for sure. He did spot Newt, then Frypan. And Aris. All of them looking as terrified as he felt, running, all eyes riveted to their goal, now just a short distance away.

Minho lost his footing and fell, slipped from Thomas's grip. Thomas stopped, turned around, pulled the burnt boy back to his feet, reset Minho's arm around his shoulder. Gripping him around the torso with both arms now, he half carried, half pulled him along. A blinding arc of lightning went right over their heads, pummeled the earth behind them; Thomas didn't look, kept moving. A Glader fell to his left; he couldn't tell who it was, didn't hear the scream he knew must've come. Another boy fell to his right, got back up. A blast of lightning, just ahead and to the right. Another to the left. One straight ahead. Thomas had to pause, blinking viciously until his sight came back. He started up again, yanking Minho along with him.

And then they were there. The first building of the city.

In the gripping darkness of the storm, the structure was all gray. Massive blocks of stone, an arch of smaller bricks, half-broken windows. Aris reached the door first, didn't bother to open it. It had been made of glass that was mostly gone, so he carefully smashed out the remaining shards with his elbow. He waved a couple of Gladers past, then went in himself, swallowed by the interior.

Thomas made it just as Newt did, and gestured for help. Newt and another boy took Minho from him, carefully dragged him backward over the threshold of the open entrance, his feet hitting the sill as they pulled him through.

And then Thomas, still in shock over the sheer power of the lightning bursts, followed his friends, stepping into the gloom.

He turned to look just in time to see the rain start falling outside, as if the storm had finally decided to weep with shame for what it had done to them.

CHAPTER 25

The rain fell in torrents, like God had sucked up the ocean and spit it out over their heads in fury.

Thomas sat in the exact same place for at least two hours as he watched it. He huddled against the wall, exhausted and sore, willing his hearing to come back. It seemed to be working—what had been a complete throb of silence had decreased its pressure, and the ringing had gone away. When he coughed, he thought it was more than just a vibration he felt. He *heard* a trace of it. And in the distance, as if from the other side of a dream, came the steady drumming sound of the rain. Maybe he wouldn't be deaf after all.

The dull gray light coming from the windows did little to fight off the cold darkness inside the building. The other Gladers sat hunched up or lying on their sides around the room. Minho was curled up in a ball at Thomas's feet, barely moving; it looked as if every shift sent waves of burning pain through his nerves. Newt was there, also, close, as was Frypan. But no one tried to talk or get things organized. No one counted off the Gladers or tried to figure out who was missing. They all sat or lay as lifeless as Thomas, probably pondering the same thing he was—what kind of messed-up world could create a storm like that?

The soft thrum of the rain grew louder until Thomas had no more doubt—he could really hear it. It was a soothing sound, despite everything, and he finally fell asleep.

★ ★ ★

By the time he woke up, his body so stiff it felt like glue had dried in his veins and muscles, all the machinery in his ears and head was back to fully functional. He heard the heavy breaths of sleeping Gladers, heard the whimpering moans from Minho, heard the now-pounding deluge of water slamming into the pavement outside.

But it was dark. Completely. At some point, night had fallen.

Pushing away his discomfort, letting the exhaustion take over, he shifted until he lay flat, his head propped on someone's leg—then he was asleep again.

Two things woke him up for good: the glow of sunrise and a sudden rush of silence. The storm was over, and he'd slept through the night. But even before he felt the stiffness and soreness he expected, he felt something much more overpowering.

Hunger.

The light came through the broken windows and dappled the floor around him. He looked up to see a ruin of a building, massive holes ripped in each floor all the way to the roof dozens of stories toward the sky; it seemed that only the steel infrastructure was keeping the whole thing from coming down. He couldn't imagine what had caused it all to happen. But jags of bright blue seemed to hover above, a sight that seemed impossible last time he'd been outside. Whatever horror that storm had been, whatever quirks in the climate of the earth could cause such a thing, it really did seem to be gone for now.

Sharp pains stabbed at his stomach, which groaned, aching for food. He glanced around to see most of the other Gladers still asleep, but Newt lay with his back against the wall, staring sadly at a blank spot in the middle of the room.

"You okay, there?" Thomas asked. Even his jaw felt stiff.

Newt slowly turned to him; his eyes were distant until he seemed to snap out of his thoughts and focus on Thomas. "Okay? Yeah, I guess I'm okay. We're alive—guess that's all that bloody matters anymore." The bitterness in his voice couldn't have been stronger.

"Sometimes I wonder," Thomas murmured.

"Wonder what?"

"If being alive matters. If being dead might be a lot easier."

"Please. I don't believe for one second you really think that."

Thomas's gaze had lowered while he'd delivered the depressing sentiment and he looked up sharply at Newt's retort. Then he smiled, and it felt good. "You're right. Just trying to sound as miserable as you." He could almost convince himself that it was true. That he *didn't* feel as if dying would be the easy way out.

Newt gestured wearily toward Minho. "What bloody happened to him?"

"Lightning strike somehow caught his clothes on fire. How it did that without frying his brain I have no idea. But we were able to beat it out before it did too much damage, I think."

"Before it did too much damage? I'd hate to see what you think *real* damage looks like."

Thomas closed his eyes for a second and rested his head against the wall. "Hey, like you said—he's alive, right? And he still has clothes on, which means it couldn't have burned his skin in *too* many places. He'll be fine."

"Yeah, good that," Newt replied with a sarcastic chuckle. "Remind me not to hire you as my buggin' doctor anytime soon."

"Ohhhh." This came from Minho, a long, drawn-out groan. His eyes fluttered open, then squinted as he caught Thomas's gaze. "Oh, man. I'm shucked. I'm shucked for good."

"How bad is it?" Newt asked him.

Instead of answering, Minho very slowly pushed himself up to a sitting position, grunting and wincing with every small move. But he finally did it, legs crossed beneath him. His clothes were blackened and ragged. In some places where skin was exposed, raw red blisters peeked out like menacing alien eyeballs. But even though Thomas wasn't a doctor and had no clue about such things, his instincts told him the burns were manageable and would heal pretty quickly. Most of Minho's face had been spared, and he still had all his hair—filthy as it was.

"Can't be too bad if you can do that," Thomas said with a sly smile.

"Shuck it," Minho responded. "I'm tougher than nails. I could still kick your pony-lovin' butt with twice this pain."

Thomas shrugged. "I do love ponies. Wish I could eat one right now." His stomach grumbled and gurgled.

"Was that a joke?" Minho said. "Did Thomas the boring slinthead actually make a joke?"

"I think he did" was Newt's response.

"I'm a funny guy," Thomas said with a shrug.

"Yeah, you are." But Minho obviously had already lost interest in the small talk. He twisted his head around to take in the rest of the Gladers, most of them asleep or lying still with blank looks on their faces. "How many?"

Thomas counted them up. Eleven. After all they'd been through, only eleven were left. And that included the new kid, Aris. Forty or fifty had lived in the Glade when Thomas first arrived, just a few weeks before. Now there were eleven.

Eleven.

He couldn't bring himself to say anything out loud after this realization, and the lighter moment only seconds earlier suddenly seemed like pure blasphemy. Like an abomination.

How could I be part of WICKED? he thought. *How could I have been any part of this?* He knew he should tell them about his memory-dreams, but he just couldn't.

"There's only eleven of us," Newt finally said. There. It was out.

"So, what, six died in the storm? Seven?" Minho sounded completely detached, as if he were counting how many apples they'd lost when the packs had blown away.

"Seven," Newt snapped, showing his disapproval of the cavalier attitude. Then, in a softer tone, "Seven. Unless people ran to a different building."

"Dude," Minho said. "How're we gonna fight our way through this city with only eleven people? There could be hundreds of Cranks in this place for all we know. Thousands. And we don't have a clue what to expect from them!"

Newt let out a big breath. "And that's all you can buggin' think about? What about the people who died, Minho? Jack's missing. So is Winston—he never had a chance. And"—he looked around—"I don't see Stan or Tim, either. What about them?"

"Whoa, whoa, whoa." Minho held his hands up, palms facing Newt. "Slim it nice and calm, brother. I didn't ask to be the shuck leader. You wanna cry all day about what's happened, fine. But that's not what a leader does. A leader figures out where to go and what to do after that's done."

"Well, guess that's why you got the job, then," Newt said. But then a look of apology washed over his face. "Whatever. Seriously, sorry. I just . . ."

"Yeah, I'm sorry, too." Minho rolled his eyes, though, and Thomas hoped against hope that Newt didn't notice because his gaze had fallen to the floor again.

Luckily Aris scooted over to join them. Thomas wanted the conversation to go in a different direction.

"Ever seen anything like that lightning storm?" the new kid asked.

Thomas shook his head because Aris was looking at him. "Didn't seem natural. Even in my klunky memories, I'm pretty sure stuff like that doesn't happen normally."

"But remember what the Rat Man said and that lady told you on the bus," Minho said. "Sun flares, and the whole world burning like hell itself. That'd screw up the climate plenty enough to make crazy storms like that pop up. I have a feeling we're lucky it wasn't worse."

"Not sure *lucky*'s the first word I'd think of," Aris said.

"Yeah, well."

Newt pointed at the broken glass of the door, where the glow of sunrise had brightened into the same white brilliance they'd grown accustomed to their first couple of days out in the Scorch. "Least it's over. We better start thinking about what we're gonna do next."

"See," Minho said. "You're just as heartless as me. And you're right."

Thomas remembered the image of the Cranks at the windows back at the dorm. Like living nightmares, missing only a death certificate to make them official zombies. "Yeah, we better figure things out before we have a bunch of those crazies show up. But I'm telling you, we gotta eat first. We gotta find food." The last word almost hurt, he wanted some so badly.

"Food?"

Thomas pulled in a gasp of surprise; the voice had come from above. He looked up just as the others did. A face looked down at them from the shredded remains of the third floor, that of a young Hispanic man. His eyes were slightly wild, and Thomas felt a belt of tension cinch inside him.

"Who're you?" Minho shouted.

Then, to Thomas's utter disbelief, the man jumped through the jagged hole in the ceilings, falling toward them. At the last second, he crumpled into a human ball and rolled three times, then sprang up and landed on his feet.

"My name is Jorge," he said, his arms outstretched as if he expected applause for his acrobatics. "And I'm the Crank who rules this place."

CHAPTER 26

For a second Thomas had a hard time believing that the guy who'd dropped in—literally—was real. He was so unexpected, and there was an odd silliness about what he'd said and the way he'd said it. But he was there, all right. And even though he didn't seem quite as gone as some of the others they'd seen, he'd already confessed to being a Crank.

"You people forget how to talk?" Jorge asked, a smile on his face that looked completely out of place in the shattered building. "Or you just scared of the Cranks? Scared we'll pull you to the ground and eat your eyeballs out? Mmm, tasty. I love a good eyeball when the grub's runnin' short. Tastes like undercooked eggs."

Minho took it on himself to answer, doing a great job of hiding his pain. "You admit you're a Crank? That you're freaking crazy?"

"He just said he likes the taste of eyeballs." This from Frypan. "I think that qualifies as crazy."

Jorge laughed, and there was a definite tone of menace in it. "Come, come, my new friends. I'd only eat your eyes if you were already dead. Course, I might help you get that way if I needed to. Understand what I'm saying?" All mirth vanished from his expression, replaced with a look of stern warning. Almost as if he was daring them to confront him.

No one spoke for a long moment. Then Newt asked, "How many of you are here?"

Jorge's gaze snapped to Newt. "How many? How many Cranks? We're all Cranks around here, *hermano*."

"That's not what I meant and you know it," Newt replied flatly.

Jorge started pacing the room, stepping over and around Gladers, taking everyone in as he spoke. "Lot of things you people need to understand about how things work in this city. About the Cranks and WICKED, about the government, about why they left us here to rot in our disease, kill each other, go completely and utterly *insane*. About how there's different levels of the Flare. About how it's too late for you—the ill is gonna catch ya if you don't already have it."

Thomas had followed the stranger with his eyes as he walked around the room making these horrible statements. The Flare. He thought he'd gotten used to the fear of having the disease, but with this Crank standing right in front of him, he was more scared than ever. And helpless to do anything about it.

Jorge stopped near him and his friends, his feet almost touching Minho. He continued to talk.

"But that's not the way it's gonna work, *comprende?* Those who are at a disadvantage are those who speak first. I want to know everything about you. Where you came from, why you're here, what in God's name your purpose could be. Now."

Minho let out a low, dangerous-sounding chuckle. "We're the ones at a disadvantage?" Minho swiveled his head around mockingly. "Unless that lightning storm fried my retinas, I'd say there are eleven of us and one of you. Maybe *you* should start talking."

Thomas really wished Minho hadn't said that. It was stupid and arrogant, and it could very well get them killed. The guy obviously wasn't alone. There could be a hundred Cranks hiding out in the torn-up remains of the upper floors, spying on them, waiting with who-knew-what kind of horrific weapons. Or worse, the savagery of their own hands and teeth and madness.

Jorge looked at Minho for a long time, his face blank. "You didn't just say that to me, did you? Please tell me you didn't just speak to me like a dog. You have ten seconds to apologize."

Minho looked over at Thomas with a smirk.

"One," Jorge said. "Two. Three. Four."

Thomas tried to shoot a look of warning to Minho, nodded at him. *Do it.*

"Five. Six."

"Do it," Thomas finally said aloud.

"Seven. Eight."

Jorge's voice was rising with each number. Thomas thought he caught a glimpse of movement somewhere far above, just a blur of streaking shadow. Maybe Minho noticed it, too; any arrogance drained from his face.

"Nine."

"I'm sorry," Minho blurted out, with little feeling.

"I don't think you meant that," Jorge said. Then he kicked Minho in the leg.

Thomas's hands clenched into fists when his friend cried out in pain; the Crank must've gotten him right in a burnt spot.

"Say it with meaning, *hermano.*"

Thomas looked up at the Crank, hated him. Irrational thoughts started swimming through his mind—he wanted to jump up and attack, beat him like he'd beaten Gally after escaping the Maze.

Jorge pulled his leg back and kicked Minho again, twice as hard in the same spot. "Say it with *meaning!*" He screamed the last word with a harshness that sounded crazed.

Minho wailed, grabbing the wound with both hands. "I'm . . . sorry," he said between heavy breaths, his voice strained and full of pain. But as soon as Jorge smiled and relaxed, satisfied with the humiliation he'd inflicted, Minho swung an arm out and slammed it into the Crank's shin. The man leaped onto his other foot, then fell, crashing to the ground with his own yelp, a shriek that was half surprise, half hurt.

Then Minho was on top of him, yelling a string of obscenities Thomas had never heard come out of his friend before. Their leader squeezed his thighs to trap Jorge's body, then started punching.

"Minho!" Thomas shouted. "Stop!" He got to his feet, ignoring the stiffness in his joints, the soreness in his muscles. He took a quick glance upward as he made for Minho, ready to tackle him off Jorge's body. There was movement up there, in several places. Then he saw people looking down, people readying to jump. Ropes appeared, dangled over the sides of the jagged holes.

Thomas rammed into Minho, sent him sprawling off Jorge's body; they crashed to the ground. Thomas quickly spun to grab his friend, wrapped his arms around his chest and squeezed against his struggles to escape.

"There's more of them up there!" Thomas screamed in his ear from behind. "You have to stop! They'll kill you! They'll kill all of us!"

Jorge had staggered to his feet, slowly wiping a thin trail of blood from the corner of his mouth. The look on his face was enough to ram a spike of fear straight through Thomas's heart. There was no telling what the guy would do.

"Wait!" Thomas shouted. "Please, wait!"

Jorge made eye contact with him just as a few more Cranks dropped to the ground from above. Some of them did the jump-and-roll like Jorge had done; others slid down ropes and landed squarely on their feet. All of them quickly gathered in a pack behind their leader, maybe fifteen of them. Men and women; a few were teenagers. All filthy and dressed in tattered clothing. Most of them skinny and frail-looking.

Minho had quit fighting, and Thomas finally loosened his grip. By the looks of it, he had only a few seconds before a dire situation turned into a slaughterhouse. He pressed one hand firmly down on Minho's back, then held the other one up toward Jorge in a conciliatory gesture.

"Please give me a minute," Thomas said, urging his heart and voice to calm down. "Won't do you people any good to . . . hurt us."

"Won't do us any good?" the Crank said; he spit a wad of red goo from his mouth. "It'll do me a lot of good. That, I can guarantee, *hermano*." He balled both hands into fists at his sides.

Then he cocked his head, barely enough to be noticed. But as soon as he did, the Cranks behind him pulled all kinds of nasty things from within the hidden depths of their ragged clothes. Knives. Rusted machetes. Black spikes that had maybe once been in a railroad somewhere. Shards of glass with red-tinged smudges on their razor-thin tips. One girl, who couldn't have been more than thirteen years old, held a splintered shovel, its metal scoop ending in a jagged edge like the teeth of a saw.

Thomas had the sudden and absolute certainty that he was now pleading for their lives. The Gladers couldn't win in a fight against these people. No way. They weren't Grievers, but there also wasn't a magic code to shut them down.

"Listen," Thomas said, slowly getting to his feet, hoping Minho wouldn't be stupid enough to try anything. "There's something about us. We're not just random shanks who showed up on your doorstep. We're valuable. Alive, not dead."

The anger on Jorge's face lessened ever so slightly. Maybe a spark of curiosity. But what he said was "What's a shank?"

Thomas almost—*almost*—laughed. An irrational response that somehow would've seemed appropriate. "Me and you. Ten minutes. Alone. That's all I ask. Bring all the weapons you need."

Jorge *did* laugh at that, more of a wet snort than anything. "Sorry to burst your bubble, kid, but I don't think I'll need any."

He paused, and it felt like the next few seconds lasted a full hour.

"Ten minutes," the Crank finally said. "Rest of you stay here, watch these punks. If I give the word, let the death games begin." He held a hand out, gesturing to a dark hallway that led from the room on the side across from the broken doors.

"Ten minutes," he repeated.

Thomas nodded. When Jorge didn't move, he went first, walking toward their meeting place and maybe the most important discussion of his life.

And maybe the last.

CHAPTER 27

Thomas felt Jorge at his heels as he entered the dark hallway. It smelled of mildew and rot; water dripped from the ceiling, sending out creepy echoes that for some awful reason made him think of blood.

"Just keep going," Jorge said from behind. "There's a room at the end with chairs. Make even the slightest move against me, everyone dies."

Thomas wanted to turn and scream at the guy but kept walking. "I'm not an idiot. You can quit the whole tough-guy routine."

The Crank only snickered in response.

After several minutes of quiet, Thomas finally approached a wooden door with a round silver knob. He reached out and opened it without hesitating, trying to show Jorge that he still had some dignity. Once inside, however, he didn't know what to do. It was pitch-black.

He sensed Jorge stepping around him; then there was the loud *flump*ing sound of heavy cloth being whipped in the air. A hot, blinding light appeared, and Thomas had to shield his eyes with his forearms. He could only squint at first, then eventually dropped his arms and was able to see okay; he realized that the Crank had pulled a large sheet of canvas from a window. An unbroken window. Outside, there was only sunlight and concrete.

"Sit down," Jorge said, his voice less gruff than Thomas would've expected. He hoped it was because the Crank had finally accepted that his new visitor was going to take a rational and calm approach to their situation. That maybe there really was something to this discussion that could end up benefiting the current residents of the dilapidated building. Of course, the guy was a Crank, so Thomas had no idea how he'd react.

The room had no furniture other than two small wooden chairs and a table between them. Thomas pulled out the one closer to him and took a seat. Jorge sat down on the other side, then leaned forward and put his elbows on the table, hands clasped. His face was blank, his eyes glued on Thomas.

"Talk."

Thomas wished he could take a second to sift through all the ideas that had run through his mind back in the larger room, but he knew there wasn't any time for that.

"Okay." He hesitated. One word. So far, not so good. He pulled in a breath. "Look, I heard you mention WICKED back there. We know all about those guys. It'd be really interesting to hear what you have to say about them."

Jorge didn't budge; his expression didn't change. "I'm not the one talking right now. You are."

"Yeah, I know." Thomas scooted his chair a little closer to the table. Then he pushed it back and put a foot up on his knee. He needed to calm down and just let the words flow. "Well, this is hard because I don't know what you know. So I guess I'll just pretend like you're stupid to the whole thing."

"I'd strongly advise you never to use the word *stupid* with me again."

Thomas had to force himself to swallow, his throat tight with fear. "Just a figure of speech."

"Get on with it."

Thomas took another deep breath. "We used to be a group of about fifty guys. And . . . a girl." A prick of pain stuck him at that. "Now we're down to eleven. I don't know all the details, but WICKED is some kind of organization that's doing a whole load of nasty things to us for some reason. We started in a place called the Glade, inside a stone maze, surrounded by these creatures called Grievers."

He waited, searching Jorge's face for any reaction to his burst of strange information. But the Crank showed no signs of confusion or recognition. Nothing at all.

And so Thomas told him everything. What it had been like in the Maze, how they'd escaped, how they thought they were safe, how it ended up being just another layer of the WICKED plan. He told him about the Rat Man, and the mission he'd set them on: to survive long enough to make it one hundred miles to the north, to a place he referred to as the safe haven. He related how they'd gone down the long tunnel, been attacked by the flying silver goop, made the trek across the initial miles of their journey.

He told Jorge the whole story. And the more he talked, the crazier it seemed that he was sharing it. Yet he kept talking because he couldn't think of anything else to do. He did it with the hope that WICKED was just as much the Cranks' enemy as it was theirs.

He didn't mention Teresa, however—she was the only thing he left out.

"So there must be something special about us," Thomas said, trying to wrap things up. "They can't be doing this just to be nasty. What'd be the point?"

"Speaking of points," Jorge responded, the first he'd spoken in at least ten minutes, the allotted time already gone. "What's yours?"

Thomas waited. This was it. His only chance.

"Well?" Jorge pushed.

Thomas went for it. "If you . . . help us . . . I mean, if you, or maybe just a few of you, go *with* us and help us make it to the safe haven . . ."

"Yeah?"

"Then maybe you'll be safe, too. . . ." And this was what Thomas had planned all along—had been building toward—the hope strung out by the Rat Man. "They told us we have the Flare. And that if we make it to the safe haven, we'll all be cured. They said they have a cure. If you help us get there, maybe you can get it, too." Thomas stopped talking and looked at Jorge earnestly.

Something had changed—slightly—in the Crank's face at that last thing he'd said, and Thomas knew he had won. The look was brief, but it was definitely *hope,* quickly replaced with a blank indifference. Yet Thomas knew what he'd seen.

"A cure," the Crank repeated.

"A cure." Thomas was determined to say as little as possible from here on out—he'd done his best.

Jorge leaned back in his chair, the wood creaking as if about to break, and folded his arms. He lowered his eyebrows in a look of contemplation. "What's your name?"

Thomas was surprised by the question. Felt sure, in fact, that he'd already told him. Or at least it seemed like he should have told him at some point. But then again, this whole scenario wasn't exactly your typical get-acquainted affair.

"Your *name?*" Jorge repeated. "I'm assuming you have one, *hermano.*"

"Oh. Yeah. Sorry. It's Thomas."

Another flash across Jorge's face—this time something like . . . recognition. Mixed with surprise. "Thomas, huh. You go by Tommy? Tom, maybe?"

That last one hurt, made him think of his dream about Teresa. "No," he said, probably a little too quickly. "Just . . . Thomas."

"Okay, Thomas. Let me ask you something. Do you have the slightest clue in that squishy brain of yours what the Flare does to people? Do I look like someone who has a hideous disease to you?"

That seemed an impossible question to answer without getting your face beaten in, but Thomas went with the safest bet. "No."

"No? No to both questions?"

"Yes. I mean, no. I mean . . . yes, the answer to both questions is no."

Jorge smiled—nothing but an uptick of the right corner of his mouth—and Thomas thought he must be enjoying every second of this. "The Flare works in stages, *muchacho*. Every person in this city has it, and I'm not shocked to hear that you and your sissy friends do, too. Someone like me is in the beginning, a Crank in name only. I caught it just a few weeks ago, tested positive at the quarantine checkpoint—government's trying their damnedest to keep the sick and the well separate. Ain't working. Saw my whole world go straight in the crap hole. Was sent here. Fought to capture this building with a bunch of other newbies."

At that word, Thomas's breath caught in his throat like a mote of dust. It brought back too many memories of the Glade.

"My friends out there with the weapons are all in the same boat as me. But you go and take a nice stroll around the city and you'll see what happens as time goes by. You'll see the stages, see what it's like to be past the Gone, though you might not live to remember it for very long. And we don't even have any of the numbing agent here. The Bliss. None."

"Who sent you here?" Thomas asked, saving his curiosity about this numbing agent for later.

"WICKED—same as you. Only we're not *special* like you say you are. WICKED was set up by the surviving governments to fight the disease, and they claim that this city has something to do with it. Don't know much else."

Thomas felt a mixture of surprise and confusion, then a hope for answers. "Who *is* WICKED? *What* is WICKED?"

Jorge looked just about as confused as Thomas felt. "I told you all I know. Why're you asking me that, anyway? I thought the whole point here was that you were special to them, that they were behind this whole story you told me."

"Look, everything I told you is the honest truth. We've been promised things, but we still don't know much about them. They don't give us any details. Like they're testing us to see if we can make it through all this klunk even though we have no idea what's happening."

"And what makes you think they have a cure?"

Now Thomas had to keep his voice steady, think back to what he'd heard from the Rat Man. "The guy in the white suit I told you about. He told us it's why we have to make it to the safe haven."

"Mmm-hmm," Jorge said, one of those noises that sounded like a yes but meant exactly the opposite. "And what in the world makes you think they'll let us just ride in on a horse with you and get the cure, too?"

Thomas had to keep playing it nice and calm. "Obviously I don't know that at all. But why not at least try? If you help us get there, you have a small chance. If you kill us, you have zero chance. Only a full-gone Crank would choose the second option."

Jorge gave that pathetic smile again, then let out a small bark of a laugh. "There's something about you, Thomas. Few minutes ago I wanted to stab your friend in the eyeballs and then do the same to the rest of ya. But I'll be licked if you haven't half convinced me."

Thomas shrugged, trying to keep his face calm. "All I care about is surviving one more day. All I want is to make it through this city, and then I'll worry about what comes next. And you know what else?" He braced himself to act tougher than he felt.

Jorge raised his eyebrows. "What's that?"

"If stabbing *you* in the eyeballs could get me to tomorrow, I'd do it right now. But I need you. We all need you." Thomas wondered if he could ever actually do such a thing even as he said it.

But it worked.

The Crank eyed Thomas for a drawn-out moment, then stuck out a hand across the table. "I believe we have ourselves a deal, *hermano*. For many reasons."

Thomas reached out and shook. And even though he was filled with relief, it took everything he had not to show it.

But then Jorge brought it all crashing down. "I just have one condition. That ratty kid who junked me on the ground? Think I heard you call him Minho?"

"Yeah?" Thomas asked in a weak voice, his heart thumping all over again.

"He dies."

CHAPTER 28

"No."

Thomas said it with every ounce of finality and firmness he could muster.

"No?" Jorge repeated with a look of surprise. "I offer you a chance to make it through a city full of vicious Cranks ready to eat you alive, and you say no? To my one little itsy-bitsy request? That does not make me happy."

"It wouldn't be smart," Thomas said. He had no idea how he was able to maintain his calm expression, where this bravery was coming from. But something told him it was the only way he could survive with this Crank.

Jorge leaned forward again, placed his elbows on the table. But this time he didn't clasp his hands; instead, he balled them into fists. His knuckles cracked. "Is it your goal in life to piss me off until I cut your arteries open one by one?"

"You saw what he did to you," Thomas countered. "You know the guts that took. If you kill him, you lose the skills he brings. He's our best fighter, and he's not scared of anything. Maybe he's crazy, but we need him."

Thomas was trying to sound so practical. Pragmatic. But if there was a person other than Teresa on the planet he could truly call a friend, it was Minho. And he couldn't handle losing him, too.

"But he made me *angry*," Jorge said tightly; his fists had not relaxed in the slightest. "He made me look like a little girl in front of my people. And that's not . . . acceptable."

Thomas shrugged like he didn't care, like it was a small and meaningless point. "So punish him. Make *him* look like a little girl. But killing him doesn't help us. The more bodies we have that can fight, the better our chances. I mean, you *live* here. Do I really need to tell you this?"

Finally, *finally*, Jorge loosened his white-knuckled grips. He also let out a breath that Thomas hadn't realized he'd been holding.

"Okay," the Crank said. "Okay. But it has nothing to do with your lame attempt to talk me into it. I'll spare him because I just made up my mind about something. Because of two reasons, actually. One of which you should have thought of yourself."

"What?" Thomas didn't mind his relief showing anymore—the effort to hide things was exhausting him. Plus, he was now too intrigued by what Jorge had to say.

"First off, you don't really know all the details behind this test or experiment or whatever it is that WICKED is putting you through. Maybe the more of you that make it back—to that safe haven—the better chances you have of getting the cure. Ever thought that this Group B you mentioned are probably your competitors? I think it's in my best interests to make sure all eleven of you make it now."

Thomas nodded, but didn't say anything. He didn't want to take the slightest chance of ruining the victory here: Jorge believed him about the Rat Man and the cure.

"Which leads to my second reason," he continued. "The thing I've made up my mind about."

"And what's that?" Thomas asked.

"I'm not taking all those Cranks out there with me. With *us*."

"Huh? Why? I thought the whole point was that you guys could help us fight our way through the city."

Jorge adamantly shook his head as he leaned back in his chair and assumed a much less threatening position, folding his arms across his chest. "No. If we're gonna do this, stealth will work way better than muscle. We've been sneaking around this hellhole ever since we got here, and I think our chances of making it through—and getting all the food and supplies we need—are way better if we take what we've learned and use it. Tiptoe our way past the long-gone-crazy Cranks instead of slashing through them like a bunch of wannabe warriors."

"You're hard to figure out," Thomas said. "Not to be rude, but it sure seems like warriors are exactly what you guys want to be. Ya know, based on all the ugly outfits and sharp things."

A long moment of silence passed, and Thomas was just starting to think he'd made a mistake when Jorge burst out laughing.

"Oh, *muchacho,* you're one lucky sucker I like you. Not sure why, but I do. Otherwise I would've killed you three times already."

"Can you do that?" Thomas asked.

"Huh?"

"Kill someone three times."

"I'd figure out a way."

"Then I'll try to be nicer."

Jorge slapped the table and stood up. "Okay. So here's the deal. We need to get all eleven of you punks to your safe haven. To do it, I'm only taking one other person—her name is Brenda, and she's a genius. We need her mind. And if we do make it, and it ends up that there's no cure for us, then I don't think I need to tell you what the consequences will be."

"Come on," Thomas said sarcastically. "I thought we were friends now."

"Pshh. We ain't friends, *hermano.* We're partners. I'll deliver you to WICKED. You get me a cure. That's the deal or there's gonna be a lot of death."

Thomas stood as well; his chair creaked against the floor. "We already agreed on that, didn't we?"

"Yeah. Yeah, we did. Now listen, don't you dare say a word out there. Getting away from those other Cranks is gonna be . . . tricky."

"What's the plan?"

Jorge thought for a minute, his eyes glued to Thomas as he did. Then he broke his silence. "Just keep your tongue-hole shut and let me do my thing." He started to move toward the door to the hallway, but stopped short. "Oh, and I don't think your *compadre* Minho is going to like it very much."

As they walked down the hallway to join the others, Thomas realized how achingly hungry he was. The cramps in his stomach had spread to the rest of his body, as if his internal organs and muscles were starting to eat each other.

"All right, everybody listen!" Jorge announced when they reentered the large torn-up room. "Me and the bird-face here have come to a resolution."

Bird face? Thomas thought.

The Cranks still stood at attention, nasty weapons gripped tightly, glaring at the Gladers, all of whom sat around the edges of the space, backs against the walls. Light beamed through the shattered windows and holes above.

Jorge came to a stop in the middle of the room and slowly turned to address the whole group. Thomas thought he looked ridiculous—like he was trying too hard.

"First, we need to get these people food. I know it seems crazy to share our hard-earned grub with a bunch of strangers, but I think we could use their help. Give 'em the pork and beans—I'm sick of that horse crap anyway." One of the Cranks snickered, a skinny runt of a kid whose eyes darted back and forth. "Second, being the grand gentleman and saint that I am, I've decided not to kill the punk who attacked me."

Thomas heard a few disappointed groans break out and wondered just how far along some of these people were with the Flare. But one girl, a pretty, older teenager with long hair that was surprisingly clean, rolled her eyes and shook her head as if she thought the noise was idiotic. Thomas found himself hoping she was the Brenda girl Jorge had mentioned.

Jorge pointed at Minho, who, not shockingly to Thomas at all, smiled and waved at the crowd.

"Pretty happy, are you?" Jorge grunted. "That's good to know. Means you'll take the news well."

"What news?" Minho asked sharply.

Thomas glanced over at Jorge, wondering what was about to come out of the guy's mouth.

The Crank leader spoke matter-of-factly. "After we get you stragglers fed so you don't go dying of starvation on us, you get to have your punishment for attacking me."

"Oh yeah?" If Minho was scared, he didn't show any sign of it. "And what's that gonna be?"

Jorge just stared back at Minho—a blank expression spread eerily across his face. "You punched me with both of your fists. So we're gonna cut a finger off each hand."

CHAPTER 29

Thomas didn't understand at all how threatening to cut off Minho's fingers was going to set the groundwork for them escaping from the rest of the Cranks. And he certainly wasn't stupid enough to trust Jorge after just one brief meeting. He began to panic that things were about to go terribly, horribly wrong.

But then Jorge looked at him, even as his Crank friends started to hoot and holler, and there was something there, in his eyes. Something that put Thomas at ease.

Minho, on the other hand, was a different story. He'd stood up as soon as Jorge had pronounced his punishment, and would've charged if the pretty girl hadn't stepped right up to him and placed her blade under his chin. It drew a drop of blood, bright red in the daylight pouring through the busted doors. He couldn't even talk without risking serious bodily harm.

"Here's the plan," Jorge said calmly. "Brenda and I will escort these moochers to the stash, let 'em eat up. Then we'll all meet on the Tower, let's say one hour from now." He looked at his watch. "Make that noon on the dot. We'll bring up lunch for the rest of you."

"Why just you and Brenda?" someone asked. Thomas didn't see who at first, then realized a man had said it—probably the oldest person in the room. "What if they jump you? There's eleven of them to two of you."

Jorge squinted—a scoffing look. "Thanks for the math lesson, Barkley. Next time I forget how many toes I have, I'll be sure and spend some counting time with you. For now, shut your flappin' lips and lead everybody to the Tower. If these punks try anything, Brenda will slash Mr. Minho to tiny bits while I beat the living hell out of the rest of 'em. They can barely stand they're so weak. Now *get!*"

Relief swam through Thomas. Once separated from the others, surely Jorge meant to run. Surely he didn't mean to go through with the punishment.

The man named Barkley was old but looked tough, veined muscles stretching the sleeves of his shirt. He held a nasty dagger in one hand and a big hammer in the other. "Fine," he said after a long stare down with his leader. "But if they do jump you and slit your throat, we'll get along just fine without ya."

"Thanks for the kind words, *hermano*. Now get, or we'll have double the fun on the Tower."

Barkley laughed as if to salvage some dignity, then started off down the same hallway Thomas and Jorge had used. He waved his arm in a "follow me" gesture and soon every last Crank was shuffling after him except Jorge and the pretty girl with the long brown hair. She still had her knife at Minho's neck, but the good part was that she had to be Brenda.

Once the main group of Flare-infected people left the room, Jorge shared an almost relieved look with Thomas; then he subtly shook his head, as if the others might still be able to hear them.

Movement from Brenda grabbed Thomas's attention. He looked to see her drop the knife away from Minho and step back, absently wiping the small trace of blood there on her pants. "I really would've killed you, ya know," she said in a slightly scratchy voice. Almost husky. "Charge Jorge again and I'll sever an artery."

Minho wiped at his small wound with a thumb, then looked at the bright red smear. "That's one sharp knife. Makes me like you more."

Newt and Frypan groaned simultaneously.

"Looks like I'm not the only Crank standing here," Brenda responded. "You're even more gone than me."

"None of us are crazy yet," Jorge added, walking over to stand next to her. "But it won't be long. Come on. We need to get over to the stash and put some food in you people. You all look like a bunch of starved zombies."

Minho didn't seem to like the idea. "You think I'm just gonna waltz over to have a sit-down with you psychos, then let you cut my freaking fingers off?"

"Just shut up for once," Thomas snapped, trying to communicate something different with his eyes. "Let's go eat. I don't care what happens to your beautiful hands after that."

Minho squinted in confusion, but seemed to pick up that something was off. "Whatever. Let's go."

Brenda stepped in front of Thomas unexpectedly, her face only a few inches from his. She had eyes so dark it made the whites seem to glow brightly. "You the leader?"

Thomas shook his head. "No—it's the guy you just nipped with your knife."

Brenda looked over at Minho, then back at Thomas. She grinned. "Well, then that's stupid. I know I'm on the verge of crazy, but I would've picked you. You seem like the leader type."

"Um, thanks." Thomas felt a rush of embarrassment, then remembered Minho's tattoo. Remembered his own, how he was supposed to be killed. He scrambled to say something to hide his sudden mood shift. "I, uh, would've picked you, too, instead of Jorge over there."

The girl leaned forward and kissed Thomas on the cheek. "You're sweet. I really hope we don't end up killing you, at least."

"All right." Jorge was already motioning everyone toward the broken doors that led outside. "Enough of this lovefest. Brenda, we have a lot to talk about once we get to the stash. Come on, let's go."

Brenda didn't take her eyes off Thomas. As for him, he still felt the tingle that had shot through his entire body when she'd touched him with her lips.

"I like you," she said.

Thomas swallowed, his mind empty of a comeback. Brenda's tongue touched the corner of her mouth and she grinned, then finally turned away from him and walked to the doors, slipping her knife into a pants pocket. "Let's go!" she yelled without looking back.

Thomas knew every single Glader was staring at him, but he refused to make eye contact with any of them. Instead, he hitched up his shirt and walked forward, not caring about the slight smile on his face. Soon the others fell into step behind him, and the group exited the building and emerged into the white heat of the sun beating down on the broken pavement outside.

Brenda led while Jorge took up the rear. Thomas had a hard time adjusting to the brightness, shielding his eyes and squinting as they walked close to the wall to stay in the scant shade. The other buildings and streets around him seemed to shine with unearthly luminescence, as if they were made of some sort of magic stone.

Brenda moved along the walls of the structure they'd just exited until they reached what Thomas thought must be the back. There, a set of steps disappeared into the pavement, reminding him of something in his past life. An entrance to some kind of underground train system, perhaps.

She didn't hesitate. Without waiting to make sure the others were behind her, she bounced down the stairs. But Thomas noticed that the knife had reappeared in her right hand, gripped tightly and held a few inches from the side of her body—a stealthy attempt at being ready to attack—or defend—on a moment's notice.

He followed her, eager to get out of the sun and, more importantly, make it to food. His insides ached more strongly for sustenance with every step he took. In fact, he was surprised he could still move; the weakness was like a poisonous growth inside him, replacing his vital parts with a painful cancer.

Darkness swallowed them eventually, welcome and cool. Thomas followed the sound of Brenda's footsteps until they reached a small doorway, through which shone a glow of orange. She went inside, and Thomas hesitated at the threshold. It was a small, damp room full of boxes and cans, with a single lightbulb hanging from the center of the ceiling. It looked far too cramped for all of them to enter.

Brenda must've sensed his thoughts. "You and the others can stay out there in the hallway, find a wall and sit. I'll start bringing out some tasty delights for you in a sec."

Thomas nodded even though she wasn't looking and stumbled back out into the hallway. He collapsed next to a wall down a ways from the rest of the Gladers, deeper into the darkness of the tunnel. And he knew for certain he'd never get back up unless he ate something.

The "tasty delights" ended up being canned beans and some type of sausage—according to Brenda, the words on the label were in Spanish. They ate it cold, but it tasted like the grandest meal ever to Thomas, and he devoured every bite. They'd already learned it wasn't smart to eat quickly after such a long period of fasting, but he didn't care. If he threw it all up, he'd just enjoy eating all over again. Hopefully a fresh batch.

After Brenda passed out the food to the starving Gladers, she walked over to sit by Thomas, the soft glow from the room illuminating the thin strands on the fringes of her dark hair. She set down a couple of backpacks—filled with more of the cans—at her side.

"One of these is for you," she said.

"Thanks." Thomas had already reached the bottom half of his can, scooping out one bite after another. No one spoke down the hall from them; the only sounds were slurping and swallowing.

"Taste good?" she asked as she dug into her own food.

"Please. I'd push my own mom down the stairs to eat this stuff. If I still *have* a mom." He couldn't help thinking of his dream and the brief glimpse he'd seen of her, but did his best to forget it—it was too depressing.

"You get sick of it fast," Brenda said, pulling Thomas out of his head. He noticed the way she sat, her right knee pressed against his shin, and his thoughts jumped to the ridiculous idea that she'd moved her leg like that on purpose. "We only have about four or five options."

Thomas concentrated on clearing his mind, bringing his thoughts back to the present. "Where'd you get the food? And how much is left?"

"Before this area got scorched by the flares, this city had several food manufacturing plants, plus a lot of warehouses to hold the food. Sometimes I think that's why WICKED sends Cranks here. They can at least tell themselves that we won't starve while we slowly go crazy and kill each other."

Thomas scooped out the last bit of sauce from the bottom of his can and licked his spoon clean. "If there's plenty, why do you only have a few options?" He had the thought that maybe they'd trusted her too quickly, that they could be eating poison. But she was eating the same food, so his worries were probably far-fetched.

Brenda pointed toward the ceiling with her thumb. "We've only scoured the closest ones. Some company that specialized, not much variety. *I'd* kill your mother for something fresh out of a garden. A nice salad."

"Guess my mom doesn't have much of a chance if she's ever standing between us and a grocery store."

"Guess not."

She smiled then, though a shadow mostly hid her face. The grin still shone through, and Thomas found himself liking this girl. She'd just drawn blood from his best friend, but he liked her. Maybe, in small part, because of that.

"Does the world still have grocery stores?" he asked. "I mean, what's it like out there after all this Flare business? Really hot, with a bunch of crazy people running around?"

"No. Well, I don't know. The sun flares killed a lot of people before they could escape to the north or south. My family lived in northern Canada. My parents were some of the first ones to make it to the camps set up by the coalition between governments. The people who ended up forming WICKED later."

Thomas stared for a second, his mouth wide open. She'd just revealed more to him about the state of the world in those few sentences than anything he'd heard since having his memory wiped.

"Wait . . . wait a second," he said. "I need to hear all this. Can you start from the beginning?"

Brenda shrugged. "Not much to tell—happened a long time ago. The sun flares were completely unexpected and unpredictable, and by the time the scientists tried to warn anyone, it was way too late. They wiped out half the planet, killed everything around the equatorial regions. Changed climates everywhere else. The survivors gathered, some governments combined. Wasn't too long before they discovered that a nasty virus had been unleashed from some disease-control place. Called it the Flare right from the beginning."

"Man," Thomas muttered. He looked down the hall at the other Gladers, wondering if they'd heard any of this, but none of them seemed to be listening, all absorbed in their food. They were probably too far away anyway. "When did—"

She shushed him, holding a hand up. "Wait," she said. "Something's wrong. I think we have visitors."

Thomas hadn't heard anything, and the other Gladers didn't seem to notice, either. But Jorge was already at Brenda's side, whispering something in her ear. She was just moving to stand up when a crash exploded down the hall—from the stairs they'd used to reach the stash. It was a horribly loud sound, the crumple and cracking of a structure falling apart, cement breaking, metal ripping. A cloud of dust fogged its way toward them, choking off the scant light from the food room.

Thomas sat and stared, paralyzed by fear. He could just see Minho and Newt and all the others running back toward the destroyed stairs, then turning down a branching hallway he hadn't noticed before. Brenda grabbed him by the shirt and pulled him to his feet.

"Run!" she screamed, and started dragging him away from the destruction and deeper into the underground.

Thomas snapped out of his stupor and swatted at her hand, though she didn't let go. "No! We have to follow my fr—"

Before he could finish, an entire section of the roof came crashing down onto the floor in front of him, blocks of cement falling on top of each other with thunderous cracks. It cut him off from the direction his friends had taken. He heard more fracturing of rock above him and realized that he no longer had any choice—or any time.

Reluctantly he turned and ran with Brenda, her hand still clutching his shirt as they sprinted into the darkness.

CHAPTER 30

Thomas didn't notice his heart pounding, or have time to contemplate what could possibly have caused the explosion. All he could think about were the other Gladers, now separated from him. Blind, he ran with Brenda—forced to entrust his life to her completely.

"Here!" she yelled. They made a sharp turn to the right; he almost stumbled and fell but she helped him stay on his feet. Once he had a good pace, she finally let go of his shirt. "Stick close to me."

The sounds of destruction behind them faded as they ran down this new path, and panic lit up inside Thomas. "What about my friends? What if—"

"Just keep going! Better for everyone to split up anyway."

The air cooled as they moved farther down the long hallway. The darkness deepened. Thomas felt his strength slowly returning and he caught his breath quickly. Behind them, the noises had almost stopped. He worried about the Gladers, but instinct told him it was okay to stay with Brenda—that his friends would be able to fend for themselves if they'd gotten out. But what if some of them had been captured by whoever had set off the explosion? Or killed? And who had attacked them? Concern seemed to bleed his heart dry as they ran along.

Brenda took three more turns; Thomas had no idea how she could know where she was going. He was just about to ask when she stopped, putting a hand to his chest to hold him back.

"You hear anything?" she said through huffs.

Thomas listened, but all he heard was their own breathing. Everything else was silence and darkness. "No," he told her. "Where are we?"

"A bunch of tunnels and secret passages connect the buildings on this side of town, maybe across the whole city—we haven't explored that far yet. They call it the Underneath."

Thomas couldn't see her face, but she was close enough that he felt and smelled her breath. It didn't reek, which surprised him, considering her living conditions. It kind of had a nonscent, somehow pleasant.

"The Underneath?" he repeated. "Sounds stupid."

"Well, I didn't name it."

"How much of it *have* you explored?" He didn't like the idea of running around down there without knowing what was ahead.

"Not much. We usually run into Cranks. The really bad ones. Way past Gone."

This made Thomas turn in a circle, searching the darkness for he didn't know what. His whole body tensed with fear as if he'd just jumped into ice water. "Well . . . are we safe? What happened with that explosion, anyway? We need to go back and find my friends."

"What about Jorge?"

"Huh?"

"Shouldn't we go find Jorge, too?"

Thomas hadn't meant to offend her. "Yeah, Jorge, my friends, all those shanks. We can't leave them behind."

"What's a shank?"

"Never mind. Just . . . what do you think happened back there?"

She sighed and stepped even closer to him, pressing her chest against his. He felt her lips brushing his ear as she spoke. "I want you to promise me something." She said it softly, in barely more than a whisper.

Chills broke out all over Thomas's body. "Um . . . what?"

She didn't pull back, just kept speaking into his ear. "No matter what happens, even if we have to go alone, you'll take me all the way back. All the way to WICKED, to that cure you promised Jorge—he told me about it in the storage room. I can't stay here and slowly go insane. I can't do it. I'd rather die."

She grabbed both of his hands in hers, squeezed. Then she rested her head on his shoulder, her nose nestled against his neck—she had to be standing on the tips of her toes. Each breath from her sent a new wave of chills across his skin.

Thomas was enjoying her being so close, but it seemed so bizarre and out of the blue. Then he had a surge of guilt, thinking of Teresa. All this was stupid. He was in the middle of a brutal and ruthless attempt to make it across a wasteland, his life on the line, his friends maybe dead. Teresa could even be dead. To sit here and cuddle with some strange girl in the dark was about the most absurd thing he could think of.

"Hey," he said. He wiggled his hands from her grip and grabbed her upper arms, pushed her away. He still couldn't see anything, but he imagined her there, looking at him. "Don't you think we need to figure things out?"

"You still haven't promised me," she replied.

Thomas wanted to scream, couldn't believe how strange she was acting. "Fine, I promise. Did Jorge tell you everything?"

"Mostly, I think. Though I'd already guessed it the second he told our group to go on without us and meet at the Tower."

"Guessed what?"

"That we were going to help you get through the city in exchange for you taking us back to civilization."

This made Thomas worry. "If you came up with that so quickly, don't you think some of your friends did, too?"

"Exactly."

"What do you mean *exactly*? Sounds like you figured something out."

She reached out and placed her hands on his chest. "I think that's what happened. At first I worried it was a group of longer-gone Cranks, but since no one chased us, I think Barkley and a couple of his buddies rigged an explosion at the Underneath entrance, tried to kill us. They know they can get plenty of food somewhere else, and there're other ways to get down here."

Thomas still didn't understand why she was being so touchy with him. "That doesn't make sense. I mean, kill us? Wouldn't they want to use us, too? Come with us?"

"No, no, no. Barkley and the others are happy here. I think they're a little more gone than we are, starting to lose their rational sides. I doubt the idea even occurred to them. I bet they just thought we were all gonna gang up and . . . eliminate them. That we were making plans down here."

Thomas let go of her, leaned his head back against the wall. She pressed in again and wrapped her arms around his middle.

"Uh . . . Brenda?" he asked. Something wasn't right with this girl.

"Yeah?" she mumbled against his chest.

"What are you doing?"

"What do you mean?"

"Don't you think it's a little weird how you're acting?"

She laughed, such an unexpected sound that Thomas thought for a second she'd succumbed to the Flare—become a full-blown Crank or something. She pulled away from him, still chuckling.

"What?" he asked.

"Nothing," she said through a schoolgirl snicker. "Guess we came from different places, that's all. Sorry."

"What do you mean?" He suddenly found himself wishing she'd hug him again.

"Don't worry about it," she said, her merriment at his expense finally subsiding. "Sorry for being so forward. It's just . . . pretty normal where I come from."

"No . . . it's okay. I . . . I mean, good that. I'm good." He was glad she couldn't see his face, because it must've burned so red she'd start laughing all over again.

He thought of Teresa then. He thought of Minho and the others. He had to take control. Now.

"Look, you said it yourself," he said, trying to pump confidence into his voice. "No one chased us. We need to go back."

"Are you sure?" She had a suspicious tone.

"What do you mean?"

"I could get you through the city. Find enough food to take with us. Why don't we leave all of them? Make it to this safe haven place on our own?"

Thomas wasn't going to have this conversation. "If you won't come back with me, fine. But I'm going." He put his hand against the wall to guide himself and started walking in the direction from which they'd fled.

"Wait!" she called out, then caught up to him. She grabbed his hand and intertwined their fingers, now walking alongside him, hand in hand like old lovers. "I'm sorry. Really. I just . . . I think it would be easier to make it through with fewer people. I'm not really great friends with any of those Cranks. Not like you and your . . . Gladers."

Had he said that word around her? He didn't remember, but anybody could've at some point without his noticing. "I really think as many of us as possible need to make it to the safe haven. Even if we do get past the city, who knows what'll be next. Maybe then we'll really want numbers."

He thought about what he'd just said. Did he really only care about having numbers in the end so they'd have a better chance to be safe? Was he really that detached?

"Okay" was all she said in response. Something had changed in her. She seemed less confident. Less in charge.

Thomas took his hand from her grip, coughing into it as an excuse. He didn't reach out for her again when he finished.

They didn't talk for the next few minutes. He followed her, sensing her even though he still couldn't see. After several turns, a light appeared up ahead, brightening quickly as they approached.

It turned out to be sunlight, pouring down from jagged holes in the roof—the aftermath of the explosion. Massive chunks of rock and twisted pieces of steel and broken pipes blocked the way to where the stairs had been—and it looked like climbing over the wreckage would be dangerous. A haze of dust clouded everything, making the rays of sunshine appear thick and alive, motes dancing like gnats. The air smelled of plaster and something burnt.

They were also blocked from the stash room with all that food, but Brenda found the two backpacks she'd brought out earlier.

"Doesn't look like anybody's here," she said. "They didn't come back. Jorge and your friends might've even gotten back up and outside somehow."

Thomas didn't really know what he'd been hoping to find, but at least one piece of good news was obvious. "No bodies, though, right? No one died in the explosion?"

Brenda shrugged. "Cranks could've dragged their bodies off. But I doubt it. No point."

Thomas nodded, as if solidifying her statement, holding on to it. But he had no idea what to do next. Did they go through the tunnels—the Underneath—searching for the other Gladers? Did they go out into the streets? Back to the building where they'd ditched Barkley and the others? Every idea sounded horrible. He looked around, as if the answer would magically present itself.

"We have to go through the Underneath," Brenda announced after a long moment; she'd probably been contemplating their options just like Thomas. "If the others went up top, then they'll be long gone by now. Plus, they'll pull any attention toward themselves and away from us."

"And if they're down here we'll find them, right?" Thomas asked. "These tunnels all come back together eventually, right?"

"Right. Either way, I know Jorge will have them moving toward the other side of the city, toward the mountains. We just have to make it so we can meet up and keep going."

Thomas looked at Brenda, thinking. Maybe only pretending to think, because he really had no option than to stick with her. She was probably his best—maybe only—bet of accomplishing anything other than a quick and horrible death at the hands of long-gone Cranks. What else *could* he do?

"Okay," he said. "Let's go."

She smiled, a sweet smile that shone through the grime on her face, and Thomas unexpectedly longed for that moment they'd had in the darkness together. Almost as quickly as his thought formed, though, it was gone. Brenda handed him one of the backpacks, then reached into hers and pulled out a flashlight, clicked it on. The beam shot through the dust as she shone it this way and that, finally aiming it down the long tunnel they'd already been down twice.

"Shall we?" she asked.

"We shall," Thomas muttered. He still felt sick about his friends, and he wondered if he was doing the right thing sticking with Brenda.

But when she started walking, he followed.

CHAPTER 31

The Underneath was a dank, miserable place. Thomas almost preferred the utter darkness to being able to see what was around him. The walls and floors were dull gray, nothing more than painted concrete, streaks of water trickling down the sides here and there. They passed a door every few dozen feet, but most of them were locked when he tried them. Dust coated the long-dark light fixtures on the ceiling, at least half of them busted, jagged glass screwed into rusty holes.

All in all, the place had the feel of a haunted tomb. The Underneath was as good a name as any. He wondered what the underground structure had been built for in the first place. Walkways and offices for who knew what kinds of jobs? Paths between buildings on rainy days? Emergency routes? *Escape* routes for things like massive sun flares and attacks from crazy people?

They didn't talk much as he followed Brenda through tunnel after tunnel, sometimes turning left at intersections or forks, sometimes turning right. His body quickly consumed any energy provided by his recent binge, and after walking for what felt like several hours he finally convinced her to stop and eat another meal.

"I'm assuming you know where we're going," he said to her when they set off again. Everything they passed looked exactly the same to him. Drab and dark. Dusty, where it wasn't wet. The tunnels were silent but for the distant drops of water and the swishing of their clothes as they walked. Their footsteps, dull thumps on the concrete.

She suddenly stopped and whirled on him, shining the light on her face from below. "Boo," she whispered.

Thomas jumped, then pushed her away. "Cut that crap," he yelled. He felt like an idiot—his heart had just about exploded from fright. "Makes you look like a . . ."

She let the flashlight fall to her side, but her eyes remained locked on his. "Look like a what?"

"Nothing."

"A *Crank*?"

The word cut to Thomas's heart. He didn't want to think of her that way. "Well . . . yeah," he murmured. "Sorry."

She turned from him and started walking again, her light shining forward. "I *am* a Crank, Thomas. Got the Flare, I'm a Crank. You are, too."

He had to run a few steps to catch up with her. "Yeah, but you're not full gone yet. And . . . me neither, right? We'll get the cure before we go nuts." The Rat Man had better have been telling the truth.

"Can't wait. And yeah, by the way. I do know where we're going. Thanks for checking."

They kept going, turn after turn, long tunnel after long tunnel. The slow but steady exercise took Thomas's thoughts off Brenda and made him feel better than he had in days. His mind drifted into a half-daze, thinking about the Maze and his splotchy memories and Teresa. Mostly about Teresa.

Eventually they entered a large room with quite a few exits branching off to the left and right, more than he'd seen previously. It almost seemed like it could be a gathering place joined by tunnels from all the buildings.

"Is this the center of the city or something?" he asked.

Brenda stopped to rest, sitting down on the ground with her back to the wall; Thomas joined her.

"More or less," she answered. "See? Already made it halfway to the other side of the city."

Thomas liked the sound of that, but he hated to think of the others. Minho, Newt, all the Gladers. Where were they? He felt like such a shuck-face for not looking for them, seeing if they were in trouble. Could they have already made it safely outside of town?

A loud pop startled Thomas, like a glass bulb breaking.

Brenda immediately shone her light back in the direction from which they'd come, but the hallway disappeared in shadow, empty except for a few ugly streaks of water on the walls, black on gray.

"What was that?" Thomas whispered.

"An old light busting, I guess." Her voice held no concern. She put her flashlight on the ground so it shone on the wall opposite them.

"Why would an old light just spontaneously break?"

"I don't know. A rat?"

"I haven't seen any rats. Plus, how would a rat walk on the ceiling?"

She gazed at him, a look of total mocking on her face. "You're right. It must be a *flying* rat. We should get the hell out of here."

A small, nervous laugh escaped before Thomas could stop it. "Hilarious."

Another pop, this time followed by the tinkle of glass sprinkling on the floor. It had definitely come from behind them—Thomas was sure of it this time. Someone had to be following them. And it couldn't be the Gladers—it sounded more like people trying to freak them out. Scare them.

Even Brenda couldn't hide her reaction. Her eyes met his, and they were full of worry.

"Get up," she whispered.

They both did it together, then quietly secured their packs. Brenda shone the light once again back the way they'd come. Nothing was there.

"Should we check it out?" she asked in a low voice. She was whispering, but in the silence of the tunnel it sounded way too loud—if anyone was close, they could hear every word she and Thomas were saying.

"Check it out?" Thomas thought that was the worst idea he'd heard in a long time. "No, we should get out of here, just like you said."

"What, you wanna just let whoever it is keep following us? Maybe gather some of his or her buddies to ambush us? Better to take care of it now."

Thomas grabbed her hand holding the flashlight and made it point to the ground. Then he leaned closer to her so he could whisper in her ear. "It could totally be a trap. There wasn't any glass on the ground back there—they had to have reached up and broken one of the old lights. Why would someone do that? It has to be someone trying to get us to go back there."

She countered. "If they have enough people to attack, why would they bait us? That's stupid. Why not just come in here and get it over with?"

Thomas thought about that. She had a point. "Well, it's even more stupid to sit here and talk about it all day. What do we do?"

"Let's just—" She had started to raise the flashlight as she spoke, but cut short her words, her eyes widening in terror.

Thomas whipped his head around to see the cause.

A man stood there, just on the edge of her flashlight's range.

He was like an apparition—there was something unreal about him. He leaned to the right, his left foot and leg jiggling slightly, like he had a nervous tic. His left arm also twitched, the hand clenching and unclenching. He wore a dark suit that had probably once been nice, though now it was filthy and tattered. Water or something more foul soaked both knees of the pants.

But Thomas took all that in quickly. Most of his attention was drawn to the man's head. Thomas couldn't help but stare, mesmerized. It looked like hair had been ripped from his scalp, leaving bloody scabs in its place. His face was pallid and wet, with scars and sores everywhere. One eye was gone, a gummy red mass where it should have been. He also had no nose, and Thomas could actually see traces of the nasal passages in his skull underneath the terribly mangled skin.

And his mouth. Lips drawn back in a snarl, gleaming white teeth exposed, clenched tightly together. His good eye glared, somehow vicious in the way it darted between Brenda and Thomas.

Then the man said something in a wet and gurgly voice that made Thomas shiver. He spoke only a few words, but they were so absurd and out of place that it just made the whole thing that much more horrifying.

"Rose took my nose, I suppose."

CHAPTER 32

A small cry escaped from deep within Thomas's chest, and he didn't know if it was audible or something he just felt inside, imagined. Brenda stood next to him, silent—transfixed, maybe—her light still fixed on the hideous stranger.

The man took a lumbering step toward them, having to wave his one good arm to keep his balance on the one good leg.

"Rose took my nose, I suppose," he repeated; the bubble of phlegm in his throat made a disgusting crackle. "And it really blows."

Thomas held his breath, waiting for Brenda to make the first move.

"Get it?" the man said, his snarl trying to morph into a grin. He looked like an animal about to pounce on its prey. "It really blows. My nose. Taken by Rose. I suppose." He laughed then, a wet chortle that made Thomas worry he might never sleep in peace again.

"Yeah, I get it," Brenda said. "That's some funny stuff."

Thomas sensed movement and looked over at her. She had pulled a can from her bag, slyly, and now gripped it in her right hand. Before he could wonder whether it was a good idea and whether he should try to stop her, she pulled her arm back and tossed the can at the Crank. Thomas watched it fly, watched it crash into the man's face.

He let out a shriek that iced Thomas to the core.

And then others appeared. A group of two. Then three. Then four more. Men and women. All dragging themselves out of the darkness to stand behind the first Crank. All just as gone. Just as hideous, consumed fully by the Flare, raging mad and injured head to toe. And, Thomas noticed, all missing their nose.

"That didn't hurt so bad," the leading Crank said. "You have a pretty nose. I really want a nose again." He stopped snarling long enough to lick his lips, then went right back to it. His tongue was a gruesomely scarred purple thing, as if he chewed it when bored. "And so do my friends."

Fear pushed up and through Thomas's chest, like toxic gas rejected by his stomach. He now knew better than ever what the Flare did to people. He'd seen it back at the windows of the dormitory—but now he faced it on a more personal level. Right in front of him, with no bars to keep them away. The faces of the Cranks were primitive and animalistic. The lead man took another lurching step, then another.

It was time to go.

Brenda didn't say anything. She didn't need to. After she pulled out another can and flung it toward the Cranks, Thomas turned around with her and they ran. The psychotic shrill of their pursuers' cries rose behind them like the battle call of a demon army.

Brenda's flashlight beam shakily crisscrossed left and right, bouncing as they sprinted straight past the slew of right and left turns. Thomas knew they had an advantage—the Cranks looked half broken, riddled with injury. Surely they wouldn't be able to keep up. But the thought that even more Cranks might be down here, maybe even waiting for them up ahead . . .

Brenda pulled up and turned right, grabbing Thomas's arm to drag him along. He stumbled the first few steps, got his feet under him, pushed himself back to full speed. The angry shouts and catcalls of the Cranks faded a bit.

Then Brenda turned left. Then right again. After this second turn she flicked off the flashlight but didn't slow.

"What're you doing?" Thomas asked. He held a hand out in front of him, sure he was going to smack into a wall at any second.

A shush was the only response he got. He wondered about how much he was trusting Brenda. He'd put his life in her hands. But he didn't see what other options he had, especially now.

She pulled up again a few seconds later, stopping completely. They stood in darkness, catching their breath. The Cranks were distant but still loud enough, coming closer.

"Okay," she whispered. "Right about . . . here."

"What?" he asked.

"Just follow me into this room. There's a perfect hiding spot in here—I found it while exploring once. There's no way they'll stumble on it. Come on."

Her hand tightened around his, pulled him to the right. He sensed that they were passing through a narrow door; then Brenda pulled him down to the floor.

"There's an old table here," she said. "Can you feel it?"

She pushed his hand out until he felt hard, smooth wood.

"Yeah," he answered.

"Just watch your head. We're gonna crawl under it and then through a small notch in the wall that leads to a hidden compartment. Who knows what it's for, but no way those Cranks'll find it. Even if they have a light, which I doubt."

Thomas had to wonder how they got around without one, but he saved the question for later—Brenda was already on the move, and he didn't want to lose her. Staying close, his fingers brushing her foot, he followed her as she scooted on her hands and knees under the table and toward the wall. Then they crawled through a small square opening into the long, narrow compartment. Thomas felt around, patting the surfaces to get a sense of where he was. The ceiling was only about two feet off the ground, so he continued to drag himself farther into the crevice.

Brenda lay with her back against the far wall of the hideout by the time Thomas awkwardly got himself in position. They had no choice but to lie stretched out, on their sides. It was a squeeze, but he fit, facing the same direction she did, his back pressed against her front. He felt her breath on his neck.

"This is real comfy," he whispered.

"Just be quiet."

Thomas scooted up a little so his head could rest against the wall; then he relaxed. He settled in, taking deep, slow breaths and listening for any sign of the Cranks.

At first the silence was so deep it had a buzz to it, a ringing in his ears. But then came the first traces of Crank noises. Coughing, random shouts, lunatic giggles. They came closer by the second, and Thomas felt a moment of panic, worried that they'd been stupid to trap themselves like this. But then he thought about it. The odds of the Cranks finding the hidden cubbyhole were slim, especially in the darkness. They'd move on, hopefully going far away. Maybe even forgetting about him and Brenda altogether. That was better than a prolonged chase.

And if worse came to worst, he and Brenda could easily defend themselves through the tiny opening into the compartment. Maybe.

The Cranks were close now; Thomas had to fight the urge to hold his breath. All they needed was for an unexpected gasp for oxygen to give them away. Despite the darkness, he closed his eyes to concentrate on listening.

The swishes of shuffling feet. Grunts and heavy breathing. Someone banged on a wall, a series of deadened thumps against the concrete. Arguments broke out, frantic exchanges of gibberish. He heard a "This way!" and a "That way!" More coughing. One of them gagged and spit violently, like he was trying to rid himself of an organ or two. A woman laughed, so full of madness the sound made Thomas shudder.

Brenda found his hand, squeezed it. Once again, Thomas felt a ridiculous surge of guilt, like he was cheating on Teresa. He couldn't help that this girl was so touchy-feely. And what a stupid thing to think when you have—

A Crank entered the room right outside their compartment. Then another. Thomas heard their wheezy intakes of breath, the scrapes of their feet against the floor. Another entered, those footsteps a long slide and thump, long slide and thump. Thomas thought it might be the first man they'd seen, the only one who'd spoken to them—the one with the arm and leg shaking and useless.

"Little boooooooy," the man said, a taunting and creepy call. Definitely him—Thomas couldn't forget that voice. "Little girrrrrrrl. Come out come out make a sound make a sound. I want your noses."

"Nothin' in here," a woman spat. "Nothin' but an old table."

The creak of wood scraping against the floor sliced through the air, then ended abruptly.

"Maybe they're hiding their noses under it," the man responded. "Maybe they're still attached to their sweet little pretty faces."

Thomas shrank back against Brenda when he heard a hand or shoe scruff along the floor just outside the entrance to their little hiding place. Just a foot or two away.

"Nothin' down there!" the woman said again.

Thomas heard her move away. He realized that his whole body had tensed into a pack of taut wires; he forced himself to relax, still careful to control his breathing.

More shuffling of feet. Then a haunting set of whispers, as if the trio had met in the middle of the room to strategize. Were their minds still sound enough to do such a thing? Thomas wondered. He strained to hear, to catch any words, but the harsh puffs of speech remained indecipherable.

"No!" one of them shouted. A man, but Thomas couldn't tell if it was *the* man. "No! No no no no no no no no." The words quieted into a murmured stutter.

The woman cut him off with her own chant. "Yes yes yes yes yes yes yes."

"Shut up!" the leader said. Definitely the leader. "Shut up shut up shut up!"

Thomas felt cold inside, though sweat was beading on his skin. He didn't know if this exchange had any meaning whatsoever or was just more evidence of madness.

"I'm leaving," the woman said, her words broken by a sob. She sounded like a child left out of a game.

"Me too, me too." This from the other man.

"Shut up shut up shut up shut up!" the leader yelled, this time much louder. "Go away go away go away!"

The sudden repetition of words creeped Thomas out. Like some control over language had snapped in their brains.

Brenda was squeezing his hand so hard it hurt. Her breath was cool against the sweat on his neck.

Shuffles of feet and swishing of clothes outside. Were they leaving?

The sounds decreased sharply in volume when they entered the hallway, tunnel, whatever. The other Cranks in their party seemed to have left already. Soon it became silent all over again. Thomas only heard the faint sounds of his and Brenda's breath.

They waited in the darkness, lying flat on the hard ground, facing the small doorway, pressed together, sweating. The silence stretched out, turned back into the buzz of absent sound. Thomas kept listening, knowing they had to be absolutely sure. As much as he wanted to leave that little compartment, as uncomfortable as it was, they had to wait.

Several minutes passed. Several more. Nothing but silence and darkness.

"I think they're gone," Brenda finally whispered. She flicked on her flashlight.

"Hello, noses!" a hideous voice yelled from the room.

Then a bloody hand reached through the doorway and grabbed Thomas by the shirt.

CHAPTER 33

Thomas shrieked, started swatting at the scarred and bruised hand. His eyes were still adjusting to the brightness of Brenda's flashlight; he squinted to see the firm grip the man had on his shirt. The Crank pulled, slamming Thomas's body against the wall. His face smashed into the hard concrete and a burst of pain exploded around his nose. He felt blood trickling down.

The man pushed him back a few inches, then pulled him forward again. Pushed and pulled again. And again, slamming Thomas's face into the wall each time. Thomas couldn't believe the strength of the Crank—it seemed impossible based on how he looked. Weak and horribly injured.

Brenda had her knife out, was trying to crawl over him, get in position to slash at the hand.

"Careful!" Thomas yelled. That knife was awfully close. He grabbed the man's wrist and wriggled it back and forth, trying to loosen that iron grip. Nothing worked, and the man kept pulling and pushing, battering Thomas's body as he hit the wall.

Brenda screamed and went for it. She swept across Thomas and her blade flashed as she drove it right into the Crank's forearm. The man let out a demonic wail and let go of Thomas's shirt. His hand disappeared through the doorway, leaving a trail of blood on the floor. His shrieks of pain continued, loud with trailing echoes.

"We can't let him get away!" Brenda yelled. "Hurry, get out there!"

Thomas, hurting all over, knew she was right and was already squirming to get his body in position. If the man reached the other Cranks, they'd all come back. They might have heard the commotion and already be turning around.

Thomas finally got his arms and head through the opening; then it became easier. He used the wall for leverage and pushed himself the rest of the way out, his eyes glued to the Crank, waiting for another attack. The man was only a few feet away, cradling his wounded arm against his chest. Their eyes met, and the Crank snarled like a wounded animal, bit at the air.

Thomas started to stand up but his head banged into the bottom of the table. "Shuck!" he yelled, then scrambled out from under the old slab of wood. Brenda was right on his heels, and soon they were both standing over the Crank, who lay on the ground in a fetal position, whimpering. Blood dripped from his wound onto the floor, already forming a small puddle.

Brenda held her flashlight in one hand, the knife in the other, its point aimed at the Crank. "Should've gone with your psycho friends, old man. Should've known better than to mess with us."

Instead of responding, the man suddenly spun on his shoulder, kicking his good leg out with shocking speed and strength. He hit Brenda first, sent her crashing into Thomas, and they both crumpled to the floor. Thomas heard the knife and flashlight clatter across the cement. Shadows danced on the walls.

The Crank staggered to his feet, ran for the knife, which had come to rest by the door to the hallway. Thomas pushed himself up and dove forward, crashing into the backs of the man's knees and tackling him to the ground. The man spun, swinging an elbow as he did so. It connected with Thomas's jaw; he felt another explosion of pain as he fell, his hand naturally flying up to his face.

Then Brenda was there. She jumped on the Crank, hit him in the face twice, stunning him, by the looks of it. She took advantage of the brief moment and somehow yanked the man around again so that he lay on his stomach, flat on the floor. She grabbed his arms and pinned them behind him, pushing up in a way that looked incredibly painful. The Crank wrenched and thrashed, but Brenda had him pinned with her legs as well. He started screaming, a horrific, piercing wail of pure terror.

"We have to kill him!" she yelled over it.

Thomas had gotten to his knees and was looking on in a stupor of inaction. "What?" he asked, drugged with exhaustion, too stunned to process her words.

"Get the knife! We have to kill him!"

The Crank kept screaming, a sound that made Thomas want to run as far away as possible. It was unnatural. Inhuman.

"Thomas!" Brenda yelled.

Thomas crawled over to the knife, picked it up, looked at the crimson goo on its sharp blade. He turned back to Brenda.

"Hurry!" she said, her eyes lit with anger. Something told him that her anger was no longer just for the Crank—she was mad at him for taking so long.

But could he do this? Could he kill a man? Even a crazed lunatic of a man who wanted him dead? Who wanted his shuck nose, for crying out loud?

He shambled back to her, holding the knife as if it were tipped with poison. As if just holding it might make him catch a hundred diseases and die a slow and agonizing death.

The Crank, arms yanked behind him, pinned to the floor, continued to scream.

Brenda caught Thomas's gaze, spoke with determination. "I'm gonna flip him—you need to stab him in the heart!"

Thomas started to shake his head, then stopped. He had no choice. He had to do this. So he nodded.

Brenda let out a cry of effort and fell to the right side of the Crank, using her body and her grip on his arms to make the man twist onto his side. Impossibly, his shrieks grew even louder. His chest was now there for the taking, arched and sticking up right in front of Thomas, just inches away.

"Now!" Brenda yelled.

Thomas tightened his grip on the knife. Then he put his other hand on it for more support, all ten fingers clasped tightly around the handle, blade pointing toward the floor. He had to do this. He had to do it.

"Now!" Brenda yelled again.

The Crank, screaming.

Sweat pouring down Thomas's face.

His heart, pumping, thumping, rattling.

Sweat in his eyes. His whole body aching. The terrible, inhuman screams.

"Now!"

Thomas used all his strength and plunged the knife into the Crank's chest.

CHAPTER 34

The next thirty seconds were a horrible, horrible thing for Thomas.

The Crank struggled. Spasmed. Choked and spat. Brenda held him while Thomas twisted the knife. Pushed it deeper. Life took its time as it drained from the man, as the light in his maddened eyes faded, as the grunts and the physical strain to hold on slowly quieted and stilled.

But finally, the Flare-infected man died, and Thomas fell backward, his whole body a tense coil of rusty wire. He gasped for breath, fought the sickening swell in his breast.

He'd just killed a man. He'd taken the life of another person. His insides felt full of poison.

"We need to go," Brenda said, jumping to her feet. "There's no way they didn't hear all that racket. Come on."

Thomas couldn't believe how unaffected she was, how quickly she'd moved on from what they'd done. But then again, they didn't have much choice. The first sign of the other Cranks came echoing down the hall, like the sounds of hyenas bouncing through a canyon.

Thomas forced himself to stand, pushed down the guilt that threatened to consume him. "Fine, but no more of this." First the head-eating silver balls. Now fighting Cranks in the darkness.

"What do you mean?"

He'd had enough of long black tunnels. Enough to last a lifetime. "I want daylight. I don't care what it takes. I want daylight. Now."

* * *

Brenda didn't argue. She guided him through several twists and turns and soon they found a long iron ladder leading toward the sky, out of the Underneath. The disturbing noises of Cranks lingered in the distance. Laughs and shouts and giggles. An occasional scream.

Moving the round manhole cover took some serious pushing, but it gave way and they climbed out. They found themselves standing in gray twilight, surrounded by enormously tall buildings in every direction. Broken windows. Garbage strewn over the streets. Several dead bodies lying about. A smell of rot and dust. Heat.

But no people. None living, anyway. Thomas felt a moment of alarm that some of the dead might be his friends, but that wasn't the case. The scattered bodies were older men and women, and decay had already set in.

Brenda slowly turned in a circle, getting her bearings. "Okay, the mountains should be down that street." She pointed, but it was impossible to tell because they didn't have a clear view and the buildings hid the setting sun.

"You sure?" Thomas asked.

"Yeah, come on."

As they set off down the long and lonely street, Thomas kept his eyes peeled, scanning every broken window, every alley, every crumbled doorway. Hoping to see some sign of Minho and the Gladers. And hoping *not* to see any Cranks.

They traveled until dark, avoiding contact with anyone. They did hear the occasional scream in the distance, or the sounds of things crashing inside a building now and then. Once, Thomas saw a group of people scurry across a street several blocks away, but they seemed not to notice him or Brenda.

Just before the sun disappeared completely for the day, they turned a corner and came into full view of the city's edge, maybe another mile farther. The buildings ended abruptly, and behind them the mountains rose in all their majesty. They were several times bigger than Thomas would've guessed upon first glimpsing them a few days earlier, and were dry and rocky. No snowcapped beauties—a hazy memory from his past—in this part of the world.

"Should we go the rest of the way?" Thomas asked.

Brenda was busy looking for a place to hide. "Tempting, but no. First off, it's too dangerous running around here at night. Second, even if we made it, there'd be no place for cover out there unless we made it all the way to the mountains. Which I don't think we could do."

As much as Thomas dreaded spending another night in this wretched city, he agreed. But the frustration and worry over the other Gladers were eating away at his insides. He weakly replied, "Okay. Where should we go, then?"

"Follow me."

They wound up in an alley that ended in a large brick wall. At first Thomas thought it was a terrible idea to sleep in a place that had only one way out, but Brenda convinced him otherwise—Cranks would have no reason to enter the alley since it didn't lead anywhere. Plus, she pointed out, there were several large, rusted trucks in which to hide.

They ended up inside one that looked like it had been torn apart for anything usable. The seats were tattered but they were soft, and the cab was big. Thomas sat behind the wheel, pushing the seat as far back as it would go. Surprisingly, he felt somewhat comfortable once settled. Brenda was just a couple of feet to his right, settling in herself. Outside, the darkness grew complete, and the distant sounds of active Cranks came through the broken windows.

Thomas was exhausted. Sore. In pain. Had dried blood all over his clothes. Earlier, he'd cleaned his hands, scrubbing them until Brenda yelled at him to quit wasting their water. But having the blood of that Crank on his fingers, on his palms . . . he couldn't take it. His heart sank every time he thought of it, but he could no longer deny a terrible truth: if he hadn't had the Flare before—a slim hope that Rat Man had lied—he'd surely caught it by now.

And now, sitting in the darkness, his head propped against the truck's door, thoughts of what he'd done earlier came storming into his mind.

"I killed that guy," he whispered.

"Yeah, you did," Brenda responded, her voice soft. "Otherwise he would've killed you. Pretty sure that's doing the right thing."

He wanted to believe it. The guy had been fully gone, consumed by the Flare. He probably would've died soon anyway. Not to mention he'd been doing everything possible to hurt them. To kill them. Thomas *had* done the right thing. But guilt still gnawed at him, crept through his bones. Killing another human. It wasn't easy to accept.

"I know," he finally responded. "But it was so . . . vicious. So brutal. I wish I could've just shot him from a distance with a gun or something."

"Yeah. Sorry it had to go down that way."

"What if I see his nasty face every night when I go to sleep? What if he's in my dreams?" He felt a surge of irritation at Brenda for making *him* stab the Crank—maybe unwarranted when he really considered how desperate they'd been.

Brenda shifted in her seat to face him. Moonlight illuminated her just enough that he could see her dark eyes, her dirty but pretty face.

Maybe it was bad, maybe he was a jerk. But looking at her made him want Teresa back.

Brenda reached out, took his hand and squeezed it. He let her, but he didn't squeeze back.

"Thomas?" She said his name even though he was looking right at her.

"Yeah?"

"You didn't just save your own skin, ya know. You saved mine, too. I don't think I could've beaten that Crank by myself."

Thomas nodded but didn't say anything. He hurt inside for so many reasons. All his friends were gone. Dead, for all he knew. Chuck was definitely dead. Teresa was lost to him. He was only halfway to the safe haven, sleeping in a truck with a girl who would eventually go crazy, and they were surrounded by a city full of bloodthirsty Cranks.

"You asleep with your eyes open?" she asked him.

Thomas tried to smile. "No. Just thinking about how much my life sucks."

"Mine does, too. Sucks big-time. But I'm glad I'm with you."

The statement was so simple and so sweet it made Thomas close his eyes, squeeze them shut. All the pain inside him transformed into something for Brenda, almost like what he'd felt for Chuck. He hated the people who'd done this to her, hated the disease that had made all this happen, and he wanted to make it right.

He finally looked at her again. "I'm glad, too. Being alone would suck even worse."

"They killed my dad."

Thomas lifted his head, surprised by the sudden shift in conversation. "What?"

Brenda nodded slowly. "WICKED. He tried to stop them from

taking me, screamed like a lunatic as he attacked them with . . . I think it was a wooden rolling pin." She let out a small laugh. "Then they shot him in the head." Tears glistened in her eyes, sparkling in the faint light.

"You're serious?"

"Yeah. I saw it happen. Saw the life go out of him before he even hit the floor."

"Oh, man." Thomas searched for words. "I'm really . . . sorry. I saw maybe my best friend in the world get stabbed. He died right in my arms." He paused again. "What about your mom?"

"She hadn't been around for a long time." She didn't elaborate, and Thomas didn't push. Didn't really want to know.

"I'm so scared of going crazy," she said after a long minute of silence. "I can already feel it happening. Things look weird, sound weird. Out of the blue I'll start thinking about stuff that doesn't make any sense. Sometimes the air around me feels . . . hard. I don't even know what that means, but it's scary. I'm definitely starting. The Flare's taking my brain to hell."

Thomas couldn't handle the look in her eyes; he let his gaze drop to the floor. "Don't give up yet. We'll make it to the safe haven, get the cure."

"False hope," she said. "Guess that's better than no hope at all."

She squeezed his hand. This time, Thomas squeezed back.

And then, impossibly, they slept.

CHAPTER 35

A nightmare woke Thomas—something about Minho and Newt being cornered by a bunch of Cranks past the Gone. Cranks with knives. Angry Cranks. The first spill of blood finally jerked Thomas awake.

He looked around, scared that he'd yelled or said something. The cab of the truck still lay in the darkness of night—he could barely see Brenda, couldn't even tell if her eyes were open. But then she spoke.

"Bad dream?"

Thomas settled himself, closed his eyes. "Yeah. I can't quit worrying about my other friends. I just hate it so bad that we were separated."

"I'm sorry that happened. I really am." She shifted in her seat. "But I seriously don't think you need to worry. Your Glader buddies seemed capable enough, but even if they weren't—Jorge is one tough monkey. He'll get them through the city just fine. Don't waste the stress on your heart. *We're* the ones you should be worried about."

"You're doing a terrible job of making me feel better."

Brenda laughed. "Sorry—I was smiling when I said that last part, but you couldn't see me, I guess."

Thomas looked at his backlit watch, then said, "We still have a few hours before the sun comes up."

After a short silence, Thomas spoke again. "Tell me a little bit more about what life's like now. They took most of our memories—some of mine came back, but they're sketchy and I don't know if I can trust them. There isn't much there about the outside world, either."

Brenda sighed deeply. "The outside world, huh? Well, it sucks. The temperatures are finally starting to go down, but it'll be forever before the sea levels do the same. It's been a long time since the flares, but so many people died, Thomas. So many. It's actually kind of amazing how everyone who survived stabilized and civilized so quickly. If it weren't for the stupid Flare, I think the world would pull through in the long run. But if wishes were fishes . . . oh, I can't remember. Something my dad used to say."

Thomas could hardly contain the curiosity that now raced inside him. "What *did* happen? Are there new countries, or just one big government? And how does WICKED fit into it all? *Are* they the government?"

"There are still countries, but they're more . . . unified. Once the Flare started spreading like crazy, they combined all their forces, technology, resources, whatever to start up WICKED. They set up this crazy elaborate testing system and have tried really hard to have quarantined areas. They slowed the Flare down, but they can't stop it. I think the only hope is to find a cure. Hope you're right that they've done it—but if they have, they sure haven't shared it with the public yet."

"So where are we?" Thomas asked. "Where are we right now?"

"In a truck." When Thomas didn't laugh, she continued. "Sorry, bad time for jokes. Judging by the labels on the food, we think we're in Mexico. Or what used to be Mexico. It makes the most sense. Now it's called the Scorch. Basically any area between the two Tropics—Cancer and Capricorn—is a complete wasteland now. Central and South Americas, most of Africa, the Middle East and southern Asia. Lots of dead lands, lots of dead people. So, welcome to the Scorch. Isn't it nice of them to send us sweet Cranks down here?"

"Man." Thoughts raced through Thomas's mind, mostly related to how he knew he was a part of WICKED—a huge part—and how the

Maze and Groups A and B and all the junk they were going through were parts of it too. But he couldn't remember enough for it to make any sense.

"Man?" Brenda asked. "That's the best you can come up with?"

"I have too many questions—I can't seem to latch on to just one to ask."

"Do you know about the numbing agent?"

Thomas looked over at her, wished he could make out more of her face. "I think Jorge said something about that. What is it?"

"You know how the world is. New disease, new drugs. Even if it doesn't do jack to the illness itself, they still come up with stuff."

"What does it do? Do you have any?"

"Ha!" Brenda shouted it with contempt. "You think they'd give us any? Only the important people, the rich people can get their hands on that junk. They call it the Bliss. Numbs your emotions, numbs your brain processes, slows you down to a drunken stupor so you don't feel much. Keeps the Flare at bay because the virus thrives in your brain. Eats at it, destroys it. If there's not a lot of activity, the virus weakens."

Thomas folded his arms. There was something very important here, but he couldn't put his finger on it. "So . . . it's not a cure? Even though it slows the virus down?"

"Not even close. Just delays the inevitable. The Flare always wins in the end. You lose any chance of being rational, having common sense, having compassion. You lose your humanity."

Thomas was quiet. Maybe more strongly than ever before, he felt that a memory—an important one—was trying to squeeze its way through the cracks in the wall blocking him from his past. The Flare. The brain. Going mad. The numbing agent, the Bliss. WICKED. The trials. What Rat Man had said, that their responses to the Variables were what this was all about.

"Did you fall asleep?" Brenda asked him after several minutes of silence.

"No. Just too much information." He felt dimly alarmed at what she had said, but he still couldn't put anything together. "It's hard to process it all."

"Well, I'll shut up, then." She turned away, rested her head against the door. "Push it out of your mind. Won't do you any good. You need rest."

"Uh-huh," Thomas mumbled, frustrated at having so many clues but no real answers. But Brenda was right—he could definitely use a good night's sleep. He got comfortable and did his best, but it took a long time before he finally dozed off. And dreamed.

He's older again, probably fourteen now. He and Teresa are kneeling on the ground, their ears pressed to the crack of a door, listening. Eavesdropping. A man and a woman are talking inside, and Thomas can hear them well enough.

The man first. "Did you get the additions to the Variables list?"

"Last night," the woman responds. "I like what Trent added for the end of the Maze Trials. Brutal, but we need it to happen. Should create some interesting patterns."

"Absolutely. Same with the betrayal scenario, if that ever has to play out."

The woman makes a noise that must be a laugh but that sounds strained and humorless. "Yeah, I had the same thought. I mean, good Lord, how much can these kids take before they'll go crazy on their own?"

"Not just that, it's risky. What if he dies? We all agree that by then he'll surely be one of the top Candidates."

"He won't. We won't let him."

"Still. We're not God. He *could* die."

There's a long pause. Then the man says, "Maybe it won't come to that. But I doubt it. The Psychs say it will stimulate a lot of the patterns we need."

"Well, there's a lot of emotion involved with something like that," the woman answers. "And according to Trent, some of the hardest patterns to create. I think the plan for those Variables is just about the only thing that will work."

"You really think the Trials are *going* to work?" the man asks. "Seriously, the scale and logistics of this thing are unbelievable. Think of how much could go wrong!"

"*Could,* you're right. But what's the alternative? Try it, and if it fails, we'll just be in the same spot as if we'd tried nothing."

"I guess."

Teresa tugs on Thomas's shirt; he looks to see her pointing back down the hall. Time to go. He nods, but leans back in to see if he can catch one last phrase or two. He does. It's the woman.

"Too bad we'll never see the end of the Trials."

"I know," the man answers. "But the future will thank us."

The first purple traces of dawn were what woke up Thomas the second time. He couldn't remember stirring once in his sleep since his middle-of-the-night talk with Brenda—not even after the dream.

The dream. It had been the strangest one yet, lots of things said that were already fading, too difficult to grasp and fit into the pieces of his past that were slowly, very slowly, beginning to come together again. He allowed himself to feel a little hope that maybe he wasn't in on as much to do with the Trials as he'd begun to think. Though he hadn't understood much in the dream, the fact that he and Teresa had been spying meant they weren't involved in every aspect of the Trials.

But what could the purpose of all this be? Why would the future thank those people?

He rubbed his eyes and stretched, then looked over at Brenda—her eyes still closed, her chest moving with slow and even breaths, her mouth slightly open. Though his body felt even stiffer than the day before, the restful slumber had done wonders for his spirit. He felt refreshed. Invigorated. Somewhat perplexed and brain-dead over his memory-dream and all the things Brenda had told him about, but invigorated all the same.

He stretched again and was just letting out a long yawn when he saw something on the wall of the alley. A large metal plaque, riveted to the wall. A sign that looked very familiar.

He pushed the door open and stumbled out onto the street and over to it. It was nearly identical to the sign in the Maze that had said WORLD IN CATASTROPHE—KILLZONE EXPERIMENT DEPARTMENT. Same dull metal, same lettering. Except this one said something very different. And he stared at it for at least five straight minutes before he moved an inch.

It said:

THOMAS, YOU'RE THE REAL LEADER

CHAPTER 36

Thomas might've gone on looking at the plaque all day if Brenda hadn't come out of the truck.

"I was waiting for the right time to tell you," she finally said, completely snapping him out of his daze.

He jerked his head to look at her. "What? What're you talking about?"

She didn't return his gaze, just kept staring at the sign. "Ever since I found out what your name was. Same with Jorge. It's probably why he decided to take his chances and go with you through the city and to this safe haven of yours."

"Brenda, what are you *talking* about?" Thomas repeated.

She finally met his eyes. "These signs are all over the city. All of them say the same thing. Exactly the same thing."

Thomas felt a weakening in his knees. He turned around and sank to the ground, resting his back against the wall. "How . . . how is this even possible? I mean, it looks like it's been there for a while. . . ." He didn't really know what else to say.

"Don't know," Brenda answered, joining him on the ground. "None of us knew what it meant. But when you guys showed up and you told us your name . . . well, we figured it wasn't a coincidence."

Thomas gave her a hard stare, anger fighting its way up inside him. "Why didn't you tell me about this? You'll hold my hand, tell me about your dad being killed, but not this?"

"I didn't tell you because I was worried about how you'd react. I figured you'd probably run off looking for the signs, forget all about me."

Thomas sighed. He was sick of all of it. He let the anger go and blew out a long breath. "I guess it's just another part of this whole nightmare that makes no sense."

Brenda twisted to look up at the sign. "How could you not know what it means? Could it be any simpler? You're supposed to be the leader, take over. I'll help you, earn my way in. Earn a spot at the safe haven."

Thomas laughed. "Here I am in a city full of whacked-in-the-brain Cranks, there's a group of girls who want to kill me, and I'm supposed to worry about who the real leader of my group is? It's ridiculous."

Brenda's face wrinkled in confusion. "Girls who want to kill you? What're you talking about?"

Thomas didn't respond, wondering if he really should tell her the whole story from beginning to end. Wondering if he had the heart to go over it all again.

"Well?" she pressed.

Deciding that it would be nice to get it off his chest, and feeling like she'd gained his trust, he caved and told her everything. He'd given her hints and small parts, but now he took the time for details. About the Maze, about being rescued, about waking up and finding that it had all gone back to crappy. About Aris and Group B. He didn't linger on Teresa, but he could tell she noticed something when he mentioned her. Maybe in his eyes.

"So do you and this Teresa girl got a little somethin' going?" she asked when he was done.

Thomas didn't know how to answer. *Did* they have a little something? They were close, they were friends, he knew that much. Though he'd only gotten back some of his memories, he sensed that he and she had maybe even been more than friends before the Maze. During that awful time when they'd actually helped design the stupid thing.

And then there'd been that kiss . . .

"Tom?" Brenda asked.

He looked at her sharply. "Don't call me that."

"Huh?" she asked, obviously startled, maybe even hurt. "Why?"

"Just . . . don't." He felt terrible for saying it, but couldn't take it back. That was what Teresa called him.

"Fine. Shall I call you Mr. Thomas? Or maybe King Thomas? Or better yet, just Your Majesty?"

Thomas sighed. "I'm sorry. Call me whatever."

Brenda let out a sarcastic laugh and then they both grew silent.

Thomas and Brenda sat, backs against the wall, and the minutes stretched on. It was almost a peaceful quiet until Thomas heard an odd thumping sound that alarmed him.

"Do you hear that?" he asked, now fully at attention.

Brenda had stilled, head cocked to the side as she listened intently. "Yeah. Sounds like someone bangin' on a drum."

"I guess the fun and games are over." He stood up, then helped Brenda do the same. "What do you think it is?"

"Chances are it's not good."

"But what if it's our friends?"

The low *bump-bump-bump* suddenly seemed to come from everywhere at once, the echoes bouncing back and forth between the alley walls. But after a long few seconds, Thomas grew certain the sound was coming from a corner of the dead end. Despite the risk, he ran in that direction to get a look.

"What're you doing!" Brenda snapped at him, but when he ignored her, she followed.

At the very end of the alley, Thomas reached a wall of cracked and faded bricks, where four stairs led down to a scratched and worn wooden door. Just above the door, there was a tiny rectangle of a window, its glass missing. One broken shard still hung at the top, like a jagged tooth.

Thomas could hear music playing, much louder now. It was intense and fast, the bass powerful, drums banging and guitars screaming. Mixed in were the sounds of people laughing and shouting and singing along. And none of it sounded very . . . sane. There was something creepy and disturbing about it.

It looked like the Cranks didn't just look for peoples' noses to bite off, and it gave Thomas a very bad feeling—this noise had nothing to do with his friends.

"We better get out of here," Thomas said.

"Ya think?" Brenda responded, standing right at his shoulder.

"Come on." Thomas turned to go just as she did, but they both froze. Three people had appeared in the alley while they'd been distracted. Two men and one woman, now standing only a few feet away.

Thomas's stomach dropped as he quickly observed the new arrivals. Their clothes were tattered, their hair messy, their faces dirty. But when he looked closer he saw that they didn't have any noticeable injuries, and their eyes showed glints of intelligence. Cranks, but not full-gone Cranks.

"Hi there," the woman said. She had long red hair pulled into a ponytail. Her shirt was cut so low that Thomas had to force himself to keep his eyes focused on hers. "Come to join our party? Lots of dancing. Lots of lovin'. Lots of booze."

There was an edge to her voice that made Thomas nervous. He didn't know what it meant, but this lady wasn't being nice. She was mocking them.

"Um, no thanks," Thomas said. "We, uh, we were just—"

Brenda cut in. "Just trying to find our friends. We're new here, just getting settled."

"Welcome to WICKED's very own Crankland." This was one of the men, a tall, ugly guy with greasy hair. "Don't worry, most of 'em down there"—he nodded toward the stairs—"are half gone at worst. You might get an elbow in the face, maybe kicked in the 'nads. But no one's gonna try to eat you."

"'Nads?" Brenda repeated. "Excuse me?"

The man pointed at Thomas. "I was talkin' to the boy. Things might get a little worse for you if you don't stick close to us. You being female and all."

This whole conversation was making Thomas ill. "Sounds like fun. But we gotta go. Find our friends. Maybe we'll come back."

The other man stepped forward. This one was short but handsome, with blond hair in a crew cut. "You two are nothin' but kids. Time you got some lessons on life. Time you had some fun. We're officially inviting you to the party." He pronounced each word of the last sentence carefully, and with no kindness whatsoever.

"Thanks, but no thanks," Brenda said.

Blondie pulled a gun from a pocket of his long jacket. It was a pistol, silver but grimy and dull. Still, it looked as menacing and deadly as anything Thomas had ever seen.

"I don't think you understood me," the man said. "You're invited to our party. That's not something you turn down."

Tall and Ugly pulled out a knife. Ponytail pulled out a screwdriver, its tip black with what had to be old blood.

"What do you say?" Blondie asked. "Would you like to come to our party?"

Thomas looked at Brenda, but she didn't look back. Her eyes were glued to the blond man, and her face said she was about to do something really stupid.

"Okay," Thomas said quickly. "We'll go. Let's do it."

Brenda snapped her head around. "What?"

"He has a gun. He has a knife. *She's* got a shuck screwdriver! I'm not in the mood to have an eyeball smashed into my skull."

"Looks like your boyfriend's not stupid," Blondie said. "Now let's go have some fun." He pointed his pistol at the stairs and smiled. "Feel free to lead the way."

Brenda was clearly angry, but her eyes also revealed that she knew they had no other choice. "Fine."

Blondie smiled again; the expression would've looked natural on a snake. "That's the spirit. Fine and dandy, nothing to worry about."

"No one's gonna hurt you," Tall and Ugly added. "Unless you get difficult. Unless you act like brats. By the end of the party, you'll wanna join our group. Trust me on that."

Thomas had to fight to keep the panic from pounding through him. "Let's just go," he said to Blondie.

"Waiting on you." The man pointed at the stairs with his gun again.

Thomas reached out and grabbed Brenda's hand, pulled her close to him. "Let's go to the party, sweetheart." He put as much sarcasm into it as he could. "This'll be so much fun!"

"That's very nice," Ponytail said. "I get weepy when I see two people in love." She feigned wiping tears from her cheeks.

With Brenda by his side, Thomas turned toward the stairs, aware the whole time of the gun pointed at his back. They made their way down the steps to the old slab of a door, the space just wide enough for them to go side by side. When they reached the bottom, Thomas didn't see a handle. Raising his eyebrows, he looked back at Blondie, who stood two steps behind them.

"Gotta do the special knock," the man said. "Three slow fist thumps, three fast ones, then two knuckle taps."

Thomas hated these people. He hated the way they spoke so calmly and said mostly nice words, all of them full of mockery. In a way these Cranks were worse than the nose-missing guy he'd stabbed the day before—at least with him they'd known exactly what they were dealing with.

"Do it," Brenda whispered.

Thomas balled his hand into a fist and did the slow fist thumps, then the fast ones. Then he rapped the wood twice with his knuckles. The door opened immediately, the pounding music escaping like a blasting wind.

The guy who greeted them was huge, ears and face pierced several times, tattoos all over. His hair was long and white, reaching well past his shoulders. But Thomas barely had time to register this before the man spoke.

"Hey, Thomas. We've been waiting for you."

CHAPTER 37

The next minute or so was a stunned blur of the five senses.

The welcome statement had shocked Thomas, but before he could respond, the long-haired man practically pulled him and Brenda inside, then started ushering them through a tightly packed crowd of dancing bodies, gyrating and jumping and hugging and spinning. The music was deafening, each beat of the drums like a hammer to Thomas's skull. Several flashlights had been strung from the ceiling; they swayed back and forth as people swatted them, sending beams of light slashing this way and that.

Long Hair leaned over and spoke to Thomas as they slowly made their way through the dancers; Thomas could barely hear him even though he was yelling.

"Thank God for batteries! Life's gonna suck when those run out!"

"How did you know my name?" Thomas yelled back. "Why were you waiting for me?"

The man laughed. "We watched you all night! Then this morning we saw your reaction to the sign through a window—figured you had to be the famous Thomas!"

Brenda had both arms wrapped around Thomas's waist, clinging to him, probably just so they wouldn't get separated. Probably. But when she heard this, she squeezed even tighter.

Thomas looked back, saw Blondie and his two friends following on their heels. The gun had been put away, but Thomas knew it could be brought right back out again.

The music blared. The bass thumped and rattled the room. People dancing and jumping all around them, the swords of light crisscrossing the dark air. The Cranks were slick and shiny with sweat, all that body heat making the room uncomfortably warm.

Somewhere right in the middle, Long Hair stopped and turned to face them, his odd white mane flopping.

"We really want you to join us!" he shouted. "There's gotta be something about you! We'll protect you from the bad Cranks!"

Thomas was glad they didn't know more. Maybe this wouldn't be so bad after all. Play along, pretend to be a special Crank, and maybe he and Brenda would get through this long enough to slip away unnoticed at the right time.

"I'll go and get you a drink!" Long Hair called out. "Enjoy yourselves!" Then he scuttled off, vanishing into the thick, writhing crowd.

Thomas turned to see Blondie and his two friends still there, not dancing at all—just watching. Ponytail caught his attention with a wave of her hand.

"Might as well dance!" she yelled. But she didn't follow her own advice.

Thomas twisted around until he was fully facing Brenda. They needed to talk.

As though she could read his mind, she brought her arms up and wrapped them around his neck, pulling him close until her mouth was right next to his ear, her breath hot and tingling against his sweat.

"How did we get into this piece-of-crap situation?" she asked.

Thomas didn't know what to do but wrap his arms around her back and waist. He felt her heat through her damp clothes. Something stirred inside him, mixed with guilt and longing for Teresa.

"I never could have imagined this an hour ago," he finally said, speaking through her hair. It was the only thing he could think of to say.

The song changed, something dark and haunting. The beat had slowed a bit, the drum somehow deeper. Thomas couldn't make out any words—it was as if the singer were lamenting some horrible tragedy, the voice wailing, high-pitched and sorrowful.

"Maybe we should just stay with these people for a while," Brenda said.

Thomas noticed then that the two of them *were* dancing, without meaning to or thinking about it. Moving with the music, slowly turning, their bodies pressed tightly together, clasping each other.

"What're you talking about?" he asked, surprised. "You're giving up already?"

"No. Just tired. Maybe we'd be safer here."

He wanted to trust her, felt like he could. But something about all this worried him—had she brought him here on purpose? It seemed a stretch. "Brenda, don't quit on me yet. The only option we have is to get to the safe haven. There's a cure for this."

Brenda shook her head slightly. "It's just so hard to believe it's really true. Hard to hope for it."

"Don't say that." He didn't want to think it, and he didn't want to hear it.

"Why would they have sent all these Cranks here if there was a cure? It just doesn't make any sense."

Thomas pulled back to look at her, worried about the sudden change in attitude. Her eyes were wet with tears.

"You're talking crazy," he said, then paused. He had his own doubts, of course, but he didn't want to discourage her. "The cure is real. We have to . . ." He trailed off, looked over at Blondie, who was still staring at him. The guy probably couldn't hear, but better safe than sorry.

Thomas leaned back in to speak directly in Brenda's ear. "We have to get out of here. You wanna stay with people who pull guns and screwdrivers on you?"

Before she could respond, Long Hair was back, a cup in each hand, the brownish liquid inside sloshing as he got bumped from all directions by the dancers. "Drink up!" he called out.

Something inside Thomas seemed to wake up then. Taking a drink from these strangers suddenly felt like a very, very bad idea. Impossibly, everything about this place and this situation had become even more uncomfortable.

Brenda had already started reaching for a drink, though.

"No!" Thomas yelled before he could stop himself, then raced to cover his mistake. "I mean, no, I really don't think we should be drinking that stuff. We've gone a long time without water—we need that first. We, um, just wanna dance for a while." He tried to act casual, but was cringing on the inside, knowing he sounded like an idiot—especially when Brenda gave him a strange look.

Something small and hard pressed against his side. He didn't have to turn to see what it was: Blondie's pistol.

"I offered you a drink," Long Hair said again, this time any sign of kindness gone from his tattooed face. "It would be very rude to turn such an offer down." He held the cups out again.

Panic swelled in Thomas. Any small doubt had gone—something was wrong with the drinks.

Blondie pressed the gun into him even harder. "I'm gonna count to one," the man said into his ear. "Just one."

Thomas didn't have to think. He reached out and took the cup, poured the liquid in his mouth, swallowed all of it at once. It burned like fire, searing his throat and chest as it went down; he broke into a lurching, wracking cough.

"Now you," Long Hair said, handing the other cup to Brenda.

She looked at Thomas, then took it and drank. It didn't seem to faze her in the least; there was just a slight tightening of her eyes as it went down.

Long Hair took the empty cups back, a huge grin now spread across his face. "That's just fine! Back to dancing ya go!"

Thomas already felt something funny in his gut. A soothing warmth, a calmness, growing and spreading through his body. He took Brenda back into his arms, held her tightly as they swayed to the music. Her mouth was against his neck. Every time her lips bumped against his skin, a wave of pleasure shot through him.

"What was it?" he asked. He felt more than heard the slur in his voice.

"Something not good," she said; he could barely hear her. "Something drugged. It's doing funny things to me."

Yeah. Thomas thought. *Something funny.* The room had begun to spin around him, far faster than their slow turn should have caused it to. People's faces seemed to stretch when they laughed, their mouths gaping black holes. The music slowed and thickened, the singing voice deepened, grew drawn-out.

Brenda pulled her head away from him, clasped the sides of his face with her hands. She stared at him, though her eyes seemed to jiggle. She looked beautiful. More beautiful than anything he'd ever seen before. Everything around them faded to darkness. His mind was shutting down, he knew it.

"Maybe it's better this way," she said. Her words didn't match her lips. Her face was moving in circles, seemingly detached from her neck. "Maybe we can be with them. Maybe we can be happy until we're past the Gone." She smiled then, a sickening, disturbing smile. "Then you can kill me."

"No, Brenda," he said, but his voice seemed a million miles away, as if it were coming from an endless tunnel. "Don't . . ."

"Kiss me," she said. "Tom, kiss me." Her hands tightened on his face. She started to pull him down toward her.

"No," he said, resisting.

She stopped, a hurt look washing over her face. Her moving, blurring face.

"Why?" she asked.

The darkness almost had him fully now. "You're not . . . her." His voice, distant. A mere echo. "You could never be her."

And then she fell away, and his mind did the same.

CHAPTER 38

Thomas awoke to darkness, and it felt as if he had been put into some type of ancient torture device, nails slowly driving into his skull from all directions.

He groaned, a halting, terrible sound that only intensified the pain in his head. He forced himself silent, tried to reach up to rub—

His hands wouldn't move. Something held them down, something sticky pressing against his wrists. Tape. He tried to kick out with his legs, but they were bound, too. The effort sent another wave of pain crashing through his head and body; he went limp, moaning softly. He wondered how long he'd been out.

"Brenda?" he whispered. No response.

A light came on.

Bright and stabbing. He squeezed both eyes shut, then opened one just enough to squint through. Three people stood in front of him, but their faces were in shadow, the light source coming from behind.

"Wakey wakey," a husky voice said. Someone snickered.

"Want some more of that fire juice?" This came from a woman. The same person snickered again.

Thomas finally grew accustomed to the light and opened his eyes fully. He was in a wooden chair, wide gray tape tightly securing his wrists to the armrests and his ankles to the chair legs. Two men and one woman stood in front of him. Blondie. Tall and Ugly. Ponytail.

"Why didn't you just whack me out in the alley?" Thomas asked.

"Whack you?" Blondie responded. His voice hadn't seemed husky before; it sounded like he'd spent the last few hours yelling out on the dance floor. "What do you think we are, some kind of twentieth-century mafia clan? If we wanted to *whack* you, you'd already be dead, bleeding in the streets."

"We don't want you dead," Ponytail interrupted. "That would spoil the meat. We like to eat our victims while they're still breathing. Eat as much as we can before they bleed to death. You wouldn't believe how juicy and . . . sweet that tastes."

Tall and Ugly laughed, but Thomas couldn't tell whether Ponytail was serious. Either way, it freaked him out.

"She's kidding," Blondie said. "We've only eaten other humans when it's gotten completely desperate. Man meat tastes like pig crap."

Another burst of giggles from Tall and Ugly. Not snickering, not laughing. Giggling. Thomas didn't believe they were serious—he was much more worried about how their minds seemed . . . off.

Blondie smiled for the first time since Thomas had met him. "Joking again. We're not quite that Cranked-out yet. But I do bet people don't taste very good."

Tall and Ugly and Ponytail nodded.

Man, these guys are really starting to lose it. Thomas thought. He heard a muffled groan to his left and looked over. Brenda was in a corner of the room, bound just as he was. But her mouth had been taped shut as well, making him wonder if she'd put up more of a fight before she passed out. It looked like she was only now waking up, and when she noticed the three Cranks, she shifted and wiggled in her chair, moaning through the gag. Her eyes lit with fire.

Blondie pointed at her. His pistol had magically appeared. "Shut up! Shut up or I'll splat your brain on the wall!"

Brenda stopped. Thomas expected her to start whimpering or

crying or something. But she didn't, and he immediately felt stupid for thinking it. She'd already shown how tough she was.

Blondie dropped the gun to his side. "Better. Good God, we should've killed her when she first started screaming up there. And biting." He looked at his forearm, where the long arc of a welt shone red.

"She's with him," Ponytail said. "We can't kill her yet."

Blondie pulled a chair from the far wall and took a seat just a few feet in front of Thomas. The others followed suit, looking relieved, as if they'd been waiting hours for permission. Blondie rested the gun on his thigh, its business end pointed straight at Thomas.

"Okay," the man said. "We've got us quite a lot to talk about. I'm not going through the normal bullcrap with you, either. If you mess around or refuse to answer or whatever, I'm gonna shoot you in the leg. Then the other one. Third time, a bullet goes into your girlfriend's face. I'm thinking somewhere right between the eyes. And I bet you can guess what happens the fourth time you piss me off."

Thomas nodded. He wanted to think he was tough, think he could stand up to these Cranks. But common sense won out. He was taped to a chair, no weapons, no allies, nothing. Though honestly, he didn't have anything to hide. He'd answer whatever the guy asked him. Whatever ended up happening, he didn't want any bullets in his leg. And he doubted the guy was bluffing.

"First question," Blondie said. "Who are you and why is your name on signs all over this piece of crap city?"

"My name is Thomas." As soon as it came out, Blondie scrunched up his face in anger. Thomas realized his stupid mistake and hurried along. "You already knew that. Well, how I got here is a really weird story and I doubt you'll believe it. But I swear I'm telling the truth."

"Didn't you come on a Berg like the rest of us?" Ponytail asked.

"Berg?" Thomas didn't know what that meant, but he just shook his head and went on. "No. We came out of some underground tunnel about thirty miles or so to the south. Before that we went through something called a Flat Trans. Before that—"

"Hold it hold it hold it," Blondie said, holding up a hand. "A Flat Trans? I'd shoot you right now, but there's no way you just made that up."

Thomas wrinkled his brow in confusion "Why?"

"You'd be stupid to try getting away with an obvious lie like that. You came through a Flat Trans?" The man's surprise was obvious.

Thomas glanced at the other Cranks, both of whom had similar looks of shock on their faces. "Yeah. Why's that so hard to believe?"

"Do you have any idea how expensive Flat Transportation is? Before the flares, it had just been revealed to the public. Only governments and billionaires can afford to use it."

Thomas shrugged. "Well, I know they have a lot of money, and that's what the guy called it. A Flat Trans. Kind of a gray wall that tingles like ice when you walk through it."

"What guy?" Ponytail asked.

Thomas had barely started and already his mind was jumbled. How could you tell a story like this? "I think he was from WICKED. They're running us through some kind of experiment or test. I don't really know everything. We . . . had our memories wiped out. Some of mine came back, but not a whole lot."

Blondie didn't react for a second, just sat there staring at him. Almost *through* him, at the wall behind. Finally, he said, "I was a lawyer. Back before the flares and this disease ruined everything. I know when someone's lying. I was very, very good at my job."

Oddly, Thomas relaxed. "Then you know I'm not—"

"Yeah, I know. I wanna hear the whole thing. Start talking."

Thomas did. He couldn't say why, but it seemed okay. His instincts told him these Cranks were just like everybody else—sent here to live out their last horrible years succumbing to the Flare. They were just trying to find an advantage, find a way out, like anybody would. And meeting a guy who had special signs about him all over the city was an excellent first step. If Thomas had been in their shoes, he'd probably have been doing the same thing. Without the gun and bindings, hopefully.

He'd told most of the story to Brenda just the day before, and related it much the same way now. The Maze, the escape, the dorms. Being given the mission to cross the Scorch. He took special care to make it sound very important, stressing the part about the cure waiting at the end. Since they'd lost the chance to have Jorge's help getting through the city, maybe he could start over with these people. He also expressed his concern over the other Gladers, but when he asked if they'd seen them—or a big group of girls—the answer was no.

Once again, he didn't talk much about Teresa. He just didn't want to take any chances of endangering her somehow, though he had no idea how talking about her might do that. He also lied a bit about Brenda. Well, he never really lied directly. He just kind of made it sound like she'd been with him from the beginning.

When he finished, ending at the part where they'd met the three people in front of him in the alley, he took a deep breath and adjusted himself in the chair. "Can you *please* take this tape off me now?"

A flick of Tall and Ugly's hand caught his attention and he looked to see that a very sharp, shiny knife had appeared there. "What do you think?" he asked Blondie.

"Sure, why not." He'd held a stoic face throughout the tale, giving no hint yet as to whether he believed the story.

Tall and Ugly shrugged and got to his feet, walked over to Thomas. He was just leaning over, knife outstretched, when a commotion broke out above. Hard thumps on the ceiling, followed by a couple of screams. Then it sounded like a hundred people running. Frantic footsteps, jumping, more thumps. More screams.

"Another group must've found us," Blondie said, his face suddenly pale. He stood, motioned for the other two to follow him. A few seconds later they were gone, vanishing up a set of stairs into the shadows. A door opened and closed. The chaos above continued.

All of this combined to scare Thomas nearly out of his wits. He looked over at Brenda, who sat perfectly still, listening. Her eyes finally met his gaze. Still gagged, she could only raise her eyebrows.

He didn't like their odds being left like this, taped to chairs. There was no way any of the Cranks he'd met that night had a chance against ones like Mr. Nose. "What if a bunch of full-gone Cranks are up there?" he asked.

Brenda mumbled something through the tape.

Thomas strained every muscle and started jumping his chair in tiny steps toward where she sat. He'd made it about three feet when the sounds of fighting and rumbling suddenly stopped. He froze, looked up at the ceiling.

Nothing for several seconds. Then a set of footsteps, maybe two, shuffling across the floor above. A loud thump. Another loud thump. Then another. Thomas imagined bodies being thrown on the ground.

The door at the top of the stairs opened.

Then footsteps, hard and heavy, running down. It was all in shadow, and a cold panic flooded Thomas's body as he waited to see who came down.

Finally, someone stepped into the light.

Minho. Dirty and bloody, burn marks on his face. Knives in both hands. *Minho.*

"You guys look comfy," he said.

CHAPTER 39

Despite everything he'd been through, Thomas couldn't remember the last time he'd been at such a loss for words. "What . . . how . . ." He stammered, trying to get something out.

Minho smiled, a very welcome sight. Especially considering how horrible the guy looked. "We'd just found you. Did you think we were gonna let these bunch of shuck-faces do anything to you? You owe me. Big-time." He walked over and started cutting the tape.

"What do you mean you'd just found us?" Thomas was so happy he wanted to giggle like an idiot. Not only were they rescued, his friends were alive. They were alive!

Minho kept cutting. "Jorge's been leading us through the city—avoiding Cranks, finding food." He finished up with Thomas and went to free Brenda, still talking over his shoulder. "Yesterday morning, we kind of spread out, spying here and there. Frypan was peeking around the corner into that alley up there just as those three shanks pulled a gun on you. He came back, we got mad, started planning our ambush. Most of those shucks were wasted or asleep."

Brenda pushed her way out of the chair and past Minho as soon as her tape was cut. She started toward Thomas, but hesitated—he couldn't tell if she was mad or just worried. Then she came the rest of the way, ripping the tape off her mouth as she reached his side.

Thomas stood up, and immediately his head pounded again, the room swaying, making him sick. He plopped back into the chair. "Oh, man. Anybody got some aspirin?"

Minho only laughed. Brenda had made her way to the bottom of the stairs, where she stood with arms folded. Something about her body language *did* make her look angry. Then he remembered what he had said to her right before passing out from the drug.

Oh, crap, he thought. He'd told her she could never be Teresa.

"Brenda?" he asked sheepishly. "You okay?" No way he was gonna bring up their odd dance and that conversation in front of Minho.

She nodded, but didn't look back at him. "I'm fine. Let's go. I wanna see Jorge." Short clips for words. No emotion in them.

Thomas groaned, glad to have the pain in his head as an excuse. Yeah, she was mad at him. Actually, *mad* might've been the wrong word. She looked more hurt.

Or maybe he assumed too much and she didn't care at all.

Minho came up to him, offered a hand. "Come on, dude. Headache or no headache, we need to go. No telling how long we can keep the shuck prisoners up there quiet and still."

"Prisoners?" Thomas repeated.

"Whatever you wanna call them—we can't risk letting them go until we get out. We've got a dozen guys holding more than twenty. And they aren't too happy. They might start thinking they can take us pretty soon. Once they get rid of their hangovers."

Thomas stood up again, this time much more slowly. The pain in his head rocked and throbbed like a steady drum, seeming to push on his eyeballs from behind with every thud. He closed his eyes until things quit spinning around him. He sucked in a deep breath, looked at Minho. "I'll be fine."

Minho flashed him a smile. "Such a man. Come on."

Thomas followed his friend to the stairs. He paused beside Brenda but didn't say anything. Minho peered back at Thomas with an expression that said, *What's up with her?* Thomas just shook his head slightly.

Minho shrugged, then stomped his way up and out of the room, but Thomas stayed back with Brenda for a second. She didn't seem to want to move just yet. And she refused to meet his eyes.

"I'm sorry," he said, regretting his harsh words right before passing out. "I think I said something kinda mean—"

Her eyes snapped up to meet his. "You think I give a crap about you and your girlfriend? I was just dancing, trying to have some fun before everything went bad. What, you think I'm in love with you or something? Just dying till the day you ask me to be your Crank bride? Get over yourself."

Her words were so full of rage that Thomas took a step back, as hurt as if she'd slapped him. Before he could respond, she disappeared upstairs, all heavy footsteps and sighs. He'd never missed Teresa so badly as at that moment. On a whim, he called out to her with his mind. But she still wasn't there.

The smell hit him before he even entered the room where they'd danced.

Like sweat and vomit.

Bodies littered the floor, some sleeping, some huddled together and shivering; some even looked dead. Jorge, Newt and Aris were there, standing guard, slowly turning in circles with knives drawn and pointing.

Thomas saw Frypan and the other Gladers, too. Though his head still throbbed, he felt a rush of relief and excitement. "What happened to you guys! Where have you been?"

"Hey, it's Thomas!" Frypan roared. "As ugly and alive as ever!"

Newt came up to him, gave a sincere smile. "Glad you're not bloody dead, Tommy. I'm really, really glad."

"You too." Thomas realized with a weird numbness that this was what his life had become. This was how you greeted people after a day or two apart. "Has everyone made it so far? Where'd you guys go? How'd you get here?"

Newt nodded. "Still eleven of us. Plus Jorge."

Thomas's questions came faster than anyone could answer. "Any sign of Barkley and the rest of them? Were they the ones who set off the explosion?"

Jorge answered—Thomas saw that he stood closest to the door, holding a very nasty-looking sword that was currently resting on the shoulder of Tall and Ugly himself. Ponytail was next to him, and they were both curled up on the ground. "Haven't seen 'em since. We got away pretty quickly, and they're too scared to come deeper into the city."

The sight of Tall and Ugly had set off a small alarm inside Thomas. Blondie. Where was Blondie? How would Minho and the others have dealt with his gun? He looked around but couldn't find him anywhere in the room.

"Minho," Thomas whispered, then motioned for him to come closer. Once he and Newt were both right next to him, he leaned in. "The guy with really short blond hair. Seemed like the leader. What happened to him?"

Minho shrugged and looked at Newt to answer.

"Must've got out," Newt replied. "A handful did—we couldn't stop all of them."

"Why?" Minho asked. "You worried about him?"

Thomas looked around, lowered his voice even further. "He had a *gun*. He's the only one I've seen with something worse than a knife. And he wasn't very nice."

"Who gives a klunk?" Minho said. "We'll be out of this stupid city in an hour. And we should go. Now."

That sounded like the best idea Thomas had heard in days. "Okay, I want to get out of here before he comes back."

"Listen up!" Minho called out as he stepped away, walking through the crowd. "We're leaving now. Don't follow us, you'll be fine. Follow us, you'll be dead. Pretty easy choice, don't ya think?"

Thomas wondered when and how Minho had taken back the leadership role from Jorge. He looked over at the older man and noticed Brenda standing silently next to a wall, staring at the floor. He felt so bad about what had happened the night before. He really *had* wanted to kiss her. But for some reason he'd felt disgusted at the same time. Maybe it was the drug. Maybe it was Teresa. Maybe it was—

"Hey, Thomas!" Minho was yelling at him. "Dude, wake up! We're leaving!"

Several Gladers had already walked through the door and into the sunlight. How long had he been out from the drug? A full day? Or just a few hours, since morning? He moved to follow, stopping by Brenda and giving her a little push. He worried for a second that she wouldn't come with them, but she only hesitated a moment before heading for the door.

Minho, Newt and Jorge waited, keeping guard with their weapons, until everyone but Thomas and Brenda were out. Thomas watched at the doorway as the three Gladers backed away, slowly sweeping the tips of their knives and swords back and forth as they did so. But it didn't look like anyone was going to put up a fuss. They were all probably ready to move on, just glad to be alive.

Everyone gathered in the alley away from the stairs. Thomas stayed close to the top step, but Brenda made her way to the other side of the group. He swore he'd get her alone as soon as they were away and safe, have a long talk. He liked her, wanted to be her friend if nothing else. More importantly, he now felt about her much the way he'd felt about Chuck. For some reason a feeling of responsibility for her had overcome him.

"—make a run for it."

Thomas shook his head, realizing that Minho had been talking. Daggers of pain shot through his skull, but he focused.

"There's only about a mile left," Minho continued. "These Cranks aren't so hard to fight after all. So let's—"

"Hey!"

The shout came from behind Thomas, loud and screechy, filled with more than a hint of lunacy. Thomas spun around to see Blondie standing down on the bottom step, by the open door, his arm extended. His white-knuckled fingers held the gun, surprisingly steady and calm. It was pointed directly at Thomas.

Before anyone could move he fired, an explosion that rocked the narrow alley with a thunderous boom.

Pure pain ripped through Thomas's left shoulder.

CHAPTER 40

The impact knocked Thomas back, spinning him around so that he fell flat on his face, smacking his nose on the ground. Somehow, through the pain and muffled buzz in his ears, he heard the gun fire again, then the sound of grunts and punches, followed by metal clacking across the cement.

He rolled onto his back, hand clasped tight to where he'd been shot; he searched for the courage to look at the wound. The ringing in his ears grew louder, and he barely noticed out of the corner of his eye that Blondie had been tackled to the ground. Someone was punching the living crap out of him.

Minho.

Thomas finally gazed down at the damage. What he saw there made his heart double its pace.

A small hole in his shirt revealed a gooey red blob right in the meaty part above his armpit, blood pouring from the wound. It hurt. It hurt *bad*. If he'd thought his headache downstairs had been tough, this was like three or four of those, all smashed into a coil of pain right there in his shoulder. And spreading through the rest of his body.

Newt was at his side, looking down with worried eyes.

"He shot me." It just came out, a new number one on the list of the dumbest things he'd ever said. The pain, like living metal staples running through his insides, pricking and scratching with their little sharp points. He felt his mind going dark for the second time that day.

Someone handed a shirt to Newt, who pressed it tightly against Thomas's wound. This sent another wave of agony through him; he cried out, not caring how wimpy he sounded. It hurt like nothing he'd ever felt before. The world around him faded another few degrees.

Pass out, he urged himself. *Please pass out, make it go away.*

Voices came from a distance again, just like his own had on the dance floor after being drugged.

"I can get that sucker out of him." This was Jorge, of all people. "But I'll need a fire."

"We can't do this here." Was that Newt?

"Let's get out of this shuck city." Definitely Minho.

"All right. Help me carry him." No idea.

Hands gripping him from underneath, grasping his legs. The pain. Someone saying something about the count of three. The pain. It really, really hurt. One. The pain. Two. *Ouch*. Three!

He rose toward the sky, and the pain exploded anew, fresh and raw.

Then his wish to pass out came true and darkness washed his troubles away.

He awoke, his mind a haze.

Light blinded him; he couldn't open his eyes all the way. His whole body jostled and bumped, hands still holding him tight. He heard the sounds of breathing, heavy and fast. Feet pounding on pavement. Someone shouting, though he couldn't understand the words. In the distance, the mad screams of Cranks. Close enough that they might be pursuing.

Heat. The air was burning hot.

His shoulder, on fire. Pain tore through him like a series of toxic explosions, and he fled to the darkness once again.

★ ★ ★

He cracked his eyes.

This time the light was much less intense. The golden gleam of twilight. He lay on his back, the ground beneath him hard. A rock dug into his lower back, but it felt heavenly compared to the rot in his shoulder. People lumbered about him, talking in short and tight whispers.

The cackle of Cranks had grown more distant. He saw nothing but sky above him, no buildings. Pain in his shoulder. Oh, the pain.

A fire licked and spit somewhere close. He felt the heat wafting across his body, hot wind through hot air.

Someone said, "You better hold him down. Legs and arms."

Though his mind still floated in fog, those words didn't sound good.

A flash of light on silver in his vision, the fading sun's reflection on . . . a knife? Was it glowing red?

"This is gonna hurt somethin' awful." No idea who said it.

He heard the hiss right before a billion pounds of dynamite exploded in his shoulder.

His mind said goodbye for the third time.

He sensed that a long spell of time had passed this go-around. When he opened his eyes again, stars like pinpricks of daylight shone down from the dark sky. Someone held his hand. He tried to turn his head to look over, but it sent a fresh wave of agony shooting down his spine.

He didn't need to see. It was Brenda.

Who else would it be? Plus, the hand was soft and small. Brenda for sure.

The intense pain of before had been replaced. In some ways, he now felt worse. Something like an illness crept through the inner workings of his body. A gnawing, itching filthiness. Something foul, like maggots squirming through his veins and the hollows of his bones and between his muscles. Eating away at him.

It hurt, but now it was more of an ache. Deep and raw. His stomach, gurgly and unstable, fire in his veins.

He didn't know how he knew, but he was sure of it. Something was wrong.

The word *infection* popped up in his mind, then stayed there.

He drifted off.

The sunrise woke Thomas in the morning. The first thing he realized was that Brenda no longer held his hand. Then he noticed the cool air of early morning on his skin, which gave him the briefest moment of pleasure.

Then he became fully aware of the throbbing pain that consumed his body, dwelling in every last molecule. It no longer had anything to do with his shoulder and the bullet wound. Something terrible had gone wrong with his entire system.

Infection. That word again.

He didn't know how he'd make it through the next five minutes. Or the next hour. How could he possibly go through an entire day? Then sleep and start the whole thing all over again? Despair sucked at him, an empty, yawning void that threatened to pull him down into an awful abyss. A panic-laced craziness struck him. Suffusing it all, the pain.

That was when things got bizarre.

The others heard it before he did. Minho and everyone else were suddenly scrambling, searching for something, many of them scanning the sky. The sky? Why would they be doing that?

Someone—Jorge, he thought—yelled the word *Berg*.

Then Thomas heard it. A deep thrumming, full of heavy thumps. It grew louder before he even realized what was going on, and soon it felt as though the noise were inside his skull, rattling his jaw and eardrums and sluicing down his spine. A constant, steady pounding, like the world's largest drums; behind it all, the massive hum of heavy machinery. A wind picked up, and at first Thomas worried that a storm was starting again, but the sky was perfectly blue. Not a cloud to be seen.

The noise worsened his pain, made him begin to shut down again. But he fought it, desperate to know the source of the sounds. Minho shouted something, pointed to the north. Thomas hurt too much to turn and look. The wind grew stronger, gusting across him, ripping at his clothes. Dust flew and clouded the air. Suddenly Brenda was beside him again, squeezing his hand.

She leaned over until her face was only inches above his. Her hair whipped all around.

"I'm sorry," she said, though he barely heard her. "I didn't mean to—I mean, I know that you . . ." She fumbled for words, looked away.

What was she talking about? Why didn't she tell him what was making that horrible noise! He hurt so bad. . . .

A look of curious horror spread across her face, eyes widening, mouth dropping open. And then she was being pushed away by two . . .

Panic seized Thomas now. Two people, dressed in the strangest outfits he'd ever seen. One-piece, baggy and dark green—letters he couldn't read scrawled across the chest. Goggles covering their faces. No, not goggles. Some kind of gas mask. They looked hideous and alien. They looked evil, like giant, demented, human-eating insects wrapped in plastic.

One of them grabbed his legs by the ankles. The other put his hands under him, gripped him by the armpits, and Thomas screamed. They lifted, and pain went coursing through his body. He'd almost grown used to the agony by now, but this felt even worse. It hurt too much to struggle, so he went limp.

Then they were moving, carrying him, and for the first time, Thomas's eyes focused enough to read the letters on the chest of the person at his feet.

WICKED.

Darkness threatened to take him again. He let it, but the pain went with him.

CHAPTER 41

Once again, he woke to a blinding white light—this one shining directly into his eyes from above. He knew immediately it wasn't the sun—it was different. Plus, it shone from only a short distance away. Even as he clenched his eyes shut again, the afterimage of a bulb floated across the darkness.

He heard voices—more like whispers. He couldn't understand a word. Too soft, just out-of-reach enough that they were impossible to decipher.

He heard the click and clack of metal against metal. Small sounds, and the first thing he thought of was medical instruments. Scalpels and those little rods with mirrors on the end. These images swam up from the murkiness of his memory bank, and combining them with the light, he knew.

He'd been taken to a hospital. A hospital. The last thing he could ever imagine existing anywhere in the Scorch. Or had he been taken away? Far away? Through a Flat Trans, maybe?

A shadow crossed the light, and Thomas opened his eyes. Someone was looking down at him, dressed in the same ridiculous outfit as those who'd brought him here. The gas mask, or whatever it was. Big goggles. Behind the protective glass, he saw dark eyes focused on him. A woman's eyes, though he didn't know how he could tell.

"Can you hear me?" she asked. Yes, a woman, even though the mask muffled her voice.

Thomas tried to nod, didn't know if he actually did or not.

"This wasn't supposed to happen." She'd pulled her head back a bit and looked away, which made Thomas think she hadn't meant that comment for him. "How'd a working gun get in the city? You have any idea the amount of rust and gunk must've been on that bullet? Not to mention the germs."

She sounded very angry.

A man replied. "Just get on with it. We have to send him back. Quickly."

Thomas barely had time to process what they were saying. A new pain blossomed in his shoulder, unbearable.

He passed out for the umpteenth time.

Awake again.

Something was off. He couldn't tell what. The same light shone from the same spot above; he looked to the side this time instead of closing his eyes. He could see better, focus more. Silver squares of ceiling tile, a steel contraption with all kinds of dials and switches and monitors. None of it made sense.

Then it hit him. Hit him with such shock and wonder that he scarcely believed it could be true.

He felt no pain. None. Nothing at all.

No people stood around him. No crazy green alien suits, no goggles, no one sticking scalpels in his shoulder. He seemed to be alone, and the absence of pain was pure ecstasy. He didn't know it was possible to feel this good.

It wasn't. Had to be a drug.

He dozed off.

★ ★ ★

He stirred at the sound of soft voices, though it came through the haze of his drugged stupor.

Somehow he knew enough to keep his eyes shut, see if he could learn anything about the people who'd taken him. The people who'd evidently fixed him up and rid his body of the infection.

A man was talking. "Are we sure this doesn't screw anything up?"

"I'm positive." This from a woman. "Well, as positive as I can be. If anything, it may stimulate a pattern in the killzone that we hadn't expected. A bonus, possibly? I can't imagine it leading him or anyone else in a direction that would prevent the other patterns we're looking for."

"Dear God above, I hope you're right," the man responded.

Another woman spoke, her voice high, almost crystalline. "How many of the ones left do you think are still viable Candidates?" Thomas sensed the capital letter in that word—*Candidates*. Confused, he tried to remain still, listen.

"We're down to four or five," the first woman answered. "Thomas here is by far our greatest hope. He responds really sharply to the Variables. Wait, I think I just saw his eyes move."

Thomas froze, tried to stare straight ahead into the darkness of his eyelids. It was hard, but he forced himself to breathe evenly, as if asleep. He didn't know exactly what these people were talking about, but he desperately wanted to hear more. *Knew* he needed to hear more.

"Who cares if he's listening?" the man asked. "He couldn't possibly understand enough to affect his responses one way or the other. It'll do him good to know we made a huge exception to get that infection out of him. That WICKED will do what it has to when necessary."

The high-pitched-voice lady laughed, one of the most pleasant sounds Thomas had ever heard. "If you're listening, Thomas, don't get too excited. We're about to dump you right back where we took you from."

The drugs coursing through Thomas's veins seemed to surge, and he felt himself fading into bliss. He tried to open his eyes, but couldn't. Before he drifted off he did hear one last thing, from the first woman. Something very odd.

"It's what you would've wanted us to do."

CHAPTER 42

The mysterious people were true to their word.

The next time Thomas woke up, he was hanging in the air, strung tightly to a canvas litter with handles, swaying back and forth. A large rope attached to a ring of blue metal held him as he was lowered from something huge, the whole time accompanied by the same explosion of hums and heavy thumps that he'd heard when they'd come to get him. He gripped the sides of the litter, terrified.

Finally, he felt a soft bump, and then a million faces appeared around him. Minho, Newt, Jorge, Brenda, Frypan, Aris, the other Gladers. The rope holding him detached and sprang up into the air. Then, almost instantaneously, the vessel from which he'd been lowered vaulted away, disappearing into the brilliance of the sun directly overhead. The sounds of its engines faded, and soon it was gone.

Then everyone spoke at once.

"What was that all about?"

"Are you okay?"

"What'd they do to you?"

"Who was that?"

"Have fun in the Berg?"

"How's your shoulder?"

Thomas ignored it all and tried to get up, but realized that the ropes holding him to the litter still bound him tightly to it. He found Minho with his eyes. "A little help here?"

As Minho and a couple of others worked on untying him, Thomas had a disturbing thought. The people from WICKED had shown up to save him pretty quickly. From what they'd said, it was something they hadn't planned on, but they'd done it anyway. Which meant they were watching and could swoop in to save them whenever they wanted to.

But they hadn't until now. How many people had died in the last few days while WICKED stood by and watched? And why did that change for Thomas, just because he'd been shot by a rusty bullet?

It was too much to think about.

Once freed, he got to his feet and stretched out his muscles, refusing to acknowledge the second volley of questions flung his way. The day was hot, brutally hot, and as he stretched, he realized that he felt no pain other than the slightest of aches in his shoulder. He looked down to see that he was wearing fresh clothes, and that there was the bulge of a bandage under the left sleeve of his shirt. But his thoughts immediately went to something else.

"What are you guys doing out in the open? Your skin is gonna bake!"

Minho didn't answer, just pointed at something behind him, and Thomas looked to see a very shabby hut. It was made out of dry wood that seemed like it might crumble to pure dust at any second, but it was big enough to provide shelter for everyone there.

"We better get back under that thing," Minho said. Thomas realized that they must've run out just to see him delivered from the huge flying . . . Berg? Jorge had called it a Berg.

The group trekked over to the shelter; Thomas told them a dozen times that he'd explain everything from beginning to end once they were settled. Brenda found him, walked right next to him. But she didn't offer her hand, and Thomas felt an uneasy relief. She also didn't say anything, and neither did he.

The miserable city of the Cranks lay a few miles distant, huddling in all its decay and madness to the south. No sign of the infected people anywhere. To the north, the mountains loomed now, only a day or so away. Craggy and lifeless, they sloped up higher and higher until they ended in jagged brown peaks. Harsh cuts in the rock made the whole range appear as though a giant had hacked at it with a massive axe for days and days, letting out all its giant frustration.

They reached the shelter, the wood dry as rotted bone. It looked as if it had stood there for a hundred years—maybe built by a farmer in the days before the world was ravaged. How it had withstood everything was a complete mystery. But one flick of a match and the thing would probably burn down in three seconds.

"All right," Minho said, pointing to a spot in the far end of the shade. "You sit there, get yourself all nice and comfy and start talking."

Thomas couldn't believe how good he felt—just a dull ache in his shoulder. And he didn't think he had any trace of drugs in him anymore. Whatever doctors WICKED had unleashed on him had been brilliant at what they did. He took a seat and waited for everyone to get situated in front of him, sitting cross-legged on the hot and dusty ground. He was like a schoolteacher readying to give a lesson—a blurry flash from his past.

Minho was the last to take a seat, right next to Brenda. "Okay, tell us about your adventures with the aliens in their big bad spaceship."

"You sure about this?" Thomas asked. "How many days left to get over those mountains, to the safe haven?"

"Five days, dude. But you know we can't go tramping around in this sun with nothing to protect us. You're gonna talk, then we're gonna sleep, then we're all gonna bust our humps walking all night. Get on it."

"Good that," Thomas said, wondering what they'd been doing

while he was away, but realizing it didn't matter all that much. "Save all your questions till the end, children." When not a single person laughed, or even smiled, he coughed and hurried on. "It was WICKED that came and got me. I kept passing out, but they took me to some doctors who totally fixed me up. I heard them saying something about how it wasn't supposed to happen, how the gun had been a factor they hadn't expected. The bullet set off a nasty infection in me, and I guess they felt pretty strongly that it wasn't time for me to die."

Blank faces stared back at him.

Thomas knew it would be hard for them to accept—even after he'd told the whole story. "Just telling you what I heard."

He went on to explain more. Every detail of what he could remember, and about the odd bedside conversation he'd listened in on. Things about killzone patterns and Candidates. More about the Variables. None of it had made much sense the first time around, and it made even less now as he tried to recall it word for word. The Gladers—plus Jorge and Brenda—looked as frustrated as he felt.

"Well, that really cleared things up," Minho finally said. "Must have something to do with all those signs about you in the city."

Thomas shrugged. "Glad to know you're so happy to see me alive."

"Hey, if you wanna be the leader, no skin off my back. I *am* happy to see you alive."

"No thanks. You keep it."

Minho didn't respond. Thomas couldn't deny that the signs weighed heavily on him—what did it really mean that WICKED wanted him to be the leader? And what should he do about it?

Newt got to his feet, his face in a deep scowl of concentration. "So we're all potential candidates for *something*. And maybe the purpose of all the buggin' klunk we've been through is to weed out those who don't qualify. But for some reason the whole gun-and-rusty-bullet thing wasn't part of the . . . normal tests. Or Variables, whatever. If Thomas is gonna croak and die, it wasn't supposed to come from a bloody infection."

Thomas pursed his lips and nodded. Sounded like a great summary to him.

"What this means is that they're watching us," Minho said. "Just like they did in the Maze. Has anyone seen a beetle blade running around anywhere?"

Several Gladers shook their heads.

"What the hell's a beetle blade?" Jorge asked.

Thomas answered. "Little mechanical lizard things that spied on us with cameras in the Maze."

Jorge rolled his eyes. "Of course. Sorry I asked."

"The Maze was definitely some kind of indoor facility," Aris said. "But there's just no way we're inside something anymore. Though they could be using satellites or long-range cameras, I guess."

Jorge cleared his throat. "What is it about Thomas that makes him so special? Those signs in the city about him being the real leader, them swooping in here and saving his butt when he got all sicky-sicky." He looked at Thomas. "I'm not trying to be mean, *muchacho*—I'm just curious. What makes you better than the rest of your buddies?"

"I'm not special," Thomas said, even though he knew he was hiding something. He just didn't know *what*. "You heard what they said. We have lots of ways to die out here, but that gun shouldn't be one of them. I think they would've saved anybody who'd gotten shot. It wasn't about me—it was the bullet that messed things up."

"Still," Jorge replied with a smirk. "I think I'll stay close to you from here on."

A few more discussions broke out, but Minho didn't let them last long. He insisted that they all needed sleep if they were planning on marching through the night. Thomas didn't complain—he'd grown more tired with every passing second of sitting in that hot air on that hot ground. Maybe it was his body healing, maybe just the heat. Either way, sleep called to him.

They didn't have blankets or pillows, so Thomas curled up on the ground in the very spot where he'd been sitting, resting his head on his folded arms. Brenda somehow ended up right next to him, though she didn't say anything, and she certainly didn't touch him. Thomas didn't know if he'd ever figure her out.

He sucked in a long, slow breath, closed his eyes, then welcomed the rest, welcomed that heavy feeling of slumber as it started pulling him into its depths. The sounds around him seemed to fade away, the air to thicken. A calm came over him, then sleep.

The sun was still blazing in the sky when a voice sounded in his mind, waking him up.

A girl's voice.

Teresa.

After days and days of utter silence, Teresa started talking to him telepathically, all at once, a rush of words.

Tom, don't even try to talk back, just listen. Something terrible is going to happen to you tomorrow. An awful, awful thing. You're gonna be hurt and you're gonna be scared. But you have to trust me. No matter what happens, no matter what you see, no matter what you hear, no matter what you think. You have to trust me. I won't be able to talk to you.

She paused, but Thomas was so stunned and trying so hard to understand what she'd said—make sure he remembered it—that he couldn't get a word in before she started up again.

I have to go. You won't hear from me for a while.

Another pause.

Not until we're back together.

He fumbled for something to say, but her voice and her presence slipped away, leaving him empty once more.

CHAPTER 43

It took a long time for Thomas to find sleep again.

He had no doubt it had been Teresa. None at all. Just like before when they'd spoken to each other, he'd felt her presence, sensed her emotions. She'd been with him, even if it had been for such a short time. And when she left, it was like opening up that vast void within all over again. As if during the days since her disappearance a thick liquid had slowly seeped in and filled that chamber, only to have it all sucked out again when she came and went.

What had she meant, anyway? Something awful was going to happen to him, but he needed to trust her? He couldn't wrap his mind around that enough for it to make any sense. And as awful as her warning sounded, his thoughts kept drifting to the last part, about them being together again. Was that some string of false hope? Or did it mean she thought he'd make it through the bad thing and end up okay? Reunited with her? Possibilities raced through his mind, but they all seemed to hit a depressing dead end.

The day only got hotter and hotter as he tossed and turned, haunted by his thoughts. He'd almost grown used to Teresa's being gone, which made him sick to his stomach. To make it worse, he felt like he'd betrayed her by letting Brenda become his friend, by growing so close to her.

Ironically, his first instinct was to reach out and wake Brenda, talk to *her* about it. Was that wrong? He felt so frustrated and stupid he wanted to scream.

All great for someone trying to fall back asleep in the miserable heat.

The sun had trudged halfway to the horizon before he finally did.

He felt a little better in the late evening when Newt shook him awake. Teresa's brief visit to his mind seemed like a dream now. He could almost believe it had never happened.

"Sleep well, Tommy?" Newt asked. "How's that shoulder?"

Thomas sat up, rubbed his eyes. Though he couldn't have slept for more than three or four hours, his sleep had been deep and undisturbed. He rubbed his shoulder to test it and was surprised all over again. "Feels really good, actually—aches a little, but not much. Hard to believe I was hurtin' so bad before."

Newt looked around at the Gladers preparing to leave, then back at Thomas. "Feels like we haven't talked much since leaving the bloody dorm. Not much time to sit around and sip tea, I guess."

"Yeah." For some reason this made Thomas think of Chuck, and all the pain of his death came rushing back. Which just made him hate the people behind all this all over again. The line from Teresa came back to him. "I don't see how WICKED can be good."

"Huh?"

"Remember what Teresa had written on her arm when she first woke up? Or did you even know about that? It said *WICKED is good*. I'm just finding that hard to believe." The sarcasm in his voice wasn't subtle.

Newt had a strange smile on his face. "Well, they just saved your buggin' life."

"Yeah, they're real saints." Thomas couldn't deny he was confused. They *had* saved his life. He also knew he'd worked for them. But what it all meant, he had no idea.

Brenda, who had been stirring in her sleep, now finally sat up, letting out a big yawn. "Morning. Or evening. Whatever."

"Another day alive," Thomas answered, then realized Newt might have no idea who Brenda was. He really had no idea what had happened in the group since he'd been shot. "I'm assuming you guys had time to get to know each other? If not, Brenda, this is Newt. Newt, Brenda."

"Yeah, we know already." Newt reached out and shook her hand mockingly. "But thanks again for making sure this bloody sissy didn't get his butt killed while you two were out partying."

The barest hint of a smile flashed across her face. "Partying. Yeah. I especially loved the part where we had people trying to cut our noses off." A look flashed across her face, part embarrassment, part despair. "Guess it won't be long before *I'm* one of those psychos."

Thomas didn't know how to respond to that. "You're probably not that much farther along than us. Remember that—"

Brenda wouldn't let him finish. "Yeah, I know. You guys are gonna take me to the magical cure. I know." She got up then, the conversation obviously over.

Thomas looked at Newt, who shrugged. Then, as he got to his knees, he leaned in and whispered, "She your new girlfriend? I'm telling Teresa." He snickered to himself and was gone.

Thomas sat there for a minute, overwhelmed by it all. Teresa, Brenda, his friends. The warning he'd received. The Flare. The fact that they only had a few days to cross those mountains. WICKED. Whatever waited for them at the safe haven and in the future.

Too much. It was all too much.

He had to stop thinking. He was hungry, and that he *could* solve. So he got up and went searching for something to eat. And Frypan didn't disappoint.

* * *

They set off just as the sun dipped below the horizon, making the dusty orange land look almost purple. Thomas was cramped and tired, itching to walk off some steam and loosen his muscles.

The mountains slowly became jagged peaks of shadow, growing taller and taller as they walked. There were no real foothills to speak of; the flat valley just stretched forward until the ground erupted toward the sky in sheer cliffs and steep slopes. All brown and ugly, lifeless. Thomas hoped an obvious path would present itself once they'd made it that far.

No one spoke much as they marched along. Brenda stayed close but quiet. She didn't even talk to Jorge. Thomas hated how it was now. How suddenly everything was awkward between him and Brenda. He liked her, probably more than he liked anyone else now besides Newt and Minho. And Teresa, of course.

Newt approached him after darkness had fallen, the stars and moon their only guides. Their light was enough—you didn't need much when the ground was flat and all you had to do was walk toward the looming wall of rock in front of you. The *crunch crunch crunch* of their footsteps on the earth filled the air.

"Been thinkin'," Newt said.

"About what?" Thomas didn't really care; he was just glad to have someone to talk to and get his mind off things.

"WICKED. Ya know, they broke their own bloody rules with you."

"How's that?"

"They said there *were* no rules. Said we had so much time to get to the bloody safe haven and that was that. No rules. People dying left and right, then they come down in a buggin' monster flying thing and save your butt. Doesn't make sense." He paused. "Not that I'm complaining—I'm glad you're alive and all."

"Gee, thanks." Thomas knew it was a good point, but he was tired of thinking about it.

"And then there were all those signs in the city. Weird."

Thomas looked over at Newt, barely able to see his friend's face. "What, you jealous or something?" he asked, trying to make a joke out of it. Trying to ignore the fact that the signs *had* to be a big deal.

Newt laughed. "No, you shank. Just dying to know what's really going on around here. What this is really all about."

"Yeah." Thomas nodded. He couldn't agree more. "The lady said only a few of us were good enough to be Candidates. And she *did* say I was the best Candidate, and they didn't want me dying from something they hadn't planned. But I don't know what it all means. Has something to do with all that klunk about killzone patterns."

They walked on for a minute or so before Newt spoke again. "Not worth bustin' our brains about, I guess. What's gonna happen'll happen."

Thomas almost told him then about what Teresa had said in his mind, but for some reason it just didn't feel right.

He stayed silent, and eventually Newt drifted away until once again Thomas walked alone in the dark.

A couple of hours passed before he had another conversation, this time with Minho. A lot of words flew back and forth between them, but in the end they hadn't really said much. Just passing time, rehashing the same questions they'd all gone over in their minds a million times.

Thomas's legs were a little tired, but not too bad. The mountains got ever closer. The air cooled considerably, and it felt wonderful. Brenda remained silent and distant.

And on they went.

★ ★ ★

When the first traces of dawn turned the sky a deep, dark blue, the stars beginning to wink away for the coming day, Thomas finally got the nerve to approach Brenda and talk about something. Anything. The cliffs loomed now, dead trees and chunks of scattered rock coming into focus. They'd reach the foot of the mountains by the time the sun popped over the horizon, Thomas was sure of it.

"Hey," he said to her. "How're your feet holding up?"

"Fine." It came out curt, but then she quickly spoke again, maybe trying to make up for it. "How about you? Your shoulder seem okay?"

"I can't believe how fine it is. Doesn't hurt much at all."

"That's good."

"Yeah." He racked his brain, trying to think of something to say. "So, um, I'm sorry about all the weird stuff that happened. And . . . for anything I said. My head's all kinds of crazy and messed up."

She looked over at him, and he could see a bit of softness in her eyes. "Please, Thomas. The last thing you need to do is apologize." She returned her gaze up ahead. "We're just different. Plus, you have that girlfriend of yours. I shouldn't have tried to kiss you and all that crap."

"She's not really my girlfriend." He regretted saying it as soon as it came out—didn't even know where it had come from.

Brenda huffed. "Don't be dumb. And don't insult me. If you're gonna resist this"—she paused and gestured to herself with a sweep of her hands from head to toe with a mocking smile—"then it better be for a good reason."

Thomas laughed—all the tension and awkwardness had just vanished completely. "Point taken. You're probably a crappy kisser anyway."

She punched him in the arm—luckily his good one. "You couldn't possibly be more wrong. Trust me on that one."

Thomas was just about to say something stupid when he stopped dead in his tracks. Somebody almost ran into him from behind, tripped around to his side, but he couldn't tell who—his eyes were glued in front of him, his heart completely frozen.

The sky had lightened considerably, and the leading edge of the mountains' slope lay just a few hundred feet away. Halfway between here and there, a girl had seemingly appeared out of nowhere, rising from the ground. And she was walking toward them at a brisk pace.

In her hands she held a long shaft of wood with a large, nasty-looking blade lashed to one end.

It was Teresa.

CHAPTER 44

Thomas didn't quite know how to compute what he saw. He felt no surprise or joy at Teresa's being alive—he'd already known that she was. She'd spoken to his mind just the day before. But seeing her in the flesh still lifted his spirits. Until he remembered her warning that something bad was going to happen. Until he thought about the fact she was holding a bladed spear.

The other Gladers noticed right after he did, and soon everyone had stopped to gawk at Teresa as she marched toward them, her hands gripping that weapon, her face hard as stone. She looked ready to start stabbing the first thing that moved.

Thomas took a step forward, not really sure what he planned to do. But then more movement stopped him.

On both sides of Teresa, girls appeared; they, too, seemed to come from nowhere. He turned to look behind him. They were surrounded, by at least twenty girls.

And they all held weapons, varying knives and rusty swords and jagged machetes. Several of the girls had bows and arrows, their menacing tips already aimed at the group of Gladers. Thomas felt an uneasy slice of fear. Regardless of what Teresa had said about something bad happening, surely she wouldn't let these people hurt them. Right?

Group B popped into his mind. And his tattoo saying how they were supposed to kill him.

His thoughts were cut short when Teresa stopped about thirty feet away from the group. Her companions did the same, forming a complete circle around the Gladers. Thomas turned again to take it all in. Each one of their new visitors stood stiffly, eyes squinted, weapons held out in front and ready. The bows scared him the most—he and the others would have no chance to do anything before those arrows could fly and find a home inside someone's chest.

He stopped, facing Teresa. Her eyes were focused on him.

Minho spoke first. "What's this crap about, Teresa? Nice way to greet your long-lost buddies."

At the mention of the name *Teresa,* Brenda spun and looked sharply at Thomas. He gave her a quick nod, and the surprise on her face made him sad for some reason.

Teresa didn't answer the question, and an eerie silence swept across the group. The sun continued to rise, inching toward the point where its heat would beat down on them unbearably.

Teresa walked toward them again, and stopped about ten feet from where Minho and Newt stood side by side.

"Teresa?" Newt asked. "What the bloody—"

"Shut up," Teresa said. She didn't snap or yell it. She said it calmly and with conviction, which only made it that much more frightening to Thomas. "And any of you makes a move, the bows start shooting."

Teresa brought her spear up to a better fighting position, swept it back and forth as she stepped past Newt and Minho and through the Gladers, acting as if she was searching for something. She came to Brenda, paused. Neither said a word, but the hatred between them was visible. Teresa moved past her, never dropping her icy stare.

And then she was in front of Thomas. He tried to tell himself that she'd never use that weapon on him, but believing it wasn't easy when you were looking at the blade's sharp edge.

"Teresa," he whispered before he could stop himself. Despite the spear, despite the hard look on her face, despite the way her muscles tensed as if she was about to slash him, all he wanted was to reach out to her. He couldn't help but remember the kiss she'd given him. The way it had felt.

She didn't move, just kept staring at him, her face unreadable except for the obvious anger there.

"Teresa, what's—"

"Shut up." That same voice of calm. Of utter command. It didn't sound like her.

"But what—"

Teresa reared back and swung the butt of her spear at him, smashing it into his right cheek. An explosion of pain shot through his skull, his neck; he crumpled to his knees, a hand to his face where she'd hit him.

"I said shut up." She reached down and grabbed him by the shirt, jerked up until he stood once again. She repositioned her hands on the wooden shaft, pointed it at him. "Is your name Thomas?"

He gaped at her. His world was crashing in on him, even though he told himself she'd warned him. Told him that no matter what, he had to trust her. "You know who I—"

She swung the spear even more violently this time, crashing the bladeless end into the side of his head, right on his ear. The pain was twice as bad as the first hit; he cried out, clutching his head. But he didn't fall this time. "You know who I am!" he screamed.

"I used to, anyway," she said in a voice that was both soft and disgusted. "Now I'm going to ask you one more time. Is your name Thomas?"

"*Yes!*" he yelled back at her. "My name is Thomas!"

Teresa nodded, then started to back away from him, the tip of the blade once again aimed at his chest. People got out of her way as she passed the group and rejoined the circle of girls who surrounded them.

"You're coming with us," she called out. "Thomas. Come on. Remember, anyone tries something, the arrows fly."

"No way!" Minho yelled. "You're not taking him anywhere."

Teresa acted as if she hadn't heard him, her eyes riveted to Thomas in that strange squinty-eyed stare. "This isn't some stupid game. I'm going to start counting. Every time I hit a multiple of five, we'll kill one of you with an arrow. We'll do it until Thomas is the only one left, then we'll take him anyway. It's up to you."

For the first time, Thomas noticed that Aris was acting strange. He stood just a few feet to Thomas's right, and he kept turning in a slow circle, staring at the girls one by one as if he knew them each well. But somehow he kept his mouth shut.

Of course, Thomas thought. If this really was Group B, Aris had been with them. He *did* know them.

"One!" Teresa shouted.

Thomas wasn't taking any chances. He walked forward, pushing past people until he reached the open, then went straight toward Teresa. He ignored the comments from Minho and the others. He ignored everything. Eyes on Teresa, trying to show no emotion, he walked until he stood almost nose to nose with her.

It was what he wanted anyway, right? He wanted to be with her. Even if she'd been turned against him somehow. Even if she was being manipulated by WICKED, like Alby and Gally had been. For all he knew, her memory had been wiped again. Didn't matter. She looked serious, and he couldn't risk having someone shoot one of his friends with a bow and arrow.

"Fine," he said. "Take me."

"I only made it to one."

"Yeah. I'm really brave that way."

She hit him with the spear, so hard that he couldn't help but drop to the ground again. His jaw and head ached like smoldering fire. He spit, saw blood splatter on the dirt.

"Bring the bag," Teresa said from above.

In his peripheral vision he saw two girls walking toward him, their weapons hidden away somewhere. One of them—a dark-skinned girl with hair cut almost to her scalp—held a large frayed burlap sack. They stopped two feet from him; he got back to his hands and knees, scared to do anything more for fear of getting pummeled again.

"We're taking him with us!" Teresa yelled. "If anybody follows, I'll hit him again and we'll start shooting you. We won't really bother aiming. Just let the arrows fly any old way they feel like."

"Teresa!" Minho's voice. "You catch the Flare that quickly? Your mind's obviously gone already."

The butt of the spear smashed into the back of Thomas's head; he collapsed onto his stomach, black stars swimming in the dirt inches from his face. How could she do this to him?

"Anything else you wanna say?" Teresa asked. After a long moment of silence, she said, "Didn't think so. Put the bag over him."

Hands roughly grabbed his shoulder and spun him onto his back—their grip dug into his bullet wound enough to send a deep ache flashing through his upper body for the first time since WICKED had fixed him up.

He moaned. Faces—they didn't even look angry—hovered over him as two girls held the open end of the sack directly above his head.

"Don't resist," the dark-skinned girl said, her face shining with sweat. "Or it'll just get worse."

Thomas was perplexed. Her eyes and voice held genuine sympathy for him. But her next words couldn't have been more different.

"Better just to go along and let us kill you. Doesn't do you any good to have a lot of pain along the way."

The bag slipped over his head, and all he could see was ugly brown light.

CHAPTER 45

They shifted him around on the ground till they got the bag slipped entirely over his body. Then they tied the open end at his feet with a rope, knotting it tight and wrapping its ends up and around the rest of him, pinning him inside the bag, cinching another knot just over his head.

Thomas felt the bag going taut; then his head was pulled up. He imagined girls holding either end of this impossibly long rope. Which could only mean one thing—they were going to drag him. He couldn't take it anymore, started squirming even though he knew what it'd get him.

"Teresa! Don't do this to me!"

This time a fist hit him right in the stomach, making him howl. He tried to double over, tried to clutch his middle, but couldn't because of the stupid bag. Nausea swept through him; he fought it, kept his food down.

"Since you obviously don't care about yourself," Teresa said, "talk again and we'll start shooting your friends. That sound good to you?"

Thomas didn't respond; he heaved a silent sob of agony. Had he really been thinking things were looking up in the world only yesterday? His infection cured and his wound healed, away from the city of Cranks, nothing but a swift and hard hike through the mountains between them and the safe haven. He should've known better after everything he'd been through.

"I meant what I said!" Teresa yelled at the Gladers. "There won't be a warning. Follow us and the arrows start flying."

Thomas saw her outline as she knelt next to him, heard her knees crunching on the dirt. Then she grabbed him through the material of the bag, put her head against his, her mouth just half an inch from his ear. She started whispering, so faintly he had to strain to hear, concentrating to separate her words from the breeze.

"They're blocking me from talking to you in our heads. Remember to trust me."

Thomas, surprised, had to fight to keep his mouth shut.

"What're you saying to him?" This came from one of the girls holding the rope attached to the bag.

"I'm letting him know just how much I'm enjoying this. How much I'm enjoying my revenge. Do you mind?"

Thomas had never heard such arrogance from her. She was either a really good actress or *had* started going crazy. Gained a split personality or two.

"Well," the other girl responded. "Glad you're having so much fun. But we need to hurry."

"I know," Teresa said. She gripped the sides of Thomas's head even harder, squeezed and shook it. Then she pressed her mouth against the rough material, pushing on his ear. When she spoke, again with that hot whisper, he could feel her hot breath through the weave of the burlap. "Hang in there. It'll be over soon."

The words numbed Thomas's brain; he had no idea what to think. Was she being sarcastic?

She released him and stood back up. "Okay, let's get out of here. Make sure you hit as many rocks as you can along the way."

His captors started walking, dragging him along behind them. He felt the rough ground below him as he was dragged across it, the big sack providing absolutely no protection. It hurt. He arched his back, putting all his weight on his feet, letting his shoes bear the brunt of the impacts. But he knew his strength couldn't hold out forever.

Teresa walked right beside him as they pulled his body along. He could just make her out through the burlap.

Then Minho started yelling, his voice already fading with distance, the sound of being dragged against the dirt making it that much harder to hear. What Thomas *did* hear, however, gave him little hope. Between garbled unflattering names, Thomas heard the words "we'll find you" and "time is right" and "weapons."

Teresa slammed her fist into Thomas's stomach again, shutting Minho up.

And across the desert they went, Thomas bouncing over the dirt like a sack of old clothes.

Thomas imagined horrible things as they went along. His legs were weakening every second, and he knew he'd have to lower his body to the ground soon. He pictured the bleeding wounds, the permanent scars.

But maybe it wouldn't matter. They planned on killing him anyway.

Teresa had said to trust her. And even though he had a hard time doing it, he was trying to believe her. Could all the stuff she'd done to him since reappearing with the weapons and Group B really be an act? If it wasn't, why would she keep whispering to him to trust her?

His mind turned it all over in circles until he couldn't concentrate anymore. His body was being rubbed raw, and he knew he needed to figure out how to prevent every inch of skin from being scratched off.

The mountains saved him.

When they started going up the steep slope, it obviously became difficult for the girls to drag his body the way they'd done across flat ground. They tried pulling him in quick jerks—slipping and letting him slide several feet back down, then hauling him back up only to let him slip again. Teresa finally said it'd probably be easier to carry him by the shoulders and ankles. And that they should do it in shifts.

An idea hit Thomas then that was so obvious he thought surely he'd missed something. "Why don't you just let me walk!" he called through the burlap, his voice muffled and cracking from thirst. "I mean, you *do* have weapons. What am I gonna do?"

Teresa kicked him in the side. "Shut up, Thomas. We're not idiots. We're waiting until your Glader buddies can't see us anymore."

He'd done his best to stifle his groan when her foot crashed into his rib cage. "Huh? Why?"

"Because that's what we were *told* to do. Now shut up!"

"Why'd you tell him that?" one of the other girls whispered harshly.

"What does it matter?" Teresa responded, not even trying to hide what she was saying. "We're gonna kill him anyway. Who cares if he knows what we were told to do?"

Told to do, Thomas thought. *By WICKED.*

A different girl spoke up. "Well, I can barely see them now. Once we reach that crevice up there, we'll be out of sight, and they'll never find us after that. Even if they do follow."

"All right, then," Teresa said. "Let's just get him that far."

Hands were soon gripping Thomas on all sides, lifting him into the air. From what he could see through the sack, Teresa and three of her new friends were carrying him. They picked their way through boulders and around dead trees, going up and up and up. He heard their heavy breaths, smelled their sweat, hated them more with each jolting step. Even Teresa. He tried one last time to reach her mind, to salvage his trust in her, but she wasn't there.

The trudge up the mountain went on for maybe an hour—with stops here and there for girls to switch off carrying duties—and it had been at least twice that long since they'd left the Gladers. The sun was reaching a point where it would become dangerous, the heat stifling. But then they rounded a massive wall, the ground leveling a bit, and entered shade. The cooler air was a relief.

"All right," Teresa said. "Drop him."

Without ceremony, they did what she said and he slammed into the ground with a heavy grunt. It knocked the wind out of him, and he lay there gasping for air as they started untying the ropes. By the time he caught his breath, the bag had been taken off.

He blinked, looking up at Teresa and her friends. They all had their weapons pointed at him, which just seemed ridiculous.

From somewhere he found a trace of courage. "You guys must think a lot of me, twenty of you with knives and machetes, me with nothing. I feel so special."

Teresa reared back with her spear.

"Wait!" Thomas cried, and she stopped. He held his hands up in deference, slowly got to his feet. "Look, I'm not gonna try anything. Just take me wherever we're going and then I'll let you kill me like a good boy. I don't have any shuck thing to live for anyway."

He looked directly at Teresa when he said this, tried to put as much spite into his words as possible. He still held on to a little hope that somehow this would end up making sense, but either way, after how he'd been treated, he wasn't in such a hot mood.

"Come on," Teresa said. "I'm sick of this. Let's get to the inside of the Pass so we can sleep the day off. Tonight we'll start heading through."

The girl with dark skin who'd helped put him in the sack spoke next. "And what about this guy we've been hauling around for the last few hours?"

"Don't worry, we'll kill him," Teresa replied. "We'll kill him just the way they told us to. It's his punishment for what he did to me."

CHAPTER 46

Thomas couldn't figure out what Teresa meant by her last statement. What had he done to her? But his mind went numb as they walked and walked and walked, apparently heading back to Group B's camp. A steady climb uphill, the effort burning his legs. A sheer cliff to their left kept them in the shade as they hiked, but everything was still red and brown and hot. Dry. Dusty. The girls gave him a few sips of water, but he was sure that every drop evaporated before it hit his stomach.

They reached a large indentation in the east wall just as the noon sun broke out overhead, a golden ball of fire bent on burning them to ashes. The shallow cave went about forty feet into the mountain face; it was obvious that this was their camp, and it looked like they'd been there for a day or two. Blankets strewn about, the remains of a fire, some trash piled on the edge. Only three people were there when they arrived—girls just like the others—which meant they'd felt they needed almost everyone to kidnap Thomas.

With the bows and arrows, the knives and machetes? It seemed almost silly. A few of them would've done just as well.

Along the way, Thomas had learned some things. The dark-skinned girl's name was Harriet, and the one who was always with her, with the reddish blond hair and white, white skin, was named Sonya. Though he couldn't tell for certain, he guessed that those two had mostly been in charge until Teresa had arrived. They acted with some authority, but always deferred to her in the end.

"Okay," Teresa said. "Let's tie him to that ugly tree." She pointed at the bone-white skeleton of an oak, its roots still clinging to the rocky soil even though it had to have been dead for years and years. "And we might as well feed him so he doesn't moan and groan all day and keep us awake."

Laying it on a little thick, isn't she? Thomas thought. Whatever her true intentions, her words had started to get a little ridiculous. And he couldn't deny it anymore—he was really starting to hate her, no matter what she'd said in the beginning.

He didn't fight as they tied his torso to the trunk, leaving his hands free. Once they had him good and secure they gave him a few granola bars and a bottle of water. No one spoke to him or met his gaze. And strangely, if he wasn't mistaken, he noticed that everyone looked a little guilty. He started eating, and as he did he carefully took in everything around him. His thoughts wandered all over the place as the rest of them began settling in to sleep out the remaining daylight. Something wasn't right about all this.

Teresa's display certainly didn't seem like an act. It never had. Was it possible that she was doing the exact opposite of what she'd told him—making him think he should trust her when her real plan had been and was to—

With a jolt he remembered the tag outside her door back in the dorm. *The Betrayer.* He'd completely forgotten about it until that moment. Things started to make more sense.

WICKED was the boss, here. They were the groups' only hope of surviving. If they'd really told her to kill him, would she do it? To save herself? And what was that line she'd spit out about his having done something to her? Could they even be manipulating her thoughts? Making her not like him anymore?

Then there was his tattoo and the signs in the city. The tattoo had warned him; the signs had told him he was the real leader. The label next to Teresa's door had been another warning.

Still—he had no weapons and he was tied to a tree. Group B outnumbered him by more than twenty and they all *had* weapons. Real easy.

Sighing, he finished up his food and felt a little better physically. And though he didn't quite know how everything added up, he had a new confidence that he was closer to understanding. And that he couldn't quit.

Harriet and Sonya had pallets laid out nearby; they kept sneaking looks at him as they readied for sleep. Again Thomas noticed those odd expressions of shame or guilt. He saw it as an opportunity to fight for his life with words.

"You guys don't really wanna kill me, do you?" He asked it in a tone that said he'd caught them in a lie. "Have you ever even killed anyone before?"

Harriet gave him a harsh glare, stopping just before she laid her head down on a wad of blankets. She propped herself up on her elbow. "Based on what Teresa told us, we escaped our Maze three days faster than your group did. Lost fewer people and killed more Grievers to do it. I think knocking off one little insignificant teenage boy won't be too tough."

"Think of the guilt you'll feel." He could only hope the thought would dig at them.

"We'll get over it." She stuck her tongue out at him—actually stuck her tongue out!—then put her head down and closed her eyes.

Sonya sat cross-legged, looking about as far from sleep as humanly possible. "We don't have a choice. WICKED said that was our only task.

If we don't do it, they won't let us in at the safe haven. We'll die out here in the Scorch."

Thomas shrugged. "Hey, I understand. Sacrifice me to save yourselves. Very noble."

She stared at him for a long time; he had to fight not to drop his gaze. She finally looked away and lay down with her back to him.

Teresa walked over, her face twisted in annoyance. "What are you talking about?"

"Nothing," mumbled Harriet. "Tell him to shut up."

"Shut up," Teresa said.

Thomas huffed a sarcastic laugh. "What're you gonna do, kill me if I don't?"

She didn't say anything, just kept looking at him, her face blank.

"Why do you hate me all of a sudden?" he asked. "What did I do to you?"

Sonya and Harriet both had turned to listen, looking back and forth between Thomas and Teresa.

"You know what you did," Teresa finally said. "So does everyone here—I told them all about it. But even still, I wouldn't have sunk to your level and tried to kill you. We're only doing that because we have no choice. Sorry. Life's tough."

Did something just flash in her eyes? Thomas wondered. What was she trying to tell him? "What are you talking about, *sink to my level*? I'd never kill a friend to save my own butt. Never."

"Me neither. Which is why I'm glad we're not friends." She started to turn away.

"So what'd I do to you?" Thomas asked quickly. "Sorry, I'm kind of havin' a memory lapse—ya know, we have those a lot around here. Remind me."

She twisted back around and glared at him with fiery eyes. "Don't insult me. Don't you dare sit there and act like nothing happened. Now shut up or I'll give you another bruise on that pretty face of yours."

She stomped away, and Thomas kept silent. He shifted until he was somewhat comfortable, his head leaning back on the dead wood of the tree. Everything about his current situation stank, but he was determined to figure it out and survive.

Eventually he slept.

CHAPTER 47

Thomas slept fitfully for a few hours, tossing and turning, trying to find a comfortable position on the hard rock. He finally fell into a deep slumber, and then came the dream.

Thomas is fifteen. He doesn't know how he knows this. Something to do with the timing of the memory. Is it a memory?

He and Teresa are standing in front of a massive bank of screens, each one showing various images from the Glade and the Maze. Some of the views are moving, and he knows why. These camera shots are coming from beetle blades, and every once in a while they have to change position. When they do, it's like looking through the eyes of a rat.

"I can't believe they're all dead," Teresa says.

Thomas is confused. Once again he doesn't quite understand what's happening. He's inside this boy who's supposed to be him, but he doesn't know what Teresa's talking about. Obviously not the Gladers—on one screen he can see Minho and Newt walking toward the forest; on another, Gally sitting on a bench. Then Alby yelling at someone Thomas doesn't recognize.

"We knew it would happen," he finally responds, not sure why he said it.

"It's still hard to take." They aren't looking at each other, just analyzing the screens. "Now it's up to us. And the people in the barracks."

"That's a good thing," Thomas says.

"I almost feel as sorry for them as I do for the Gladers. Almost."

Thomas wonders what this means as his younger dream version clears his throat. "Do you think we've learned enough? Do you really think we can pull this off with all the original Creators dead?"

"We have to, Tom." Teresa steps over to him and grabs his hand. He looks down at her but he can't read her expression. "Everything's in place. We have a year to train the replacements and get ready."

"But it's not right. How can we ask them to—"

Teresa rolls her eyes and squeezes his hand so hard it hurts. "They know what they're getting into. No more talking like that."

"Yeah." Somehow Thomas knows this version of himself in the vision he's seeing feels dead inside. His words mean nothing. "All that matters now are the patterns. The killzone. Nothing else."

Teresa nodded. "No matter how many die or get hurt. If the Variables don't work, they'll end up the same anyway. Everyone will."

"The patterns," Thomas says.

Teresa squeezes his hand. "The patterns."

When he woke up, the light dimming to a dull gray as the sun sank to a horizon he couldn't see, Harriet and Sonya were sitting just a few feet from him. Both staring at him strangely.

"Good evening," he said with false enthusiasm, the troubling dream still fresh in his mind. "Can I help you ladies?"

"We want to know what you know," Harriet said quietly.

The lingering fog of sleep quickly vanished. "Why should I help you?" He wanted to sit and think about what he'd dreamed, but he knew something had changed—he could see it in Harriet's gaze—and he couldn't pass up the chance to save himself.

"I don't think you have much choice," Harriet said. "But if you share whatever you've learned or figured out, maybe we can help *you*."

Thomas looked around for Teresa but couldn't see her. "Where is—"

Sonya interrupted him. "She said she wanted to scout the area to see if your friends followed us. Been gone for about an hour."

In his mind, Thomas could see the Teresa of his dream. Watching those screens, talking about dead Creators and the killzone. Talking about *patterns*. How did it all fit together?

"Forget how to talk?"

His eyes focused on Sonya. "No, um . . . does this mean you guys are having second thoughts about killing me?" The words sounded stupid to him, and he wondered how many people in the history of the world had ever asked a question like that.

Harriet smirked. "Don't go jumping to conclusions. And don't think we've gone all righteous. Let's just say we have our doubts and want to talk—but your odds are slim."

Sonya picked up her line of thought. "The smartest thing right now seems to be to do what we were told. There are a lot more of us than you. I mean, come on. If it was *your* decision, what would you do?"

"Pretty sure I'd choose the option of not killing myself."

"Don't be a jerk. This isn't funny. If you could choose, and the two options were you die or all of us die, which one would you pick? This is all about you or us."

Her face showed she was very serious, and the question hit Thomas like a thump to his chest. She was right, on some level. If that really would happen—they'd all die if they didn't get rid of him—then how could he expect them not to do it?

"You gonna answer?" Sonya pushed.

"I'm thinking." He paused, wiped some sweat off his forehead. Once again, the dream tried to creep to the front of his mind and he had to push it back. "Okay, I'm being honest here. I promise. If I were in your shoes, I'd choose not to kill me."

Harriet rolled her eyes. "Easy for you to say, since it's your life on the line."

"It's not just that. I think it's some kind of test and maybe you're not really supposed to do it." Thomas's heartbeat picked up—he really did mean what he said, but he doubted they'd believe him even if he tried to explain it. "Maybe we *should* share what we know, figure something out."

Harriet and Sonya exchanged a long look.

Sonya finally nodded; then Harriet said, "We've had our doubts about this whole thing from the beginning. Something about it isn't right. So yeah, you better talk. But let us get everybody over here first." They stood up to go rouse the others.

"Hurry, then," Thomas said, wondering if he really did have a chance to get out of this mess. "We better do this before Teresa gets back."

CHAPTER 48

It didn't take long for them to gather everyone—Thomas figured the intrigue of hearing what the dead-guy-walking had to say was just too good to pass up. The girls stood in a tight group in front of him; he remained tied to the ugly, lifeless tree.

"All right," Harriet said. "You talk first, then we will."

Thomas nodded and cleared his throat. He began talking even though he hadn't totally planned what to say yet.

"All I know about your group is what I learned from Aris. And it seems like we all went through pretty much the same thing inside the Maze. But since we escaped, lots of things have been different. And I'm not sure what you know about WICKED."

Sonya cut in. "Not much."

This encouraged Thomas, made him feel like he had an advantage. And it seemed a big mistake for Sonya to have admitted what she did. "Well, I've learned a lot about them. All of us are special in some way—we're being tested or something because they have plans for us." He paused then, but no one showed much of a reaction, so he went on.

"A lot of the things they're doing to us don't make sense because they're just part of the trials—what WICKED calls the Variables. Seeing how we react in certain situations. I don't understand all of it, not even close, but I think this whole thing about killing me is just another layer. Or another lie. So . . . I think this is just another Variable to see what we'll all do."

"In other words," Harriet said, "you want us to risk *our* lives because of this brilliant deduction."

"Don't you see? Killing me has no *point*. Maybe it's a test for you, I don't know. But I do know that I can help you if I'm alive, not if I'm dead."

"Or," Harriet replied, "we're being tested to see if we have the guts to kill our competitors' leader. Isn't *that* the whole point? See which group succeeds? Weed out the weak and leave the strong?"

"I haven't even *been* the leader—Minho has." Thomas shook his head adamantly. "No, think about this. How are you showing any strength by killing me? I'm way outnumbered and you have all these weapons. How does that prove who's stronger?"

"Then what *does* it have to do with?" a girl from the back called out.

Thomas paused, choosing his words carefully. "I think it's a test to see if you'll think for yourself, change plans, make rational decisions. And the more of us there are, the better odds we have of making it to the safe haven. Killing me makes no sense, does no one any good. You've proven any power you needed to by capturing me. Show them you won't blindly take it all the way."

He stopped, relaxed back against the tree. He couldn't think of anything else. It was up to them now. He'd given it his best shot.

"Interesting stuff," Sonya said. "Sounds a lot like something a person who's desperate not to die would say."

Thomas shrugged. "I really feel like it's the truth. I think that if you kill me, you'll have failed the real test WICKED is throwing at you."

"Yeah, I *bet* you think that," Harriet said. She stood up. "Look, to be honest, we've been thinking the same types of things. But we wanted to see what you had to say. Sun should be down soon, and I'm sure Teresa will be back any minute. We'll talk about it when she gets here."

Thomas spoke up quickly, worried that Teresa wouldn't be swayed.

"No! I mean, she's the one who seems the most gung ho about killing me." He said this even though deep down he hoped he didn't mean it. As badly as she'd treated him, surely she wasn't serious about taking it all the way to murder. "I think you guys should make the decision."

"Calm down," Harriet said, a half-smile on her face. "If we decide not to kill you, there's nothing she can freaking do about it. But if we . . ." She stopped, a strange look flashing across her face. Was she worried she'd said too much? "We'll figure it out."

Thomas tried not to show his relief. He might have appealed to their pride a little bit, but he tried not to let his hopes get too high.

Thomas watched as the girls gathered their belongings and packed them into backpacks—*Where'd they get* those? he wondered—readying for the night's journey, to wherever that might be. Murmurs and whispers of conversation floated through the air as people kept glancing his way, obviously discussing what he'd said.

The darkness grew deeper and deeper, and Teresa finally appeared from the direction they'd come in earlier that day. She noticed right away that something was different, probably by the way everyone kept looking between her and Thomas.

"What?" she asked, the same hard look on her face she'd worn since the day before.

It was Harriet who answered. "We need to talk."

Teresa looked confused, but went to the far side of the recess in the cliff with the rest of the group. Furious whispers immediately filled the air, but Thomas couldn't make out a word anybody said. His stomach clenched in anticipation of the verdict.

From where he stood he could see that the conversation had started to get passionate, and Teresa looked as riled up as anyone. He watched her expression intensify as she tried to make some point. It seemed like it was her against the rest of them, which made Thomas very nervous.

Finally, just as nightfall was almost complete, Teresa turned, stomped from the group of girls, and started walking away from the camp, heading north. She had her spear slung over one shoulder, a backpack over the other. Thomas watched her go until she disappeared between the narrow walls of the Pass.

He glanced back at the group, many of whom looked relieved, and Harriet came walking over. Without saying a word, she knelt down and untied the rope securing him to the tree.

"Well?" Thomas finally asked. "Did you guys decide anything?"

Harriet didn't answer until she'd completely freed him; then she sat back on her heels and looked at him, her dark eyes reflecting the faint light of the stars and moon. "It's your lucky day. We decided not to kill your puny butt after all. It can't be a coincidence that we've all been thinking the same things deep down."

Thomas didn't feel the expected rush of relief. In that moment he realized that he'd known that was what they would decide all along.

"But I tell you what," Harriet said as she stood up, holding a hand out to help him do the same. "Teresa does *not* like you. I'd watch my back around her if I were you."

Thomas let Harriet pull him up, confusion and hurt warring for dominance inside him.

Teresa really did want him dead.

CHAPTER 49

Thomas was quiet as he ate with Group B and prepared to leave. Soon they started making their way through the dark pass of the mountains, heading for the safe haven that was supposed to wait on the other side. It felt odd to suddenly be friendly with these people after what they'd done to him, but they acted like nothing unusual had ever happened. They treated him like, well, like one of the girls.

But he did keep his distance a little, hanging toward the back, wondering if he could fully trust their change of heart about him. What was he supposed to do? Even if Harriet and the others *let* him leave, should he try to find his own group, Minho and Newt and everyone else? He desperately wanted to be with his friends and Brenda again. But he knew time was running out, and he had no food or water to make it on his own. He had to hope they'd find their own way to the safe haven.

So he kept walking, staying close to Group B but not too close.

A couple of hours went by, nothing but tall cliffs of stone and the crunching of dirt and rock under his feet to keep him company. It felt good to move again, to stretch his legs and muscles. The deadline was fast approaching, though. And who knew what obstacle might spring up next? Or had the girls planned something else for him? He thought a lot about the dreams he'd been having, but still couldn't put enough together to truly understand what was going on.

Harriet drifted back until the two of them were walking side by side.

"Sorry we dragged you through the desert in a bag," she said. He couldn't see her face in the dimming light very well, but he imagined a smirk there.

"Oh, no problem, it felt good to take a load off for a while." Thomas knew he had to play the part, show some humor. He couldn't trust the girls completely yet, but he had no other options.

She laughed, a sound that put him at ease a bit. "Yeah, well, the man from WICKED gave us very specific instructions about you. But it was Teresa who got all obsessed about it. Almost like killing you was her idea."

This dug at Thomas, but he finally had a chance to learn some things and he wasn't going to let that go. "Did the guy have a white suit and kind of look like a rat turned human?"

"Yeah," she said without hesitating. "Same guy who talked to your group?"

Thomas nodded. "What were the . . . specific instructions he gave you?"

"Well, most of our trip has been through underground tunnels. That's why you didn't see us in the desert. The first thing we were supposed to do was that weird thing where you and Teresa spoke in that building on the south side of the city. Remember?"

Thomas's stomach fell. She'd been with her group at that point? "Uh, yeah, I remember."

"Well, you've probably figured it out, but all of that was an act. Kind of a prepper to give you some false security. She even told us they somehow . . . *controlled* her long enough to make her kiss you. Is that true?"

Thomas stopped walking, bent down and put his hands on his knees. Something had sucked the breath right out of him. That was it. He'd officially and completely lost any trace of doubt. Teresa had turned against him. Or maybe she had never really been on his side.

"I know this sucks," Harriet said softly. "It seems like you used to feel really close to her."

Thomas stood up again, slowly sucked in a long breath. "I . . . just . . . I had hoped it was the other way around. That they were forcing her to try to hurt us, that she broke away long enough to . . . to kiss me."

Harriet put a hand on his arm. "Ever since she joined us, she's made you out to be a monster who did something really awful to her, only she'd never tell us what it was. But I gotta tell ya—you're not anything like how she described you. That's probably the real reason we changed our minds."

Thomas closed his eyes and tried to calm his heart. Then he shook it off and started walking again. "Okay, tell me the rest. I need to hear it. All of it."

Harriet got in stride with him. "Everything else about the instructions to kill you had to do with catching you in the desert like we did and bringing you back here. We were even told to keep you in the bag until we got out of Group A's sight. Then . . . well, then the big day was supposed to be the day after tomorrow. There's supposed to be a place built into the mountain on the north side. A special place to . . . kill you."

Thomas wanted to stop again but kept his feet moving. "A *place*? What does that mean?"

"I don't know. He just told us we'd know what to do when we got there." She paused, then snapped her fingers as if she'd just thought of something. "I bet that's where she went earlier."

"Why? How close are we to the other side?"

"No idea, actually."

They fell into silence and kept walking.

★ ★ ★

It took longer than Thomas would've thought. They were in the middle of the second night of marching when shouts up ahead announced that they'd reached the end of the Pass. Thomas, who'd stayed at the back of the group, broke into a run to catch up; he desperately wanted to see what lay on the north side of the range. One way or another, his fate waited there.

The group of girls had clustered in a wide swath of broken rock that fanned out from the narrow canyon of the Pass before dropping in a steep slope to the bottom of the mountain far below. The three-quarter moon shone down on the valley in front of them, making it look dark purple and eerie. And very flat. With nothing for miles and miles but sparse, dead land.

Absolutely nothing.

No sign of anything that could be a safe haven. And they were supposed to be within a few miles of it.

"Maybe we just can't see it." Thomas didn't know who said it, but he knew every person there understood exactly why she did. Trying to hold on to hope.

"Yeah," Harriet added, sounding upbeat. "It might just be another entrance to one of their underground tunnels. I'm sure it's there."

"How many more miles do you think we have left?" Sonya asked.

"Can't be more than ten, based on where we started and how far the man said we had to go," Harriet answered. "Probably more like seven or eight. I thought we'd come out over here and we'd see a nice big building with a smiley face on it."

Thomas had been searching the darkness the whole time, but he couldn't see anything, either. Just a sea of black stretching to the horizon, where it seemed like a curtain of stars had been pulled down. And no sign of Teresa anywhere.

"Well," Sonya announced. "Not much choice but to keep heading north. We should've known better than to expect something easy. Maybe we can make it to the bottom of the mountain by sunrise. Sleep on flat ground."

The others agreed with her and were just about to set off down a barely visible footpath leading from the fan of rock when Thomas spoke up. "Where's Teresa?"

Harriet looked back at him, the moonlight bathing her face in a pale luminescence. "At this point, I don't really care. If she's a big enough girl to go runnin' around when she doesn't get her way, she's big enough to catch up and find us when she gets over it. Come on."

They started off, heading down the switchback-laden path, the loose soil and rock crunching underfoot. Thomas couldn't help but take a look behind him, searching the mountain face and the narrow entrance to the Pass for signs of Teresa. He was so confused about everything, but still had a strange urge to see her. He gazed across the dark slopes, but saw only dim shadows and reflections of the moonlight's glow.

He turned and started walking, almost relieved he hadn't spotted her.

The group made their way down the mountain, crisscrossing back and forth on the trail in silence. Thomas lingered in the back again, surprised at how blank his mind felt. How numb. He had absolutely no idea where his friends were, no idea what dangers might be waiting for him.

After an hour or so of traveling, his legs starting to burn from the awkward downhill walk, the group came across a pocket of dead trees that arrowed up the mountain in a big swath. It almost looked as if at one time a waterfall might have irrigated to the odd formation of trees. Though if it had, the last drop had long since surrendered to the Scorch.

Thomas, still last in line, was just passing the far side of the trees when a voice spoke his name, startling him so much he almost tripped. He turned sharply to see Teresa step out from behind a thick knot of white wood, spear gripped in her right hand, her face hidden in shadow. The others must not have heard, because they kept walking.

"Teresa," he whispered. "What . . ." He didn't even know what to say.

"Tom, we need to talk," she responded, almost sounding like the girl he thought he knew. "Don't worry about them, just come with me." She gestured to the trees behind her with a quick jerk of her head.

He looked back to the girls of Group B, still heading away from him, then turned to face Teresa again. "Maybe we should—"

"Just come on. The act is over." She turned away without waiting for a response and stepped into the lifeless forest.

Thomas thought hard for two whole seconds, his mind spinning in confusion, instinct screaming at him not to do it. But he followed her.

CHAPTER 50

The trees might have been dead, but their branches still pulled on Thomas's clothes and scratched at his skin. The wood shone white in the moonlight, and the streaks and pools of shadow across the ground gave the whole place a haunted feel. Teresa kept walking in silence, floating up the mountainside like an apparition.

Finally, he found the courage to speak. "Where're we going? And you really expect me to believe all that was an act? Why didn't you stop when everybody else agreed not to kill me?"

But her reply was strange. Barely turning her head, she asked, "You've met Aris, right?" She didn't break stride, just kept moving.

Thomas stopped for a second, completely taken aback. "*Aris?* How do you even know about him? What's he got to do with this?" He hurried to catch up with her again, curious but dreading the answer for some reason.

She didn't respond right away, picking her way through a particularly tight pack of branches; one flew back and smacked him in the face after she let it fly. Once through, she finally stopped and turned to him, right where a shaft of moonlight illuminated her face. She looked unhappy.

"I happen to know Aris very well," she said in a tight voice. "Much better than you're going to like. Not only was he a big part of my life before the Maze, he and I can speak in our minds, just like you and I used to do. Even when I was in the Glade, we communicated all the time. And we knew they'd eventually put us back together."

Thomas searched for a response. What she'd said was so unexpected he thought it must be a joke. Another trick by WICKED.

She waited, arms folded, as if she enjoyed seeing him struggle to speak.

"You're lying," he finally said. "That's all you do is lie. I don't understand why, or what's going on, but—"

"Oh, come *on,* Tom," she said. "How could you *possibly* be so stupid? After all that's happened to you, how could anything surprise you anymore? Everything about us was part of some ridiculous test. And it's over. Aris and I are going to do what we were told to do, and life goes on. WICKED's all that matters now. That's it."

"What are you *talking* about?" He couldn't have felt any emptier.

Teresa looked past him, over his shoulder. He heard the snap of breaking twigs on the ground, and somehow he held on to his dignity enough to not turn around to see who had snuck up on him.

"Tom," Teresa said. "Aris is right behind you, and he has a very big knife. Try anything and he'll slice your neck. You're coming with us and you're gonna do exactly what we tell you. Understand?"

Thomas stared at her, hoping the rage he felt inside showed clearly on his face. He'd never felt so angry in his life—what he could remember of it.

"Say hi, Aris," she said. And then, the worst thing yet—she smiled.

"Hi, Tommy," the boy said from behind. It was definitely him, just not as friendly as before. "Such a thrill to be with you again." The point of his knife just touched Thomas's back.

Thomas remained silent.

"Well," Teresa said. "At least you're acting like a grown-up about this. Just keep following me—we're almost there."

"Where are we going?" Thomas asked in a steely voice.

"You'll find out soon enough." She turned and started walking through the trees again, using her spear like a staff.

Thomas hurried to follow before Aris got the satisfaction of pushing him. The trees got thicker and closer together, and the moonlight flitted away. Darkness pressed in, sucking light and life right out of him.

They reached a cave, the thick copse of trees serving as a tight wall at its entrance. Thomas didn't have any warning—one minute they were picking their way through prickly branches, the next they were in a tall, narrow hole in the side of the mountain. A dull light source shone from deep inside, a sickly green rectangle that made Teresa look like a zombie when she moved to the side for the other two to enter.

Aris stepped around him, his blade aimed like a gun at Thomas's chest as he backed to the wall opposite Teresa and leaned against it. Thomas could do nothing but look back and forth between them. Two people who every instinct had told him were his friends. Until now.

"Well, we're here," Teresa said, looking at Aris.

He didn't take his eyes off Thomas. "Yep, we're here, all right. You're serious about him talking the others into sparing him? What is he, some kind of superpsychologist?"

"It kind of helped, actually. Made it easier to get him here." Teresa threw a condescending glance toward Thomas, then crossed the cave to Aris. As Thomas watched, she stood on her toes to kiss Aris on the cheek and grinned. "I'm so glad we're finally back together."

Aris smiled. He shot Thomas a look of warning, then risked looking away long enough to tilt his head toward Teresa. And kiss her on the lips.

Thomas tore his eyes away and closed them. Her pleas for him to trust her, her quick whisper to hang in there—it had all been to get him here. To bring him more easily to this point.

So that she could fulfill some evil purpose concocted by WICKED.

"Get it over with," he finally said, not daring to open his eyes again. He didn't want to know what they were doing, why they were quiet. But he wanted them to think he'd given up. "Just get it over with."

When they didn't answer, he couldn't help but take a peek. They were whispering to each other, stealing kisses between words. Something like burning oil filled his stomach.

He looked away again, focusing on the odd source of light in the back of the cave. A large rectangle of pale green, set into the dark stone, pulsed with an ethereal glow. It was as tall as an average man, maybe four feet wide. Stains streaked across its dull surface—a grimy window to something that looked like radioactive sludge, glowing and dangerous.

Out of the corner of his eye, he saw Teresa step away from Aris, their lovefest evidently over. He looked at her, wondering if his eyes showed just how much she had crushed him.

"Tom," she said. "If it helps, I'm really sorry I hurt you. I did what I had to do back in the Maze, and being all buddy-buddy seemed like my best shot at getting the memories we needed to figure out that code and escape. And I didn't have much choice here in the Scorch. All we had to do was get you here to pass the Trials. *And it's either you or us.*"

Teresa paused for a second, and there was a strange glint in her eye. "Aris is my best friend, Tom," she said calmly, evenly.

And that was what finally made Thomas crack. "I . . . don't . . . *care!*" he screamed, though nothing could've been further from the truth.

"I'm just saying. If you care about me, then you should understand why I'd be willing to do whatever it takes to make it through this and keep him safe. Wouldn't you have done the same for me?"

Thomas couldn't believe how far away he felt from the girl he'd once thought was his best friend. Even in all of his memories—it was always the two of them. "What is this? Are you trying to come up with all the ways possible in the universe to hurt me? Just shut your shuck mouth and do whatever it is you brought me here to do!" His chest heaved with angry breaths, his heart thumping a deadly pace.

"Fine," she replied. "Aris, let's open the door. Time for Tom to go."

CHAPTER 51

Thomas was done talking, to either of them. But he certainly wasn't going down without a fight. He resolved to wait and watch for the best opportunity.

Aris kept his knife pointed at him as Teresa made her way toward the big rectangle of illuminated green glass. Thomas couldn't deny his curiosity about the door.

She reached a point where the glow silhouetted her whole body. It made her edges fuzzy, as if she were dissolving. She walked across the cave until she'd left the light completely, then reached for the stone wall, started punching a finger on what had to be some sort of keypad that Thomas couldn't see.

She finished up and stepped back toward him.

"We'll see if that actually works," Aris said.

"It will," Teresa replied.

A loud pop sounded, followed by a sharp hiss. Thomas watched as the right edge of the glass began to swing outward like a door. As it opened, wispy streams of white mist swirled through the widening crack, almost immediately evaporating into nothing. It was like a long-abandoned freezer releasing its cold air into the heat of the night. Darkness lurked inside even as the rectangle of glass continued to emit its strange green radiance.

So the door wasn't a window at all, Thomas thought. Just a green door. Maybe toxic waste *wasn't* in his near future. He hoped.

The door finally stopped, thumping with an icy screech against the wall of jagged rock. A pit of black now lay where the door had once been—there wasn't enough light to reveal what lay inside. The mist had completely stopped as well. Thomas felt an abyss of anxiety open up beneath him.

"Do you have a flashlight?" Aris asked.

Teresa put her spear on the ground, then pulled her backpack off and dug through its contents. A moment later she pulled out a flashlight and flicked it on.

Aris nodded back toward the opening. "Take a look while I watch him. Don't try anything, Thomas. I'm pretty sure what they have planned for you is easier than getting stabbed to death."

Thomas didn't answer, keeping his pathetic oath to stay silent from here on out. He thought about the knife and whether he could take it from Aris.

Teresa had stepped up right to the side of the gaping rectangular hole; she shone her flashlight inside. Swept it up and down, left to right. It cut through a fine cloud of mist as she did so, but the dwindling moisture was thin enough to reveal the interior.

It was a small room, only several feet deep. Its walls appeared to be made of some silvery metal, their surfaces broken up by small protrusions maybe an inch high, each ending in a black hole. The little knobs or spouts were set about five inches apart, making a square grid across the walls.

Teresa turned to Aris, flicking off the flashlight as she did so. "Looks about right," she said.

Aris snapped his head back to look at Thomas, who had been so focused on the strange room he'd missed another chance to do something. "Exactly like they said it would be."

"So . . . I guess this is it?" Teresa asked.

Aris nodded, then switched his knife to the other hand, holding it more tightly. "This is it. Thomas, be a good boy and go on inside. Who knows, maybe this is all a big test and once you're in they'll let ya go and we can all have a happy reunion."

"Shut up, Aris," Teresa said. It was actually the first thing she'd said in quite some time that didn't make Thomas want to punch her. She then turned back to Thomas, avoiding his eyes. "Let's get this over with."

Aris waved his blade, indicating that Thomas should walk forward. "Come on. Don't make me drag you in."

Thomas looked at him, struggling to keep a blank expression as his mind spun in a million directions. A surge of panic boiled inside him. It was now or never. Fight or die.

He turned his gaze to the open doorway and started slowly walking toward it. Three steps and he'd halved the distance. Teresa had straightened, her arms tensed in case he caused trouble. Aris kept his weapon trained on Thomas's neck.

Another step. Another. Now Aris stood directly to his left, just two or three feet away. Teresa was behind him, out of sight, the open doorway and the odd silver room with walls covered in holes right in front of him.

He stopped, looked sideways at Aris. "What did Rachel look like as she bled to death?" It was a gamble, a pitch to throw him off.

Shocked and hurt, Aris froze, giving Thomas the split second he needed.

He jumped toward the other boy and swung his left arm in an arc to smack the knife out of his hand. It clattered across the rocks. Thomas slammed his right fist into Aris's stomach, sending him to the ground, desperately trying to suck in a breath.

The click of metal against rock stopped Thomas from kicking the boy at his feet. He looked up to see that Teresa had picked up her spear.

They locked eyes for an instant; then she charged him. Thomas threw his hands up to protect himself but it was too late—the butt of the weapon swung through the air and smacked him on the side of the head. Stars floated before his eyes as he fell, fighting to stay conscious. As soon as he hit the ground, he scrambled to his hands and knees to get away.

But he heard Teresa scream, and a second later the wood came crashing down on the top of his skull. With a thump Thomas collapsed again; something wet oozed through his hair and trickled onto both temples. Pain tore through his head, as if an axe had been driven straight into his brain. It spread to the rest of his body, making him nauseated. He somehow pushed off the ground and flopped onto his back to see Teresa with the weapon raised above her once more.

"Get in the room, Thomas," she said through heavy breaths. "Get in the room or I'll hit you again. I swear I'll keep doing it till you pass out or bleed to death."

Aris had recovered and gotten back to his feet; he stood right next to her.

Thomas reared both legs back and kicked out, connecting with a knee on both of them. They screamed and crumpled, falling on top of each other. The physical effort sent a horrible rush of pain raging through Thomas. White flashes blinded him; the world was spinning. He groaned as he struggled to move, got back on his stomach, tried to get his hands under himself. He'd barely pushed a few inches off the ground when Aris landed on his back, slamming him down. Soon the boy's arm wrapped around Thomas's neck, squeezing.

"You're going in that room," Aris spit in his ear. "Help me, Teresa!"

Thomas couldn't find any strength to fight them off. The double blow to his head had somehow sapped him of everything, as if all his muscles had gone dormant because his brain didn't have enough energy to tell them what to do. Soon Teresa had grabbed both of his arms; she started dragging him toward the open doorway, Aris pushing him. Thomas kicked feebly. Rocks dug into his skin.

"Don't do this," he whispered, giving in to desperation. Every word sent a surge of pain across his nerves. "Please . . ." All he saw now were flashes of white on black. A concussion, he realized. He had a terrible, terrible concussion.

He was barely aware of his body crossing the threshold, of Teresa resting his arms against the cool metal of the back wall, stepping over him, helping Aris flip his legs up and over so that he now lay in a heap, facing the side. Thomas couldn't even find the strength to look at them.

"No," he said, but it was merely a whisper. The image of the sick boy, Ben, being Banished back in the Glade swam into his brain. An odd time to think it, but now he knew how that kid had felt in those last seconds before the walls slammed shut, trapping him in the Maze forever.

"No," he repeated; it was so quiet he couldn't imagine they heard him. He ached from head to toe.

"You're so stubborn," he heard Teresa say. "You had to make it harder on yourself! Harder on all of us!"

"Teresa," Thomas whispered. He dug through the pain and tried to call out to her telepathically, even though it hadn't worked in a long time. *Teresa.*

I'm sorry, Tom, she answered back, in his mind once again. *But thanks for being our sacrifice.*

He hadn't realized the door was swinging closed, but it slammed shut just as that last horrible word floated across his darkening thoughts.

CHAPTER 52

The back of the door they'd shut on him glowed green, turning the small room into a creepy, sickening prison. He might've cried, might've gushed tears and snot and wailed like a baby if his head didn't hurt so much. The pain drilled through his skull, and his eyes felt as if they were boiling in lava.

But even then, through all that, the deeper ache of truly losing Teresa gnawed away at his heart. He just couldn't let himself cry.

He lost all concept of time as he lay there. It was as if whoever was behind it all wanted to give him a chance to reflect on what had happened while he waited for the end. On how Teresa's message to trust her no matter what had ended up being a cruel trick that only magnified her two-faced treachery.

An hour passed. Maybe two or three. Maybe only thirty minutes. He had no idea.

And then the hissing started.

The faint light of the glowing door revealed sprays of mist shooting from the holes that dotted the metal walls in front of him. He turned his head, sending a fresh wave of pain across his skull, and saw that all the openings were expelling similar jets of fog.

And it all hissed like a squirming nest of poisonous vipers.

So this is it? he thought. After everything he'd been through, after all the mysteries and fighting and fleeting moments of hope, they were just going to kill him with some kind of poison gas? Stupid, that was what this was. Stupid. He'd battled Grievers and Cranks, survived a gunshot and infection. WICKED. They were the ones who'd saved him! And now they were just going to gas him to death?

He sat up, actually crying out from the jolt of pain it caused. He looked around, looked for anything he might be able to . . .

Tired. So tired.

Something in his chest felt wrong. Sick.

The gas.

Tired. Hurt. Body exhausted.

Breathing in gas.

Couldn't help himself.

So . . . tired . . .

Inside him. Wrong.

Teresa. Why did it have to end that way?

Tired . . .

Somewhere on the edge of his consciousness, he was aware of his head thumping against the floor.

Betrayal.

So . . .

Tired . . .

CHAPTER 53

Thomas didn't know if he was dead or alive, but it felt like he was asleep. Aware of himself, but as if through a haze. He slipped into yet another memory-dream.

Thomas is sixteen. He's standing in front of Teresa and some girl he doesn't recognize.

And Aris.

Aris?

All three of them are looking at him with grim faces. Teresa is crying.

"It's time to go," Thomas says.

Aris nods. "Into the Swipe, then into the Maze."

Teresa does nothing but wipe away some tears.

Thomas reaches out a hand and Aris shakes it. Then Thomas does the same with the girl he doesn't know.

Then Teresa rushes forward and pulls him into an embrace. She's sobbing, and Thomas realizes that he's also crying. His tears wet her hair as he hugs her tightly.

"You have to go now," Aris says.

Thomas looks at him. Waits. Tries to enjoy this moment with Teresa. His last moment of full memory. They won't be like this again for a very long time.

Teresa looks up at him. "It's going to work. It's all going to work."

"I know," Thomas says. He feels a sadness that makes every last bit of him ache.

Aris opens a door and beckons for Thomas to follow him. Thomas does, but manages to look back at Teresa one last time. Tries to look hopeful.

"See ya tomorrow," he says.

Which is true, and it hurts.

The dream faded, and Thomas fell into the blackest sleep of his life.

CHAPTER 54

Whispers in the dark.

That was what Thomas heard when he began returning to consciousness. Low but harsh, like sandpaper rubbing across his eardrums. He didn't understand any of it. It was so dark it took him a second to realize that his eyes were open.

Something cool and hard pressed against his face. The ground. He hadn't moved since the gas had knocked him out. Shockingly, his head didn't hurt anymore. In fact, nothing did. Instead, a feeling of refreshed euphoria swam through him, almost made him dizzy. Maybe he was just happy to be alive.

He got his hands under himself and pushed up into a sitting position. A look around did nothing—not even the faintest glimmer of light broke up the utter darkness. He wondered what had happened to the green glow of the door that Teresa had shut on him.

Teresa.

His elation drained away. Remembering what she'd done to him. But then . . .

He wasn't dead. Unless the afterlife was just a crappy room of blackness.

He rested for a few minutes, letting his mind wake up and settle before he finally got to his feet and started feeling around. Three cool metal walls with evenly spaced upraised holes. One smooth wall that felt like plastic. He was definitely in that same little room.

He pounded on the door. "Hey! Anybody out there?"

His thoughts started spinning. The memory-dreams, several now—so much to process, so many questions. The things that had first come back to him with the Changing in the Maze were slowly starting to come into focus, solidify. He'd been part of WICKED's plans, part of all this. He and Teresa had been close—best friends, even. All of it had seemed right. Doing these things for the greater good.

Only, Thomas didn't feel so good about it now. All he felt was anger and shame. How could anything justify what they'd done? What WICKED—what *they*—were doing? Though he certainly didn't think of himself this way, he and the others were just kids. Kids! He didn't like himself very much anymore. He wasn't sure when he'd reached this turning point. But something had cracked within him.

And then there was Teresa. How could he ever have felt so much for her?

Something cracked, then hissed, interrupting his line of thinking.

The door started to open, slowly swinging outward. Teresa stood there in the pale light of early morning, her face streaked with tears. As soon as there was enough room, she threw her arms around him, pressing her face against his neck.

"I'm so sorry, Tom," she said; her tears were wet against his skin. "I'm so, so, so sorry. They said they'd kill you if we didn't do everything just like they told us. No matter how horrible. I'm sorry, Tom!"

Thomas couldn't answer, couldn't bring himself to hug back. Betrayal. The sign on Teresa's door, the conversation between the people in his dreams. Pieces were falling into place. For all he knew, she was just trying to trick him again. The betrayal meant he couldn't trust her anymore, and his heart told him he couldn't forgive her.

On some level, he realized that Teresa had kept her initial promise to him after all. She had done those awful things against her will. What she had said in the shack had been true. But he also knew that things could never, never be the same between them.

He finally pushed Teresa away. The sincerity in her blue eyes did little to diminish his lingering doubt. "Uh . . . maybe you should tell me what happened."

"I told you to trust me," she answered. "I told you that bad, bad things would happen to you. But the bad stuff was all an act." She smiled then, and it was so pretty Thomas longed to find a way to forget what she'd done.

"Yeah, but you didn't seem to struggle too much, beating the klunk out of me with a spear and throwing me into a gas chamber." He couldn't hide the mistrust raging in his heart. He glanced at Aris, who looked sheepish, like he'd intruded on a private conversation.

"I'm sorry," the boy said.

"Why didn't you tell me we knew each other before?" Thomas responded. "What . . ." He didn't know what to say.

"It was all an *act,* Tom," Teresa said. "You have to believe us. We were promised from the very beginning that you wouldn't die. That this chamber thing had its own purposes and then it'd be over. I'm so sorry."

Thomas looked back at the still-gaping door. "I think I need some time to process all this." Teresa wanted him to forgive her—for everything to be how it used to be immediately. And instinct told him to hide his bitter feelings, but it was hard.

"What happened in there, anyway?" Teresa asked.

Thomas returned his gaze to her. "How about you talk first, then me. I think I earned that much."

She tried to take his hand but he moved it, pretending he had an itch on his neck. When he saw the flash of hurt cross her face, he felt the slightest bit of vindication.

"Look," she said. "You're right. You deserve an explanation. I think it's okay to tell you everything now—not that we know too much of the *why*."

Aris cleared his throat, an obvious interjection. "But, um, we better do it while walking. Or running. We only have a few hours left. Today is the day."

Those words jarred Thomas completely out of his stupor. He looked down at his watch. Only five and a half hours remained if Aris was right that they'd reached the end of the two weeks—Thomas had kind of lost track himself, not knowing how long he'd been in the chamber. And none of this other stuff mattered at all if they didn't make it to the safe haven. Hopefully Minho and the others had already found it.

"Fine. Let's just forget this for now," he said, then changed the subject. "Is anything different out there? I mean, I saw it in the dark, but—"

"We know," Teresa interrupted. "There's no sign of a building. Nothing. It looks even worse in the daylight. Just forever and ever of flat wasteland. There isn't a tree or a hill, much less any *safe haven*."

Thomas looked at Aris, then back at Teresa. "Then what're we supposed to do? Where do we go?" He thought of Minho and Newt, the Gladers, Brenda and Jorge. "Have you seen any of the others?"

Aris answered. "All the girls from my group are down there, walking north like they're supposed to, already a couple miles out. We spotted your friends at the base of the mountain a mile or two west of here. Can't tell for sure, but looks like no one new is missing, and they're heading in the same direction as the girls."

Relief filled Thomas. His friends had made it—hopefully all of them.

"We gotta get moving," Teresa said. "Just because nothing's there doesn't mean anything. Who knows what WICKED is up to? We just have to do what they told us. Come on."

Thomas had been experiencing a brief moment of wanting to give up, to sit down and forget it all—let whatever was going to happen, happen. But almost as fast as it came out, it disappeared. "Okay, let's go. But you better tell me everything you know."

"I will," she answered. "You guys up for running once we're out of these dead trees?"

Aris nodded, but Thomas rolled his eyes. "*Please*. I'm a Runner."

She raised her eyebrows. "Well, then, we'll just have to see who stops before who."

In answer, Thomas stepped out of the small clearing and into the lifeless forest first, refusing to dwell on the storm of memories and emotions that tried to weigh him down.

The sky didn't lighten much as morning ticked on. Clouds blew in, gray and thick, so thick that Thomas wouldn't have had any idea of the time if it weren't for his watch.

Clouds. Last time that had happened . . .

Maybe this storm wouldn't be so bad. Maybe.

Once they left the dense pack of dead trees, they didn't pause. An obvious trail led toward the valley below, switching back and forth like a jagged scar on the mountain face. Thomas estimated it would take a couple of hours just to get to the bottom—running on the steep, slippery slopes looked like a good way to break an ankle or leg. And if that happened, they'd never make it.

The three agreed they'd hike quickly but safely, then book it once they were on flat land. They started down—Aris, then Thomas, then Teresa. The dark clouds churned above them as wind gusted in seemingly every direction. Just as Aris had said, Thomas could see two separate packs of people in the desert below—his Glader friends, not far from the base of the mountain, then Group B, maybe a mile or two farther out.

Once again Thomas was relieved, and his step felt lighter as he made his way.

After the third switchback, Teresa spoke up from behind him. "So, guess I'll start the story from where we left off."

Thomas just nodded. He couldn't believe how good he felt physically—his stomach miraculously full, the pain from being beaten up gone, fresh air and brisk wind to make him feel alive. He had no idea what was in that gas he'd breathed, but it seemed far from poisonous. Still, his mistrust of Teresa itched at him; he didn't want to be overly nice.

"It all started right when we were talking to each other in the middle of the night—that very first one right after the rescue from the Maze. I was kind of half asleep and then these people were in my room, all dressed funny. Creepy. Baggy jumpsuits and goggles."

"Serious?" Thomas asked over his shoulder. They sounded just like the people he'd seen after being shot.

"Freaked me out—and I tried calling to you, but it suddenly cut out. The telepathy thing, I mean. I don't know how I knew, but it just vanished. From then until now it's only come and gone in spurts."

Then she spoke in his mind. *You can hear me perfectly now, right?*

Yeah. Did you and Aris really talk while we were in the Maze?

Well . . .

She trailed off, and when Thomas looked back at her, she had a worried look on her face.

What's wrong? he asked, turning his attention back to the trail before he did something stupid like trip and go tumbling down the mountain.

I don't wanna go into that yet.

"Go—" He stopped himself before he said it out loud. *Go into what?*

Teresa didn't answer.

Thomas tried as hard as he could to shout inside her mind. *Go into what!*

She stayed silent a few seconds longer before finally answering.

Yeah, he and I have been talking since I first showed up in the Glade. Mostly while I was in that stupid coma.

CHAPTER 55

It took every ounce of Thomas's willpower not to stop and turn toward her. *What? Why didn't you tell me about him back in the Maze?* As if he needed another reason to dislike either of them.

"Why'd you guys stop talking?" Aris suddenly asked. "You yappin' about me in those pretty little heads of yours?" Impossibly, he didn't seem the least bit sinister at all anymore. It was almost as if everything that had happened back in the dead forest had been a creation of Thomas's imagination.

Thomas let out a heavy breath that had been building in his lungs. "I can't believe this. You two've been—" He stopped, realizing that maybe he wasn't so surprised after all. He'd *seen* Aris in the splotchy memories of his most recent dream. He was a part of this, whatever *this* was. And the way they'd acted toward each other in that brief recall seemed to say they were on the same side. *Used* to be, anyway.

"Shuck it," Thomas finally said. "Just keep talking."

"All right," Teresa said. "There's a lot of stuff to explain, so from now on just keep quiet and listen. Got it?"

Thomas's legs were starting to burn from their steady pace on the slope. "Okay, but . . . how do you know when you're talking to me and when you're talking to him? How does that work?"

"It just does. That's like me asking how you know when you're telling your right leg to move and when you're telling your left leg to move. I just . . . know. It's built into my brain somehow."

"We've done it, too, man," Aris said. "Don't you remember?"

"Of course I remember," Thomas muttered, annoyed and frustrated on so many levels. If only he could have everything back—every last memory—he knew the pieces would fall into place and he could just move forward. He couldn't fathom why WICKED felt it was so important to keep their minds clean of memory. And why the occasional leakage lately? Was that on purpose or an accident? A lingering effect of the Changing?

Too many questions. Too many shuck questions, all without answers. "All right," he finally said. "I'll keep my mouth and brain shut. Keep going."

"We can talk about Aris and me later. I don't even remember what we spoke about—I lost almost everything when I woke up. Our comas had to be part of the Variables, so maybe we could communicate just so we wouldn't go crazy. I mean, we *were* part of setting it all up, right?"

"Setting it all up?" Thomas asked. "I don't—"

Teresa reached forward and swatted him on the back. "Thought you were gonna be quiet?"

"Yeah," Thomas grumbled.

"Anyway, these people came into my room dressed in those creepy outfits and my telepathy with you cut off. I was scared and only half awake. Part of me thought it was just a bad nightmare. Then the next thing I knew, they put something over my mouth that smelled horrible and then I passed out. When I woke up I was lying in a bed in a different room and a bunch of people were sitting in chairs on the opposite side of this weird glass wall. I couldn't see it until I touched it—almost like a force field or something."

"Yeah," Thomas said. "We had something like that, too."

"So then they started talking to me. That's when they told me this whole plan of what Aris and I had to do to you—and they expected me to tell him. By, you know, speaking in his mind, even though he was now with your group. Our group. Group A. They took me from my room and sent me to be with Group B; then they told us about the mission to the safe haven, about having the Flare. We were scared, confused, but we had no choice. We went through these underground tunnels until we got to the mountains—we avoided the city altogether. When you and I met in that little building, and then everything that happened from the time we came down to you in the valley with all those weapons—all of that was planned."

Thomas thought about the sketchy memories he'd had in his dreams. Something told him he'd known that a scenario like this might need to happen before he ever went to the Glade and the Maze. He had a hundred questions to ask Teresa, but decided to hold back for a little while longer.

They turned at another switchback; then Teresa continued. "I only know two things for sure. One, they said that if I did anything against their plan they'd kill you. Said they 'had other options,' whatever that means. The second thing I know is that the reason for all this was that you had to truly and absolutely feel betrayed. The whole purpose of what we did to you was to ensure that that happened."

Again Thomas thought of the memories. He and Teresa had both used the word *patterns* right before he left her. What did it mean?

"So?" Teresa asked after they'd walked in silence for a while.

"So . . . what?" Thomas replied.

"So what do you think?"

"That's it? That's your whole explanation? I'm supposed to feel all happy now?"

"Tom, I couldn't take any chances. I was convinced they'd kill you unless I went along. No matter what, in the end you had to feel like I'd completely betrayed you. That's why I put so much into it. But why this was all so important? I have no idea."

Thomas realized suddenly that all this information had started another headache. "Well, you sure were good at it. What about in that building? When you kissed me? And . . . why did Aris need to be involved in all this?"

Teresa grabbed his arm and made him stop and turn to face her. "They had everything calculated. All for the Variables. I don't *know* how it all fits together."

Thomas slowly shook his head. "Well, none of this crap makes any sense to me. And excuse me for feeling a little ticked off."

"Did it work?"

"Huh?"

"For some reason they wanted you betrayed, and it worked. Right?"

Thomas paused, looked into her blue eyes for a long time. "Yeah. It did."

"I'm sorry for what I did. But you're alive, and so am I. And so is Aris."

"Yeah," he repeated. He really didn't feel like talking to her anymore.

"WICKED got what they want, and I got what I want." Teresa looked at Aris, who'd kept walking for a while and now stood down on the next level of the path. "Aris, turn around, face the valley."

"What?" he replied. He looked confused. "Why?"

"Just do it." She didn't have the mean streak in her voice anymore, hadn't since the gas chamber, but if anything, that made Thomas even more suspicious. What was she up to now?

Aris sighed and rolled his eyes, but did what she said, turning his back to them.

Teresa didn't hesitate. She wrapped her arms around Thomas's neck, pulling him in. He didn't have enough will to resist.

They kissed, but nothing stirred inside Thomas. He felt nothing.

CHAPTER 56

The wind intensified, whipping and swirling.

Thunder rumbled in the darkening sky, giving Thomas an excuse to pull away from Teresa. He decided again to hide his hard feelings. Time was running out and they still had a long way to go.

Doing his best acting job, he gave Teresa a smile and said, "Guess I got it—you did a bunch of weird stuff, but you were forced to, and now I'm alive. That's it, right?"

"That's about it."

"Then I'm gonna quit thinking about it. We need to catch up with the others." The best chance he had to make it to the safe haven was to work with Teresa and Aris, so he would. He could think about Teresa and all she'd done later.

"If you say so," she said with a forced smile, as if she sensed that something wasn't quite right. Or maybe she didn't like the prospect of facing the Gladers after what had happened.

"Are you guys done up there?" Aris yelled, still facing the other direction.

"Yes!" Teresa called back. "And don't expect me to ever kiss *you* on the cheek again. I think my lips have a fungus now."

Thomas almost gagged at hearing that. He set off down the mountain again, moving before Teresa tried to hold his hand.

★ ★ ★

It took another hour to get to the bottom of the mountain. The slope leveled a bit as they got closer, allowing them to increase their pace. Eventually the switchbacks stopped altogether, and they jogged the last mile or so to the flat and desolate wasteland stretching to the horizon. The air was hot, but the overcast sky and the wind kept it bearable.

Thomas still couldn't get a very good look at the slowly converging Groups A and B up ahead, especially now that he'd lost the bird's-eye view and dust had clouded the air. But both the boys and the girls still moved in their own tight packs, heading north. Even from his vantage point, they appeared to be leaning into the stiffening wind as they walked.

Thomas's eyes stung from the dirt flying through the air. He kept wiping at them, which only made it worse, made the surrounding skin feel raw. The world continued to darken as the clouds thickened in the sky above.

After a quick break to eat and drink—their remaining supplies were dwindling fast—the three of them took a moment to observe the other groups.

"They're just walking up there," Teresa said, pointing ahead with one hand while shielding her eyes from the wind with the other. "Why aren't they running?"

"Because we still have over three hours until the deadline," Aris responded, looking at his watch. "Unless we totally figured wrong, the safe haven should be only a few miles from this side of the mountains. But I don't see anything."

Thomas hated to admit it, but the hope that they were just missing something from a distance had faded away. "By the way they're dragging, they obviously can't see it, either. It must not be there—they don't have anything to run to but more desert."

Aris glanced at the gray-black sky. "Looks ugly up there. What if we get another one of those nice lightning storms?"

"We'd be better off staying in the mountains if that happens," Thomas said. Wouldn't that be a perfect way to end all this, he thought. Burned to a crisp by bolts of electricity while searching for some safe haven that had never been there in the first place.

"Let's just catch up to them," Teresa said. "Then we can figure out what to do." She turned to look at both boys and put her hands on her hips. "You guys ready?"

"Yeah," Thomas said. He was trying not to sink into the pit of panic and worry that threatened to swallow him. There had to be an answer to all this. Had to.

Aris just shrugged in response.

"Then let's run," Teresa said. And before Thomas could answer she was already gone, with Aris close at her heels.

Thomas took a deep breath. For some reason it all reminded him of the first time he'd run out into the Maze with Minho. Which worried him. He exhaled and set off after the other two.

After maybe twenty minutes of running, the wind forcing him to work twice as hard as he'd ever had to in the Maze, Thomas spoke out to Teresa in his mind. *I think I've had some more memories come back to me lately. In my dreams.* He'd been wanting to tell her, but not really in front of Aris. A test, more than anything, to see how she responded to what he'd remembered. See if he could find any clues to her true intentions.

Really? she answered.

He could sense her shock. *Yeah. Weird, random things. Stuff from when I was a little kid. And . . . you were there, too. I had glimpses of how WICKED treated us. A little about right before we went to the Glade.*

She paused before answering, maybe afraid to ask the questions that eventually came to him. *Does any of it help us? Do you remember much of it?*

Most of it. But there wasn't enough there to really mean a whole lot.

What did you see?

Thomas told her about each little segment of memory—or dream—he'd seen over the last couple of weeks. About seeing his mom, about overhearing conversations about surgery, about him and her spying on members of WICKED, hearing things that didn't make a whole lot of sense. About them testing and practicing their telepathy. And, finally, about saying goodbye right before he went to the Glade.

So Aris was there? she asked, but before he could answer, she continued. *Of course, I already knew that. That the three of us were all part of this. But weird about everyone dying, the replacements, all that. What do you think it means?*

I don't know, he answered. *But I feel like if we had the time to just sit and talk about it we could help each other bring it all back.*

Me too. Tom, I'm really sorry. I can tell you're having a hard time forgiving me.

Would you be any different?

No. I kind of accepted it, in a way. That saving you was worth losing what we might've had.

Thomas had no clue how to respond to that.

Not that they could've talked much more even if he wanted to. With the wind howling and the dust and debris flying through the air and the clouds churning and blackening and the distance to the others getting shorter . . .

There just wasn't time.

And so they kept running.

* * *

The two groups ahead of them eventually met up in the distance. More interesting to Thomas, though, was that it didn't appear to be an accident at all. The girls of Group B had reached a point and stopped; then Minho—Thomas could make him out now and was relieved to see him alive and well—and the Gladers had changed direction to go east to meet them.

And now, just a half-mile away, they all stood around something Thomas couldn't see, packing in a tight circle to look at whatever it was.

What's going on up there? Teresa asked Thomas in his mind.

Don't know, he answered.

The two of them, along with Aris, picked up the pace.

It only took another few minutes across the dusty wind-whipped plain before they reached Groups A and B.

Minho had stepped away from the larger pack of people and stood facing them when they finally made it. His arms were folded, his clothes filthy, his hair greasy, his face still showing signs of his burns. But somehow he was smiling. Thomas couldn't believe how good it felt to see that smirky grin again.

"It's about time you slowpokes caught up with us!" Minho yelled at them.

Thomas stopped right in front of him and doubled over to catch his breath for a few seconds, then straightened. "I thought you'd be fightin' tooth and nail with these girls after what they did to us. To me, anyway."

Minho looked back at the now-mingling group of boys and girls, then returned his gaze to Thomas. "Well, first of all, they have nastier weapons, not to mention bows and arrows. Plus, some chick named Harriet explained everything. We're the ones who should be surprised—

that you're still with them." He gave a nasty glare to Teresa, then Aris. "Never trusted either one of those shuck traitors."

Thomas tried to hide his mixed emotions. "They're on our side. Trust me." And in a twisted, backward way he really was starting to believe it. As sick as it made him feel.

Minho laughed bitterly. "Figured you'd say something like that. Let me guess, it's a long story?"

"Yeah, very long story," Thomas answered, then changed the subject. "Why'd you all stop here? What's everybody looking at?"

Minho stepped to the side, sweeping his arm behind him. "Have a peeky-peek yourself." Then he yelled to the two groups, *"You guys make a path!"*

Several Gladers and girls looked back, then slowly shuffled to the side until a narrow break in the crowd formed. Thomas immediately saw that the object that held everyone's attention was a simple stick poking out of the arid ground. An orange strip of ribbon hung from the top, whipping in the wind. Letters were printed on the thin banner.

Thomas and Teresa exchanged a look; then Thomas pushed ahead for a closer inspection. Even before he got there, he could read the words printed on the ribbon, black on orange.

THE SAFE HAVEN

CHAPTER 57

Despite the wind and the hubbub of people, the world quieted around Thomas for a minute, as if his ears had been stuffed with cotton. He fell to his knees and numbly reached out to touch the flapping orange ribbon. *This* was the safe haven? Not a building, a shelter, *something*?

Then, as quickly as it had disappeared, sound rushed back in, snapping him back to reality. Mostly the rush of wind and the chatter of conversation.

He turned back to Teresa and Minho, who stood side by side, Aris behind them peeking over their shoulders.

Thomas glanced at his watch. "We have over an hour left. Our safe haven is a stick in the ground?" Confusion muddled his mind—he wasn't quite sure what to think or say.

"Wasn't so bad, when you think about it," Minho said. "More than half of us made it here. Looks like even more of the girlie group."

Thomas stood up, trying to control his anger. "The Flare turn you crazy already? Yeah, we got here. Safe and sound. To a *stick*."

Minho scoffed at him. "Dude, they wouldn't send us here for no reason. We made it in the time they gave us. Now we just wait until the clock ticks down and something'll happen."

"That's what worries me," Thomas said.

"Hate to say it," Teresa added, "but I agree with Thomas. After everything they've done to us, it'd be way too easy to have a little sign here, and then they come get us in a nice helicopter as a reward. Something bad's gonna happen."

"Whatever you say, traitor," Minho said, his face hiding none of the hatred he felt for Teresa. "I don't want to hear another word from you." He walked away, angrier than Thomas had ever seen him.

Thomas looked at Teresa, who was visibly taken aback. "You shouldn't be surprised."

She just shrugged. "I'm sick of apologizing. I did what I had to do."

Thomas couldn't believe she was serious. "Whatever. I need to find Newt. I want—"

Before he could finish, Brenda appeared out of the crowd, glancing back and forth between him and Teresa. The wind tore through her long hair, whipping it frenziedly so that she kept pushing it behind her ears only to have it fly out again.

"Brenda," he said. For some reason he felt guilty.

"Hey there," Brenda said, walking up to stand right in front of him and Teresa. "This the girl you were tellin' me about? When you and I were snuggling in that truck?"

"Yeah." The word popped out of Thomas's mouth before he could stop it. "No. I mean . . . yeah."

Teresa held her hand out to Brenda, who shook it. "I'm Teresa."

"Nice to meet you," Brenda replied. "I'm a Crank. I'm slowly going crazy. I keep wanting to chew off my own fingers and randomly kill people. Thomas here promised to save me." Though she was obviously joking, she didn't even crack a smile.

Thomas had to hide a wince. "Funny, Brenda."

"Glad to see you still have a sense of humor about it," Teresa said. But her face could've turned water to ice.

Thomas looked down at his watch. Fifty-five minutes left. "I, um, need to talk to Newt." He turned and quickly walked away before either girl could say anything. He wanted to be as far away from both of them as possible.

Newt was sitting on the ground with Frypan and Minho, all three looking as if they were waiting for the end of the world.

The tearing wind had gained a moisture to it, and the billowing, churning clouds above them had lowered considerably, like a dark fog dropping to swallow the earth. Glimpses of light flashed here and there in the sky, burning patches of purple and orange in the grayness. Thomas hadn't seen an actual lightning bolt yet, but he knew they were coming. The first big storm had begun just like this.

"Hey, Tommy," Newt said when Thomas joined them. He sat down next to his friend and wrapped his arms around his knees. Two simple words with nothing behind them. It was as if Thomas had just gone for a leisurely walk instead of being kidnapped and almost killed.

"Glad to see you guys made it here," Thomas said.

Frypan snorted his usual animal-like bark of a laugh. "Same back at ya. Looks like you had more fun, though. Hangin' with your love goddess. Guess you two kissed and made up?"

"Not exactly," Thomas said. "It wasn't fun."

"Well, what happened?" Minho asked. "How can you trust her after all that?"

Thomas hesitated at first, but he knew he had to tell them everything. And there was no better time than the present. He sucked in a deep breath and started talking. He told them about WICKED's plan for him, the camp, his talk with Group B, the gas chamber. Still none of it made sense, but he felt a little better telling his friends.

"And you forgave that witch?" Minho asked when Thomas finally finished. "I won't. Whatever those shuck WICKED people wanna do, fine by me. Whatever you wanna do, fine by me. But I don't trust her, I don't trust Aris, and I don't like either one of them."

Newt seemed to consider it more deeply. "They went through all that—all that planning and acting—just to make you feel *betrayed*? Doesn't make any bloody sense."

"Tell me about it," Thomas muttered. "And no, I haven't forgiven her. But for now I think we're in the same boat." He looked around—most people were sitting down, staring off into the distance. Not much conversation, and not a whole lot of mingling between the two groups. "What about you guys? How'd you make it here?"

"Found a gap through the mountains," Minho answered. "Had to fight through some Cranks camping in a cave, but other than that, no problems. Food and water's almost out, though. And my feet hurt. And I'm pretty sure another big bolt of shuck lightning's about to come down and make me look like a piece of Frypan's bacon."

"Yeah," Thomas said. He glanced back at the mountains, guessed that all in all they'd probably come about four miles from the base. "Maybe we should bag this whole safe haven thing and try to find shelter." But even as he said it, he knew it wasn't an option. At least not until the time ran out.

"No way," Newt replied. "We didn't come this far to go back now. Let's just hope the buggin' storm holds off a little longer." He looked up at the almost black clouds with a grimace.

The other three Gladers had grown silent. The wind had continued to pick up, and its rushing roars and whips now made it hard to hear each other anyway. Thomas looked at his watch.

Thirty-five minutes. No way this storm would hold for—

"What's that!" Minho shouted, jumping to his feet; he pointed at a spot over Thomas's shoulder.

Thomas turned to look as he stood up, alarm igniting inside him. The terror on Minho's face had been unmistakable.

About thirty feet from the group, a large section of the desert ground was . . . opening. A perfect square—maybe fifteen feet wide—pivoted on a diagonal axis as the dirt-packed side slowly spun away from them and what had lain underneath rose up to replace it. The sound of groaning, twisting steel pierced the air, louder than the roaring wind. Soon the rotating square had fully flipped, and where once had been desert ground now lay a section of black material, with an odd object sitting on top of it.

It was oblong and white with rounded edges. Thomas had seen something just like it before. Several of them, in fact. After they'd escaped the Maze and entered the huge chamber where the Grievers had come from, they'd seen several of these coffinlike containers. He hadn't had much time to think about it then, but seeing it now, he thought those must've been where the Grievers stayed—slept?—when not hunting humans in the Maze.

Before he had time to react, more sections of the desert floor—surrounding their group in a large circle—started to rotate open like dark, gaping jaws.

Dozens of them.

CHAPTER 58

The squeal of metal was deafening as the square sections slowly spun on their axles. Thomas had his hands to his ears, trying to keep the sound out. The others in the group were doing the same. All around them, scattered evenly and fully encircling the area in which they stood, patches of desert ground rotated until they disappeared, each one eventually replaced with a large black square when it finally settled with a loud clank, one of those bulbous white coffins resting on top. At least thirty in all.

The scream of metal rubbing against metal stopped. No one spoke. The wind ripped across the land, blowing dust and dirt in streams across the rounded containers. It made a gritty pinging sound. There was so much of it, it blended into a noise that made Thomas's spine itch; he had to squint to keep stuff out of his eyes. Nothing else had moved since the foreign, almost alien objects had been revealed. There was only that sound and wind and cold and stinging eyes.

Tom? Teresa called to him.

Yeah.

You remember those, right?

Yeah.

You think Grievers are inside?

Thomas realized that was exactly what he thought, but he'd also finally accepted that he could never expect anything. He reasoned it out for a second before he answered. *I don't know. I mean, the Grievers had really moist bodies—it'd be hard on them out here.* It seemed like a stupid thing to say, but he was grasping for anything.

Maybe we're meant to . . . get inside them, she said after a pause. *Maybe they* are *the safe haven, or they'll transport us somewhere.*

Thomas hated the idea, but thought that maybe she was right. He tore his eyes away from the large pods and looked for her. She was already walking toward him. Fortunately, she was alone. He couldn't handle both her and Brenda right then.

"Hey," he said out loud, but the wind seemed to carry the sound away before it even left his mouth. He started to reach out for her hand but then pulled it back, almost forgetting how things had changed. She didn't seem to notice as she walked over to Minho and Newt and nudged both of them in greeting. They turned to face her and Thomas moved closer to conference with them.

"So what do we do?" Minho asked. He gave Teresa an annoyed look like he didn't want her to be any part of the decision making.

Newt answered. "If those things have bloody Grievers in 'em, we best start gettin' ready to fight the shuck buggers."

"What're you guys talking about?"

Thomas turned to see Harriet and Sonya—it'd been Harriet who'd spoken. And Brenda stood right behind them, with Jorge by her side.

"Oh, great," Minho muttered. "The two queens of glorious Group B."

Harriet just acted like she hadn't heard. "I'm assuming you all saw those pods back in your WICKED chamber, too. They had to be where the Grievers charged up or whatever it was they did."

"Yeah," Newt said. "Gotta be that."

In the sky above, thunder crackled and boomed, and those flashes of light grew brighter. The wind tore at everyone's clothes and hair and everything smelled wet but dusty—a strange combination. Thomas checked the time again. "We've only got twenty-five minutes. We're either gonna be fighting Grievers or we need to get inside those big coffins at the right time. Maybe they're the—"

A sharp hiss cut through the air from all directions. The sound pierced Thomas's eardrums and he clamped his hands to the sides of his head again. Movement on the perimeter surrounding them caught his attention, and he watched carefully what was happening with the large white pods.

A line of dark blue light had appeared on one side of each container, then expanded as the top half of the object began to move upward, opening on hinges like the lid of a coffin. It made no sound, at least not enough to be heard over the rushing wind and rumbling thunder. Thomas sensed the Gladers and the others slowly moving closer together, forming a tighter knot. Everyone was trying to get as far away from the pods as possible—and soon they were a coiled pack of bodies encircled by the thirty or so rounded white containers.

The lids continued moving until they'd all swung open and dropped to the ground. Something bulky rested inside each vessel. Thomas couldn't make out much, but from where he stood he couldn't see anything like the odd appendages of the Grievers. Nothing moved, but he knew not to let his guard down.

Teresa? he said to her mind. He didn't dare try talking loudly enough to be heard—but he had to talk to someone or go nuts.

Yeah?

Someone should go take a look. See what's in it. He said it, but he really didn't want to be the one to do it.

Let's go together, she said easily.

She surprised him with her courage. *Sometimes you have the worst ideas,* he responded. He'd tried to make it *feel* sarcastic, but he knew the truth of it far more than he wanted to admit to himself. He was terrified.

"Thomas!" Minho called. The wind, still wild, was drowned out by the approaching thunder and lightning now, cracking and exploding in brilliant displays above them and on the horizon. The storm was about to fully beat down its fury on them.

"What?" Thomas yelled back.

"You, me, and Newt! Let's go check it out!"

Thomas was just about to move when something slipped out of one of the pods. A collective gasp escaped those closest to Thomas, and he turned for a better look. Things were moving in all the pods, things he couldn't quite understand at first. Whatever they were, they were definitely coming out of their oblong homes. Thomas focused on the pod nearest to him, strained his eyes to discern what exactly he was about to face.

A misshapen arm hung over the edge, and its hand dangled a few inches above the ground. On it were four disfigured fingers—stubs of sickly beige flesh—none of them the same length. They wiggled and grasped for something that wasn't there, as if the creature inside was searching to get a grip to pull itself out. The arm was covered with wrinkles and lumps, and there was something completely strange right where what passed for an elbow was located. A perfectly rounded protrusion or growth, maybe four inches in diameter, glowing bright orange.

It looked like the thing had a lightbulb glued to its arm.

The monster continued to emerge. A leg flopped out, its foot a fleshy mass, four knobs of toes wriggling as much as its fingers. And on the knee, another one of those impossible orange spheres of light, seemingly growing right out of its skin.

"What is that thing?" Minho shouted over the noise of the surging storm.

No one answered. Thomas was dazed, staring at the creature—

mesmerized and terrified at the same time. He did finally look away long enough to see that similar monsters were coming out of every pod—all at the same pace—then returned his attention to the closest one.

It had somehow gained purchase enough with its right arm and leg to begin pulling the rest of its body out. Thomas looked on in horror as the abominable thing flopped and wiggled until it lurched over the edge of the open pod and stumbled to the ground. Roughly human-shaped, though at least a couple of feet taller than anyone around Thomas, its body was naked and thick, pockmarked and wrinkled. Most disturbing were more of those bulbous growths, maybe two dozen total, spread over the thing's body and glowing with brilliant orange light. Several on its chest and back. One on each elbow and knee—the bulb on the right knee had busted in a flurry of sparks when the creature landed on the ground—and several sticking out of a big lump of . . . what had to be a head, though it didn't have any eyes, nose, mouth or ears. No hair, either.

The monster got to its feet, swayed a bit as it balanced, then turned to face the group of humans. A quick glance around showed that each pod had delivered its creature, all of them now standing in a circle around the Gladers and Group B.

In unison, the creatures raised their arms until they pointed toward the sky. Then, all at once, thin blades shot out of the tips of their stubby fingers, out of their toes, out of their shoulders. The flashes of lightning in the sky glittered off their surface, sharp and gleaming silver. Though there was no sign of any kind of mouth, a deathly, creepy moan emanated from their bodies—it was a sound Thomas could feel more than hear. And it had to be loud to be heard over the terrible thunder.

Maybe Grievers would've been better, Teresa said inside Thomas's mind.

Well, they're enough alike that it's obvious who created these things, he said back, straining to stay calm.

Minho turned quickly and faced the crowd of still-gaping people surrounding Thomas. "There's about one for each of us! Grab whatever you got for a weapon!"

Almost as if they'd heard the challenge, the lightbulb creatures started moving, walking forward. Their first couple of steps were lumbering, but then they recovered, growing steady and strong and agile. Coming closer with every step.

CHAPTER 59

Teresa handed Thomas a really long knife, almost a sword. He couldn't imagine where she'd been hiding these things, but she now held a short dagger in addition to her spear.

As the lighted giants stepped closer and closer, Minho and Harriet spoke to their respective groups, moving them around, positioning them, their shouts and commands torn away by the wind before Thomas could hear anything. He dared take his eyes off the approaching monsters long enough to look at the sky. Tendrils of lightning forked and arced across the bottom of the dark clouds, which seemed to hang only a few dozen feet above them. The acrid smell of electricity permeated the air.

Thomas looked back down, concentrated on the creature closest to him. Minho and Harriet had been able to get the groups to stand together in an almost perfect circle, facing outward. Teresa stood next to Thomas, and he would've said something to her if he could've thought of anything. He was speechless.

WICKED's latest abominations were only thirty feet away.

Teresa finally elbowed him in the ribs. He looked to see her pointing at one of the creatures, telling Thomas—making sure he knew—that she'd chosen her foe. He nodded, then gestured toward the one he'd been thinking was his all along.

Twenty-five feet away.

Thomas had the sudden thought that it was a mistake to wait for them—that they needed to be spread out more. Minho must've had the same idea.

"Now!" their leader yelled, a bare and distant bark because of the storm's sounds. "Charge them!"

A slew of thoughts spun through Thomas's mind in that instant. Worry for Teresa, despite the changes between them. Worry for Brenda—standing stoically just a few people down the line from him—and regret over how they had barely spoken since being reunited. He imagined her having come all this way only to be killed by a vicious man-made creature. He thought of the Grievers, and his and Chuck and Teresa's charge back in the Maze to get to the Cliff and the Hole, the Gladers fighting and dying for them so they could punch in the code and stop it all.

He thought of all they'd gone through to arrive at this point, once again facing a biotech army sent by WICKED. He wondered what it all meant, whether it was worth trying to survive anymore. The image of Chuck taking that knife for him popped into his head. And that did it. Snapped him out of those nanoseconds of frozen doubt and fear. Screaming at the top of his lungs, he wielded his huge knife with both hands above his head and rushed forward, straight for his monster.

To his left and right, the others also charged, but he ignored them. He had to, forced himself to. If he couldn't take care of his own assignment, worrying about others wouldn't amount to anything.

He closed in. Fifteen feet. Ten feet. Five. The creature had stopped walking, bracing its legs in a fighting stance, hands outstretched, blades pointing directly at Thomas. Those shining orange lights pulsed now, flaring and receding, flaring and receding, as if the hideous thing actually had a heart somewhere inside. It was disturbing to see no face on the monster, but it helped Thomas think of it as nothing more than a machine. Nothing more than a man-made weapon that wanted him dead.

Right before he reached the creature, Thomas made a decision.

He dropped to slide on his knees and shins and swung the swordlike weapon in an arc behind and around him, slamming the blade into the monster's left leg with a full and powerful two-handed thrust. The knife cut an inch into its skin but then clanked against something hard enough to send a jolt shivering up both of Thomas's arms.

The creature didn't move, didn't retract, didn't let out any sort of sound, human or inhuman. Instead it swiped downward with both blade-studded hands where Thomas now knelt before it, his sword embedded in the monster's flesh. Thomas jerked it free and lunged backward just as those blades clattered against each other where his head had been. He fell on his back and scooted away from the creature as it took two steps forward, kicking out with the knives on its feet, barely missing Thomas.

The monster let out a roar this time—a sound almost exactly like the haunted moans of the Grievers—and dropped to the ground, thrashing its arms, trying to impale Thomas. Thomas spun away, rolling three times as he heard metal tips scraping along the dirt-packed ground. He finally took a chance and jumped to his feet, immediately sprinting several yards away before turning around, sword gripped in his hands. The creature was just getting to its own feet, slicing at the air with its stubby bladed fingers.

Thomas sucked in huge gulps of air and could see the others battling in his peripheral vision. Minho jabbing and stabbing with knives in both hands, the monster actually taking steps backward, away from him. Newt scrambling across the ground, the creature he fought lumbering after him, obviously injured. Slowing. Teresa was the closest to him, jumping and dodging and poking her foe with the butt of her spear. Why was she doing that? Her monster seemed to be badly hurt as well.

Thomas pulled his attention back to his own battle. A blur of silver movement made him duck, a wisp of wind in his hair from the swipe of the creature's arm. Thomas spun, crouched close to the ground, stabbing at anything he could as the monster pursued him, barely missing him with several more attacks. Thomas connected with one of the orange bulb growths, smashing it in a flash of sparks; the light died instantly. Knowing his luck had to be running short, he dove toward the ground, tucking and rolling again until he sprang to his feet a couple of yards away.

The creature had paused—at least as long as it had taken Thomas to make his escape move—but now it came after him again. An idea formed in Thomas's mind, and it grew to clarity when he looked back at Teresa's fight, her creature now moving in jilted, slow attacks. She kept after the bulbs, popping them as they exploded in that same display of fireworks. She'd destroyed at least three-fourths of the odd growths.

The bulbs. All he needed to do was destroy the bulbs. Somehow they were linked to the creature's power or life or strength. Could it really be that easy?

A quick glance around the rest of the battlefield showed that a few others had also gotten the idea, but most hadn't, fighting with bloody desperation to hack at limbs, muscles, skin, missing the bulbs entirely. A couple of people already lay on the ground, covered in wounds, lifeless. One boy. One girl.

Thomas changed his whole method. Instead of charging recklessly, he jumped in and took a jab at one of the bulbs on the monster's chest. He missed, slicing into the wrinkled, yellowish skin. The creature swiped at him, but he pulled back just as the very tips of the blades ripped jagged holes in his shirt. Then he thrust again, poking once more at the same bulb. He connected this time, bursting it and sending out a spray of sparks. The creature halted for a full second, then snapped back to battle mode.

Thomas circled the creature, jumping in and back again, poking, jabbing, thrusting.

Pop, pop, pop.

One of the monster's blades sliced across his forearm, leaving a long line of bright red. Thomas went in again. And again. Again.

Pop, pop, pop. Sparks flying, the creature shuddering and jerking with each break.

The pause got a little bit longer with every successful stab. Thomas felt a few more scrapes and slices, but nothing serious. He kept at it, attacking those orange spheres.

Pop, pop, pop.

Every small victory sapped the creature's strength, and it gradually began to visibly slump, though it didn't stop trying to cut Thomas to pieces. Bulb by bulb, each one easier than the one before it, Thomas attacked relentlessly. If only he could quickly finish it off, make it die. Then he could run around and help others. End this thing once and for—

A blinding light flashed behind him, then a sound like the entire universe exploding ripped away his brief moment of exhilaration and hope. A wave of invisible power knocked him over and he fell flat onto his stomach, the sword clattering away from him. The creature fell, too, and a burnt smell singed the air. Thomas rolled onto his side to look, saw a massive black hole in the ground, charred and smoking. A bladed foot and hand from one of the monsters lay on the hole's edge. No sign of the rest of the body.

It'd been a lightning strike. Right behind him. The storm had finally broken.

Even as he had the thought, he looked up to see thick shards of white heat start falling from the black clouds above.

CHAPTER 60

The lightning exploded all around him with deafening cracks of thunder; plumes of dirt flew into the air from every direction. Several people screamed—one was cut off abruptly, a girl. And that burning smell. Overwhelming. The strikes of electricity subsided as quickly as they had begun. But light continued to flash in the clouds, and rain started to pour down in sheets.

Thomas hadn't moved during that first flurry of lightning. There was no reason to think he'd be any safer in another spot than where he lay. But after the onslaught, he scrambled to his feet to look around, see what he could do or where he could run before it happened again.

The creature he'd been fighting was dead, half of its body blackened, the other half gone. Teresa stood over her foe, slamming the butt of her spear down and smashing the last bulb; its sparks died with a hiss. Minho was on the ground, but slowly getting to his feet. Newt stood there, breathing in and out, deep heaving breaths. Frypan doubled over and threw up. Some were lying on the ground; others—like Brenda and Jorge—still fighting the monsters. Thunder boomed all around them and lightning glinted in the rain.

Thomas had to do something. Teresa wasn't too far away; she stood a couple of steps from her dead creature, bent over, hands on her knees.

We have to find shelter! he said in her mind.

How much time do we have left?

Thomas squinted at his watch closely. *Ten minutes.*

We should get inside the pods. She pointed at the closest one, which still lay open like a perfectly cut eggshell, its halves surely full of water by this point.

He liked the idea. *What if we can't close it?*

Got any better plans?

No. He grabbed her hand and started running.

We need to tell the others! she said as they approached the pod.

They'll figure it out. He knew they couldn't wait—more strikes could hit them at any second. They'd all be dead by the time he and Teresa tried to communicate with anyone. He had to trust his friends to save themselves. *Knew* he could trust them.

They reached the pod just as several bolts of electricity came zigzagging down from the sky, striking in blistering explosions all around them. Dirt and rain flew everywhere; Thomas's ears rang. He looked inside the left half of the container, saw nothing but a small pool of dirty water. A horrible smell wafted up from it.

"Hurry!" he yelled as he climbed in.

Teresa followed him. They didn't need to speak to know what to do next. They both got on their knees, then leaned forward to grab the far end of the other half—it had a rubbery lining, easy to grip. Thomas braced his midsection on the lip of the pod, then pulled up, straining with every bit of strength he had left. The other half lifted and swung toward them.

Just as Thomas was repositioning himself to sit, Brenda and Jorge ran up to them. Thomas felt a rush of relief at seeing them okay.

"Is there room for us?" Jorge screamed over the noise of the storm.

"Get in!" Teresa yelled back in answer.

The two of them slipped over the edge and splashed into the large container, a tight fit but manageable. Thomas scooted to the far end to give them more room, holding the cover just barely open—the rain drummed on its outer surface. Once everyone was settled, he and Teresa ducked their heads and let the pod close completely. Other than the hollow thrum of the rain and the distant explosions of lightning and the gasping of breaths, it grew relatively silent. Though Thomas still heard that same ringing in his ears.

He could only hope his other friends had made it safely to pods of their own.

"Thanks for letting us in, *muchacho*," Jorge said when everyone seemed to have caught their breath.

"Of course," Thomas replied. The darkness inside the container was absolute, but Brenda was right next to him, then Jorge, then Teresa on the far end.

Brenda spoke up. "Thought you might've had second thoughts about bringing us along. Would've been a good chance to get rid of us."

"Please," Thomas muttered. He was too tired to care how it sounded. Everyone had almost died, and they might not be out of the woods yet.

"So is this our safe haven?" Teresa asked.

Thomas clicked the little light button on his watch; they had seven minutes till the time was up. "Right now, I sure hope so. Maybe in a few minutes these shuck squares of land will spin around and drop us into some nice comfy room where we can all live happily ever after. Or not."

Crack!

Thomas yelped—something had slammed into the top of the pod and made the loudest sound he'd ever heard, an earsplitting crash. A small hole—just a sliver of gray light—had appeared in the ceiling of their shelter, beads of water forming and dropping quickly.

"Had to be lightning," Teresa said.

Thomas rubbed his ears, the ringing worse now. "Couple more of those and we'll be right back where we started." His voice sounded hollow.

Another check of the watch. Five minutes. The water *drip-drip-drip*ped into the puddle; that horrible smell lingered; the bells in Thomas's head lessened.

"This isn't quite what I imagined, *hermano*," Jorge said. "Thought we'd show up here and you'd convince the big bosses to take us in. Give us that cure. Didn't think we'd be holed up in a stinking bathtub waiting to be electrocuted."

"How much longer?" Teresa asked.

Thomas looked. "Three minutes."

Outside, the storm raged, bursts of lightning slamming into the ground, the rain pounding.

Another boom and crack shook the pod, widened the split in the ceiling enough that water began rushing in, splashing all over Brenda and Jorge. Something hissed and steam seeped in as well, the lightning having heated up the outside material.

"We're not gonna last much longer no matter what happens!" Brenda shouted. "It's almost worse sitting here and waiting for it!"

"There's only two minutes left!" Thomas yelled back at her. "Just hold on!"

A sound started up outside. Faint at first, barely discernible over the noises of the storm. A humming. Deep and low. It grew in volume, seemed to vibrate Thomas's whole body.

"What *is* that?" Teresa asked.

"No idea," Thomas answered. "But based on our day, I'm sure it's not good. We just have to last another minute or so."

The sound got louder and deeper. Overwhelming the thunder and rain now. The walls of the pod vibrated. Thomas heard a rushing wind outside, different somehow from what had been blowing all day. Powerful. Almost . . . artificial.

"There's only thirty seconds left," Thomas announced, suddenly having a change of heart. "Maybe you guys are right. Maybe we're missing something important. I . . . I think we should look."

"What?" Jorge responded.

"We need to see what's making that sound. Come on, help me open this back up."

"And if a nice big lightning bolt comes down and fries my butt?"

Thomas put the palms of his hands on the ceiling. "We gotta take a chance! Come on—push!"

"He's right," Teresa said, and she braced her hands to help.

Brenda copied her, and soon Jorge joined them.

"Just about halfway," Thomas said. "Ready?"

After getting a few positive grunts, he said, "One . . . two . . . three!"

They all pushed toward the sky, and their strength ended up being way too much. The lid flipped up and over and crashed to the ground, leaving the pod fully open. Rain pummeled them, flying horizontally, captured by a ferocious wind.

Thomas leaned on the edge of the pod and gaped at what hovered in the air just thirty feet off the ground, lowering rapidly to land. It was huge and round, with flickering lights and burning thrusters of blue flame. It was the same ship that had saved him after he was shot. The Berg.

Thomas glanced at his watch just in time to see the last second tick down. Looked back up.

The Berg touched down on clawlike landing gear and a huge cargo door in its metal belly began to open.

CHAPTER 61

Thomas knew they couldn't waste any more time. No questions, no fear, no bickering. Only action.

"Come on!" he yelled, pulling Brenda's arm as he stepped out of the pod. He slipped and toppled over, landing with a wet *smush* in the mud. He pushed himself up, spitting the slimy stuff out of his mouth and rubbing it from his eyes, and scrambled back to his feet. The rain poured down, thunder cracked from all directions, lightning bolts lit the air in ominous flashes.

Jorge and Teresa had made it out, Brenda helping them. Thomas looked over at the Berg—maybe fifty feet away—its cargo door now fully open, a gaping maw of an entrance to warm light inside. Shadowy forms stood there, holding guns, waiting. They obviously didn't intend to come out and assist anybody onto the safe haven. The *real* safe haven.

"Run!" he screamed, already on the move. He held his knife in front of him, gripped tightly, in case any of those creatures were still alive and looking for a fight.

Teresa and the others kept pace next to him.

The rain-softened ground made it hard to get good traction; Thomas slipped twice, fell down once. Teresa grabbed his shirt and yanked until he was up and running again. Others were around them, making the same dash for the safety of the ship. The darkness of the storm and the veil of rain and brilliant flashes of lightning made it hard to see who was who. No time to worry about it.

From the right side, lumbering around the back end of the plane, a dozen of the bulb creatures appeared; they headed for a spot cutting off Thomas and his friends from the open cargo door. Their blades were slick with rain, some stained crimson. At least half of their creepy glowing bulbs had been busted, and their jerky movements showed it. But they looked as dangerous as ever. And still, the people in the Berg did nothing, only watched.

"Go right through 'em!" Thomas yelled. Minho appeared, along with Newt and a few other Gladers, joining the charge. Harriet and a few of the Group B girls, too. Everyone seemed to understand the plan, as slight as it was: fight off these last few monsters and get out of there.

Maybe for the first time since entering the Glade weeks earlier, Thomas felt no fear. He didn't know if he'd ever feel it again. He didn't know why, but something had changed. Lightning exploded around him, someone screamed, the rain intensified. Wind tore through the air, pelting him with small rocks and drops of water that hurt equally. The creatures swiped their blades through the air, screaming their disturbing roar as they waited for battle. Thomas ran on, knife held above his head.

No fear.

Three feet from the center creature he jumped into the air, kicking forward, both legs held tightly together. He slammed his feet into one of the orange bulbs protruding from the middle of the monster's chest. It burst and sizzled; the creature wailed something hideous and fell backward, slamming to the ground.

Thomas landed in the mud and rolled to the side. Immediately jumped up and danced around the creature, slashing and poking, bursting the glowing growths.

Pop, pop, pop.

Dodging and jumping away from the futile slashes of the creature's blades. Retaliating, stabbing. *Pop, pop, pop.* Only three bulbs were left; it could barely move. Thomas straddled the thing in a burst of confidence and quickly threw down the final vicious thrusts to end it.

The last bulb burst and fizzled out. Dead.

Thomas got up, spun around to see if someone else needed help. Teresa had finished off hers. Minho and Jorge as well. Newt was there, favoring his bad leg, Brenda helping him stab out the remaining bulbs on his foe.

A few seconds later it ended. No creature moved. No orange lights shone. It was over.

Thomas, breathing heavily, looked up at the entrance to the ship, only twenty feet away. Even as he did, its thrusters ignited and the ship started to lift off the ground.

"It's leaving!" Thomas screamed as loudly as he could, pointing frantically at their only means of escape. "Hurry!"

The word had barely escaped his mouth when Teresa grabbed him by the arm, pulling as she ran for the ship. Thomas stumbled, then righted himself, pounding his feet in the mud. He heard the crack of thunder behind them, saw a flash of lightning fill the sky. Another scream. Others beside him, around him, in front of him now, all running. Newt with his limp, Minho next to him, eyeing him to make sure he didn't fall.

The Berg had reached a point three feet off the ground, slowly rising and turning at the same time, ready at any second to shift those thrusters and zip away. A couple of Gladers and three girls reached it first, dove onto the platform of the open cargo door. Still it rose. Others reached it, climbed on, scrambled inside.

Then Thomas made it with Teresa. The open hatch was chest-high now. He jumped and pushed his hands down on the flat metal, arms stiff, stomach pressed against the thick edge. Swung his right leg up, got leverage, rolled his body fully onto the door. The ship, still rising. Others climbing on, reaching to pull others up. Teresa, halfway on, trying to find a handhold.

Thomas reached out and grabbed her hand, pulled her in. She collapsed on top of him, shared a brief look of victory. Then she was off, and both of them approached the edge of the door to see if anyone needed help.

The Berg was now six feet above the ground, starting to tilt. Three people still hung from the edge. Harriet and Newt were pulling a girl in. Minho was helping Aris. But Brenda held on only with her hands, her body dangling as she kicked her feet and tried to pull herself up.

Thomas dropped to his stomach and scooted closer, reached out and grabbed her right arm. Teresa got the other one. The metal of the cargo door was wet and slick; when Thomas pulled on Brenda he started sliding out, but then stopped abruptly. A quick look behind him revealed that Jorge had planted his butt and feet, holding tightly to both Thomas and Teresa.

Thomas looked back at Brenda, started pulling again. With Teresa's help, she finally came over the edge enough for her stomach to gain purchase; it was easy from there. As she crawled on and farther in, Thomas took another look outside at the ground, slowly moving away. Nothing but those horrific creatures, lifeless and wet, full of saggy pockets of flesh that had once been full and brightly lit. A few dead human bodies, but not many, and no one Thomas was close to.

He scooted backward, away from the edge, feeling an immense amount of relief. They'd made it, most of them. They'd made it through Cranks and lightning and hideous monsters. They'd made it. He bumped into Teresa, turned toward her, pulled her in and hugged her tightly, forgetting what had happened for a second. They'd made it.

"Who are these two people?"

Thomas jerked away from Teresa to see who'd shouted—it was a man with short red hair, holding a black pistol pointed at Brenda and Jorge, who sat next to each other, shivering and wet and bruised.

"Somebody answer me!" the man yelled again.

Thomas spoke up before he could think about it. "They helped us get through the city—we wouldn't be here if it weren't for them."

The man snapped his head toward Thomas. "You . . . *picked them up* along the way?"

Thomas nodded, not liking where this was going. "We made a deal with them. Promised they'd get the cure, too. We still have fewer people than we started with."

"Doesn't matter," the man said. "We didn't say you could bring citizens!"

The Berg continued to climb higher in the sky, but the gaping door didn't close. Wind whipped through the wide hole; any one of them could go tumbling to their death if they hit turbulence.

Thomas got to his feet anyway, determined to defend the pact he'd made. "Well, you told us to come here, and we did what we had to do!"

Their gun-toting host paused, seemed to consider this line of reasoning. "Sometimes I forget how little you people understand what's going on. Fine, you can keep one of 'em. The other goes."

Thomas tried not to show the jolt this gave him. "What do you mean . . . the other goes?"

The man clicked something on the gun, then held its end closer to Brenda's head. "We don't have time for this! You have five seconds to choose the one who stays. Don't choose and they both die. One."

"Wait!" Thomas looked at Brenda, at Jorge. They both stared at the floor, said nothing. Their faces pale with fear.

"Two."

Thomas suppressed the rising panic, closed his eyes. There was nothing new here. No, he understood things now. Knew what he had to do.

"Three."

No more fear. No more shock. No more questioning. Take what comes. Play along. Pass the tests. Pass the Trials.

"Four!" The man's face reddened. "Choose right now or they both die!"

Thomas opened his eyes and stepped forward. Then he pointed at Brenda and said the two most foul words to ever pass through his lips.

"Kill *her*."

Because of the odd pronouncement that only one could stay, Thomas thought he understood, thought he knew what would happen. That it was yet another Variable and they'd take whomever he *didn't* choose. But he was wrong.

The man jammed his gun into the waistband of his pants, then reached down and grabbed Brenda's shirt with two hands, yanking the girl to her feet. Without a word, he moved toward open air, taking her with him.

CHAPTER 62

Brenda looked at Thomas with panicked eyes, her face full of pain as the stranger dragged her across the metal floor of the Berg. Toward the hatch and certain death.

When he was halfway there, Thomas acted.

He jumped forward and slammed into the man's knees, tackling him to the floor; the gun clattered on the ground next to him. Brenda fell to the side, but Teresa was there to catch her, pull her back from the dangerous edge of the door. Thomas put his left forearm against the man's throat and reached for the gun with his other hand. His fingers found it, gripped it, pulled it close to him. He jumped up and away and held the pistol with both hands, pointing it at the stranger sprawled on his back.

"No one else dies," Thomas said, breathing heavily, somewhat shocked at himself. "If we haven't done enough to pass your stupid tests, then we fail. The tests are over." As he said it, he wondered if this was *supposed* to happen. But even that didn't matter—he meant every word he'd said. The senseless killing and dying had to end.

The stranger's face softened into the slightest hint of a smile and he sat up and scooted backward until he bumped into the wall. As he did so, the large cargo door began closing, the squeak of its hinges like squealing pigs. No one said anything until it clanked shut, one last rush of wind surging through before it did.

"My name's David," the man said, his voice loud in the new silence, broken only by the low hum of the ship's engines and thrusters. "And don't worry, you're right. It's over. It's all over."

Thomas nodded mockingly. "Yeah, we've heard that before. This time we mean it. We're not going to sit back and let you treat us like rats anymore. We're done."

David took a moment to scan the large cargo hold, maybe seeing whether the others agreed with what Thomas had just said. Thomas didn't dare break his gaze, though. He had to believe that they were all behind him.

Finally, David looked back at Thomas, then slowly got to his feet, raising a hand in conciliation as he did so. Once he was standing, he put both hands in his pockets. "What you don't understand is that everything has gone and will continue to go as planned. But you're right, the Trials are complete. We're taking you to a place of safety—a *real* place of safety. No more tests, no more lies, no more setups. No more pretending."

He paused. "I can only promise one thing. When you hear why we've put you through this, and why it's so important that so many of you survived, you'll understand. I promise you'll understand."

Minho snorted. "That's the biggest bunch of klunk I've ever heard in my life."

Thomas couldn't help but feel a little relief that his friend hadn't lost his fire. "And what about the cure? We were promised. For us and the two who helped us get here. How can we believe anything you tell us?"

"Think what you want for now," David said. "Things will change from here out, and you'll get the cure, just like you were told. As soon as we get back to headquarters. You can keep that gun, by the way—we'll even give you some more, if you'd like. There'll be nothing else for you to fight against, no tests or trials to ignore or refuse. Our Berg will land, you'll see that you're safe and cured, and then you can do what you want. The only thing we'll ever ask you to do again is to listen. Only to listen. I'm sure you're at least intrigued by what's behind all this?"

Thomas wanted to scream at the man but knew it'd serve no point. Instead he answered in as calm a voice as possible. "No more games."

"First sign of trouble," Minho added, "we start fighting. If that means we die, then so be it."

David smiled fully this time. "You know, that's exactly what we predicted you'd do at this point." He motioned with an arm toward a small door at the back of the cargo hold. "Shall we?"

Newt spoke up this time. "What's next on the bloody agenda?"

"Just thought you'd like to eat something, maybe take a shower. Sleep." He started walking around the crowd of Gladers and girls. "It's a very long flight."

Thomas and the others spent a few seconds exchanging glances. But in the end they followed. They really had no other option.

CHAPTER 63

Thomas tried hard not to think about things as the next couple of hours passed.

He'd made a stand, but then all that tension and courage and victory kind of trickled away as the group went through the motions of the most ordinary of activities. Hot food. Cold drinks. Medical attention. Wonderfully long showers. Fresh clothes.

Through it all, Thomas recognized the chance that it was all happening again. That he and the others were being pacified, slowly being led to another shock like the one they'd had when they awakened in the dormitory after being rescued from the Maze. But really, what else was there to do? David and the others on his staff made no threats, did nothing to raise alarm.

Refreshed and full of food, Thomas ended up sitting on a couch that ran along the narrow middle section of the Berg, a vast room full of mismatched drab-colored furniture. He'd been avoiding Teresa, but she came over and sat next to him. He still had a hard time being near her, a hard time talking to her or anyone else. His insides burned with turmoil.

But he put it all away because there was nothing else to do. He didn't know how to fly a Berg and wouldn't know where to go even if he could take it over. They'd go wherever WICKED took them, they'd listen, they'd make their decision.

"What're you thinkin' about?" Teresa finally asked.

Thomas was glad she'd spoken aloud—he wasn't sure he wanted to communicate telepathically with her anymore. "What am I thinking about? Mostly trying not to."

"Yeah. Maybe we should just enjoy the peace and quiet for a while."

Thomas looked at Teresa. She sat next to him as if nothing had changed between them at all. As if they were still best friends. And he couldn't stand it anymore.

"I hate that you're acting like nothing happened."

Teresa looked down. "I'm trying to forget just as much as you probably are. Look, I'm not stupid. I know that we can never be the same. But I still wouldn't change anything. It was the plan and it worked. You're not dead and that's worth it to me. Maybe you'll forgive me someday."

Thomas almost hated her for sounding so reasonable. "Well, all I care about right now is stopping these people. It's not right what they've done to us. It doesn't matter how much I was a part of it. It's wrong."

Teresa stretched out a little so she could rest her head against the arm of the couch. "Come on, Tom. They might've erased our memories, but they didn't remove our brains. We were both part of this, and when they tell us everything—when we remember why we put ourselves through this—we're going to do whatever they tell us to."

Thomas thought about that for a second and realized he couldn't possibly have disagreed more. Maybe at one time he'd felt that way, but not now. Though discussing it with Teresa was the last thing he wanted to do. "Maybe you're right," he murmured.

"When's the last time we slept?" she asked. "I swear I can't remember."

Again with the act that all was well. "I do. For me, anyway. It had something to do with a gas chamber and you whacking me over the head with a big spear."

Teresa stretched. "I can only say sorry so many times. At least you got some rest. I didn't sleep for one second while you were out. I think I've been awake for two full days."

"Poor baby." Thomas yawned. He couldn't help himself—he was tired, too.

"Mmmm?"

He looked over to see her eyes closed, her breathing slowed. She'd fallen asleep just like that. He glanced around at the other Gladers and Group Bs. Most of them were zonked out, also. Except Minho—he was trying to talk to some cute girl, but her eyes were closed. Jorge and Brenda were nowhere to be found—something that struck Thomas as strange, not to mention at least a bit worrisome.

It was then that he realized he missed Brenda terribly, but his own eyelids began to droop, and weariness and fatigue crept in. As he sank deeper into the couch, he decided he'd have time to look for her later. Then he finally gave in and allowed the sweet darkness of unconsciousness to take him.

CHAPTER 64

He awoke, blinked, wiped his eyes and saw nothing but pure white. No shapes, no shadows, no variation, nothing. Just white.

A flicker of panic until he realized he must be dreaming. Strange, but a dream for sure. He could feel his body, feel his fingers against his skin. Feel himself breathing. *Hear* himself breathing. Yet he was surrounded by a complete and seamless world of bright nothing.

Tom.

A voice. *Her* voice. Could she talk to him while he was dreaming? Had she done it before? Yes.

Hey, he responded.

Are you . . . okay? She sounded troubled. No, *felt* troubled.

Huh? Yeah, I'm fine. Why?

Just thought you'd be a little surprised right now.

He felt a stab of confusion. *What are you talking about?*

You're about to understand more. Very soon now.

For the first time, Thomas realized the voice wasn't quite right. There was something off about it.

Tom?

He didn't answer. Fear had crept into his gut. A horrible, sickening, toxic fear.

Tom?

Who . . . who are you? he finally asked, terrified of the answer.

A pause before she answered.

It's me, Tom. It's Brenda. Things are about to get bad for you.

Thomas screamed before he knew what he was doing. He screamed and screamed and screamed until it finally woke him up.

CHAPTER 65

He sat straight up, covered in sweat. Even before he could fully compute his surroundings, before all the information traveled through the nerve wires and cognitive functions of his brain, he knew that everything was wrong. That everything had been taken from him all over again.

He lay on the ground, alone, in a room. The walls, the ceiling, the floor—everything was white. The floor beneath him was spongy, hard and smooth but with enough give to be comfortable. He looked at the walls—they were padded, with large buttoned indentations across them, about four feet apart. Bright light shone down from a rectangle in the ceiling, too high for him to reach. The place had a clean smell to it, like ammonia and soap. Thomas looked down to see that even his clothes had no color: a T-shirt, cotton pants, socks.

A brown desk sat about a dozen feet in front of him. It was the only thing in the entire room that wasn't white. Old and battered and scratched, it had a bare wooden chair pushed into the sitting well on the other side. Behind that was the door, padded like the walls.

Thomas felt a strange calm. Instinct told him he should be on his feet, screaming for help. He should be banging on the door. But he knew that door wouldn't open. He knew no one would listen.

He was in the Box all over again, should've known better than to get his hopes up.

I'm not going to panic, he told himself. It had to be another phase of the Trials, and this time he'd fight to change things—to end it all. It was strange, but just knowing he had a plan, that he'd do whatever it took to find freedom, caused a surprising calm to pass over him.

Teresa? he called out. He knew that at this point she and Aris were his only hope for communication with the outside. *Can you hear me? Aris? You there?*

No one responded. Not Teresa. Not Aris. Not . . . Brenda.

But that had only been a dream. It had to have been. Brenda couldn't be working with WICKED, couldn't be speaking in his mind.

Teresa? he said again, throwing hard mental effort into it. *Aris?*

Nothing.

He stood and walked over to the desk, but two feet in front of it he ran into an invisible wall. A barrier, just like back in the dormitory.

Thomas didn't let the panic rise. Didn't let fear overcome him. He took a deep breath, walked back toward the corner of the room, then sat down and leaned into it. Closed his eyes and relaxed.

Waited. Fell asleep.

Tom? Tom!

He didn't know how many times she said it before he finally responded. *Teresa?* He woke with a jolt, looked around and remembered the white room. *Where are you?*

They put us in another dormitory after the Berg landed. We've been here a few days, just sitting around doing nothing. Tom, what happened to you?

Teresa was worried—scared, even. That much he knew for sure. As for himself, he mostly felt confused. *A few days? What—*

They took you away as soon as the Berg landed. They keep telling us it was too late—that the Flare is too rooted in you. They said you've gotten crazy and violent.

Thomas tried to hold it together, tried not to think about how

WICKED could wipe memories. *Teresa . . . it's just another part of the Trials. They've got me locked up in this white room. But . . . you've been there for days? How many?*

Tom, it's been almost a week.

Thomas couldn't respond. Almost wanted to pretend he hadn't heard what Teresa had just said. The fear he'd been holding back began to slowly seep into his chest. Could he trust her? She'd lied to him so much already. And how did he even know this was really her? It was high time to cut off ties with Teresa.

Tom? Teresa called to him again. *What's going on here? I'm really confused.*

Thomas felt a rush of emotion, a burning inside him that almost brought tears to his eyes. He had once considered Teresa his best friend. But it could never be like that again. Now all he felt when he thought of her was anger.

Tom! Why aren't you—

Teresa, listen to me.

Hello? That's what I'm trying to—

No, just . . . listen. Don't say anything else, okay? Just listen to me.

She paused. *Okay.* A quiet, scared voice in his mind.

Thomas couldn't control it anymore. Rage pulsed inside of him. Luckily, he only had to think the words, because he could never have spoken them aloud.

Teresa. Go away.

Tom—

No. Don't say another word. Just . . . leave me alone. And you can tell WICKED that I'm done playing their games. Tell them I'm done!

She waited a few seconds before responding. *Okay.* Another pause. *Okay. Then I just have one thing left to say to you.*

Thomas sighed. *I can't wait.*

She didn't say it right away, and he would've thought she'd left him except that he still felt her presence. Finally, she spoke again.

Tom?

What?

WICKED is good.

And then she was gone.

EPILOGUE

WICKED Memorandum, Date 232.2.13, Time 21:13
TO: My Associates
FROM: Ava Paige, Chancellor
RE: SCORCH TRIALS, Groups A and B

This is not a time to let emotions interfere with the task at hand. Yes, some events have gone in a direction we didn't foresee. Not all is ideal—things have gone wrong—but we've made tremendous progress and have collected many of the needed patterns. I feel a great amount of hope.

I expect all of us to maintain our professional demeanor and remember our purpose. The lives of so many people rest in the hands of so few. This is why it's an especially important time for vigilance and focus.

The days to come are fundamental to this study, and I have every confidence that when we restore their memories, every one of our subjects will be ready for what we plan to ask of them. We still have the Candidates we need. The final pieces will be found and put into place.

The future of the human race outweighs all. Every death and every sacrifice are well worth the ultimate outcome. The end of this monumental effort is coming, and I believe that the process will work. That we'll have our patterns. That we'll have our blueprint. That we'll have our cure.

The Psychs are deliberating even now. When they say the time is right, we'll remove the Swipe and tell our remaining subjects if they are—or are not—immune to the Flare.

That's all for now.

END OF BOOK TWO

ACKNOWLEDGMENTS

I can't really say it better than I did in Book One. To all the same people, especially Lynette, Krista, Michael and Lauren, thank you. You've changed my life forever. Thanks also to all the people at Random House who have worked so hard to make this series a success, including my publicists, Noreen Herits and Emily Pourciau, and all the amazing sales reps out there. I seriously can't believe how incredibly lucky and blessed I am. Thank you. And finally, to my readers: you rock and I love you.

THE #1 *NEW YORK TIMES* BESTSELLING MAZE RUNNER SERIES FROM
JAMES DASHNER

READ THEM ALL!

TheMazeRunner.com

/MazeRunner @JamesDashner

TURN THE PAGE TO START READING BOOK 3 IN THE MAZE RUNNER SERIES.

BOOK 3 IN THE #1 *NEW YORK TIMES* BESTSELLING SERIES BY
JAMES DASHNER

SOON TO BE A MAJOR MOTION PICTURE

THE DEATH CURE

THE MAZE RUNNER SERIES

Excerpt copyright © 2011 by James Dashner.
Published by Delacorte Press, an imprint of Random House Children's Books,
a division of Penguin Random House LLC, New York.

CHAPTER 2

Thomas had imagined this happening, countless times. What he would do, what he would say. How he'd rush forward and tackle anyone who came in, make a run for it, flee, escape. But these thoughts were almost for amusement more than anything. He knew WICKED wouldn't let something like that happen. No, he'd need to plan out every detail before he made his move.

When it *did* happen—when that door popped open with a slight puffing sound and began to swing wide—Thomas surprised himself by how he reacted. He did nothing. Something told him an invisible barrier had appeared between him and the desk—like back in the dorms after the Maze. The time for action hadn't arrived. Not yet.

He felt only the slightest hint of surprise when the Rat Man walked in—the guy who'd informed the Gladers of the last trial they'd been forced on, through the Scorch. Same long nose, same weasel-like eyes; that greasy hair, combed over an obvious bald spot that took up half his head. Same ridiculous white suit. He looked paler than the last time Thomas had seen him, though, and he was holding a thick folder filled with dozens of crinkled and messily stacked papers in the crook of his arm and dragging a straight-backed chair.

"Good morning, Thomas," he said with a stiff nod. Without waiting for a response, he pulled the door shut, set his chair behind the desk and took a seat. He placed the folder in front of him and opened it, started flipping through pages. When he found what he'd been looking for he stopped and rested his hands on top of everything. Then he flashed a pathetic grin, his eyes finally settling on Thomas.

When Thomas finally spoke, he realized that he hadn't done so in weeks, and his voice came out more like a croak. "It'll only be good if you let me out."

"Yes, yes, I know. No need to worry—you're going to be hearing plenty of positive news today. Trust me."

Thomas thought about that, ashamed that he let it lift his hopes, even for a second. He should know better by now. "*Positive* news? Didn't you choose us because you thought we were intelligent?"

Rat Man remained silent for several seconds before he responded. "Intelligent, yes. Among more important reasons." He paused and studied Thomas before continuing. "Do you think we *enjoy* all this? You think we *enjoy* watching you suffer? It's all been for a purpose, and very soon it will make sense to you." The intensity of his words had built until he'd practically shouted that last word, his face now red.

"Whoa," Thomas said, feeling bolder by the minute. "Slim it nice and calm there, old fella. You look three steps away from a heart attack."

The man stood from his chair and leaned forward on the desk, the veins in his neck standing out in taut cords. He slowly sat back down, took several deep breaths. "You would think that almost four weeks in this white box might humble a boy. But you seem more arrogant than ever."

"So are you going to tell me that I'm not crazy, then? Don't have the Flare, never did?" Thomas couldn't help himself. The anger was rising in him and he felt like he was going to explode. But he forced a calmness into his voice. "That's what kept me sane through all this—deep down I know you lied to Teresa, that this is just another one of your tests. So where do I go next? Gonna send me to the shuck moon? Make me swim across the ocean in my undies?" He smiled for effect.

The Rat Man had been staring at Thomas with blank eyes throughout his rant. "Are you finished?"

"No, I'm not finished. I want you to tell me everything. Now."

"Oh, Thomas." The Rat Man said it quietly, as if delivering sad news to a small child. "We didn't lie to you. You *do* have the Flare."

A cold chill cut through the heat of Thomas's rage. He was sure they'd lied to him before—though Rat Man could just be lying again now. He took a deep breath and shrugged, as if the news was something he heard every day. "Well, even so, I haven't started going crazy yet." At a certain point—after all that time crossing the Scorch, being with Brenda, surrounded by Cranks—he'd come to terms with the fact that he'd catch the virus eventually. But he told himself that for now he was still okay. Still sane. And that was all that mattered at the moment.

Rat Man sighed. "You don't understand. You don't understand what it is that I came in here to tell you."

"Why would I believe a word that comes out of your mouth?"

Thomas realized that he'd stood up, though he had no

memory of doing so. His chest lurched with heavy breaths. He had to get control of himself. Rat Man's stare was cold, his eyes black pits. Regardless of whether this man lied to him, Thomas knew he was going to have to hear him out if he ever wanted to leave this white room. He forced his breathing to slow. He waited.

After several seconds of silence, his visitor continued. "I know we've lied to you. Often. We've done some awful things to you and your friends. But it was all part of a plan that you not only agreed to, but helped set in place. We've had to take it all a little farther than we'd hoped in the beginning—there's no doubt about that. However, everything has stayed true to the spirit of what the Creators envisioned—what *you* envisioned in their place after they were . . . purged."

Thomas slowly shook his head; he knew he'd been involved with these people once, somehow, but the concept of putting anyone through what he'd gone through was incomprehensible. "You didn't answer me. How can you possibly expect me to believe anything you say?" He recalled more than he let on, of course. Though the window to his past was caked with grime, revealing little more than splotchy glimpses, he knew he'd worked with WICKED. He knew Teresa had too, and that they'd helped create the Maze. There'd been other flashes of memory.

"Because, Thomas, there's no value in keeping you in the dark," Rat Man said. "Not anymore."

Thomas felt a sudden weariness, like all the strength had seeped out of him, leaving him with nothing. He sank to the floor with a heavy sigh. He shook his head. "I don't even know what that means."

Rat Man kept talking, but his tone became less detached and clinical and more teacherly. "You are obviously well aware that we have a horrible disease eating the minds of humans worldwide. Everything we've done up to now has been for one purpose and one purpose only—to analyze your brain patterns and build a blueprint from them. The goal is to use this blueprint to develop a cure for the Flare. The lives lost, the pain and suffering—you knew the stakes when this began. We all did. It was all to ensure the survival of the human race. And we're very close. Very, very close."

Memories had come back to Thomas on several occasions. The Changing, the dreams he'd had since, fleeting glimpses here and there, like quick lightning strikes in his mind. And right now, listening to the white-suited man talk, it felt as if he stood a few feet back from a cliff and all the answers were just about to float up from the depths for him to see in their entirety.

But he was still wary. He knew he couldn't trust anything, despite being aware that he'd been a part of it all, had helped design the Maze, had taken over after the original Creators died and kept the program going with new recruits. "I remember enough to be ashamed of myself," he admitted. "But living through this kind of abuse is a lot different than planning it. It's just not right."

Rat Man scratched his nose, shifted in his seat. Something Thomas said had gotten to him. "We'll see what you think at the end of today, Thomas. We shall see. But let me ask this— are you telling me that the lives of a few aren't worth losing to save countless more?" Again, the man spoke with passion, leaning forward.

Thomas only stared. It was a question he couldn't answer.

The Rat Man might have smiled, but it looked more like a sneer on his face. "Just remember that at one time you did think that, Thomas." He started to collect his papers as if to go but didn't move. "I'm here to tell you that everything is set and our data is almost complete. Once we have the blueprint, you can go boo-hoo with your friends all you want about how *unfair* we've been."

Thomas wanted to cut the man with harsh words. But he held back. "How does torturing us lead to this blueprint you're talking about?"

Rat Man sighed heavily. "Boy, soon you'll remember everything, and I have a feeling you're going to regret a lot. In the meantime, there's something you need to know right now and maybe it'll bring you back to your senses."

"And what's that?" Thomas really had no idea what the man would say.

His visitor stood up, smoothed the wrinkles out of his pants and adjusted his coat. Then he clasped his hands behind his back. "You're *immune* to the Flare, Thomas. The virus lives in every molecule of your body, yet it has no effect on you, nor will it ever."

Thomas swallowed.

"On the outside, in the streets, they call you people Munies," Rat Man continued. "And they really, really hate you."

**BEFORE THE MAZE,
THERE WAS THE FEVER CODE.
READ ON FOR A SPECIAL PREVIEW
OF THE FINAL BOOK!**

BOOK 5 IN THE #1 *NEW YORK TIMES* BESTSELLING SERIES BY

JAMES DASHNER

THE FEVER CODE

THE STORY OF HOW THE MAZE WAS BUILT

THE MAZE RUNNER SERIES

Excerpt copyright © 2016 by James Dashner. Published by Delacorte Press, an imprint of Random House Children's Books, a division of Penguin Random House LLC, New York.

PROLOGUE

NEWT

It snowed the day they killed the boy's parents.

An accident, they said much later, but he was there when it happened and knew it was no accident.

The snow came before they did, almost like a cold white omen, falling from the gray sky.

He could remember how confusing it was. The sweltering heat had brutalized their city for months that stretched into years, an infinite line of days filled with sweat and pain and hunger. He and his family survived. Hopeful mornings devolved into afternoons of scavenging for food, of loud fights and terrifying noises. Then evenings of numbness from the long hot days. He would sit with his family and watch the light fade from the sky and the world slowly disappear before his eyes, wondering if it would reappear with the dawn.

Sometimes the crazies came, indifferent to day or night. But his family didn't speak of them. Not his mother, not his father; certainly not him. It felt as if admitting their existence aloud might summon them, like an incantation calling forth devils. Only Lizzy, two years younger but twice as brave, had the guts to talk about the crazies, as if she were the only one smart enough to see superstition for nonsense.

And she was just a little kid.

The boy knew he should be the one with courage; he should be the one comforting his little sister. *Don't you worry, Lizzy. The basement is locked up tight; the lights are off. The bad people won't even know we're here.* But he always found himself speechless. He'd hug her hard, squeezing her like his own personal teddy bear for comfort. And every time, *she'd* pat *him* on the back. He loved her so much it made his heart hurt. He'd squeeze her tighter, silently swearing he'd never let the crazies hurt her, looking forward to feeling the flat of her palm thumping him between his shoulder blades.

Often, they fell asleep that way, curled up in the corner of the basement, on top of the old mattress his dad had dragged down the stairs. Their mother always put a blanket over them, despite the heat—her own rebellious act against the Flare, which had ruined everything.

That morning, they awoke to a sight of wonder.

"Kids!"

It was his mother's voice. He'd been dreaming, something about a football match, the ball spinning across the green grass of the pitch, heading for an open goal in an empty stadium.

"Kids! Wake up! Come see!"

He opened his eyes, saw his mother looking out the small window, the only one in the basement room. She'd removed the board his dad had nailed there the night before, like he did every evening at sunset. A soft gray light shone down on his mother's face, revealing eyes full of bright awe. And a smile like he hadn't seen in a very long time lit her even brighter.

"What's going on?" he mumbled, climbing to his feet. Lizzy rubbed her eyes, yawned, then followed him to where Mum gazed into the daylight.

He could remember several things about that moment. As he looked out, squinting as his eyes adjusted, his father still snored like a beast. The street was empty of crazies, and clouds covered the sky, a rarity these days. He froze when he saw the white flakes. They fell from the grayness, swirling and dancing, defying gravity and flitting up before floating back down again.

Snow.

Snow.

"What the bloody hell?" he mumbled under his breath, a phrase he'd learned from his father.

"How can it snow, Mummy?" Lizzy asked, her eyes drained of sleep and filled with a joy that pinched his heart. He reached down and tugged on her braid, hoping she knew just how much she made his miserable life worth living.

"Oh, you know," Mum replied, "all those things the people say. The whole weather system of the world is shot to bits, thanks to the Flares. Let's just enjoy it, shall we? It's quite extraordinary, don't you think?"

Lizzy responded with a happy sigh.

He watched, wondering if he'd ever see such a thing again. The flakes drifted, eventually touching down and melting as soon as they met the pavement. Wet freckles dotted the windowpane.

They stood like that, watching the world outside, until shadows crossed the space at the top of the window. They were gone as soon as they appeared. The boy craned his neck to catch a glimpse of who or what had passed, but looked too late. A few seconds later, a heavy pounding came on the front door above. His father was on his feet before the sound ended, suddenly wide-awake and alert.

"Did you see anyone?" Dad asked, his voice a bit croaky.

Mum's face had lost the glee from moments earlier, replaced

with the more familiar creases of concern and worry. "Just a shadow. Do we answer?"

"No," Dad responded. "We most certainly do not. Pray they go away, whoever it is."

"They might break in," Mum whispered. "I know I would. They might think it's abandoned, maybe a bit of canned food left behind."

Dad looked at her for a long time, his mind working as the silence ticked by. Then, *boom, boom, boom*. The hard cracks on the door shook the entire house, as if their visitors had brought along a battering ram.

"Stay here," Dad said carefully. "Stay with the children."

Mum started to speak but stopped, looking down at her daughter and son, her priorities obvious. She pulled them into a hug, as if her arms could protect them, and the boy let the warmth of her body soothe him. He held her tight as Dad quietly made his way up the stairs, the floor above creaking as he moved toward the front door. Then silence.

The air grew heavy, pressing down. Lizzy reached over and took her brother's hand. Finally he found words of comfort and poured them out to her.

"Don't worry," he whispered, barely more than a breath. "It's probably just some people hungry for food. Dad will share a bit, and then they'll be on their way. You'll see." He squeezed her fingers with all the love he knew, not believing a word he'd said.

Next came a rush of noises.

The door slammed open.

Loud, angry voices.

A crash, then a thump that rattled the floorboards.

Heavy, dreadful footsteps.

And then the strangers were pounding down the stairs. Two men, three, a woman—four people total. The arrivals were dressed sharply for the times, and they looked neither kind nor menacing. Merely solemn to the core.

"You've ignored every message we've sent," one of the men stated as he examined the room. "I'm sorry, but we need the girl. Elizabeth. I'm very sorry, but we've got no choice."

And just like that, the boy's world ended. A world already filled with more sad things than a kid could count. The strangers approached, cutting through the tense air. They reached for Lizzy, grabbed her by the shirt, pushed at Mum—frantic, wild, screaming—who clutched at her little girl. The boy ran forward, beat at the back of a man's shoulders. Useless. A mosquito attacking an elephant.

The look on Lizzy's face during the sudden madness. Something cold and hard shattered within the boy's chest, the pieces falling with jagged edges, tearing at him. It was unbearable. He let out an enormous scream of his own and threw himself harder at the intruders, swinging wildly.

"Enough!" the woman yelled. A hand whipped through the air, slapped the boy in the face, a snakebite sting. Someone punched his mother right in the head. She collapsed. And then a sound like the crack of thunder, close and everywhere at once. His ears chimed with a deafening buzz. He fell back against the wall and took in the horrors.

One of the men, shot in the leg.

His dad standing in the doorway, gun in hand.

His mum screeching as she scrambled off the floor, reaching for the woman, who had pulled out her own weapon.

Dad firing off two more shots. A ping of metal and the crunch of a bullet hitting concrete. Misses, both.

Mum yanking at the lady's shoulder.

Then the woman threw an elbow, fired, spun, fired three more times. In the chaos, the air thickened, all sound retreating, time a foreign concept. The boy watched, emptiness opening below him, as both of his parents fell. A long moment passed when no one moved, most of all Mum and Dad. They'd never move again.

All eyes went to the two orphaned children.

"Grab them *both,* dammit," one of the men finally said. "They can use the other one as a control subject."

The way the man pointed at him, so casually, like finally settling on a random can of soup in the pantry. He would never forget it. He scrambled for Lizzy, pulled her into his arms. And the strangers took them away.

CHAPTER 1

221.11.28 | 9:23 a.m.

Stephen, Stephen, Stephen. My name is Stephen.

He'd been chanting it over and over to himself for the last two days—since they'd taken him from his mom. He remembered every second of his last moments with her, every tear that ran down her face, every word, her warm touch. He was young, but he understood that it was for the best. He'd seen his dad plummet into complete madness, all anger and stink and danger. He couldn't take seeing it happen to his mom.

Still, the pain of their separation swallowed him. An ocean that had sucked him under, its coldness and depth never-ending. He lay on the bed in his small room, legs tucked up to his chest and eyes squeezed shut, curled into a ball, as if that would bring sleep down on him. But since he'd been taken, slumber had come only in fits, snatches full of dark clouds and screaming beasts. He focused.

Stephen, Stephen, Stephen. My name is Stephen.

He figured he had two things to hold on to: his memories and his name. Surely they couldn't take the first away from him, but they were trying to steal the second. For two days they'd pressed him to accept his new name: Thomas. He'd refused, clinging desperately to the seven letters his own flesh and blood had chosen for him. When the people in the white coats called him Thomas, he didn't respond; he acted as if he couldn't hear them or as if he thought they were talking to someone else. It wasn't easy when only two people stood in the room, which was usually the case.

Stephen wasn't even five years old, yet his only glimpse of the world had been full of darkness and pain. And then these people took him. They seemed intent on making sure he realized that things could only get worse, every lesson learned harder than the one before it.

His door buzzed, then immediately popped open. A man strode in, dressed in a green one-piece suit that looked like pajamas for grown-ups. Stephen wanted to tell him he looked ridiculous, but based on the last few encounters he'd had with these people, he decided to keep his opinion to himself. Their patience was beginning to wear thin.

"Thomas, come with me," the man said.

Stephen, Stephen, Stephen. My name is Stephen.

He didn't move. He kept his eyes squeezed shut, hoping the stranger hadn't noticed that he'd taken a peek when the man had first entered. A different person had come each time. None of them had been hostile, but then, none had been very nice either. They all seemed distant, their thoughts elsewhere, removed from the boy alone in the bed.

The man spoke again, not even trying to conceal the impatience in his voice. "Thomas, get up. I don't have time for games, okay? They're running us ragged to get things set up, and I've heard that you're one of the last ones resisting your new name. Give me a break, son. This is seriously something you want to fight about? After we saved you from what's happening out there?"

Stephen willed himself not to move, the result only a stiffness that couldn't possibly look like someone sleeping. He held his breath until he finally had to suck in a huge gulp of air. Giving up, he rolled onto his back and glared at the stranger dead in the eye.

"You look stupid," he said.

The man tried to hide his surprise but failed; amusement crossed his face. "Excuse me?"

Anger flared inside Stephen. "I said, you look stupid. That ridiculous green jumpsuit. And give up the act. I'm not going to just do whatever you want me to do. And I'm definitely not putting on anything that looks like those man-jammies you're wearing. And don't call me Thomas. My name is Stephen!"

It all came out in one breath, and Stephen had to suck in another huge gulp of air, hoping it didn't ruin his moment. Make him look weak.

The man laughed, and he sounded more amused than condescending. It still made Stephen want to throw something across the room.

"They told me you had . . ." The man paused, looked down at an electronic notepad he carried. ". . . 'an endearing, childlike quality' about you. Guess I'm not seeing it."

"That was before they told me I had to change my name," Stephen countered. "The name my mom and dad gave me. The one you took from me."

"Would that be the dad who went crazy?" the man asked. "The one who just about beat your mom to death he was so sick? And the mom who asked us to take you away? Who's getting sicker every day? *Those* parents?"

Stephen smoldered in his bed but said nothing.

His green-clothed visitor came closer to the bed, crouched down. "Look, you're just a kid. And you're obviously bright. Really bright. Also immune to the Flare. You have a lot going for you."

Stephen heard the warning in the man's voice. Whatever came next was *not* going to be good.

"You're going to have to accept the loss of certain things and think of something bigger than yourself," he continued. "If we don't find a cure within a few years, humans are done. So here's what's going to happen, *Thomas*. You're going to get up. You're going to walk with me out that door. And I'm not going to tell you again."

The man waited for a moment, his gaze unwavering; then he stood and turned to leave.

Stephen got up. He followed the man out the door.

CHAPTER 2

221.11.28 | 9:56 a.m.

When they entered the hallway, Stephen got his first glimpse of another kid since he'd arrived. A girl. She had brown hair and looked like she might be a little older than him. It was hard to tell, though; he only got a brief look at her as a woman escorted her into the room right next to his. The door thumped closed just as he and his escort walked by, and he noticed the plaque on the front of its white surface: 31K.

"Teresa hasn't had any problem taking her new name," the man in green said as they moved down the long, dimly lit hallway. "Of course, that might be because she wanted to forget her given one."

"What was it?" Stephen asked, his tone approaching something like politeness. He genuinely wanted to know. If the girl had really given up so easily, maybe he could hold on to her name as well—a favor to a potential friend.

"It'll be hard enough for you to forget your own," came the response. "I wouldn't want to burden you with another."

I'll never forget, Stephen told himself. *Never.*

Somewhere at the edge of his mind, he realized that he'd already changed his stance, ever so slightly. Instead of insisting on calling himself Stephen, he'd begun to merely promise not to *forget* Stephen. Had he already given in? *No!* He almost shouted it.

"What's *your* name?" he asked, needing a distraction.

"Randall Spilker," the man said without breaking his stride. They turned a corner and came to a bank of elevators. "Once upon a time, I wasn't such a jerk, trust me. The world, the people I work for"—he gestured to nothing in particular all around him—"it's all turned my heart into a small lump of black coal. Too bad for you."

Stephen had no response, as he was busy wondering where they were going. They stepped onto the elevator when it chimed and the doors opened.

Stephen sat in a strange chair, its various built-in instruments pressing into his legs and back. Wireless sensors, each barely the size of a fingernail, were attached to his temples, his neck, his wrists, the crooks of his elbows, and his chest. He watched the console next to him as it collected data, chirping and beeping. The man in the grown-up jammies sat in another chair to observe, his knees only a couple of inches from Stephen's.

"I'm sorry, Thomas. We'd usually wait longer before it came to this," Randall said. He sounded nicer than he had back in the hallway and in Stephen's room. "We'd give you some more time to choose to take your new name voluntarily, like Teresa did. But time isn't a luxury we have anymore."

He held up a tiny piece of shiny silver, one end rounded, the other tapered to a razor-sharp point.

"Don't move," Randall said, leaning forward as if he were going to whisper something into Stephen's ear. Before he could question the man, Stephen felt a sharp pain in his neck, right below his chin, then the unsettling sensation of something burrowing into his throat. He yelped, but it was over as fast as it had begun, and he felt nothing more than the panic that filled his chest.

"Wh-what was that?" he stammered. He tried to get up from the chair despite all the things attached to him.

Randall pushed him back into his seat. Easy to do when he was twice Stephen's size.

"It's a pain stimulator. Don't worry, it'll dissolve and get flushed out of your system. Eventually. By then you probably won't need it anymore." He shrugged. *What can you do?* "But we can always insert another one if you make it necessary. Now calm down."

Stephen had a hard time catching his breath. "What's it going to do to me?"

"Well, that depends ... *Thomas*. We have a long road ahead of us, you and me. All of us. But for today, right now, at this moment, we can take a shortcut. A little path through the woods. All you need to do is tell me your name."

"That's easy. Stephen."

Randall let his head fall into his hands. "Do it," he said, his voice little more than a tired whisper.

Until this moment, Stephen hadn't known pain outside of the scrapes and bruises of childhood. And so it was that when the fiery tempest exploded throughout his body, when the agony erupted in his veins and muscles, he had no words for it, no capacity to understand. There were only the screams that barely reached his own ears before his mind shut down and saved him.

Stephen came to, breathing heavily and soaked in sweat. He was still in the strange chair, but at some point, he'd been secured to it with straps of soft leather. Every nerve in his body buzzed with the lingering effects of the pain inflicted by Randall and the implanted device.

"What...," Stephen whispered, a hoarse croak. His throat

burned, telling him all he needed to know about how much he'd screamed in the time he lost. "What?" he repeated, his mind struggling to connect the pieces.

"I tried to tell you, Thomas," Randall said, with perhaps, *perhaps,* some compassion in his voice. Possibly regret. "We don't have time to mess around. I'm sorry. I really am. But we're going to have to try this again. I think you understand now that none of this is a bluff. It's important to everyone here that you accept your new name." The man looked away and paused a long time, staring at the floor.

"How could you hurt me?" Stephen asked through his raw throat. "I'm just a little kid." Young or not, he understood how pathetic he sounded.

Stephen also knew that adults seemed to react to *pathetic* in one of two ways: Their hearts would melt a little and they'd backtrack. Or the guilt would burn like a furnace within them and they'd harden into rock to put the fire out. Randall chose the latter, his face reddening as he shouted back.

"All you have to do is accept a name! Now—I'm not playing around anymore. What's your name?"

Stephen wasn't stupid—he'd just pretend for now. "Thomas. My name is Thomas."

"I don't believe you," Randall responded, his eyes pools of darkness. "Again."

Stephen opened his mouth to answer, but Randall hadn't been speaking to him. The pain came back, harder and faster. He barely had time to register the agony before he passed out.

"What's your name?"

Stephen could barely speak. "Thomas."

"I don't believe you."

"No." He whimpered.

The pain was no longer a surprise, nor was the darkness that came after.

"What's your name?"

"Thomas."

"I don't want you to forget."

"No." He cried, trembling with sobs.

"What's your name?"

"Thomas."

"Do you have any other name?"

"No. Only Thomas."

"Has anyone ever called you anything else?"

"No. Only Thomas."

"Will you ever forget your name? Will you ever use another?"

"No."

"Okay. Then I'll give you one last reminder."

Later, he lay on his bed, once again curled up into himself. The world outside felt far away, silent. He'd run out of tears, his body numb except that unpleasant tingle. It was as if his entire being had fallen asleep. He pictured Randall across from him, guilt and anger mixed into a potent, lethal form of rage that turned his face into a grotesque mask as he inflicted the pain.

I'll never forget, he told himself. *I must never, never forget.*

And so, inside his mind, he chanted a familiar phrase, over and over and over. Though he couldn't quite put a finger on it, something *did* seem different.

Thomas, Thomas, Thomas. My name is Thomas.

If you love
THE MAZE RUNNER,
don't miss this sneak peek at the first book in James Dashner's bestselling Mortality Doctrine series:

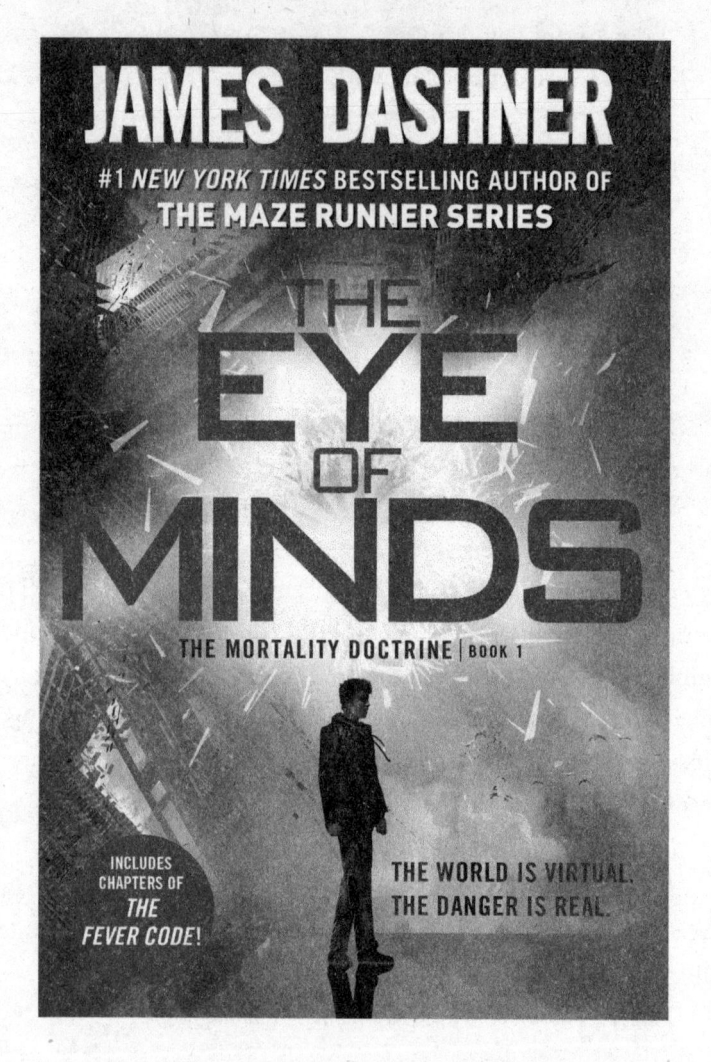

JAMES DASHNER

#1 NEW YORK TIMES BESTSELLING AUTHOR OF
THE MAZE RUNNER SERIES

THE EYE OF MINDS

THE MORTALITY DOCTRINE | BOOK 1

INCLUDES CHAPTERS OF *THE FEVER CODE*!

THE WORLD IS VIRTUAL.
THE DANGER IS REAL.

Excerpt copyright © 2013 by James Dashner.
Published by Delacorte Press, an imprint of Random House Children's Books,
a division of Penguin Random House LLC, New York.

CHAPTER 1

THE COFFIN

1

Michael spoke against the wind, to a girl named Tanya.

"I know it's water down there, but it might as well be concrete. You'll be flat as a pancake the second you hit."

Not the most comforting choice of words when talking to someone who wanted to end her life, but it was certainly the truth. Tanya had just climbed over the railing of the Golden Gate Bridge, cars zooming by on the road, and was leaning back toward the open air, her twitchy hands holding on to a pole wet with mist. Even if somehow Michael could talk her out of jumping, those slippery fingers might get the job done anyway. And then it'd be lights-out. He pictured some poor sap of a fisherman thinking he'd finally caught the big one, only to reel in a nasty surprise.

"Stop joking," the trembling girl responded. "It's not a game—not anymore."

Michael was inside the VirtNet—the Sleep, to people

who went in as often as he did. He was used to seeing scared people there. A lot of them. Yet underneath the fear was usually the *knowing*. Knowing deep down that no matter what was happening in the Sleep, it wasn't real.

Not with Tanya. Tanya was different. At least, her Aura, her computer-simulated counterpart, was. Her Aura had this bat-crazy look of pure terror on her face, and it suddenly gave Michael chills—made him feel like *he* was the one hovering over that long drop to death. And Michael wasn't a big fan of death, fake or not.

"It *is* a game, and you know it," he said louder than he'd wanted to—he didn't want to startle her. But a cold wind had sprung up, and it seemed to grab his words and whisk them down to the bay. "Get back over here and let's talk. We'll both get our Experience Points, and we can go explore the city, get to know each other. Find some crazies to spy on. Maybe even hack some free food from the shops. It'll be good times. And when we're done, we'll find you a Portal, and you can Lift back home. Take a break from the game for a while."

"This has nothing to do with *Lifeblood*!" Tanya screamed at him. The wind pulled at her clothes, and her dark hair fanned out behind her like laundry on a line. "Just go away and leave me alone. I don't want your pretty-boy face to be the last thing I see."

Michael thought of *Lifeblood Deep,* the next level, the goal of all goals. Where everything was a thousand times more real, more advanced, more intense. He was three years away from earning his way inside. Maybe two. But right then he needed to talk this dopey girl out of jumping to her date with the fishes or he'd be sent back to the Suburbs for a week, making *Lifeblood Deep* that much further away.

"Okay, look . . ." He was trying to choose his words carefully, but he'd already made a pretty big mistake and knew it. Going out of character and using the game itself as a reason for her to stop what she was doing meant he'd be docked points big-time. And it was all about the points. But this girl was legitimately starting to scare him. It was that face—pale and sunken, as if she'd already died.

"Just go away!" she yelled. "You don't get it. I'm trapped here. Portals or no Portals. I'm trapped! He won't let me Lift!"

Michael wanted to scream right back at her—she was talking nonsense. A dark part of him wanted to say forget it, tell her she was a loser, let her nosedive. She was being so stubborn—it wasn't like any of it was really happening. *It's just a game.* He had to remind himself of that all the time.

But he couldn't mess this up. He needed the points. "All right. Listen." He took a step back, held his hands up like he was trying to calm a scared animal. "We just met—give it some time. I promise I won't do anything nutty. You wanna jump, I'll let you jump. But at least talk to me. Tell me why."

Tears lined her cheeks; her eyes had gone red and puffy. "Just go away. Please." Her voice had taken on the softness of defeat. "I'm not messing around here. I'm done with this—all of this!"

"Done? Okay, that's fine to be done. But you don't have

to screw it up for me, too, right?" Michael figured maybe it was okay to talk about the game after all, since she was using it as her reason to end it—to check out of the Virtual-Flesh-and-Bones Hotel and never come back. "Seriously. Walk back to the Portal with me, Lift yourself, do it the right way. You're done with the game, you're safe, I get my points. Ain't that the happiest ending you ever heard of?"

"I hate you," she spat. Literally. A spray of misty saliva. "I don't even know you and I hate you. This has nothing to do with *Lifeblood*!"

"Then tell me what it *does* have to do with." He said it kindly, trying to keep his composure. "You've got all day to jump. Just give me a few minutes. Talk to me, Tanya."

She buried her head in the crook of her right arm. "I just can't do it anymore." She whimpered and her shoulders shook, making Michael worry about her grip again. "I can't."

Some people are just weak, he thought, though he wasn't stupid enough to say it.

Lifeblood was by *far* the most popular game in the VirtNet. Yeah, you could go off to some nasty battlefield in the Civil War or fight dragons with a magic sword, fly spaceships, explore the freaky love shacks. But that stuff got old quick. In the end, nothing was more fascinating than bare-bones, dirt-in-your-face, gritty, get-me-out-of-here real life. Nothing. And there were some, like Tanya, who obviously couldn't handle it. Michael sure could. He'd risen up its ranks almost as quickly as legendary gamer Gunner Skale.

"Come on, Tanya," he said. "How can it hurt to talk to me? And if you're going to quit, why would you want to end your last game by killing yourself so violently?"

Her head snapped up and she looked at him with eyes so hard he shivered again.

"Kaine's haunted me for the last time," she said. "He can't just trap me here and use me for an experiment—sic the KillSims on me. I'm gonna rip my Core out."

Those last words changed everything. Michael watched in horror as Tanya tightened her grip on the pole with one hand, then reached up with the other and started digging into her own flesh.

2

Michael forgot the game, forgot the points. The situation had gone from annoying to actual life-and-death. In all his years of playing, he'd never seen someone code out their Core, destroying the barrier device within the Coffin that kept the virtual world and the real world separate in their mind.

"Stop that!" he yelled, one foot already on the railing. "Stop!"

He jumped down onto the catwalk on the outer edge of the bridge and froze. He was just a few feet from her now, and he wanted to avoid any quick movements that might cause her to panic. Holding his hands out, he took a small step toward her.

"Don't do that," Michael said as softly as he could in the biting wind.

Tanya kept digging into her right temple. She'd peeled back pieces of her skin; a stream of blood from the wound quickly covered her hands and the side of her face in red gore. A look of terrifying calmness had come over her, as if she had no concept of what she was doing to herself, though Michael knew well enough that she was busy hacking the code.

"Stop coding for one second!" Michael shouted. "Would you just talk about this before you rip your freaking *Core* out? You know what that means."

"Why do you care so much?" she responded, so quietly that Michael had to read her lips to understand. But at least she'd stopped digging.

Michael just stared. Because she *had* stopped digging and was now reaching inside the torn mass of flesh with her thumb and forefinger. "You just want your Experience Points," she said. Slowly, she pulled out a small metallic chip slick with blood.

"I'll forfeit my points," Michael said, trying to hide his fear and disgust. "I swear. You can't mess around anymore, Tanya. Code that thing back in and come talk to me. It's not too late."

She held up the visual manifestation of the Core, gazed at it with fascination. "Don't you see the irony in all this?" she asked. "If it weren't for my coding skills, I probably wouldn't even know who Kaine was. About his KillSims and his plans for me. But I'm good at it, and because of that . . . *monster*, I just programmed the Core right out of my own head."

"Not your real head. It's still just a simulation, Tanya. It's not too late." Michael couldn't remember a time in his entire life when he'd felt that ill.

She looked at him so sharply that he took a step backward. "I can't take it anymore. I can't take . . . *him* anymore. He can't use me if I'm dead. I'm done."

She curled the Core onto her thumb, then flicked it toward Michael. It flew over his shoulder—he saw flashes of sunlight glint off it as it spun through the air, almost like it was winking at him, saying, *Hey, buddy, you suck at suicide negotiations.* It landed with a *plink* somewhere out in the traffic, where it would be crushed in seconds.

He couldn't believe what he was witnessing. Someone so sophisticated at manipulating code that she could destroy her Core—the device that essentially protected players' brains while they were in the Sleep. Without your Core, your brain wouldn't be able to filter the stimulation of the VirtNet properly. If your Core died in the Sleep, you'd die in the Wake. He didn't know *anyone* who'd seen this before. Two hours earlier he'd been eating stolen bleu chips at the Dan the Man Deli with his best friends. All he wanted now was to be back there, eating turkey on rye, enduring Bryson's jokes about old ladies' underwear and listening to Sarah tell him how awful his latest Sleep haircut was.

"If Kaine comes for *you*," Tanya said, "tell him that I won in the end. Tell him how brave I was. He can trap people here and steal all the bodies he wants. But not mine."

Michael was done talking. He couldn't take one more word out of this girl's blood-smeared mouth. As quickly as anything he'd ever done in his life, as any character in any game, he jumped toward the pole she clung to.

She screamed, momentarily frozen by his sudden action, but then she let go, actually pushed herself away from the bridge. Michael grabbed for the railing to his left with one hand and reached for her with the other but missed both. His feet hit something solid, then slipped. Arms flailing, he felt nothing but air, and he fell, almost in sync with her.

An incredible shriek escaped his mouth, something he would've been embarrassed about if his only companion wasn't about to lose her life. With her Core coded out, her death would be real.

Michael and Tanya fell toward the harsh gray waters of the bay. Wind tore at their clothes, and Michael's heart felt like it was creeping along the inside of his chest, up his throat. He screamed again. On some level he knew he would hit the water, feel the pain; then he'd be Lifted and wake up back home, safe and sound in his Coffin. But the VirtNet's power was feigned reality, and right now the reality was terror.

Somehow Michael's and Tanya's Auras found each other on that long fall, chest to chest, like tandem skydivers. As the churning surface below rushed toward them, they wrapped their arms around each other, pulling closer together. Michael wanted to scream again but clamped his jaw shut when he saw the complete calmness on her face.

Her eyes bored into Michael's, searched him, and found him, and he broke somewhere on the inside.